THE PLAGUE CHARMER

THE PLAGUE CHARMER

KAREN MAITLAND

REVIEW

First published in Great Britain in 2016 by
HEADLINE REVIEW
An imprint of HEADLINE PUBLISHING GROUP

1

Cataloguing in Publication Data is available from the British Library

ISBN 978 1 4722 3582 4 (Hardback)
ISBN 978 1 4722 3583 1 (Trade paperback)

Typeset in Adobe Garamond Pro by Palimpsest Book Production Ltd, Falkirk, Stirlingshire

Printed and bound in Great Britain by CPI Group (UK) Ltd, Croydon, CR0 4YY

MIX
Paper from
responsible sources
FSC
www.fsc.org FSC® C104740

Headline's policy is to use papers that are natural, renewable and recyclable
products and made from wood grown in well-managed forests and other
controlled sources. The logging and manufacturing processes are expected to conform
to the environmental regulations of the country of origin.

HEADLINE PUBLISHING GROUP
An Hachette UK Company
Carmelite House
50 Victoria Embankment
London, EC4Y 0DZ

www.headline.co.uk
www.hachette.co.uk

KEY PLACES

1. Will's cave
2. Marshes
3. Porlock Manor
4. Clifftop cairn
5. Road to Porlock Weir

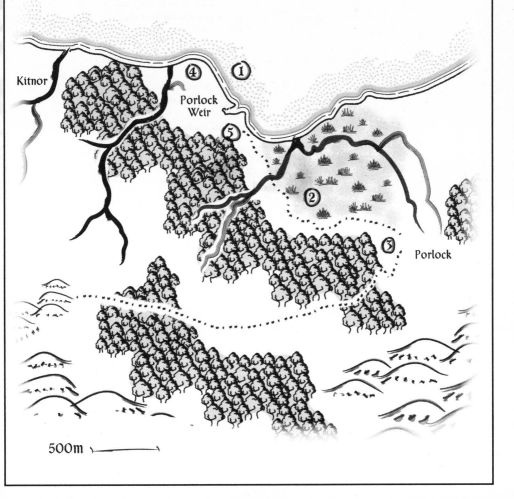

The cruellest month in all the year
is the month of Janiveer.

Weather lore saying

Are those her ribs through which the Sun
Did peer, as through a grate?
And is that Woman all her crew?
Is that a DEATH? and are there two?
Is DEATH that Woman's mate? . . .
The naked hulk alongside came,
And the twain were casting dice;
"The game is done! I've won! I've won!"
Quoth she, and whistles thrice.

From The Rime of the Ancient Mariner *written 1797–8 by
Samuel Taylor Coleridge. In 1797, the poet lived for a time on
a farm near Porlock, Somerset, where this novel is set.*

Cast of Characters

Porlock Weir

Will – dwarf, former court jester to Sir Nigel Loring
Janiveer – the woman from the sea
Sara – wife of **Elis**, a packhorse man, mother to sons
  Hob and **Luke**
Aldith – sister-in-law to Sara, wife of **Daveth**, a fisherman,
  mother to **Col**, **Ibb** and **Kitto**
Goda – Aldith's sister and seaman **Jory**'s lover
Matilda – devout woman, wife of **George**, a ship's
  carpenter, and owner of **Gatty**, the cat
Sybil – owner of the village bake-house and brew-house
Cador – village bailiff, husband to **Isobel**
Katharine – married to the drunkard, **Skiener**
Father Cuthbert – parish priest of Porlock and Porlock Weir
Harold – youth in Minor Orders, acolyte to Father Cuthbert
Bald John – blacksmith and husband to **Cecily**
Abel – elderly fisherman
Meryn – man with a withered leg
Crabfish – lad regarded as simple

Porlock Manor

Sir Nigel Loring – absentee lord of the manor
Christina – niece of Sir Nigel, daughter of **Lady Aliena**,
  and new bride of **Sir Randel**

Baby Oswin – Christina's secret son

Lady Pavia – cousin to Sir Nigel and Christina's mother and widow of **Hubert**

Sir Harry Gilmore – guest at Porlock Manor

Helen, **Mary** and **Anne** – three young wards of Sir Nigel, chaperoned by **Lady Margery**

Master Wallace – steward of Porlock Manor

Eda – elderly tiring maid to Christina's mother, now Christina's maid

Rosa – stillroom maid

In the Burial Cave

Brother Praeco – Prophet and leader of the Chosen Ones

Uriel – spiteful first wife of the Prophet

Phanuel – timid second wife of the Prophet

Raguel – third and youngest wife of the Prophet

Friar Tom – an elderly member of the Chosen Ones

David and **Noll** – henchmen and trusted disciples of Brother Praeco

Alfred – an apostate who left the Chosen Ones

*Note: Exmoor ponies were known locally as **horsebeasts** or **widgebeasts**. The word 'pony' was not used on the moor until the 1700s.*

Prologue

The storytellers say that . . .

Once, long ago, in the land of the Celts, a boy was born who was possessed of great power and strength. From a small child, Cadeyrn could transform himself into a bear and in that form he would pass through the Gate of Mist to journey into the realms of darkness and light. The druids recognised special gifts in the boy and were determined that he should become one of them, perhaps even the greatest among them. But Cadeyrn was also skilled with the axe and the sword, and others foretold he would become a mighty warrior and leader.

Cadeyrn grew in stature and his skills grew with him, but even when he had become a man, the two paths lay stretched out before him and none in his tribe could tell which he would follow.

Then one day when he was out hunting, he saw a youth set his dogs upon a she-bear that was protecting her cubs. Filled with rage, Cadeyrn pursued her attacker into a grove of oak trees. Mistletoe grew upon the branches and the law decreed that, even in the midst of battle, upon seeing the sacred herb a man must lay down his weapon and depart in peace, without shedding blood. But Cadeyrn's wrath was so great that he did not notice the mistletoe. He raised his axe and chopped off the youth's head with a single blow.

Blood spurted from the severed neck, splashing the branches of the tree beneath which the youth had taken refuge. Only when Cadeyrn saw the drops of scarlet staining the white berries did he realise he had strayed into a sacred grove. When the druids saw that blood had been shed in that holy place, they cursed him.

That night when Cadeyrn tried to pass through the Gate of Mist, it closed against him and he could no longer enter the other realms. He knew then that his destiny had been sealed: he would become a warrior. And when Cadeyrn went into battle, his path to glory seemed assured, for he slaughtered dozens with his axe and his enemies fled in terror before him. But just as victory seemed within his grasp, the druid priests appeared. At once, the battle turned against Cadeyrn and, with his men, he was forced to flee for his life across the sea to England. There he fought again and this time he conquered the people of those lands, vanquished their leader and was proclaimed king.

Now, the people who lived in those parts were Christians and they were afraid that this bloody warrior would slaughter them and sack their church, so they drew lots and sent to him a young boy, who offered himself as sacrifice. He said he would willingly die any death Cadeyrn chose for him, however agonising and terrible, if only the king would spare the people and their church. Cadeyrn was so moved by his courage that he asked the boy the name of the god he worshipped and vowed that he, too, would pray to this god, as well as to the gods of his own ancestors. Cadeyrn swore a solemn oath that anyone who called upon the name of Christ would be granted the king's protection, and he would defend them even to his own death.

But though he had spared the daughter of the Christian

ruler he had vanquished and had treated her with honour, she and her maids were filled with hatred against Cadeyrn and sought vengeance. She collected the poison of the viper and the venom of the toad and coated the holy chalice in the church with them, knowing that when the king came to Mass he would be offered the cup first.

As Cadeyrn raised the chalice to his lips, a raven flew down and dashed it from his hand. The wine spilled in a pool across the floor of the church and the raven dipped its beak in it to drink. The bird had taken only a sip before it dropped dead. When the king saw how the raven had saved him, he took up the carcass with his right hand, intending to give the bird an honoured burial, but as he touched it, the bird revived and flew up on to the roof of the church.

At that, the Christian princess and her maids became even more vengeful. They plotted with Cadeyrn's enemies, revealing to them the means by which they could invade his lands while he was absent. They attacked without warning, burning his villages and carrying off his women and his cattle.

When Cadeyrn returned and discovered what his enemies had done, he marched on their stronghold that very night and camped before their gates ready to give battle at dawn. But the princess had hidden her maids among the servants who travelled with the warriors and she had given instructions that they should add dwale to the food they prepared for the king.

The herb made the king drowsy, and when dawn came, he could not fully rouse himself. He fought with the heart of a bear, but the dwale had fuddled his senses and made him clumsy. He was overpowered and taken prisoner.

Cadeyrn begged to be allowed to die in combat, but his enemies tied him to a tree in the middle of the forest. They chopped off the hand with which he'd given battle. But instead of blood, a stream of pure water flowed from the wound and became a mighty river. In fear, they shot him with arrows, but still he lived, and finally they cut off his head.

His enemies left his corpse for the ravens to peck and the beasts in the forest to devour, but the ravens covered his severed head with their wings and beasts guarded his body. That night, the priest of the church saw a wondrous sight. A great bear came out of the forest bearing the body of the king and laid the corpse gently on a stone slab on the hillside. All that night, a golden light hung over the place where Cadeyrn's body lay, vanishing only when that greater light, the sun itself, rose.

The body of Cadeyrn was buried under a great cairn of earth and stones at the place where the bear had laid him, with much gold and many precious objects. But Cadeyrn's hand and head were borne away by the Christian priests as holy relics.

And they say that each evening at sunset a raven brings a stone to add to the cairn that stands over the resting place of the warrior king, and when that mound is high enough to reach the sky, Cadeyrn will awaken and ride once more to battle.

Chapter 1

Will

Riddle me this: How many calves' tails would it take to
reach from the earth to the sky?

She appears without warning, standing in the mouth of the cave staring in at me. Tattered skirts and long strands of hair flap wildly in the sea wind, like the feathers of the dead gull washed up on the shore. Her face is in darkness. Her eyes glitter like a wild beast's in the firelight. She stands there so long, so silently, that I think she may be the ghost of a drowned soul come to drag me down into the green waves below. I am not afraid. I would almost go willingly with her now. Almost, but not quite.

She crouches and from the depths of her cloak she pulls out a bundle, which she lays reverently on the rocky floor in front of my fire, an offering, as if I am a pagan god or Christian saint.

'You will look after him? Keep him safe from them?'

The bundle stirs. A tiny fist clenches the air. The thing gives a faint mewing sound, like a cat demanding to be let in. I shuffle closer. The baby is naked, wrapped only in a goatskin. But not a cured skin: the inside is black with dried blood as if it has only just been ripped from the carcass, or perhaps it is stained with the woman's birth blood. The infant looks to have been no longer in the world than the goat has been out of it.

'Is the child sick?' I ask her.

'No . . . but he will be. They'll make him sick . . . dead, like the others. I heard the owl. Owls know when death is coming.' Her fingers pluck repeatedly at the rags of her skirt. She is crazed, poor creature, and little wonder.

'Take it away. How do you expect me to care for it? What am I to feed it – mackerel?' I drag myself backwards, deeper into the cave, making it plain I want nothing to do with the infant. 'Even a grown man could freeze to death at night in this place – that's if the sea doesn't drown him first.'

'But you'll protect my baby. Creatures like you can keep us from evil spirits and make the sick well. I know it. I heard the stories. You're a—' She breaks off, as if even the name for *creatures* like me can conjure a power she dare not summon.

She's wrong, though. A fraud is what I am, an imposter. They expect miracles of me, but they might as well stick bluebells up their arses and dance naked on the seashore for all the good it will do them. I am fool's gold, though even now I do not admit it aloud.

The owls knew it was coming. The villagers knew it was coming. Even *I* knew it was coming. It was only a matter of time. But, you see, that's exactly why it caught us unawares. It crept up on us and pulled our breeches down, cackling with laughter. Time is the tricksiest of all tricksters, and I should know. I was a jester by profession, but I never had the skills of Mistress Time. She can stretch herself into a

6

shadow that reaches so far you think it'll never come to an end or she can shrink to the shortest of mouse-tails.

You ask any man under sentence of execution, and I've seen a good many of those. I've mocked and pranced in front of them as they were hauled to the gallows. My lords and ladies have to be entertained while they wait for the main spectacle. Heaven forbid that time should drag for them. But for those piteous felons, desperately praying for more time, she races away from them. Yet the moment they fall to pleading for the pain and agony to be quickly over, Mistress Time wantonly slows to the pace of a hobbled horse. That is her way, the naughty harlot, to do exactly the opposite of whatever a man begs her to do.

The rumours of what was coming were brought by packhorse over the high moors, and ships that carried word to shore. It could not be ignored, should not have been ignored, but it was, even by me. Maybe we thought that there in that isolated village, with the steep hills protecting our backs and the raging sea as our ramparts in front, we were safe in an impregnable fortress. But when time lays siege to a castle, there is no fortress that she cannot take in the end.

I, above all, should have known the games Mistress Time plays. I was her creation or, rather, the creation of my master, who was in her pay. My master was proud of his handiwork, of me. You see, I am a *nain*, a dwarf. But I am not a *natural* dwarf, though you'd never guess to look at me. As my master constantly reminded me all the days I was growing up, or in my case not growing *up*, I am a sculpture, a carving, a work of art that took years of patient craftsmanship to perfect.

Not that I could ever disclose that to a living soul. My

7

old master was paid a handsome purse for the purchase of a genuine dwarf, for they are valuable creatures. But it would've been my miserable carcass upon which my new lord would have vented his fury if he'd ever discovered he'd been cheated. You see, *real* dwarfs, natural-born dwarfs, are bringers of good luck. They protect the household from all kinds of evil and misfortune, like the relic of a saint or an amulet, only we dwarfs have more uses than simply to hang around on a wall. We can protect you from any sickness and cure any ailment. Just rub us on the affected part, like bear grease on to a bald pate, and see the miracle we can perform . . . which *they* can perform, but not me. I am a fake. I am the alchemist's stone, which is nothing but a polished pebble, the finger of the holy saint, which is merely a dried chicken bone.

I watched my master create other dwarfs as he had made me and he was right: it requires rare talent and much time to create us little people. But I'll tell you the secret, give it to you for nothing. Now that is a bargain you can't refuse.

First you take a lusty infant – they must be strong to survive the moulding – and fit it with an iron frame over its baby head and face. One of the iron bars with hooks on either end goes in that little toothless mouth to stretch the lips into a permanent wide grin. Dwarfs are supposed to look cheerful, and it spares us the effort of having to fix our mouths into a grin in company. It wouldn't do for that smile to slip, now, would it?

The other iron bars of the bridle flatten the baby's button nose and squeeze its skull so that the forehead bulges with wisdom and intelligence. Next you must rub the infant spine daily with the fat of tiny creatures – shrews or dormice, bats or moles are thought to be most efficacious. Finally you strap the infant in its iron bridle into a snug, stout box, open at the front, of course, for you don't want to suffocate your little homunculus – think of all that wasted time and money. Suckle it daily on the juices of dwarf elder, knotgrass and daisies mixed with milk from a dwarf goat. As the baby grows in its box, it will be compressed and deformed, squished and squashed ever tighter till it emerges from its mould, formed like a gingerbread manikin into the squat little dwarf that lords and ladies so desire.

My master was a kindly man, as he always reminded us whenever he beat us. It wrought his heart to hear the infants cry out with pain from the cramp and sores, and being so tender-hearted he could never bring himself to break their limbs to hasten the process, or dislocate their joints to make them bendy as acrobats. Dwarfs could be fashioned in a fraction of the time by such methods, he told me, though he never thought the results looked truly authentic. As a craftsman, he prided himself on the slow, careful moulding of the tender clay.

And when I was ready, fully baked so to speak, he sold me for a heavy purse to a sycophant who bought me as a gift for Sir Nigel Loring, the powerful envoy and confidant of Edward, the Black Prince, the hero of the battles of Crécy and Poitiers. As I was to discover, my new lord owned several manors, including Porlock, not that he ever spent much time at any of them, but my service for him proved to be the beginning of the journey, which, years later, was to end with me freezing my cods off in a damp sea cave only a few miles from that same manor at Porlock. As I say, Mistress Time plays some merry tricks.

I had been trained by my old master to be a jester – that

is the job of the dwarf, to tumble and conjure, mock and mimic at feasts and festivals. But we do much more than that. We are also dispensers of punning wit that our lords fancy are words of profound truth, for we're children with the faces of old men and *out of the mouths of babes and sucklings*, as the priests say.

Actually, I never minded that part so much. Those were the times I could make fools of the longshanks. All I had to do was turn a somersault, put on a droll face and declaim utter gibberish. The more nonsensical the words, the more attention they gave them.

'I am the son of water, but when water touches me I die. Pray who am I, my lord?'

'Let me think . . . I know this . . . Ice! The son of water is ice.' Sir Nigel beams at the company triumphantly. His sycophantic guests applaud their host's cleverness.

'Aah, but the sun is a golden egg that none may eat, my lord. Beware the day water touches that sun for all will die.' Now they nod as sagely as if I had just revealed a prophecy from St John himself.

You see, give them an easy one to make them think they're clever, then you can babble complete drivel and get tossed a coin for it, because they would never admit before all the company that they cannot fathom the wisdom of a fool.

So innocently wise and so utterly truthful do the long-shanks believe dwarfs to be that the fate of thrones and whole kingdoms is entrusted to the little people. Dwarfs are sent as gifts into the courts of rivals to act as spies. They're entrusted to carry the secret documents of kings and traitors alike. They stand in plain view while their masters and attendants are searched, for who remembers to search the grinning child-fool? Dwarfs are sent out alone on battle-grounds, carrying the white flag with its offer of parley. They are trusted to approach even by the most wary, though we might wear the assassin's knife: none can believe we could reach up to strike the victim's heart.

But I never reached the battlefield, which would have granted me at least a little honour and glory. No, I was used as a bed-warmer to heat the feather mattress of Sir Nigel and Lady Margaret before they retired, so that they should not endure the shock of slipping naked between cold sheets. In winter, I was also foot-warmer to Lady Margaret's mother when she was being carried in a litter between two horses. I crouched beneath the old woman's skirts – her own lapdog, intended for the purpose, would not stop bounding from side to side across her lap, barking at every hound that was running alongside the riders.

When the old woman wanted to relieve herself on the journey, she'd rest her pisspot on my back. It was, as she said, a convenient height. But the indignity of that was nothing. After all, a jester loses his dignity so many times a day, he wouldn't recognise it if he fell over it. No, the task I really hated was kiss-bearer.

It was the fashion then that when a woman wished to flirt with a man who was not her husband, she would seize a dwarf and smother him with wet kisses, then bid him deliver them to the object of her affections. The dwarf was supposed to climb upon the man's knee and bestow on him the kisses he had received. Worse still, if the man was of a mind to return her advances, the longshanks would kiss the dwarf as many times as he desired to kiss the maiden or married woman and send the little person back to deliver them. As you can imagine, this mummery could continue for hours until the dwarf was as wet as if he'd been slobbered over by a pack of hounds.

That was not the worst of it. Sometimes this flirtation by proxy – or should I call it dwoxy? – went well beyond mere kissing. Every disgusting touch, each illicit fondling by both parties had to be endured by the dwarf, then re-enacted by him on the lover for whom it was intended. Inevitably the most enthusiastic players of this game were men and matrons of advancing years and foul breath. They trusted dwarfs, you see, for we always carried the truth. Poor fools, they never suspected that I was not a real dwarf. If one man in particular had known, he would never have entrusted me with the kiss that would shatter both my life and hers. It was a curse, not a kiss, I carried.

I turn around and the woman is gone, vanished as if a wave has licked her up out of the cave's mouth and the sea has swallowed her. But the baby still lies where she left him, mewing resentfully and staring up at the roof of the cave where firelight and shadows dance out a thousand stories. I waddle over and scoop him up. I should toss him into the sea. It would be kinder. A few moments and it would be over. No pain, no fear, no agonising death that lasts too long and yet is far, far too short.

Instead, I find myself tearing my only spare shirt into strips to make swaddling bands. If you don't bind those pliable limbs straight, the infant will grow bandy, not as bandy as me, of course, but if this baby must grow, let it be into a man, not a manikin. That much at least even a fake dwarf can manage.

I carry him to the cave entrance and stare out into the darkness. The waves foam white, rearing up and crashing

12

down on to the pebble beach as if they mean to smash every stone to sand. Clouds race across the moon, like herds of animals fleeing some nameless predator. There is a storm coming, a storm greater even than the last one that brought so much destruction. I do not need the owls or even the gulls to tell me that. A storm was how it all began; maybe another will finish it. Finish it for us all.

May 1361

Before the face of God nothing remains unavenged.
Medieval Proverb

Chapter 2

Vigil of Ascension Day
Porlock Weir, Exmoor

Sara

The herring shoals are ruled by a royal herring, a fish which is of uncommon size. If this fish is harmed, the shoals will vanish and come no more to the shore.

'The sea's gone, Mam. Come and look!' Little Hob's shrill voice cut through the morning air, like the screech of a gull.

'Tide's always going out,' I snapped. 'Does it twice a day, boy, you know that.'

I'd no patience with his games that morning. The fire wouldn't draw. It smouldered, sulky as a witch in irons, and the fish stew in the pot hanging above it was barely warm. There was no knowing when my husband would come down from the high moor with the packhorses, but when he did, he'd be ravenous and I'd have nothing to give him, save raw cod. Kneeling on the beaten-earth floor of our cottage, I thrust kindling sticks into the embers and tried to blow them into a blaze.

'Haven't you fetched the water yet, Hob?' I called through

the open door. 'I told you to go at first light. And carry it carefully, mind. Don't spill it.'

The spring near the cottage was usually gushing out of the hillside this time of year, but these past few weeks it had been just trickling down the rocks as if it was already late summer. My granddam told me that whenever the spring ran dry, it was because there was a great toad squatting in a cave deep inside the hill sucking up the water, and the only way to get it to move was to offer it gold. That toad would be sucking water for a long time afore it got any gold from me. I'd not a coin in the cottage, nor would I have till Elis came down from the moors.

'Mam! Come and look now!'

My head was aching and Hob's shriek went through it like a blade. Why do boys have to shout every word they utter, as if they're yelling over a howling storm?

'Sea's really gone, Mam! I swear!'

'Giss on!' Luke, my eldest son, bellowed scornfully. 'Last week you reckoned you'd seen a mermaid by the cliffs and it was nothing but a seal. Then you came running home, wailing like that old sour-face Matilda, saying a great brown bear chased you in the forest. Some bear! It was that mangy pedlar in his tattered old cloak, is all. Nug-head!'

'You're the nug-head for not coming to look,' Hob taunted. 'You'll be sorry when everyone else has seen it and you've not.'

From the clatter of wood I guessed Luke had thrown down the load he was carrying. He flashed past the door, chasing after his brother.

'Come back! There's work to be done. If you don't come here right now, I'll send you both to Kitnor to live with the ghosts and witches.'

18

I don't know why I wasted my breath. Once those two took off they'd only return when their bellies reminded them they were hungry. The one person Luke paid any heed to was his father, and not always then unless he saw Elis reach for the whip. I rocked back on my heels, rubbing my throbbing temples. The fire was at least stirring itself now, but if I didn't put a log on the flames, it would soon die down again. Sighing, I heaved myself to my feet to fetch the wood Luke was supposed to be bringing in.

But as soon as I stepped outside, I knew something was wrong. It took a few moments before I could reason what was making me uneasy. Three hobbled mares stood in the small clearing just above me on the hillside, their bellies round as barrels, swollen with unborn foals. The morning was fine and sunny, yet they were not nibbling the tender spring grass. They were pressed hard against each other, their ears pricked, rolling their eyes and tossing their heads as if they could sense a wolf creeping towards them. I glanced fearfully at the dense mass of trees that rose up the steep hillside behind the cottage, but the horses were not looking towards the forest. They were turning their heads in every direction as if they couldn't tell where danger threatened, only that they sensed it was coming.

Something else was wrong too. The bees! There was usually a steady trail of them flying between the flowers on the currant bushes and the skeps, but I couldn't see a single one on the white flowers. My hand flew to my mouth. Blessed Virgin, surely we hadn't lost them too! With our crops withering from lack of rain before they were even grown, we'd be sorely in need of all the honey the bees could make.

I ran towards the low stone wall in which the skeps were set to give them shelter from the sea wind. As I drew near

I could hear a low, irritated humming coming from inside each one. I breathed deeply, muttering a prayer of thanks. They were alive, but why weren't they flying? Something was amiss.

Our cottage sat in a dip, partway up the hill above the village, protected from the worst of the winter winds by a tree-covered rise in front and the broad back of the hill behind. I hurried down the stony track that led round the curve of the rise, until I reached the place where I could look down at the pebbly beach.

The sea had not vanished, as my son had sworn, but I could see at once what had so excited him. For the tide had ebbed out much further than usual, further than he had ever seen it in the seven years of his life. Even I'd seen it retreat as far only a few times, and then always on Lady Day or Michaelmas, when the incoming tides were at the highest, never at this season.

A small crowd of villagers was standing on the wooden jetty, but more swarmed over the mud flats. Out in the bay, far beyond the long stone walls of the fish weirs, I could just make out tiny figures, bending to gather something, perhaps stranded fish or crabs from the exposed seabed, though they were too far away for me to make out what they were collecting.

From their height and the way they moved, I could see that some of the villagers furthest out were just children. It was not safe for them to wander so far on that mud. Even the normal low tide exposed patches of quicksand beyond the fish weirs that could suck down a horse, and if the sea rolled back in along the channels, no one could outrun it, not in that ooze. What were their mothers thinking to let their young ones venture so far? A sudden chill gripped me.

Hob! Luke! Where were they? I anxiously scanned the crowd on the jetty and the beach, but I couldn't see any sign of them.

Picking up my skirts, I ran down the path, past the small stone cottages and the wooden smoke huts, towards the shore. As I ran, I stared wildly round at the groups of villagers, desperate to see the faces of Hob and Luke among them. I stumbled down on to the beach, wobbling on the broad pebbles, and picked my way over to where my sister-in-law, Aldith, stood, her baby son balanced on her hip, her little girl grasped tightly by the hand.

'Aldith, you seen the chillern?'

Whenever Luke was missing or in mischief, I could always count on him being with her eldest son, Col.

'Col's with his father picking fish from the weir pool. He wanted to go far out in the bay with Luke and the other lads, but his father's more sense than to let him. Couldn't stop your Luke, though. He's way out there.' She turned to look at me, her eyes creased with anxiety. 'If he were mine, Sara, I'd fetch him back straightway. When the tide goes out so far, she'll surge back in like horses at the gallop and if your boy gets his feet stuck fast in that mud . . .'

Aldith didn't need to finish her warning. Even strapping men could find themselves held tight in that ooze and drowned by the incoming tide.

'Luke! Luke!' I shouted. 'Come back here at once!'

None of the figures in the far distance turned or made any move towards the shore. But if Luke had heard me, he'd ignore me anyway. He always did whatever he wanted and refused to think about the consequences, even a thrashing, till he had to face it. But this was far more serious than slipping away to go egging with his friends when he should have been hoeing the weeds.

Aldith gave me a sympathetic glance, still holding tight to her wriggling daughter. 'He'd take notice if his father shouted for him.'

'Elis took the widgebeasts over the moors yesterday. Could be sundown afore he returns, tomorrow even.' I dragged off my shoes. 'My Hob, is he out there too?'

Aldith jerked her head back towards the quayside. 'Tried to follow Luke out, but Matilda grabbed him. Last I saw, she was telling him the devil would come for him in the night and drag him down to Hell if he didn't repent his sins.'

That bitterweed, Matilda, would terrify the wits out of the boy with her spiteful sermons, but for once I was grateful to her. At least she'd keep Hob safely away from the sea. I hurried down to where the shingle beach gave way to wet, muddy sand, rocks and weed.

I glanced up. I could have sworn it was growing darker, though it was not yet noon, and the wind was rising, changing direction too. Was there a storm brewing? I searched the sky to see which way the gulls were flying. If they were heading inland, it would be a sure sign of bad weather. But there was not a single gull to be seen. On any other day the air above would be full of their screeching, but I realised I couldn't hear the cry of any bird. I shivered, but not from the wind.

Holding my skirts above my knees, I ran down across the wet mud. Behind me, Aldith called something, but I couldn't make out the words. I was too busy shouting for Luke. I picked my way round the outside of the thick stone walls of the nearest weir. The pebbles underfoot were slimed with bright-green weed and several times I had to grab for the wall to stop myself slipping.

The stones gave way to cold mud again, numbing the feet. It wasn't until I felt the sharp salt sting and saw the scarlet blood running from beneath my instep that I realised I must have slashed it on a razor shell or a fragment of old iron stuck in the mud. At least I hadn't trodden on a viper-fish. Their poison made grown men weep in agony.

I squelched forward, shouting for Luke all the while, but I dared not lift my eyes to search for him as I picked my way between the sharp rocks.

Painful though it was, I tried to walk only on the patches of sharp stones or glistening swathes of bladder wrack, for though the smooth stretches of wet silt looked so soft and inviting, I knew they could conceal those viperfish or, worse still, might be quicksand from which there was no escape.

I paused and glanced up to get my bearings. Five boys were out ahead of me. I could see Luke now, furthest away from the others. There were shouts from the beach. I couldn't catch the words, but some of the boys heard them and lifted their heads. Two began to wade back towards the shore. But Luke, oblivious to all, was crouching down and digging with his hands in the mud, trying to pull something free.

The sky was definitely growing darker, I was sure of that now, a strange half-light that leached the colour from land and sea, turning all to grey. I glanced up, expecting to see thick, black clouds, but there were only a few skeins of white on the horizon, no sign of any storm. Yet it was growing colder. The wind blew strange, whirling eddies across the pools of water trapped in the hollows of the rock and sand. The ripples were turning widdershins, against the sun. I knew it for an evil omen.

'Hurry,' I yelled at the nearest boys, waving my arms. 'Get back to the shore now! Quickly!'

The boys looked alarmed, but they moved swiftly, or as swiftly as they could, weighed down by baskets of crabs, flapping fish and dripping slime-covered treasures, which might have been anything from broken swords to sea-sculpted driftwood.

Finally, Luke raised his head and stared at me, startled, as if he couldn't understand what I was doing there.

'Leave it, Luke. We must get back to the shore, there's a storm coming.'

He squinted up at the wisps of white cloud in disbelief and waved a muddy hand at me. 'I've almost got it, Mam, just have to dig a bit more.'

'No, Luke, you have to come now.'

Why was it growing so dark? I glanced at the sky again. For a moment I thought a giant leech was crawling across the edge of the sun. Blinded by the dazzle, I rubbed my eyes and, squinting, tried to look up again. Blackness was oozing across the bright disc, obliterating the light as if the sun was slowly being swallowed by its own evil shadow.

'Luke!' I yelled, floundering towards him.

His head jerked up again and he suddenly seemed to notice that daylight had turned to twilight. As he straightened up, I saw that he was holding something covered with mud, but I didn't stop to wonder what it was. My son waded towards me, his eyes wide with fear. I pulled him into my arms and hugged him fiercely, staring around. Luke clung to me. It was growing darker and colder with every panting breath we took.

'What's happening, Mam? The sun . . . is it gone?'

For one terrible moment, I didn't know which way I was

facing – towards the safety of the shore or the treacherous sea. Even on a moonless night the fishermen say they can still see Porlock Weir from the sea by the candles glimmering through the windows of the cottages and the fires in the yards glowing red. But it was noon and no lantern burned to guide our way back to the shore.

The sky, the earth, the sea had melted into one formless black mass. No birds cried above us. No animals called from the hill. The only sound was the desolate moan of the wind. It was as if we were ghosts wandering through the dark, icy caverns of the dead.

Then I heard a cry. I couldn't make out the words, but knew it was human. I prayed it was coming from the shore. Grasping at the sound, as if at a rope thrown to guide me, I held Luke tight against me and urged him forward. We slipped on seaweed and grazed our legs on the shell-covered rocks. I heard Luke gasp at the pain, but I wouldn't let him stop. Day had turned to night yet there was an eerie bone-white glow above us, like the ghosts of drowned sailors risen from the depths of the sea. I was afraid to look up, but I couldn't help myself. The sun had turned as dark as a pool of tar. It hung as a black disc in the sky, with only a halo of a deathly cold flame snaking about it, like ice burning.

By then I scarcely knew if Luke was pulling me or I was dragging him. My legs were aching from the effort of trying to hurry through the cloying mud.

The voice drifted out towards us, pulling us to the shore. *Domini venit crudelis . . . plenus et irae furorisque . . . peccatores eius conterendos de ea . . .*

I could tell they were words now, though they made no sense to me, but I knew it for the same tongue as the priest used when he spoke the words of the Mass. But

25

Father Cuthbert's tone was dull and flat, like the beat of the flail when we threshed the corn in the barn. This was a woman's voice, harsh and accusing as the skeins of greylag geese that cry, *Winter, winter*, as they fly. I glanced behind me, thinking to see a flock of angels screeching through the darkened sky, calling out that the Day of Judgment had come.

I thought I would trudge through that endless wasteland of mud and darkness for eternity. Then without warning my feet were scrabbling over shingle and I felt hands reaching out, tugging me up on to the track above the beach. I stood trembling, clutching Luke. I could feel him shivering and for the first time in many months he did not pull away from me.

A huddle of villagers silently faced the sea, only their clothes and hair moving in the wind. No one spoke. They just stared out into the strange twilight.

'*Behold, the day of the Lord is coming, a cruel day of wrath, and fury, to lay the land desolate, and to destroy the sinners. For the stars of Heaven shall not display their light: the sun shall be darkened in his rising . . .*' The woman's voice rang out. 'It is a warning. The prophecy of Isaiah has come to pass this very day. Fall to your knees and pray for forgiveness, pray that you may be spared!'

I could dimly make out a figure standing on a low wall, her head and shoulders raised above the villagers. She shook her fist and pointed into the sky as if she was commanding the darkness to obliterate us. Now that I was safely back on land, my head began to clear and I recognised the voice I'd heard shouting above the wind. It was no avenging angel, only Matilda, and the villagers were taking as much notice of her as of a pissing dog.

26

Someone in the crowd pointed upwards, relief bubbling in his voice: 'Look, sun's escaping!'

We all shielded our eyes and gazed up. A bright crescent of light was emerging from the circle of blackness, and as it grew, so the skies began to lighten again. We rubbed our eyes, blinded by the dazzling glare. The sun was sliding free. Light and warmth were returning, and as if to reassure us, two jackdaws glided down over the hillside and on to the shore, uttering their mocking *tchack-tchack* as if they had hidden the sun to play a joke on the world and were laughing at us all for our fear.

Matilda was still shouting: '*And the Lord says I will visit the evils of the world against the wicked for their iniquity: and I will make the pride of infidels to cease, and will bring down the arrogance of the mighty.* The sun is God's warning, take heed.'

But with every passing moment the sky was growing lighter and the birds had begun calling, as if it was dawn. Even the goats and pigs had started to forage as if they had just been let out of the byres after winter. Neighbours, grinning sheepishly, were slapping each other on the backs and shoving their friends as if to show they'd never been afeared, not for one moment, and were teasing those who had. All the same the laughter was uneasy. The sun does not grow dark at midday for no reason. It was an omen, but an omen of what? Nothing good, that was for sure.

Col came racing along the path and barged into Luke. 'What's you got there?'

I glanced down. Luke was kneeling on the track, trying to prise open the lid of a small box, covered in the tracks and holes from ship's worms. But the rusty lock held.

'I bet it's gold!' Col breathed, glowering reproachfully

towards his father, whom he evidently blamed for preventing him searching for treasure too. He pulled a gutting knife from his belt and proffered it to Luke, who wriggled it into the crack.

'Mind you don't snap that blade, Luke,' I warned. 'I've not the money to go buying Col's father another.'

But both lads ignored me. Luke rocked the knife back and forth. The lock held but a narrow strip from the edge of the lid splintered and fell away. Luke tipped the box, but no shower of gold coins or jewels tumbled out. He poked two fingers through the small hole.

'There's summat in there,' he said, screwing up his face as he struggled to reach it.

I felt a sudden pang of unease. Whatever was in that box had not been washed up on the shore as a gift from the sea. It had been stolen from the sea. It belonged to her and she would demand something or someone in return. And the sea always exacted her price three times over.

I hauled Luke to his feet. 'Throw it back. It doesn't belong to you.'

I tried to pull the box from him, but Luke clung to it. 'It's mine. I found it. 'Sides, I can't throw it back, less you want me to go out there again.'

He took a threatening step towards the beach. The fear I'd felt for him out there boiled up into anger. I raised my hand with every intention of slapping him, but he dodged away and raced up the track towards the cottage.

'When your father gets home he'll give you the thrashing of your life,' I called after him furiously.

But we both knew he wouldn't. He'd probably chuckle at the boy's 'high spirits', as it pleased him to call Luke's defiance.

'When the tide floods in, she'll bring a storm wi' her,' old Abel muttered grimly. 'Taste it, I can, on the wind.'

'Aye, well, for once I'm glad of it,' Bald John said. 'Good drop of rain is what's needed, make streams start running again.'

I scanned the horizon in the hope of seeing rain clouds, but even the few wisps of white had vanished. But something was approaching, something evil – I could feel it. As if in a distant land the devil had just unfurled his wings and was even now flying over the sea towards us, his shadow reaching out before him.

Chapter 3

Porlock Manor

From the foolish tongue come many troubles.

Medieval Proverb

'Give *it* to me,' Eda demanded, looming over the girl.

'He's a baby not a dog,' Christina whispered. She gazed down into the forget-me-not-blue eyes staring trustingly up into her own. The tiny mouth blew a bubble in the milk that dribbled out from between his lips. 'You must call him Oswin.'

'I call him a bastard, for that's what he is,' Eda retorted. 'A bastard without a name.'

The girl's head jerked up. 'How dare you speak to me like—'

'Like what, m'lady? Like a whore, an adulterer?'

Eda ripped the sleepy infant from her arms. Christina half rose, trying to tuck the shawl tighter around her son, but her hand was slapped away.

Her mother's tiring maid shuffled the few paces to the thick oak door of the tiny turret chamber. Eda always reminded Christina of an aged ferret standing on its hind legs, whip-thin and mangy. The maid turned, clutching Oswin tightly against the folds of her white wimple, as if she was about to sink her fangs into his neck. Christina was overwhelmed with a desire to snatch the helpless child back, but she had learned painfully, weeks ago, not to attempt that again.

'The steward tells me that your mother's cousin, Lady Pavia, is expected to arrive here shortly,' Eda announced. 'She is withdrawing from London. Many are leaving . . .' She pressed her lips tightly together as if she feared words would escape from them without her consent.

Christina frowned. 'Why?'

Eda gave that dry little cough of hers, which always meant she had no intention of answering the question but, as a servant, could not say as much.

Christina had encountered Lady Pavia only half a dozen times in her life, but that was more than enough. The first time she'd been brought to her, the old dowager had stood so close that, as a small child, all Christina had been able to see of her face was a pair of sharp eyes peering down over the great mounds of her breasts. Even a few minutes of her sharp questions always left Christina feeling like a chicken that had been weighed and pinched by a cook to determine if she was fat enough to kill.

'Your mother has informed her ladyship that you have been sent to Porlock Manor because you have an oppression of the spleen and the physician has advised removing you from the evil miasmas of the towns. I doubt that Lady Pavia will want to see you, but if she does feel obliged to visit you as a courtesy to your mother, you must pretend that you're weak and need to sleep. That should not be difficult. You're well practised in deception.'

The invention of an illness of some kind had been required to explain why a new bride of just sixteen summers should

31

have been sent away to such a remote manor and kept in isolation away from the rest of her uncle's household. Rumours of a contagion, however vague, would alarm the servants and Christina looked too healthy to be suffering from the green sickness, which often affected young girls. So Christina's mother and Eda had settled upon a safe and respectable illness – *oppression of the spleen*. It would also usefully explain Christina's frequent bouts of weeping, for everyone knew such a malady caused melancholia and, furthermore, the spleen could continue to be oppressed for as many weeks or months as might prove expedient.

Eda stared at the milk-stained top of Christina's gown and wrinkled her long, thin nose as if some foul smell had assaulted it. 'Don't allow Lady Pavia to linger. She has sharp eyes, and even if you cover yourself, she's sure to notice those are no longer the paps of a virgin maid.'

Christina's breasts had never been any larger than half-peaches, for her whole body was slender, but they had swelled alarmingly during the last few weeks before Oswin's birth. Indeed it was her breasts rather than her belly that could not be concealed beneath the folds of her gown, and had first aroused Eda's suspicions. The tiring maid had wasted no time in reporting her suspicions to her mistress.

A hollow echo rang through the stone walls as Eda pulled the stout door shut behind her. It muffled any sound beyond, so that Christina could not hear the maid's soft leather shoes retreating down the stairs, but she knew that Oswin would be taken straight to the stillroom that stood alone in the courtyard, where the woman now slept. Eda had told the other servants that the baby was her own niece's child. Her niece, she said, had died giving birth and she was obliged to tend the infant until its father, a drover, returned.

Eda was also well practised in deception. It was an art required of many a loyal servant if they were faithfully to serve their noble masters and mistresses.

When Eda had first taken charge of her son, Christina had been terrified the old woman would find a way of ensuring that Oswin did not survive. She imagined Eda leaving him naked in a draught from a casement so he would die of cold, dropping him on the hard flags or smothering him. But she had come to realise that the maid would protect the child with her life; to do otherwise would be to fail in her duty to her mistress.

Besides, even Eda didn't know for certain he was not Sir Randel's son. None of them did. The maid might make her foul accusations in the privacy of Christina's chamber, but she'd never bring disgrace upon her mistress, Lady Aliena, by uttering such suspicions about her daughter outside that chamber or in the presence of another servant. Eda was rarely obliged to hold her tongue up in the turret: except for a scurrying of serving girls who twice a day brought food and emptied the pisspot, no one else climbed those stairs. It was a prison without locks, for Christina was forbidden to set foot beyond the door, and knew full well that life could be made very much worse for her if she attempted to do so.

At least, Christina told herself, she was allowed to give suck to her son, snuggle him and drink in the sweet-sour smell of infant skin and milk that lingered in his hair as soft as thistledown. No other niece of Sir Nigel Loring would ever be permitted to suckle children at her noble breasts. It would not have been fitting for any female relative of a man who was the 'dear and beloved knight' of the Black Prince, his envoy, his diplomat, his protector, his '*cher et très bien ami*'.

No, such treasured babies were whisked away the hour the cord was cut and delivered into the arms of stout wet-nurses with teats as long as cows' udders. The noble offspring were returned only when they were weaned and walking. But Eda had dared not employ a wet-nurse for little Oswin. Such women knew they would never be paid to give suck to a great-nephew of a lowly maid. The tale of a dead mother would not fool them for an instant, and they could build a bonfire of scandal from the merest wisp of smoke.

If Christina's mother could have been sure that the child was not Randel's, Oswin would never have drawn breath, and maybe Christina would have died with him. She often lay awake in that turret room wondering if Eda would have procured some poison, or if her mother would have done the deed with her own hand. Throughout her childhood, she had felt her mother's whip descend mercilessly on her fragile little body enough times to know that she was more than capable of coldly dispatching both daughter and grandson should it prove necessary. *Death before dishonour*: that was the code of chivalry.

But until Randel had returned from France to settle the matter, Christina's mother was taking no chances. No word of Christina's condition or her banishment to Porlock would reach him there. *Blessed and Holy Virgin, let him never return to learn of it.* But the words had barely been whispered to the empty chamber before Christina shuddered with the horror of what she had said. To pray for a man's death must be a terrible sin, and to pray for your own husband's death – that was nothing short of treason.

Randel was the son-in-law of every mother's dreams, gilded with enough lands and manors to satisfy even the most avaricious dowager. It had been a marriage Christina's mother had long schemed to bring about. And if Randel publicly acknowledged the boy to be his son, she'd be only too eager to boast of a daughter so fecund that noble sons came tumbling from her belly after only a single night in the marriage bed. For once in her life, she might even praise Christina.

But if Randel refused to acknowledge the child as his own . . . Christina shivered once more. Unbidden her hand strayed to her shoulder. The bruises had faded months ago, but not the memory. One night over dinner in her uncle's great hall she had innocently offered the last two lines of a poem about a knight, which Randel, in his cups, had misquoted. He'd laughed when those around had praised his betrothed's sharp wits and joked he should take care he did not find himself impaled on the point of them. But later in the garden, when she found herself alone with him, his words had turned savage and his fist merciless.

Suppose Randel had now found a wealthier match or a woman he lusted after, it would be easy for him to rid himself of an inconvenient wife by denying the boy and proclaiming his mother unfaithful. Not even her uncle's favoured position would save Christina then. Indeed, it would make her dishonour worse. She would be forced to do public penance, so that all the world could see her shame, then be walled up in a nunnery till she withered and died. Her son would be sold to a tanner to spend his life collecting dog dung. That was if they were both lucky.

Christina knew only too well that a girl suffering from oppression of the spleen could make a full and miraculous recovery, but just as easily such a malady could suddenly prove fatal.

Chapter 4

Matilda

St Antony is the patron saint of swineherds and he cures ailments of the skin, for pork fat is a fair remedy for such maladies.

The shutter rattled violently in the gust of wind. The leather hinge was almost cracked through, but there was no one to mend it. My husband should have attended to it before he went back to sea. There is much he should have seen to before he departed. He was a ship's carpenter, and had the smallest peg wanted hammering in on the hull, or a sea-hatch needed rehanging, it would have been done before the master had finished giving the order, but he never stirred himself to mend half the things that needed seeing to in my cottage, even when I scolded him to it a dozen times a day.

Gatty half turned her head as the wooden shutter rapped at the casement, but she didn't move, save to wriggle herself a little closer to the fire. When I'd returned from saying the Nones prayers at St Olaf's chapel, she was dashing about the cottage as if she was possessed of a demon, leaping on and off the table, racing about the room. Cats are always agitated when they sense a wind is coming. But when it arrives they settle themselves down somewhere warm and sheltered, as if their work is done.

A cry outside made us both turn our heads. Had I caught the thief at last?

I lit the lantern that hung ready, and slid my longest, sharpest knife into my belt. I tried to ease the door open quietly, but it was snatched from my grasp and slammed against the wall. The wind shrieked through the cottage, lifting the bracken on the floor and sending the flames in the hearth guttering. The smoke whirled out in choking clouds. Gatty scrambled up the ladder into the half-loft to hide. I was compelled to set the lantern down and use both hands to pull the door closed behind me. It was as black as the devil's soul outside.

Holding my skirts tightly against the wind, I edged towards the pigsty and raised the lantern. The sow had ushered her remaining six piglets into the round stone shelter. She lay with her back to the hole to shelter them. She'd farrowed eleven, but crushed two and three had vanished in the night. 'Foxes,' my neighbours said, 'or wolves.' One even told me it was a bear, for he swore he'd seen tracks in the forest. But I knew exactly what manner of beast had taken my piglets. I'd set iron caltrops around the sty, burying the spikes beneath a thin layer of leaf mould. But I had not set them to catch any animal.

When a storm is coming, pigs run about with straw hanging from their jaws. Like cats, they sense its approach. Not many cottagers in Porlock Weir kept pigs. If they were fishermen or sailors, they wouldn't even utter the name. *The things*, they called them, or else *grunters*, and if a pig crossed their path on their way to the boats, they'd turn tail for home. They'd rather let their children go hungry than put to sea. They were quick enough to read omens in the dumb beasts, but spat in the face of our Lord, even when He turned the golden sun black in the sky above them. It was the villagers I called grunters.

I swept the feeble beam from the lantern over the places where I'd buried the caltrops. I'd caught him at last! There he was, rolling helplessly on the ground, his foot impaled by a spike. But I felt a pang of disappointment as I moved closer and saw it was nothing but an empty sack that had snagged on a bush and was flapping in the wind. It was probably the sack the thief had brought with him to steal yet another of my piglets.

Suppose he'd snatched one already, but dropped the sack and piglet when he heard me coming. It might be running loose close by. I cast my lantern about again, poking under bushes and listening for the piglet's squeals. But a herd of wild boar might have been running through my herb garden and I wouldn't have heard them over that wind.

A violent gust almost sent me stumbling on to one of my own caltrops. If I continued blundering about in that storm I'd likely break a leg and my idle neighbours wouldn't trouble to answer my cries. Best to wait till morning light then search again. I consoled myself with the thought that if the piglet was hiding close by, it would return to the sound of its dam's grunts when she stirred at daybreak.

I fought my way back towards the cottage door. The sea thundered against the cliffs, roaring as if it was determined to out-shout the wind. The glimmer of lights from the lanterns set in the casements of the cottages caught the white tops of the waves, which were already crashing over the track that ran along the shore. More pinpricks of yellow light were swaying up the hill. Some of the villagers who lived closest to the beach must be moving their families to higher ground.

The wind knocked me hard against the stone wall of my cottage. I groped along it, setting my lantern down to try to stop the door being snatched from its hinges as I opened it. As I turned to retrieve the lantern, my attention was caught by something bright gleaming far out in the raging sea. I blinked furiously as the salt-wind blurred my eyes with tears. Three tiny lights rose up out of the darkness, only to vanish again. I knew them at once for the lights of a ship, and one that was perilously close to the cliffs. Again they rose, like fish leaping to escape the maw of a whale, only to vanish once more. The lights reappeared, but there were only two this time and set at such an angle I knew the ship must have struck the rocks.

I muttered a fervent prayer to the Blessed Virgin and to all the saints for those poor souls on board that stricken vessel. God grant them a miracle. Bring them safe ashore! But even as I watched, the ship's lantern lights were swallowed by the waves, and they did not rise again.

Chapter 5

Will

Riddle me this: What is the distance from the surface of the sea to its deepest part?

The old besom nearly caught me. It was that evil cat of hers, more savage than any watchdog. I could almost believe what some of the village women mutter about that imp being her familiar. I swear it whispered in her ear and told her when I was creeping around her cottage. How else would she have heard me above the wind?

I never thought she'd go so far as to lay caltrops, though. Where had the Holy Hag got hold of those? I'd come within a mouse's whisker of standing on one the first time she hid them beneath the leaf litter, but my bandy legs saved me from being impaled. Longshanks put their feet straight down, I rock from side to side, which, I can assure you, is agony on the hips and knees. But for once I was grateful for, as my foot lifted sideways, the edge of my shoe knocked against one of the spikes, sending the caltrop rolling. After that I took care always to take a stick to prod the ground whenever I went there to purloin another piglet.

I know what you're thinking – what kind of man steals food from an elderly woman? But how much meat can one old besom eat all by herself? I couldn't claim to be starving. Fish I could catch a-plenty, gather seaweed too, even limpets and razor shells. But meat and bread, pies and puddings were what I was used to in my lord's employ, and fish alone just doesn't satisfy the belly, not when you eat nothing else morning, noon and night. I salivated for meat. I dreamed of meat. I craved it.

In the beginning I offered Matilda several fishes for just a small piece of pork. But she picked up her broom and shoved me away from her threshold, as if I was a flea-bitten dog begging for scraps. 'Get away, you filthy little creature.'

Well, you can't say I hadn't offered to trade fairly, and you know us stray dogs: we'll snatch any food left unattended. We are just dumb creatures, after all.

But she'd almost caught me this time. I hadn't heard the door open over the wind, and only just reached the back of her house before the light from the lantern caught me. I hadn't managed to fasten the neck of the sack and, as I dived for cover, the wretched piglet wriggled free and ran off into the darkness, while the wind snatched away the sack. I didn't dare move until I saw the lantern light disappear as she shuffled around the house. But I couldn't risk trying again. She was probably lying in wait just round the corner. I'd be back, though. She needn't think she'd won.

One of the advantages of being a dwarf, real or fake, is that you're already low to the ground so I didn't need to duck as I scuttled along the back of her cottage and away down the track. A light burst in the dark sky above me, startling me so much that I tripped and only my stick saved me from falling on my face. The beacon on the watchtower had been set ablaze. Flames were leaping into

41

the night, whipped up like demons in the wind. I heard shouts and glimpsed lanterns bobbing up and down as men hurried towards the shore. Maybe a ship or boat was foundering.

I scuttled down the hill. Waves were surging over the path that ran above the beach, the dark water swirling about the lowest cottages. The red glow of the beacon flames revealed a jagged gap in the row of houses below. One of the wooden smoke huts had already been smashed and swept away. Others in that row would surely follow before the night was out. If there was a ship out there in that storm, there was little hope of any man being saved from it. Anything – or anyone – that fell into those waves would be swept out to sea or, if they were carried towards the beach, dashed to pieces against the stone banks of the fish weirs or smashed against a cottage wall.

I joined the other men standing on the slope looking down at the shore below. The lanterns did little more than illuminate the troubled faces of their owners. I stared out over the black water of the bay. Even at that distance, salt spray and skeins of white foam were caught up by the wind and flung into our stinging eyes, drenching our faces. But though I strained to peer into the darkness, I could glimpse no ship out there. It must either have broken its back on the rocks and sunk or had rounded the headland if, by some miracle, it had survived.

'Hey, what's that?' a man shouted. He was crouching down, holding his lantern as low as he could, but the light was too feeble to illuminate anything except the grass and wind-whipped bushes. We edged further down the slope.

'Someone's there,' Daveth shouted. 'See, in the water, 'tween the cottages.'

'Just a bit of sailcloth being tossed about,' another bellowed back, over the roar of the wind.

'Looks human to me.'

'If it is, it'll be a corpse. No sense in risking a living man just to pull out a dead 'un.'

'Head's sticking up – that's no corpse,' Daveth shouted. 'But if we don't get him out of there he soon will be. He'll not be able to hold on long in that swell. He'll be dragged back out.'

The men crowded together, all trying to peer down into the gap between the cottages below. I was squashed between them, a mass of stinking breeches pressing into my face, but I was used to that. At least the longshanks had their uses: they kept off the worst of the wind.

Daveth gazed round at the knot of men and suddenly noticed me, wedged up against his crotch. 'Use the little man. Tie a rope round him and drop him down there to take a squint.'

The men held up their lanterns and studied me, as if I was a strange fish they'd just dragged up in their nets. I thought they were going to hitch a rope around me and toss me into the water without so much as a by-your-leave.

But at least the packhorse man, Elis, had the courtesy to ask, 'You willing? You being so light, we can lower you down quicker than any of us.'

I didn't doubt that, though I wasn't at all sure they'd bother to haul me back up. But if there was some poor bastard clinging on in that sea, they'd be growing colder and weaker with every wave that crashed over them. Besides, if I refused, the villagers would probably throw me down anyway. I nodded and tried to assure myself that at least fishermen and packmen between them could be trusted to tie a secure knot.

The wind hit me the moment I began to descend, knocking me from my feet. I slid down the slope of the rise, bumping over every stone and scraping against every thorny shrub on the way. Waves were surging in on both sides of the cottages, splashing against the walls and bank, so that before I'd even reached the bottom of the slope I was dripping from the spray. I was forced to grab a particularly prickly bush to stop myself slipping straight into the water, and tried to rub the salt water from my stinging eyes with my sodden sleeve.

The light from the lanterns the men were dangling above me grazed the black water, giving it an oily sheen, but it was impossible to judge just how deep it was. I cursed myself with every name of fool. Light I might be, but down there what was needed was a giant, not a dwarf, to wade through the surge. The rope was slack. I edged down. My foot slipped and I plunged straight into the freezing water, just as another wave crashed over. Choking and gagging, I was so panic-stricken I didn't even realise the men above had tightened the rope and were hauling me out, like a mackerel on a line.

As I rose, I glimpsed something white beneath me. The poor wretch was tangled in the struts of a fish-drying rack. The face vanished as another wave surged over it. Long dark hair streamed out as the wave dragged the head back, and the face floated to the surface again. In the flickering red glow from the beacon it was hard to distinguish any features, but I was sure of two things: it was a woman, not a man, who floated down there, and whoever she was, she was dead.

What I should have done then was to tug on the rope and signal for them to haul me up. What was the sense in risking my life to drag up a corpse, when in all likelihood the fishermen would simply hurl her back into the sea? They always said a corpse that the sea had claimed for her own should never be stolen from her. But dwarfs, even unnatural ones like me, are contrary creatures, perverse. And, after all, as my erstwhile master would be only too willing to testify, I am a thief.

With one huge effort I flung myself forward, lunging towards the woman and grabbing her by the hair, just as another wave broke over us both. I clung to her as the wave sucked back with such power I was sure it would drag me off the rope. If I'd had even a grain of hope that the woman was alive, one touch of her fish-cold skin banished it. But somehow that made me more determined the sea would not keep her.

My legs may be as bowed as a tar barrel, though my arms are strong, thanks to years of having to haul myself up on to benches and beds made for longshanks. But my hands were growing numb in the icy water, and the waves crashed over me several times before I managed to get the rope looped over both of us.

The men above were yelling down, but their words might as well have been the screech of gulls for all the sense I could make of what they were saying above the roar of wind and waves. I could scarcely move my fingers for the cold, but I tore with my teeth until her gown suddenly ripped free from the rack, and for a terrifying moment we were both floating free in the water. She lay like a lover in my embrace, her head flopped on to my shoulder, the wet strands of her hair tangled about my neck.

I tugged sharply on the rope, and felt an answering jerk as it tightened, dragging us from the sucking water. My crooked back smashed against the slope. Then came the slow, painful ascent, as we were jerked and hauled over grass and through bushes, inch by inch up the rise, with the rope cutting and burning into my flesh. The woman's head hung against my shoulder, her body limp in my arms as if I was carrying a sleeping lover to my bed. For all the pain it was causing me, I wanted that slope to grow even higher, so that I could hold her just a few minutes more. But Mistress Time was playing her usual tricks and would not spread herself for me.

'Look at that! The little man's caught himself a woman.'

'Easy does it. Don't jerk her. She could have broken bones.'

They were going to be bloody furious when they realised they'd been hauling up a corpse, but she was *my* corpse. And I was the thief who had stolen her from the sea.

Chapter 6

Sara

*Fish bones must never be burned, but cast back into the
sea else the fish will not return.*

'Twas to my door they brought her. Not that my cottage
wasn't already full to the rafters with Elis's sister, Aldith,
her husband Daveth and their three chillern, as well as
Goda, Elis's youngest sister, whose belly was swollen with
a babe.

Elis and Daveth carried the poor woman in. They brought
the wind in with them an' all, sending the dried bracken
on the floor whirling and the flames of the hearth fire
gusting so wildly it was a mercy the one didn't set the other
ablaze. Even the crowd of menfolk who squashed in the
doorway, peering in curiously, could not keep out the blast
of the storm. I snatched away some pots and wooden bowls
as Elis and Daveth laid the woman down on the narrow
table, for there was no place else to put her.

'Should I fetch Father Cuthbert?' someone called.

'By the time you find him, it'll be too late, I reckon,'
another said.

'Already is, I'd say. Should've tossed her straight back.
She'd have taken the storm back out to sea with her.'

47

'Out, out, all of you,' I ordered, 'and shut that door behind you afore the wind lifts the thatch clean off.'

But they couldn't seem to drag their eyes from the bedraggled woman, especially that queer little dwarf who lives in the cave on the shore. Makes my skin crawl, he does, the way he's always grinning, even when there's nothing to laugh at. He was doing it again right there in my cottage, as if a poor drowned woman was a huge joke to him. Spiteful, I call it.

Exasperated, I poked a couple of the men in the belly with the end of my broom, pushing them out of my doorway until they finally retreated, dragging the door closed behind them.

The flames of the fire steadied and the bracken fell back to cover the beaten-earth floor, but none of us stirred. We just stared at the woman on the table, as seawater dripped from her sodden skirts and long hair. Her eyes were closed, her lips blue.

Elis, who was closest, pressed the flat of his hand over the woman's chest, then grimly shook his head.

Aldith bustled forward, pushed him aside, rubbed the blade of her knife against her skirts and held it close to the woman's lips. She peered at the blade. 'She's breathing. See? It's misty!'

'That'll be naught but damp from her skin rising in the heat of the fire,' Elis said.

Aldith rounded on her brother. 'I've brought enough babbies into this world to tell if a body's breathing or not.'

Goda whimpered and her hand flew to her swollen belly.

'Don't you fret,' I said quickly. 'This 'un'll come out alive, won't it, Aldith?'

Goda had been with child once before, but that baby had

never drawn breath. Aldith reckoned it had died days before in her womb, though Goda had refused to admit that anything was wrong till the fever had taken hold. It was a miracle she'd not died too.

Aldith was vigorously chafing the woman's hands between her own. 'Here, help me turn her over. She'll have swallowed a barrel of seawater and sooner that's out of her the better. Course, if the menfolk had thought to carry her face down, she'd have coughed it up b'now. But that's the trouble with men, don't think, do they?'

'She'd still be under waves if we'd not pulled her out,' her husband said indignantly.

Aldith ignored him, though Daveth was used to that. She nodded to me. 'Need to get her wet clothes off too. Chill her to the marrow, they will.'

As soon as the woman was turned, water dribbled from her mouth and by the time we'd stripped her and rubbed her cold, clammy limbs and chest vigorously with warm goose-fat, she was coughing and her chest was rising and falling rapidly, though she'd still not opened her eyes.

All the time Aldith and I worked, my Elis and Daveth crouched by the fire spooning down bowls of pottage to warm themselves, but their eyes kept darting back to the woman as if she was the rarest beauty they'd seen. When they thought I'd seen them gawping, they'd sheepishly look away again, like youths caught peeking at a naked girl through a casement. But they were not boys and the stranger was no blushing maid.

She was handsome enough in her own way, I suppose. Well, she would have been, if she'd had a peck of flesh on her to fill out those hollow cheeks. It was hard to place her age in the dim light of the rush candles: maybe forty or so.

49

Her hair was long, thick and dark, but streaked with white. She was no high-born lady. Used to hard work by the looks of it, for her body, though bruised and bleeding from the rocks, was lean and tough, the muscles of her arms and belly hard. She'd a livid scar on her shoulder, a wound not long healed, and a mark on her belly low down near her bush of black hair. Dark blue it was, the colour of a new bruise, and that's what I thought it was at first, just another bruise. But then I realised it was the picture of an eye, wide open, staring right at you. I mean, who would paint an eye on their body and down there too? I tried to scrub it off with a bit of rag, but it wouldn't budge. So I covered it quick afore the menfolk could see it.

She was alive and breathing, but even strong vinegar wafted under her nose wouldn't rouse her. Nor could she be induced to swallow so much as a sip of warmed ale. So, there was no help for it but to lay her down on the old sheepskins we used under the packs of the horses and wait to see if, come dawn, she'd be among the living or the dead.

I snuffed out the rush lights and banked down the fire as we all settled down for what was left of the night, squashed tight as herrings in a barrel. The others were soon grunting and snoring but, exhausted though I was, I couldn't sleep. Now that the voices in the cottage had fallen silent, the wind shrieked louder than ever, rattling and banging every loose thing. I lay in the only bed in the cottage, alongside Goda, wondering if the next creak or groan meant a tree was about to crash down on our roof or the rocks from the hillside above were hurtling towards us.

A flash of blue lightning burst through the cracks in the shutters. Startled, I turned my head. The woman's eyes were wide open, like the eye on her belly. I sat up, thinking that if she'd recovered her senses only to find herself lying in some strange place, she'd be afeared.

'You're safe now,' I whispered, 'among friends . . . Shall I fetch you some ale . . . a bowl of pottage?'

But as another flash lit up the cottage, I saw the woman's eyes were closed again and she lay as still as death.

Aldith's youngest son, Kitto, woke first. His wails dragged the rest of us groaning from our sleep. Soon as I remembered, I glanced over to the pile of sheepskins, fearing the worst, but the place where the woman had lain was empty. Maybe she'd not been human at all, but a sea-sprite or the ghost of a drowned woman who had vanished with the first light. But Aldith's daughter, Ibb, pointed to the door, which was unlatched. Sprites and wraiths have no need of doors, and the woman's clothes, which I'd laid near the fire to dry, had also gone. Elis stretched and, rubbing his back, wandered out into the grey dawn. Daveth and I followed.

Elis jerked his chin towards the meadow on the slope above us, where the hobbled packhorses were grazing. 'At least the widgebeasts came through the storm without hurt. Brought a fair few branches down, that wind has, but ground's still as dry as a beggar's loaf. As soon as we've had a bite, I'll go down with you to your cottage, Daveth, see what damage's been done.'

Daveth grimaced. 'Be a mercy if the walls are still standing.' His gaze strayed back to the open door of the cottage, where Aldith stood, dandling little Kitto on her hip. 'Strange that maid going off without a word.'

Aldith snorted. 'That'll teach you to go dragging queer fish from the sea. Your father used to say, "If you pull anything out you can't name, throw it back."'

51

Aldith and I set about chivvying the older boys to stir themselves. But there was scarcely room for us to move in the cottage, and as fast as one of us tried to pick up a blanket, someone else would step back on it. Aldith was soon pushing the children out through the door to fetch wood and water to give us space enough to mend the fire.

I peered into the pot. What I'd prepared yesterday should have fed Elis and the boys for supper and breakfast as well. But the menfolk had shovelled down most of it after they'd brought the woman back, just to warm their bones, and the scrapings that were left wouldn't fill the bellies of my own family, never mind Aldith's brood and Goda too. But I couldn't send them back to a cold, wet cottage without a bite of something hot inside them. Besides, who knew if they even had a cottage to return to?

This was always a hungry time of year, with the last of the winter's stores gone and precious little yet to harvest. If I thinned the pottage enough to make it stretch round all of us, it would be as weak as whey. Hot would be the best you could say of it, but it wouldn't stave off the men's hunger even till midday, and what would I give them then?

The tang of salt-weed wafted into the cottage and a shadow fell across the room, as someone blocked the doorway. I half turned, thinking it to be Elis or Daveth, meaning to warn them the meal wasn't ready. But it was the woman from the sea who stood there. She ambled towards me, dangling a dozen good-sized fish from a cord threaded through their gills and an armful of dripping kelp. She dropped both on to the table where only hours ago she had lain as limp as a gutted mackerel. Aside from the grazes on her face, she looked remarkably lively for a corpse.

She gestured towards the fire. 'Many people to feed. We

must roast the fish, so we can eat quickly. There is much work to be done.'

She spoke as if she was the mistress of the house and I the servant. I could understand her well enough, but she had a queer way of saying the words. The pedlars from the other side of the moors, who come here to trade, have a strange tongue too, but not like hers.

I pointed at the fish. 'You get those from the weirs?' She said nothing. 'There's people own those weirs. Can't just take—'

'Fish were washed up behind the cottages,' she said, giving me a cold stare. 'Gulls and cats eat well today.'

I cursed myself. Of course there'd be fish stranded on the shore after that storm. I should have thought of it myself and sent the boys out early to collect what they could. But the whole village would be out scavenging by now, as well as that monstrous cat of Matilda's. Overfed beast it was, always hanging about the nets. It'ud maul a dozen fish, just to spoil them from spite.

I set the boys to building a fire outside, big enough to roast all the fish at once, while I gutted them. Some I put on the spit to cook. But the sea woman wrapped the rest in the fronds of kelp – *devil's apron*, Aldith calls it – baking them on stones she placed among the hot embers. Aldith watched her wrapping the fish as if she was a madman fishing for the moon and, later, when we were all gathered round and pulling the steaming fragments of flesh from the bones, I noticed that Aldith was careful to eat only the fish that I had spit-roasted. The kelp gave the fish an odd salt-sweet taste, but the menfolk didn't seem to mind it.

The sea woman worked and ate in silence, asking us nothing and saying not a word about her rescue until I began to wonder if she even remembered how she'd come to be here. Aldith can't abide not knowing everything about a body, so I knew she'd not be able to contain her curiosity for long, but the woman told her only what she asked, no more.

Her name, she said, was Janiveer.

'Queer sort of a name,' Aldith grunted. 'You come from Wales?'

'I come from a ship.'

Had she seen others in the water? She'd seen nothing. Did the ship strike the rocks? She didn't know. Where was the ship bound? They hadn't told her.

'But where are *you* going?' Aldith persisted.

Janiveer gazed up into the grey-clouded sky, watching a rust-coloured kite flapping over the cottage towards its usual hunting grounds of Kitnor. Those birds seldom came east to Porlock Weir, preferring to feast on the creatures of the forest and moors, rather than the fish-scraps from our village. She marked its flight into the far distance where its fellows were mere specks in the sky, gliding above the distant hills.

'I go or I stay – you will choose.'

It soon became plain that if the choice was left to Aldith, Janiveer would be going – and going a lot further than Kitnor too. All the time we were eating, Daveth could scarcely keep his eyes off her, and my Elis wasn't much better. Janiveer didn't flaunt herself, like some of the captains' harlots who sail on the ships, quite the opposite: she ignored the menfolk completely, but her indifference to them seemed only to captivate them the more.

Aldith scarcely waited for Daveth to finish eating before she chivvied him down the hill to see what could be done to dry out their cottage. She left her two youngest, Ibb and Kitto, with me to mind, for they'd be more of a hindrance than a help, but much to her annoyance her eldest, Col, had disappeared with my Luke and Hob. As Aldith hurried down the path, I assured her that I'd send Col down to help his father as soon as he returned and Luke, too, though privately I doubted I'd see any of the lads until their empty bellies drove them home.

Janiveer was standing on top of the rise in front of the cottage, staring down at the beach below. I wondered if she was searching for any sign of the ship or those she'd sailed with. I didn't know if she'd had a husband or family on board. As if she could feel me watching, she clambered back down, running the last few yards to keep her balance on the steep slope.

'You want your sons? Up there.' She pointed to the dense thicket above the cottage. 'The box they took from the sea . . . it is . . .' She wrapped her arms about her as if she was suddenly chilled. 'They must not open it. Throw it back into deep water where it cannot be found. I warn you, do it quickly.' She stretched out her hand, and lightly touched her finger to my forehead. 'A life for a life.'

Then she walked away towards the shore. I stood staring after her. The spot she had touched on my face burned cold as if I had been touched with ice.

The sea had taken what little remained of the villagers' winter stores, paying for what it took with the fish it had cast up on the shore for us. Everyone in the village had gathered what they could, even collecting fishes that had already been mauled by gulls, otters or Matilda's brute of a cat. If just a mouthful or two of uneaten flesh remained, it could always be added to the pottage pots. And I would need every scrap we could gather, for Goda, Aldith and her family had returned to lodge with us at least for the next few days. Their cottage was too wet and cold to sleep in. Puddles of seawater lay on the beaten-earth floor. Their bed boards were sodden, and every pot they owned was slimed with mud and weed.

There were too many of us to stay inside my cottage to eat, so that evening we built a great fire outside and cooked the fish the sea had given us. Seeing the blaze, others in the village climbed the slope to share the warmth, for the wood-piles next to the beach cottages had either been soaked in seawater or swept away. They brought what little food they had to share – fish, of course. What did anyone have left but fish? Old Abel tottered up and Meryn on his crutches. The dwarf sidled in, worming his way closest to the fire. Even that bitterweed Matilda came shuffling along, though her cottage had not been touched.

But I knew what had drawn her, what had drawn all of them: not the warmth of the fire, or the smell of roasted fish, but their curiosity about Janiveer. For it's not every day a woman is plucked alive from the sea and, stranger still, we had found no other soul from the ship, either cast on to the rocks or drifting on the waves. A few planks and spars that might have come from a stricken vessel had washed up, and a couple of staved-in barrels, but no bodies. If others had drowned, they must have been swept out to sea. In a day or so, they might drift ashore in one of the many bays further along the coast. But if they did, not even Aldith could winkle any gossip from the mouth of a corpse.

Janiveer said little at first, no more than she had told Aldith and me, but when Matilda asked her if God had turned the sun black over the ship, Janiveer nodded. She stared for a long time at Matilda, as if she was trying to read something in her face, like a sailor gazes at the sky, trying to read the stars.

She gestured towards the sea, softly hissing over the shingle. 'On the far shores, there have been many signs. In Burgundy, rain fell as blood.'

'Do you all hear that?' Matilda crowed. 'Blood! The waters were turned to blood, just as in the plagues of Egypt.'

'Burgundy – that in Egypt, then, is it?' the lad, Crabfish, said, beaming stupidly at everyone as if he'd at last understood what someone was saying.

People smiled indulgently and shook their heads. It was a land beyond France somewhere, they told the lad, but poor Crabfish had no notion where France was either, so he quickly lost interest and stuffed more fish into his slack mouth.

'I seen it rain frogs once,' Cador, the bailiff, said.

'Aye, and fishes too,' old Abel added.

'Rained those last night, I reckon,' Elis said, jerking his head towards the many that were roasting or boiling on the fire. 'Could do with some real rain, though. Never known rivers run so low. Falls at Silcombe are naught but a trickle of gnat's piss.'

A chunter of voices broke out, all telling of this stream or that spring that had dried up or near to it.

Janiveer's voice rang out in the darkness, scything through the chatter. 'In Bologna, a cross of fire hung in the skies all the day. In the sixth hour it fled across the heavens. It plunged into the sea. The water around it burned scarlet and gold.'

'Are you listening?' Matilda called out. 'Do you heed God's warnings?'

We hushed her impatiently as Janiveer continued: 'Men

swear they have seen two castles rise from the ground where there was not even a stone before. They stood strong and tall as if they had taken a hundred years to build. At dawn a band of knights rode out from the first castle, pennants streaming. From the other castle, came men dressed in black, their faces hidden. All day they gave battle. First the knights defeated the men in black, then the fortunes of battle turned and the knights were defeated. But those who saw them fall from their horses, or their helmets knocked from their heads, said there were not living men inside the armour but the white skulls and bones of the dead. At sunset the slain rose up from the ground and all the warriors rode back through the castle gates. Then the castles sank into the earth. Only the ground churned up from the horses' hoofs marked where the fierce battle had been fought.'

The menfolk huddled round the blazing fire gave a pleasurable shudder. Some murmured that this foreigner was as entertaining as any of the travelling storytellers you could hear at Porlock market. 'Tell us more,' someone urged.

'Foxes,' Janiveer said, gazing not at us, but up at the dark sky. 'Running in packs, swarming out of the forests into villages and towns, savaging babies in their cradles, attacking their parents when they tried to drive them off. Wolves, too, coming into the villages even while it is day, devouring men alive.'

'Foxes are the devil's beasts,' Matilda said triumphantly. 'Demons in disguise.'

Little Ibb, clutching the rag doll she always carried, gazed fearfully over her shoulder towards the dark forest and began to wail. She tried to bury herself in Aldith's arms, almost knocking baby Kitto off her lap.

Elis raised his head. 'Heard the same tale about those ghost castles from a pedlar up on the moors. Been seen here too. Wales it was.'

'Wales bain't here,' old Abel said firmly. 'Foreigners, they are. Can't believe a word that comes out of a Welshman's mouth, no more than you can any foreigner.' He jerked his head in the direction of Janiveer to make his meaning plain to the gathering. 'That's if you can understand a word they say to start with.'

'I'll tell you something that isn't just talk,' Elis said. 'Something that's worse than all the foxes and wolves and demon castles put together. The Great Pestilence has returned.'

The crackle of the fire, the distant sucking of waves, the creaking of the trees seemed suddenly to be growing louder. But there were no human sounds at all. No one spoke or even moved, waiting for Elis to continue.

He glanced anxiously at the bailiff. 'I was all set to bring you the news last night, Cador, soon as I returned, but by the time I came down from the high moor, the storm was raging and the beacon had been fired. And this morning . . .' he grimaced '. . . with all that cleaning up to be done, well, I reckoned the news would get no worse for the keeping. But it'll not come as much of a surprise to any, I reckon. We've all heard rumours of it from the sailors and pedlars these past weeks.'

'Aye, and that's exactly what they are,' Cador said. 'Just rumours, pedlars' tales to frighten you into buying their potions and charms. It's a trick as old as the sea, like the merchants tell you some new war's broken out 'twixt us and France so you'd best buy pepper afore the ports are blocked, or there's been a plague of insects in the north that's eaten half the grain, so they've had to raise their prices.'

'It's more than rumours now, Cador,' Elis said. 'Every pedlar, merchant and drover on t'other side of the moor brings some fresh tale of it. Broke out in London. Been raging there since Lent, at back end of March. Any man who can afford to is fleeing the city. Any who can't lie dead in the streets.'

There was a sudden stirring as if a violent gust had blown through the gathering. Some villagers crossed themselves. Others clenched their fists around their thumbs to ward off the evil. Sweethearts felt for each other's hands. Women pressed their faces against their babies.

I pulled Hob to me, hugging him so hard he squealed and tried to wriggle out of my arms. He had no notion of the dread those words conjured. Nor did the other chillern. They were not even born when pestilence first swept across the land, leaving villages deserted and babbies starving beside the rotting corpses of their dead parents. But I remembered it only too well: the men taking turns, night and day, up in that watchtower, ready to light the beacon fire the moment they saw any ship that appeared to be adrift. They'd run to the shore and row out as close as they dared, throwing lighted barrels of tar on to the ship's deck and firing burning arrows at the sails to set the vessel ablaze, for fear that the crew were dying from the contagion. I was barely thirteen summers the year the pestilence struck, only two years older than my Luke, but even now in my nightmares I still saw the bloated corpse of my mother and woke with the sickly stench of her death in my nostrils.

Suddenly there was a torrent of voices, as if someone had pulled a bung from a keg of brine. Every man and woman around that cooking fire in the darkness began yelling questions.

'How far has it spread? How close is it?'

'Is the king doing nothing to stop it?'

'What about the physicians? The priests?'

'Quiet, woman! Let the man speak, will you?'

Elis stared down at his calloused fingers. 'They say King Edward tried what he might. His physicians said it was a great cattle market they call Smithfield that was the cause of it all. The blood and entrails were giving off bad humours and poisoning the air. So the king gave orders that no beasts were to be slaughtered there. But it did no good. Even bishops and noblemen who can afford the most expensive physic have died. The pestilence takes a man so quick that some are dead afore the physician can even be fetched. King and his court have fled to the New Forest, walled themselves up in Beaulieu Abbey till it's over.'

'London's many days' ride from here,' Daveth said. 'We're safe enough.'

Others murmured in agreement. 'If the king's taken his wife and chillern to the New Forest, he must reckon it'll not spread out of the city, least not that far at any rate.'

'It did before,' Elis said.

'But who's to know if this is the same fever?' Cador protested. 'Last time the Great Pestilence came on ships from foreign parts. But if this fever broke out in London, it'll more than likely be poisoned wells that's the cause of their sickness or, like the king says, the bad humours from those great beast markets of theirs. Sir Nigel's steward says they get the bloody flux in that city every year, regular as the tides, but we don't suffer it.'

'It rages all across France too,' Janiveer said quietly. 'It will spread.'

61

'But not to here!' Aldith spat on her fingers to ward off the evil words, as if Janiveer was calling the sickness to us.

Matilda rose, her eyes shining in the firelight. She pointed up at the night sky, where the stars hung like shards of ice. 'Are you blind and deaf? The wells and springs have been shut up against us. Only yesterday the sun turned black right over the village. Then came a great storm without rain. What more warning do you need? The Great Pestilence will strike us here, in the heart of the village. It will destroy you, your wives and children, your horses and goats. You must repent – repent before you are dragged down to Hell by your heinous sins.'

She strode away, back down the path towards her cottage. Long after we lost sight of her, we could hear her, flinging psalms and prophecies up into the heavens.

'That old hag has set the babby off now with her ranting,' Aldith grumbled, pushing Ibb from her lap and gathering the wailing Kitto into her arms. 'Little wonder her poor husband spends so many months at sea – it's the only peace he gets from her bitter tongue. When he comes home this time, someone ought to cut him a stick and teach him how to use it on her back.' She was rocking Kitto so violently that he bellered even louder. 'Why doesn't she go and preach to them as has the pestilence? Stands to reason, it's London that has all the sinners 'cause that's where the pestilence has struck. I'm telling you, it'll not come here,' she repeated emphatically.

Several others nodded. 'Course it won't.'

'The pestilence will come,' Janiveer said. 'And it will come soon.'

Unlike Matilda's raving, her tone was calm and flat, but it served only to make her words all the more chilling, as if she really knew.

'My darling's dead,' Goda shrieked, wrapping her arms round her swollen belly. 'The pestilence's taken him. I know it has. He's dead!'

Aldith gave her young sister a little shake. 'It's done nothing of the sort. You mustn't dwell on such things. It's thinking dark thoughts that poisons the womb. Your man'll be back from the sea just as soon as may be, with a purse full of coins to take care of you and the babby. You think on that.'

She rounded on Janiveer. 'My sister's already lost her first. You want to fright her into losing this 'un and all? Anyhow, what do you know about the pestilence? Reckon yourself cleverer than the king's physicians, do you?'

'I know how to save you from it,' Janiveer answered quietly, 'how to save you all.'

Bald John, the blacksmith, gave a roar of laughter. 'Cador's right. Every friar, pedlar and camelot on the road'll be claiming they have the certain cure, from the blood of St Sebastian to the alchemist's stone and every manner of potion and amulet between. Seen it all afore, I have. If the man who's fool enough to buy their cure lives, then he thinks it's money well spent. And if the pestilence kills him, he's not likely to come asking for his coins back, is he? It's an easy way to earn a living, that's for sure.'

Cador nodded his agreement. 'Aye, so if you've some bless-vore you're trying to sell us, woman, you'd best take it to London. There are enough fools there who'll buy it. Sir Nigel's steward reckons some of them have got heads stuffed full of gold pieces instead of brains. But we've no coins to waste in Porlock Weir and we've more wit than to part with them, if we did.'

There's many would have flown into a rage to be mocked

like that, but Janiveer remained as calm as if the bailiff had been telling her the price of beans.

'What I offer you cannot be bought with coins. I have a price, but it is not to be paid in gold or silver.' She swept her sea-cold gaze around the circle of villagers huddled in the firelight. 'I will save this village if just one among you has the courage to give me what I ask.'

Chapter 7

The eye sends a person into a ditch and a camel into a cauldron.

Medieval Proverb

The woman from the sea watches the people of the land, and she waits, her great grey-blue eyes unblinking in the firelight. Her mother taught her how to watch and wait. Sometimes it is the only weapon a woman can wield. But in Janiveer's hand it is sharper and more deadly than any sword even the strongest knight can raise. Under her unblinking gaze she knows the villagers will fall silent, shiver. They will glance at her and, finding her gaze too piercing, too knowing, their eyes will dart away, like a shoal of little fishes.

But an incubus will creep into their mouths and speak with their tongues. They will find themselves asking the very question they resolved not to ask. But only when they are forced to ask it will they be ready to hear the answer. And that time, she knows, is not yet. Now she watches.

Her mother gave Janiveer her eyes, all three of them. Two were fashioned in the womb, twins of her mother's and her grandmother's before that, stretching back into a time beyond even the stories they tell around the fires in winter. The third eye she received from her mother's hand, not her womb.

One frosted night when she was no more than eleven

summers, her mother woke Janiveer. Her grandmothers and aunts, wearing their coracles, like shells, upon their backs, waited for her outside her hut. They stripped her of the deer-pelt she had wrapped herself in against the cold and pulled her down to the seashore, naked as a newborn. The women set their coracles on top of the lapping waves and paddled out through the moon-gilded water to the island where no man ever set foot, like a swarm of turtles returning to the shore where they had been hatched. The icy sea breeze had ruffled Janiveer's skin into goose pimples. But it was not the chill breeze alone that made her shiver. She was afraid of this island, rarely glimpsed behind its curtain of mist. But the child had always known that she would be taken there one day, the day her blood first flowed out like the tide in answer to the moon's call, the day a girl becomes a woman.

The aunts had bathed her in saltwater and put a crow's stone in her mouth to give her knowledge. They had rubbed an ice-smooth pebble, the size and shape of a chicken's egg, on her human eyes to make her see what was not visible. Then they had held her down while her mother stitched the third eye into her belly with a bone needle, drawing threads soaked in copper and soot beneath the skin, until the blue eye was indelibly marked above her woman's mound. That was the eye that no man looked upon twice.

A skein of golden light had risen across the far horizon of the inky sea before the delicate and painful task was completed. Tears had flowed, her own and her mother's, but Janiveer had not uttered a sound. The lesson in pain had been learned and learned well. But it was only the first of many before she understood what she had been born to do.

Now Janiveer watches the villagers in silence. They bluster and mutter, laugh and jeer, trying to dismiss her words. But no one rises, no one leaves. They are afraid to turn their backs on the fragile light of the fire, to venture out alone into the vastness of the night, afraid to enter the darkness of their own homes, for a grave, too, has a roof and four walls and it is a cold dwelling.

Only Aldith stares at her, glowering. If looks could kill . . . but they can. Janiveer knows that better than most. She saw the hostility in Aldith's eyes the moment she opened her own. The fisherman's wife has done nothing to conceal her jealousy. Janiveer wants to laugh. These village women are fearful that their menfolk will be seduced from their beds as easily as puppies are lured from their masters simply by dangling a morsel of fresh meat. What do they imagine she would do with such dull-wits? Are they trying to convince themselves that they have something worth the stealing?

But Sara is not one of those. She, too, sits in silence. A white scar like a new moon glows on her cheek. Her brown hair gleams copper in the flames. Janiveer has been watching her all day and knows her fear is not that her husband might stray but that she is already losing her first-born son. He is drifting away from her and she cannot understand where he is going or why. She hugs her younger son to her now, gripped by a new and greater terror. Her fists tighten around his shoulders as if she would drag him back from the claws of death. He squeaks and pulls away, pouting resentfully, like a fretful infant. They are all falling silent now, gazing into the fire as if the answer is written there in the twisting flames. And it is, for those who know how to read it, which they do not.

In the end it is Sara who breaks the silence, her halting voice startling the villagers out of their reverie. 'You said you could stop the pestilence coming . . . if we had the courage to pay the price.'

'I said, when it comes, I could save you. That is different.'

Cador gives a snort. 'Listen to her, words as slippery as a barrelful of eels. Tell your wife to save her breath, Elis. You'll no more get a straight answer out of this foreigner than you'll get an honest handshake from a Frenchman.'

Elis rocks sideways on his hams as if he is farting, glowering at his feet. It shames a man to be told to control his own wife, and it amuses Janiveer to see it.

'It's naught but sparrow's shit whether the foreigner answers straight or not,' he mutters petulantly. 'How could she turn back the pestilence, when king's own physicians can't?'

'But if there's a chance,' Sara says hotly, 'what else are we to do? Sit here like goats staked out as wolf-bait, waiting for it to come? I have to do something to protect my chillern. And you heard her, she says she's not after coin. So maybe she's a holy woman, maybe she *has* got the touch. Saints can perform miracles.'

'Her? A saint?' Aldith sneers.

'She came alive from that sea, didn't she?' Sara says. 'That's as close to a miracle as I've ever seen. She was dead, or near enough. Now look at her. Maybe she was saved and cast up here so she could protect us. Besides, there's none of you would decide whether or not to buy so much as a peck of grain till you knew what price was being asked for it. So where's the harm in asking her?'

Sara ignores the mew of outrage from Cador's wife, Isobel, at a mere packman's woman usurping the authority of the bailiff. She jerks up her chin in the firelight, her eyes boldly meeting Janiveer's. 'So, come on, you tell us what this price is of yours. I'm not saying we'll pay it, but we'll not know till we've heard it.'

Janiveer gazes round at the tense faces. 'A human life. That is my price.'

There is a stunned silence. It pulses on the air, unlike any that has gone before.

Bald John shatters it with a forced belly laugh, reaching over and slapping the dwarf on his crooked back. 'What about this 'un? If it's a sacrifice you want, you can have the dwarf and welcome. We'll even deliver him trussed up, like a suckling pig, for the spit. Though whether creatures like him are human, you'd best be asking Father Cuthbert.'

Several of the villagers chuckle, though it is a tense, mirthless laughter. But Janiveer does not smile. Her tone when she speaks again is measured, cold.

'If it is your village that is to be saved, it is your village that must pay. The life must be one of your own – a man, woman or child born on the earth of this village, one who has breathed its air, drunk from its veins. Someone whose flesh *is* Porlock Weir. Without that, I can do nothing to save you. Which family will offer me one life, just one, to save you all?'

The villagers stare at one another, as if for a moment they really believe that one death will save them. They want to believe it, they are desperate to believe it, and they are willing one another to step forward and say, *Take me, take mine.* But no one does, and in their hearts they know no one will.

'If no one offers themselves,' Janiveer says, 'then ask the gods. Draw lots. Let their mark fall on whoever they will choose. Let the gods decide who among you will die.'

Hope shatters into fury. The villagers are on their feet,

shouting and screaming. Their faces contort into grotesques in the flickering light of the Hell-red flames. Men push forward, bellowing their rage. Mothers clutch their children, dragging them back to hide them in the darkness as if they are afraid their neighbours might snatch a precious baby from their arms and toss his little body into the sacrificial fire. Old men and women shrink away for fear that someone will decide their life is over and they can be offered up. Suddenly the villagers' hands are full of filth and stones, though, come morning, no one will remember who bent to snatch up the first.

But Janiveer does not move, does not flinch. She watches and waits. Her steady gaze chills the villagers. Their arms feel like lead, their fingers grow numb around the stones. One by one the raised arms fall.

Cador pushes to the front. 'You have your answer,' he growls. 'There's no one'll pay your price. There's other villages might, but not here, not in Porlock Weir. We take care of our own. Even if any was willing, I'd not let them do it. I swore on the holy book that I'd do all in my power to see that no harm comes to any man, woman, child or beast in this village, not while I'm bailiff. I mean to keep that oath till death takes me.'

He turns his head towards the crowd. His face is glistening with sweat in the firelight, though the night breeze is cold. 'Get you to your beds and forget this nonsense. There is nothing to fear. The pestilence'll not come here, that I swear.'

'What of her?' Bald John bellows.

'I reckon we should fling her off the cliff back into the sea,' old Abel says. 'No good ever came from taking back what the sea has claimed.'

'He's right,' Meryn says, brandishing one of his crutches. 'If you catch a fish that's poison, throw it back.'

But though the villagers squawk and snarl their desire to do just that, no one moves. Cador, as bailiff, must be the first to lay hands on her. Janiveer fixes her gaze on him, challenging, warning. He hesitates, transfixed by the twin flames of the reflected fire dancing in those two great eyes. Then, as if she has reached out and pushed him, he stumbles a pace backwards, turning his face away.

'No call for that,' he says tersely. 'Sir Nigel would not take kindly to us killing a woman without proper trial. He's not a man to show mercy if the king's law's been broken. And I've no mind to find myself swinging on the gallows.'

The grumbling breaks out again, muttering about cowards and men who are too afraid to stand up and act.

Cador, plainly stung, rounds on Janiveer. 'But as bailiff I'm ordering you to leave this village. I want you gone afore the sun is clear over the horizon and don't set foot here again, else I'll put you in irons and drag you all the way to the manor court myself.'

The woman from the sea wonders what crime he would conjure up against her. Maybe sorcery, an old favourite. But she does not ask. It would not be wise to put the word in their mouths, much less the thought in their minds.

'Since you ask it, I will go,' she says. 'You can shut me out. You can shut out all the signs and the rumours, even the truth. But you cannot shut out death. A single life is all I ask, and before this year has ended you will be begging me to take it.'

Chapter 8

Porlock Manor

Poor men suffer lice, rich men suffer guests.
Medieval Proverb

Lady Pavia stood under the archway that led into the great hall. She positioned herself as gracefully as a woman of her ample proportions could without splitting the seams of her tightly fitted scarlet bodice. She raised her hand, laying it elegantly on the carved wood, the better to display the white tippet of her sleeve, which was so long it brushed the rushes on the floor. Behind her back, the maidservants, unfamiliar with the latest court fashions, goggled at those extravagant sleeves and rolled their eyes. It was as plain as a prick on a rutting goat that *she* never had to empty a pisspot or baste a roast goose. The male servants tried to squeeze past her without treading on the hem of her trailing skirts, balancing ewers of wine and great platters of rabbit, hare and every wild bird, from a heron to a lark, that could be snared, netted, caught with lime or brought down by the falconer's art.

Lady Pavia blithely ignored the chaos she was causing behind her. She was a widow twice over, but though she was rapidly approaching her sixty-third year she had no intention of quietly retreating to a nunnery or ending her days in some draughty corner of one of her sons' houses under the rule of their pinch-faced wives. She fully intended to catch another husband and install herself as the unequalled mistress of her own household. Her eyes, though they could no longer comfortably read the words in her psalter, still had the keenness of a kestrel when it came to spotting prey. But she could see at a glance there was no quarry worth pursuing in this hall.

In spite of the quantities and richness of the dishes being borne in, the only people seated at the high table on the dais were Lady Margery, an elderly aunt of Sir Nigel and chaperon to his three giggling young wards, and a solitary man sitting at the other end of the table. Lady Pavia studied him. Probably in his thirties and comely enough to be worth the chase but, alas, the candlelight revealed the gleam of his freshly shaved tonsure. She sniffed her disappointment.

The high table was laid with a fresh white cloth, and strewn with cowslips, primroses and wild apple blossom. The silver and pewter gleamed under the candlelight and the lavers had been filled with rosewater. If Sir Nigel had chosen to descend on this one of his many manors, without warning, he would have found everything to his satisfaction, but Lady Pavia knew that His Holiness the Pope was more likely to pay a visit to this remote corner of England than her cousin and his retinue.

She would not be here herself, so far from the hunting grounds for eligible men, had Sir Nigel not been so insistent. 'No safer corner of the realm,' he had told her. 'The Great Mortality will never blow so far from London.'

She knew that other members of his wide family circle would have been grateful, not even to say highly flattered, that such a busy man, whose presence the Black Prince constantly demanded, should have given the safety of a dowager cousin so much as a fleeting thought. But Lady Pavia had not buried two husbands and raised five sons without learning that if a powerful man concerns himself with the welfare of a mere woman he must be using her as a shield for his own rump. Her cousin had sent her here for some purpose but, as yet, not even she could discern quite what that might be.

As her gaze ranged about the hall, it alighted on the wizened figure of Eda edging along the wall towards the table occupied by the higher-ranking servants. The woman's furtive movements always irritated her and normally she would have ignored her, but she was reminded she had intended to have words with her. As Eda looked up, Lady Pavia beckoned with a plump finger, like an executioner inviting the condemned to climb up on to the scaffold.

The elderly maid shuffled across and bent her stiff knees in obeisance far more deeply than was wise for a woman of her age, wincing as she rose.

Lady Pavia barely waited for her to recover her balance. 'I have this afternoon visited your young mistress, in spite of the most arduous climb up those stairs. It is little wonder she is weary and melancholic, confined to that miserable, dark little chamber. She is a girl, not a bat. Young women need companionship. They must be occupied, else they start imagining all kinds of foolishness. You will have her moved at once to the solar where she may keep company with Sir Nigel's wards. I grant they are younger than her and inclined to childish prattle, but that will divert her admirably. And those chattering jays may learn to follow Christina's example and keep silent in the presence of their elders. With luck a little of her melancholy will rub off on them, which would indeed be a blessing to us all.'

Eda, though keeping her gaze respectfully lowered, spoke with a firmness that equalled Lady Pavia's. 'The physician prescribed complete rest and quiet. He said she was to be kept away from any excitement and to be given draughts of rhubarb, columbine and parsley, morning and evening. My mistress charged me to follow his instructions faithfully.'

'Faddle.' Lady Pavia waved her hand dismissively, her long tippet snaking out like a whip with the movement of her arm. 'A day's hunting will do more to cure any girl than an apothecary's draught or barber's bloodletting. You will move her tomorrow.' She peered suspiciously at Eda. 'Unless, of course, there is another reason for the girl being kept in confinement.'

Eda bowed the knee again, as submissively as any well-trained servant, and shuffled away, but not before Lady Pavia had seen a flash of alarm in those hooded eyes. So, the arrow had found its mark, she thought, with satisfaction.

When Lady Pavia had bracingly assured Christina that her new bridegroom was certain to return soon from France and that his attentions would bring the roses back to her cheeks, she had been startled to see fear in the girl's face. It was only fleeting and Christina had recovered herself well, saying how much she was looking forward to Randel's return, but her words had not deceived Lady Pavia. Was the girl being recalcitrant over the brilliant match that her mother and Sir Nigel had arranged for her? Was that why she'd been sent to this remote manor, to bring her to obedience or, more worryingly, keep her from eloping with another swain?

But perhaps the fear she had shown was simple anxiety about the marriage bed – that was only natural and proper.

75

But keeping her isolated with only an old spinster maid to confide in was hardly likely to allay her fears. Lady Pavia grimly recalled her own nursemaid, who had terrified her by recounting the dreadful fates that awaited innocent girls. Some men, the nursemaid had told her, were hung like stallions, their members so long that when they pierced their new brides the girls burst open, as if they'd been impaled on a spear, and those who survived their husband's animal demands had borne such huge children that they could not give birth to them and their babies had had to be cut out of their bellies in front of their very eyes.

No, indeed, it would not do to leave Christina to the tender mercy of that old crone and her tales. If the girl needed to be taught how to embrace the joys and trials of marriage, then Lady Pavia considered it her duty to do just that.

She was jerked from her thoughts by a discreet cough at her elbow. 'If you will allow me to escort you, my lady.'

She found herself gazing up into the brown eyes of one of those men whose age was hard to determine. He was by no means a stripling, but not yet running to middle-age portliness. His face was tanned, but his small neat beard and dark hair showed only a trace of grey. His clothes would have passed as fashionable enough for the king's court. His sleeves were buttoned down to his knuckles and the closely fitting blue gypon was padded over the upper chest, giving him the appearance of a puffed-up pigeon. But Lady Pavia observed that the panels of silver embroidery which decorated the front were frayed and worn as if they had been unpicked from a much older garment and sewn on this new one. Was that a sign of the man's thrift or of his empty coffers?

He straightened from a deep bow and impudently extended

his arm, palm downwards so that she might place her own hand upon it. The blood-red stone set into his gold thumb-ring was the size of a blackbird's egg but, she noticed, cracked. She did not take the proffered arm.

'And who is it wishes to squire me?'

He lowered his arm and inclined his head. 'Your pardon, my lady. In my eagerness to escort such a rare beauty, I neglected to introduce myself. Sir Harry Gilmore.' He bowed again.

Lady Pavia granted him the ghost of a smile and this time when he offered his arm she permitted her hand to rest lightly over his. But she was not flattered. Fine words, like fine nets, are cast to snare a goose, and she was not pleased to be taken for a fool. All the same, she was prepared to overlook the insult for the moment. Men who had been at the king's court soon acquired the habit of making pretty, empty speeches.

Lady Pavia's soft leather shoes sank into the deep spongy mat of old rushes on the floor. Dried bracken and herbs had been strewn on top of the mouldy and compacted layers beneath, but they had done little to sweeten the stench of rotting food or the dog and cat dung that the mice and insects feasted on below. It was a wonder the smaller page boys hadn't vanished beneath it. When she had been mistress of her husbands' halls, she had always insisted that the whole stinking mess be cleared out completely once a year and burned, just to keep the fleas and lice in check. She would see to it that Master Wallace did the same, just as soon as the new bracken and reeds had grown long enough to be gathered in any quantity.

Sir Harry seated her between himself and the cleric, whose name she learned was Father Cuthbert. The three young wards chattered and laughed at the far end of the table, oblivious to Lady Pavia's frowns. The elderly aunt did nothing to reprove them, too busy marking the progress of each and every servant in case she should miss the arrival of some new dish she had not tasted.

As if he were the host, instead of merely another guest, Sir Harry sliced into the breast of a fat rabbit with his own sword-sharp knife and placed the tender flesh on Lady Pavia's trencher of bread, before wrenching off the rabbit's leg and sinking his teeth into it with all the relish of a man devouring his first meat after the Lenten fast.

Introductions had scarcely been made when Father Cuthbert leaned towards her, as if he was expecting to hear her confession. 'Master Wallace tells me you were lately in London, Lady Pavia. I have heard disturbing rumours that the Great Mortality has returned and is ravaging the city. Can it be—'

Sir Harry rapped the handle of his knife on the table. 'Now, Father, let us have no talk of that. The royal physician who attends both the Black Prince and Sir Nigel insists that if a man dwells on thoughts of the Great Mortality he will bring upon himself the very sickness that he dreads. It is the foul poison in the air that mixes with the blood and destroys the heart.'

'Are you quite sure you have understood this learned physician?' Lady Pavia said tartly, slightly piqued that Sir Harry was addressing the priest across her. 'First you tell us it is *thinking* about the Great Mortality that causes it, then that the cause is poison in the air. Though I don't blame you for being confused. My own physician's explanations are so long and tortuous they are better than any of the sleeping draughts he prescribes.'

Father Cuthbert laughed so heartily that even the chattering girls glanced up. Lady Pavia was under no illusion that her wit was the cause of his merriment, rather it was the dull flush that had spread across Sir Harry's countenance.

'I trust my poor explanation will not send you to sleep, Lady Pavia,' Sir Harry said frostily. 'The foul poison, as I explained, is in the air, so we must breathe only odours that are pleasant. Likewise, if a man looks upon a pestilent corpse that same poison shall enter his body through his eye, and if he thinks on it, the poison will enter his brain. The royal physician was most insistent that we must think only pleasant thoughts, smell good odours, and look upon gold, jewels and all things lovely. It is for this very reason the king has taken his family to the safety of Beaulieu Abbey, where he will see and smell nothing that might allow poison to enter his eyes or nostrils.'

'And is that why you are here, Sir Harry, to look upon pleasant things?' Lady Pavia stared pointedly at the three young girls. Though none of them was yet ripe enough for marriage, she was aware that many men find the bud far more irresistible than the flower in full bloom. Was this why Sir Nigel had sent her here, to guard the virtue of his valuable investments? Clearly the old aunt was not equal to the task. 'I warn you, Sir Harry, my cousin has already promised these chicks to wealthy and powerful men. He will not tolerate them being plucked of their feathers before they are safely delivered. And Sir Nigel is not a merciful man, as his enemies at Crécy and Poitiers would testify, if they still had tongues.'

This time it was Sir Harry who laughed, though somewhat shakily. He lifted her hand and slowly sucked a smear of thick blood sauce from her finger, all the while gazing into her face as if he was entranced. 'When a man sees a swan gliding upon a lake, he does not notice the chattering sparrows in the bush.'

The look of disgust that spread across the priest's face almost matched Lady Pavia's own revulsion, but she was too well schooled to betray it, though she firmly extricated her hand. 'Swans may look innocent, Sir Harry, but they have been known to break a man's arm if he intrudes upon their nests.'

'Then I shall take the greatest care not to ruffle one by so much as a single feather while I am hunting in these parts, Lady Pavia. I am told there is good hunting to be had here. Do you enjoy the chase, Father Cuthbert?'

The priest bit into a roasted songbird wrapped in bacon, crunching noisily on the bones. He delicately dabbed at his mouth with a white linen napkin, before replying.

'I am most partial to the sport. I often ride out with the steward, though there have been wretchedly few birds to be had recently because of this drought. Why, on the feast of St Francis last year we brought down so many swans, herons and ducks that we were obliged to send a boy running back to the manor to fetch two more horses to carry them.' Warming to his favourite subject, Father Cuthbert had lost his scowl. 'But this year, there is scarcely a bittern or hare to be found, much less—'

'But what of the noble beasts – the stag and boar?' Sir Harry interrupted. 'These forests must be teeming with such quarry.'

Father Cuthbert's scowl returned. He was plainly not accustomed to having his discourses cut short. 'There is such game, certainly. But these are not the flat lands of the New Forest, which you are doubtless accustomed to hunting. Here all is steep hillsides and deep ravines. A rider galloping after a stag on these treacherous slopes may easily find it is his own corpse that is borne home, not the stag's. Besides, there are so many hidden valleys, even a good lymer would be hard put to track a beast gone to cover, however keen its nose.'

Sir Harry gave a thoughtful smile. 'I have heard it said that if there is a place in the forest where a king is buried, the hart that leads the herd will go every evening at sunset to the place to speak with his noble brother, king to king.'

Father Cuthbert snorted. 'The souls of kings sit at the hand of God in Heaven. They do not wander the forests communing with dumb beasts.'

'Ah, but if the hart discovers that the sweetest grass and herbs grow on such graves, will it not return there to graze each evening? They are creatures of habit, are they not? A man might lie in wait there with his bow and bring down the noblest of beasts without any danger to himself or his horse. I understand there are a great many earthen mounds in these parts where the ancients buried their dead, even their kings.' His eyes fastened on the priest's face. 'Do you know of such graves, Father Cuthbert?'

The priest fixed his gaze on a platter of snipe, which had been skewered with their own beaks. He was studying them so intently that Lady Pavia half expected him to command them to rise and fly away. 'There are mounds, I believe,' he muttered at last, 'but the burial sites of pagans are of no concern to the Holy Church and therefore of no interest to its priests.' He raised his head. 'But as I was endeavouring to explain, if you have come here in search of good hunting, you will be sadly disappointed.'

Sir Harry spread his hands. 'If my only care was the chase, Father Cuthbert, I would have gone to the New Forest with the king's court.'

'Then may I enquire what does bring you to Porlock Manor, sir?'

Sir Harry hesitated, only for a moment, but it was long enough to make Lady Pavia's senses prick, like the ears of a watchdog. 'Why, to ensure that Sir Nigel's favourite cousin and his wards are well protected in his absence. With so many people fleeing the cities, manors remote as this become easy prey for thieves or bands of cutthroats and vagabonds seeking shelter.'

'Sir Nigel knows he can rely on me to assist Master Wallace in keeping order,' Father Cuthbert said stiffly.

'When the Great Mortality struck last time, many servants abandoned their places of employment, looting as they went. Many priests fled too,' Sir Harry added pointedly. 'In the end, Father Cuthbert, those who are paid to serve cannot be relied upon to do so, especially if they think that pay will not be forthcoming. Only true friends can be trusted to do their duty.'

Lady Pavia smiled grimly to herself. As her late husband, Hubert, was frequently heard to remark: '*A full purse never wants for friends.*' And Sir Nigel's purse was better stuffed than most. But she would have wagered a casket of jewels that neither friendship nor duty was what had brought Sir Harry to Porlock.

Chapter 9

Matilda

St Adjutor comes to the aid of swimmers and those who are drowning, for he stilled a whirlpool by throwing into it holy water and the chains of his captivity.

It was only by chance that I saw what she did. Usually I keep the door of St Olaf's chapel firmly shut, but it was so dark inside I'd been obliged to pull it open before I was ready to leave. The drawstring of my pigskin bag, which always hangs from my belt, had tangled and I needed daylight to unknot it. I keep my precious skull chalice inside the bag. Pigskin is soft and constantly polishes the chalice, so that the bone and pewter gleam. Such an object must be cared for reverently, tenderly.

The sun had barely risen, so I had not expected anyone to be abroad that early. But as I opened the chapel door, I caught sight of a woman on the track that leads into the forest, towards a hidden forsaken village known as Kitnor. A century ago the Church had sent blasphemers and witches there to keep them safely away from decent people, so they could do no harm. But Kitnor had been abandoned for a hundred years and it lay in ruins, or so the pedlars said, for no one from Porlock Weir ever ventured there, though I could think of many in the village who should have been banished to that desolation of ghosts.

As I watched from the shadow of the doorway, the woman bent to pick up a small branch that had fallen in the storm and used one end of it to gouge out a shallow hole in the middle of the path. As I watched her, I realised she was the woman they had dragged from the sea, Janiveer. Dropping the stick, she reached into a pouch that hung from her waist and drew out a flat, round stone. She held it out towards the sea, the sun glinting from its smooth white surface. I wondered where she had found it for it is rare to see such a flattened stone on our beach.

She laid it carefully in the hole she'd dug, walking round it several times, staring at it intently, as if it was a rare treasure she wished to examine from every angle. Then she bent down and turned the stone round and round in the shallow hole, as if it was a tiny grinding stone, though no Christian woman would ever turn a grinding stone widdershins, for that is to call upon the devil himself.

Janiveer straightened up and, with her bare foot, scraped the dirt back over the hole, burying the stone, then flattening the earth with her heel. She brushed the dust from her feet, then, without a single glance behind her, strode off down the path and vanished into the trees.

As soon as I was sure she had gone, I slipped out of the chapel and hurried along the track, searching for the place where I'd seen her digging. I was determined to take a closer look. But the ground was so dry that the dirt and dust she had kicked over the hole were the same hue as the rest of the path and I couldn't see where she'd buried the stone.

I scolded myself for wasting time. It was only a stone and there were thousands more on the beach. All the same, I was uneasy. She had buried it with such care. She must have had her reasons. I felt a sudden chill, as if Satan's shadow had touched me. Though it was scarcely dignified, I found myself scrambling up the bank to get off the path, fearing that I might accidentally walk over the place where the stone was buried.

It was only as I reached out to pull myself up that I realised the pigskin bag dangling from my waist was empty. I'd left the skull chalice in the chapel for anyone to steal! I hurried along the grassy bank, slipping and stumbling, not stopping to draw breath until I was safely inside. It was still where I'd left it on the altar. No one had entered. They never set foot inside except when Father Cuthbert said Mass. If it wasn't for me, days would pass without a single prayer rising from that holy place. I clutched the chalice to my chest, my heart still thumping from the fright. It was valuable, a temptation to any thief.

I had taken the skull to a silversmith along the coast at Mynedun. I'd heard he had worked the bones of holy men or enemies slain in battle into objects before. I had him cut and polish the top of the skull to make a cup, which he fixed to a stem made from an arm bone. The base of the goblet was fashioned from the broad part of a shoulder blade. I had wanted the rim of the chalice finished with a silver band, but I could afford only pewter. Nevertheless, it gleamed handsomely enough by candlelight.

My hands still shaking, I dipped the bone chalice into the holy water stoop by the door, and sprinkled the blessed water over my head, hands and feet, just to be certain I had washed the dust of that path away and with it whatever curse the woman had buried there, for I was certain that was what she had done.

As I tucked the chalice safely away in the bag I became aware of a distant clamour. The commotion was coming from the shore. I peered down towards the harbour. A small knot of people had gathered on the beach behind the weirs and others were hurrying down the track. I made haste to join them.

The tide was ebbing, though not yet fully out, but it had retreated from the weirs – three sets of thick V-shaped walls, which jutted up out of the mud in the bay, built of rocks piled high and wide. They pointed towards the sea, with a gap in the apex of each one into which long wicker traps had been fixed. The massive arms of the walls stretched out on either side as if they were reaching out to crush the whole village. Trenches ran along the base of the walls on the shoreward side, and the fish pulled in there by the receding tide were flailing in the shallow water, as they tried in vain to escape.

Usually the men and children who worked the weirs would be scooping them out and carrying them up the beach to the women who sat gutting them, but today the fish were left to live, as attention focused on one of the great woven baskets. Something bigger than the usual fish or crabs had become trapped inside and several men clustered round it as they tried to ease it out. Mostly likely it was a porpoise or a seal. Like the fish, they would swim over the wall at high tide chasing their prey, but as the tide retreated they, too, would be trapped, funnelled into the long baskets as the water ran out. If the seal was still alive, it was hard to coax it out without getting mauled. Seal bites were stubborn to heal and often went foul. Fishermen were wary of them.

A cry went up from the men and something flopped from

the mouth of the basket on to the mud, like a foal being pulled from the womb of his dam, except this was no foal. It was hard to make out what it was. At that distance, the creature looked as if it had two heads. The men lifted it between them and began to carry it back towards the shore, splashing through the shallows and slipping on patches of weed. The two heads of the beast lolled away from each other, swaying limply, as the men bore it over the pebbles. A foul monster risen from the dark depths of the sea. It was another bad omen,

Daveth and Skiener, a habitual drunkard, carried the creature up the beach, with the rest of the fishermen following. They laid it, dripping, on the stones and we all crowded round, expecting . . . I don't know what we expected to see. A grotesque giant fish? A savage sea snake? But it was not a beast. It was a human child, or rather two children bound face to face by a rope wound around their bodies. Daveth drew his knife and sawed through the wet cord. As soon as it broke the two corpses rolled apart to sprawl side by side on the shore. A wail of sorrow rose up from Sara and several of the other women.

The boy's eyes were shut, but the girl's were wide open, staring sightlessly up at the wheeling gulls above, the pupils so dilated they seemed like two black holes. Her mouth was wide open too, as if she had been screaming when she plunged into the sea. But their bodies were not bloated; neither was the skin beginning to peel. Strands of livid green seaweed and the broken limb of an orange starfish lay tangled in the girl's long hair. As we watched, a tiny transparent crab crawled out from the boy's nostril, scuttled over his face and vanished beneath his body.

'Brother and sister, by the look of it,' Aldith said, crossing

87

herself. 'One's the near spit of t'other. You reckon they were from the same ship as the foreign woman?'

'Don't look like they've been in the sea two nights,' her husband said. 'Fish would have started nibbling at them by now. But they must have been in the water afore the tide turned this morning, else they'd not have got trapped in the weir. I reckon they fell in during the night, but no more than a mile or two up the coast. They've not been drifting long.'

'Fell?' Skiener said scornfully. 'That rope was knotted, not tangled. Tied up deliberately they were, and thrown in.'

'You reckon they were alive when . . .' His wife, Katharine, looked stricken. 'The poor mites!' She knelt down and tried in vain to close the eyes of the dead girl.

Skiener hauled her roughly to her feet. Then he crouched himself, peering and prodding at the bodies, before straightening up again. 'Reckon the boy was already dead, but the maid . . . See there . . .' He nudged her arm with his bare toe. It was badly grazed and bruised. 'She struggled against the rope that bound her, fought like an eel on a hook to free herself. She'd have done better letting the sea take her straight off. She'd never have got herself free.'

'Who'd do such a thing to innocent chillern?' Sara demanded.

'Pirates, more than like,' Skiener muttered. 'Devil take them.' He spat copiously as if to clean his mouth of the word.

'Why seize them only to drown them?'

He shrugged. 'Maybe they found them on a ship they captured, but thought them not worth the bother of taking to slave markets in the Holy Land. Cost them too much to feed, see. Sailor told me once they drown the nisselers as a warning to the others not to make trouble.'

I could see that nothing was to be gained by standing

around guessing the fate that might have befallen the children. 'If they were captured by pirates, they were probably snatched from an English village, so they should be given a Christian burial. It's our duty.'

'Should give 'em back to the sea, that's what we should do,' one of the fishermen muttered.

'Not chillern, we won't,' Sara said. ''Sides, Skiener reckons boy was dead afore water took him, so the sea's no claim on him.'

All the women nodded.

Old Abel spat out the wad of brown dulse he was chewing. 'Violent death, it is,' he said. 'If bailiff was here he'd say we must send for the coroner.'

There was a sullen murmur among the men crowded round. Several darted sour looks at him.

'And if we do, 'tis us that'll get the fine,' Daveth said, 'besides losing a day's work.'

Skiener nodded vigorously. 'Coroner'll be here for hours drinking our ale and stuffing himself on our meat, and after all that, what's he going to tell us?' He lifted his chin and thrust out his belly. 'My good fellows, I am come to tell you the children drowned, which, being ignorant fishermen, you'd never have guessed.' He made a flourishing bow and his friends laughed. 'But,' he resumed in his own voice, 'the luggins'll not be able to tell who threw them in any more than we can.'

'Probably accuse us of doing it,' Daveth said. 'Justices always have to have someone to hang the blame on and they generally hang it round the neck of the poor whelk who found the corpse. So I say we bury 'em quickly and quietly before they bring a heap of trouble down on our heads.'

'Graves will need to be dug,' I said, taking charge. 'I'll prepare the winding sheets if someone will come to help me. Sara?'

A look of alarm flashed over her face. 'I think Aldith needs . . .'

'I need Sara to help me wash the bodies,' Aldith said firmly, but I caught the smile that Sara threw her.

'As you please,' I snapped, 'but *someone* had better fetch Father Cuthbert from Porlock town or there will be no burial.'

Daveth glared at me. 'No one's fetching any priest. He'll only go sending for the coroner. We'll bury them ourselves. Skiener here – he's watched a few dropped overboard in his time. He knows the words.'

'We are not at sea,' I reminded him tersely. 'I intend to ensure those children are given a proper Christian burial by Father Cuthbert, even if I have to fetch him myself.' I took a step forward to show them I meant to set off at once.

But Skiener rudely barred my way. 'You set one foot out of this village afore those chillern are safely below ground and I swear on the devil's arse you'll find yourself lying in a grave alongside them.'

Chapter 10

Sara

The chad is called 'chuck-cheeld' or 'choke-child'. For St Levan caught two chad on one hook and gave them to his sister, St Breage, to cook for her children, but the children choked on the bones.

'Where do you want them laid for the washing and winding? In the chapel, is it?' Daveth asked me.

'Can't take a murdered corpse into a church, you know that. Blood pollutes it, makes it unclean. There'd be no chance of stopping Matilda running to Father Cuthbert if she thought we'd desecrated the chapel. Spends half her life in there.'

'No blood on those corpses. Sea's already washed them.'

'And I'll wash them again,' I said, hands on hips, so he knew I'd brook no arguments. 'If they're not to be buried by a priest, least we can do is lay them in the ground decently. Their poor souls will never rest easy, if we don't.'

Aldith gnawed her lip. 'If it wasn't for the storm, I'd fetch them into our cottage, but there's nowhere to lay them. Table's smashed and you'd be up to your knees in mud and seaweed.'

'Take them up to mine, Daveth,' I said. 'And while

91

you're there, send the boys to fetch water from the stream. What's coming out of that spring wouldn't wash a sparrow's toenail.'

The little bodies looked even more helpless and pitiful when we'd laid them side by side on the table. Wherever you stood, the girl seemed to be looking straight at you, accusing. Somewhere in my head I could hear her screaming, like a far-off storm out at sea. Luke, Hob and Col returned with the pails of water far quicker than they usually shifted themselves. They dumped the buckets and crowded round the table, daring each other to touch an arm or leg or even put a finger inside the girl's open mouth, teasing each other that her jaws would suddenly snap together and bite it off.

'Stop that, you little hellers!' Aldith yelled.

I peered into the buckets. They were only half full and the water was muddy.

'If I wash anything in this, it'll be blacker than when I started. Take this out to the herb patch and water the beans with it, then march back to that stream and fetch more. Full pails this time and take them from upstream above where the beasts drink, not where they've muddied it. Go on! And,' I called after them, 'leave the pails outside the door when you bring them back. I don't want you back in here till these poor chillern are in their graves.'

They weren't listening, too busy boasting and taunting each other with tales of dead bodies and ghosts.

A lock of Aldith's sandy hair had escaped its binding and was snaking over her freckled brow. She pulled off the cloth wrapping her head and flipped her long hair forward, so that she could rewind it. The locks brushed the boy's leg and I wondered if he'd watched his own mother binding her hair. Where was she now? A slave on some stinking ship?

Drowned? Maybe she was grieving in a cottage just like mine, not knowing what had befallen her chillern, who'd simply walked out of her door one day and vanished. I hoped she hadn't seen them die. I prayed she hadn't. It must be the hardest thing in the whole world to watch your boy dying and be powerless to snatch him back to life. There is no name for such a grief.

Aldith tucked the end of the bleached cloth under the twist about her head. 'Best get these clothes off them while we're waiting for the water.' She drew her knife. 'May as well cut them off.' She grimaced. 'If it were a drowned man's clothes I'd save them, but murdered chillern . . . I'd not see any living child put in those. A dead child always takes a living one to play with. Doesn't do to tempt the ninth wave.'

She'd no need to explain. As soon as we could both toddle, every mam and granddam in the village had warned us to beware the ninth wave. That's how we'd learned to count, by watching the waves. *Eight waves will gently break, the ninth wave will take you.* The spirits of dead children rode on that wave. The ninth wave was a child stealer and it had surely stolen these little ones.

Aldith began to slit the girl's sodden kirtle, motioning me to unbutton the boy's short tunic. But the cord fastenings had swelled in the water, and wouldn't slide over the horn buttons, so I, too, drew out my knife and began to cut. Aldith worked deftly, slicing up the girl's sleeve, as I swept the pieces of the boy's tunic on to the bracken on the floor.

Aldith shrieked, dropping the knife with a clatter on to the table. For a moment, I thought she must have sliced her finger, then an evil stench, worse even than rotting fish or foul meat, burst into the room. Aldith was staring down at the point of her knife, which was covered with a thick yellowish black ooze. Giving me a stricken glance, she pushed me aside and ran round the table until she was standing behind the girl. Grasping the child's bruised wrist between a trembling finger and thumb, she lifted the arm so that the light from the door fell on it. There, under the armpit, was a dark swelling, as big as a hen's egg. Thick pus and blackened blood oozed from the boil where the tip of Aldith's knife had nicked the skin.

Aldith let the child's arm fall with a thud on to the table. Grabbing me, she pulled me out into the sunshine and sank on to the bench outside, pale and shaking, her forehead beaded with sweat.

Bile rose in my throat and it was all I could do not to vomit. How many nights in the past thirteen years had I woken shaking with terror, that smell filling my nostrils? How many times had I relived the burning shame of turning from my mam, of pulling my fingers from her hot sticky hand, of running from that cottage, running from that terrible, nauseating stench? When I'd finally steeled myself to return, it was too late. She was dead. She had died alone. Her last thought, that I had fled from her.

A chatter of shrill voices made me look up. Luke, Hob and Col were straggling back up the path towards us, bent sideways to balance the pails of water. In a daze I watched them come closer and closer. Then I was on my feet, running towards them, shouting and waving my arms.

'Get away! Get away! Don't come any closer. Go!'

The boys stopped and stared at me in alarm. Little Hob dropped his pail so suddenly the cold water drenched his legs. His face crumpled and, letting out a wail, he tried to run to my arms. But I backed away, screaming at Luke to take his brother down to their father. Hob, sobbing with fright, fought his brother to get to me, but Luke dragged him down the track, clearly convinced that I had gone mad.

'Mam?' Col stood a few yards off, gazing uncertainly at his mother. She lifted her head as if she had only just realised he was there. 'Set the water down carefully, boy,' she said. 'You go find your father. Tell him . . . tell him to get those graves dug quick, but deep. Deep as he can.' Her tone was flat and dead, and that seemed to frighten Col more than my shouting. For once he asked no questions, but ran.

Chapter 11

Matilda

*St Antony the Abbot is the patron saint of gravediggers,
for he walled himself up in a desert tomb and struggled
with the afflictions with which the devil tormented him
– slothfulness, boredom and the ghosts of women.*

As soon as I approached Sara's cottage I knew that I had
been vindicated. God had written His warning across the
heavens for all to see, and now, as closely as a shadow follows
a man, His curse had fallen upon the village. Sara and Aldith
sat on the bench outside. Sara had always been a small,
slight woman, but she seemed to have shrunk even smaller
in the hour since I'd last seen her. Her beechnut hair was
half tumbled from its cap, and the crescent scar on her
cheek where a widgebeast had kicked her seemed to stand
out white as bone against her wind-tanned skin.

The two women scarcely lifted their heads as I approached.
Sara murmured a warning, but I could smell and see all I
needed the moment I glanced through the open doorway.
I pulled the door firmly closed – had they no understanding
of what must be done? – and hurried several paces away,
lifting my head into the breeze from the sea and trying to
rid my lungs of the poisonous miasma.

'I warned this village. God is not mocked. The stench of wickedness rises up to the throne of Heaven itself and He has come to cleanse it.'

Aldith heaved herself from the bench. 'Satisfied are you now, you bitter old hag? Suppose you want me to tell that foreigner, Janiveer, she was right too.'

I saw again Janiveer turning that glittering white stone on the path, around and around, against the sun. It must have been just at the moment those drowned children were discovered in the fish trap. Had she summoned their corpses here? Drawn them towards her through the waves by some invisible thread? Had she infested their bodies with this sickness? God permits witches and demons to succeed in their wickedness to punish sinners. If they had allowed me to fetch Father Cuthbert perhaps even then God would have stayed His hand, but they took no more notice of that saintly man than they did of me.

Aldith was pulling at the winding sheets I had tucked under my arm. 'Since you're so set on them having a decent burial let's get on with it. Sooner we get those bodies wrapped and in the ground, the safer we'll all be.'

'Safer!' I hissed. 'Do you not know that stench? Do you not understand what lies inside? All your family may carry the contagion now. You may all die!'

'No!' Sara stumbled to the door and stood against it as if she meant to keep death out, like a beggar that could be driven from her threshold. 'My chillern've not been near the bodies. They'll not fall sick.'

Aldith glanced sharply at her, frowning. Sara flushed slightly and lowered her head.

'But you both have,' I said, 'and her husband.'

Aldith snatched the winding sheets from my arm. 'Give

me those, 'less you're offering to wrap the bodies yourself. Good mind to wind you in these. Keep your poisonous tongue still.' She nodded at Sara. 'You stay out here. I'll do it. No sense in both of us . . .'

Sara lifted her chin like a defiant child, glaring at me as if this was my fault. 'It's my cottage they're in. My table they're laid on.' She flung the door open with a crash.

The stench of rotting flesh rolled out again. They both recoiled, gagging, and stood swaying for a moment. Then, taking a deep gulp of air, Aldith followed Sara inside.

Chapter 12

Will

Riddle me this: How may a man discern a cow in a flock of sheep?

I reckon the whole of the village was gathered outside Sybil's brew- and bake-house that afternoon. Those who arrived first were perched on kegs or upturned boats. Others leaned against walls or even on the mud-horses they used as sledges to cross the bay at low tide. The only families who weren't present were Elis's and Daveth's.

When people get scared they huddle up like sheep, bleating for any scrap of news. Me? Well, the villagers might call me *skiddy-arse*, but I feel fear just as keenly as any longshanks. And if I was going to have to flee that village at least I wanted to be sure I was running away from danger and not straight back into its jaws. Believe me, I had every intention of going, if the rumours turned out to be true. I'd no family or home or trade to leave behind. The only thing that had kept me in Porlock Weir so long was sheer idleness. But the threat of death is a surer cure for that vice than any priest's sermon.

Sybil, never one to let a sale pass her by, bustled among the villagers with two great flagons of ale in her brawny arms, refilling beakers and dropping the coins into the purse

99

dangling from the belt that was squeezed around her great sow-belly. Crabfish, a simple lad, who lolloped along with a sideways gait, edged closer. Curiosity always drew him to any crowd. He held out his own beaker, grinning eagerly up at Sybil, though he had no coin. She shook her head sternly. Then, glancing round to make sure no one was watching – Sybil would never let any man think she was growing soft – she poured a good measure of ale into Crabfish's beaker and swiftly moved on.

After a deal of muttering and murmuring, and no sign of the bailiff Cador being in any hurry to start the meeting, Skiener drained his beaker in a single swallow and thumped on the barrel. 'We have to make sure news of this doesn't get out of the village.'

'But it's my duty to report it,' Cador protested. 'I'll lose my job, my cottage, everything if Sir Nigel discovers the matter. He's a hard man, not given to mercy.'

'And not given to visiting his manor at Porlock neither,' Skiener retorted. 'When have you ever seen him in these parts? Too busy fighting the Black Prince's battles.'

'I see his steward enough, though. Always nosing around, he is,' Cador said sullenly. 'If so much as a rabbit dies in one of his warrens, Master Wallace gets to hear of it and demands a reckoning.'

'Then you'd best make sure he doesn't hear of this. Else you'll not be the only one without food in your belly or a roof to sleep under. Once 'tis known abroad, do you think any goodwife'll buy fish from us, or any merchants pay us to carry ship's cargoes up over the moors? As it is, not a soul, save us, knows those chillern were ever here, or what killed them. And none outside the village will know, unless folk go whispering and pistering.'

The Holy Hag, Matilda, stepped forward. I knew she'd never be able to resist having her say. I would have smiled to myself, if my face wasn't permanently set in a grin.

'But we all know the children *were* here,' she said primly. 'Sara and Aldith stripped the bodies. Those women could already be infested with the contagion . . . them and their families, too.'

'If that's true, you can tell them to stay away from my hearth,' Cecily, the blacksmith's wife, said, wiping the sweat from her nose. 'I'll not have them coming here, or any of their kin. My John was living out Exeter way last time the pestilence ran through this land. Saw it with his own eyes – you tell them, John. Priest who was perfectly well that morning went to shrive a woman who was dying, and by the next morning the priest hisself were dead of pestilence and so were a half-dozen other souls he'd met in the street on his way home. Isn't that right, John?' Her husband half opened his mouth to reply, but couldn't squeeze in a single word. 'If those women go wandering about the village,' Cecily continued, 'we'll all be stricken. Won't matter then if the other villages don't trade with us 'cause we'll all be dead.'

There was a swelling murmur of agreement. The bailiff held up his hand for silence.

'Then Sara and Aldith must stay inside, till it be proved if they're sick or not. The two of them can stay in Sara's. It's a good step from the other houses in the village. No one's to cross their threshold or—'

'But there's no cause to go painting signs on her door for all the world to see,' Skiener interrupted. 'We all know which cottage it is to avoid it.'

'It's not just the women should be shut in,' Matilda said.

'Their boys were in that cottage when the mothers were stripping the bodies. Sara tried to deny it, but I saw the look that passed between her and Aldith. I know she was lying.'

'Then the boys will have to be kept in the cottage too,' Cador said. 'And the door sealed so none of them can go wandering about.'

'Those chillern of theirs run around the village, like flies round the backside of a sheep,' his wife, Isobel, added. 'Locking them in will give us all a few days of peace, sick or not.' She brushed down her skirts as if the very thought had ruffled her fine feathers.

'All very well saying they've to be shut in,' Bald John said, 'but how's it to be done? If there's one thing that'll get Elis riled up it's anyone threatening his family. He's a big man, handy with his fists too.' He massaged his jaw. 'I wouldn't count on Elis and Daveth standing idly by while we shut up their wives and sons in the cottage. And what's to stop them letting their kin out the moment we leave?'

'Then we must keep them locked up 'n' all,' the bailiff said impatiently. 'Aldith and Daveth are still sleeping up at the cottage with Elis, aren't they?'

He paused and looked round the assembled villagers. With a nod and a flick of his hand, he picked out a half-dozen or so of the brawnier men. 'You meet me back here soon as it's good and dark. Rest of you keep to your homes tonight. You've heard naught. You say naught and you do naught.'

There are times in a dwarf's life when he might almost be grateful to the god or man who fashioned him into a bandy-legged runt. At least we're not called upon to wall up children alive with the angel of death. But fear was already lapping around the cottages, trickling in beneath each closed door. You could see the cold tide of it rising in the eyes of every man and woman who was old enough to remember. With it came the savage instinct to lash out, drive off, even kill if they were cornered. And, believe me, there is no cruelty a man will shrink from inflicting on others to protect his own flesh and blood.

Chapter 13

Sara

A fresh fish and poor friend soon grow ill-favoured.

I'd never have said, of course, but truth was I couldn't wait for Aldith's cottage to dry out so they could return to their own home. With all those bodies crowded into mine, I couldn't breathe. I felt as if they were all piled on top of me, like stones over a grave. Goda was so near her time she needed to be off the cold earth floor, but she couldn't climb up the ladder into the hayloft, so Elis gave up his space in our bed, leaving me to share it with her. Aldith, with her two youngest and my little Hob, slept up in the loft, while Elis, Daveth, Luke and Col bedded down on the bracken on the floor. From the snores and snuffles, it sounded as if the whole pack of them was fast asleep, save me. I couldn't rest.

We'd thrown the drowned chillern's clothes on the fire outside, stirring up the embers and piling dried seaweed on top till they caught ablaze in spite of being sodden. We opened the door wide, burned sprigs of wild thyme and scrubbed the table with kneeholly and sand. Aldith and the menfolk said the stench had been driven out, but I could still smell it. And I could still see the face of that little girl, her eyes staring up at me, her mouth open as if she was crying out to me. I wanted to comfort her, soothe her to sleep. Wrapping the winding sheet over her face felt like smothering my own child.

No one but Daveth, Aldith and I had gone to mourn those nameless pieces of flotsam, for word of what they carried had flashed around the village faster than a lightning ball. There were no words spoken. Skiener never came. As I watched clods of earth falling on to the cloth, saw the dint where they landed, I winced as if the flesh beneath could still feel them and be bruised. I urged Daveth to cover them quickly and I carried the rocks to pile over the grave to seal that foul black cloud down in the pit, but it was all I could do to stop myself digging through the earth with my bare hands to rescue those little ones.

The day they had laid my mam in that long trench next to all the others, faceless, nameless beneath their winding sheets, I'd known the guilt of wanting that foul corpse hidden away quickly, yet the pain of wanting to drag Mam out. A voice kept crying out in my head telling me that if I could rip the smothering cloth away from her face, she would look up at me from clear blue eyes and smile as if she'd woken from a sleep. In the end, they'd had to drag me from her grave.

I shivered, pulling the blanket tighter around me, but Goda, in her sleep, tugged it back, whimpering like a babby. The ladder to the hayloft creaked. Hob clambered down and stumbled to the door, ignoring the groans of protest as he tripped over the bodies of the men and his brother on the way. Even though it was dark, he refused to use the pisspot, for his cousin Col teased him mercilessly about his 'little worm', as he dubbed it, and though I told him it would grow in time, Hob had taken to hiding himself away from Luke and Col whenever he pissed.

105

Hob dragged on the cord to lift the wooden latch. I wondered if he would remember to close it behind him, to keep the mice out. But he pulled it shut. I lay tense listening for his return, but there were so many snores, snuffles, creaks and rustles from those sleeping all around, it was hard to make out any sounds outside but the wind in the trees and the distant roar of the sea.

A sharp cry made me sit up. A bird? A vixen? Goda mumbled in her sleep pulling the blanket closer. Packs of foxes had come out of the forest to savage children, that was what Janiveer had said, but I hadn't really believed it, thought it was just a tale. But the pestilence had come to the village, like she said. A cold sweat drenched me. Hob was out there alone in the dark. The foxes, their green eyes glowing, were creeping towards him between the twisted tree trunks. I could hear their paws on the path, their snarls, their snapping teeth.

Ignoring the whimpers of protest from Goda, I struggled out of bed and blundered towards the door.

Elis grabbed my leg as I stepped over him. 'What's amiss?' he mumbled, only half awake.

'Hob. I need to fetch him,' I whispered. 'Not safe out there.'

I pulled the cord to raise the latch, but the door only opened an inch or two before it was snatched from my hand and slammed shut. Startled, I cried out. Elis scrambled to his feet, Daveth too and the boys, but they were falling over each other in the dark. I tried to pull the door open again, but it was being held on the other side.

'Hob, is that you? Let go of the door.'

A roar exploded outside, shouting, hammering, thumping. The door and shutters were rattling as if a hundred wild boar were charging repeatedly at the cottage. Round the edges of the shutters and through the cracks I glimpsed a flickering red glow. Fire! I was tugging frantically at the thick oak door, trying to force it open. We had to get out. Elis shoved me aside as he struggled to open it. Somewhere behind me a woman's shrieks cut through the howling of baby Kitto.

'Hold hard!' a man's voice shouted outside. And suddenly all fell quiet, save for the babby's cries.

'Elis? Daveth?'

'That you, Cador?' Elis called out.

The rope of terror that had tightened around my chest eased a little. The bailiff had come to help. He'd driven off whatever was out there.

'We are safe now, safe,' I murmured.

Reaching for Luke, I gripped his shoulder to reassure him, but he jerked away.

'Put your shoulder to the door, will you, Cador? 'Tis stuck,' Elis yelled.

'Can't do that, Elis,' Cador shouted back. 'Got to seal you in, you and your kin, till we're sure the pestilence is not in this house.'

Elis let out a bellow of rage, like a wounded boar, and started to pound on the door.

'Elis!' Cador raised his voice still louder. 'Listen to me. Men in the village got their own families to think of. They see you and your boys wandering abroad, and there's no knowing what some'll do. You know what happened last time in these parts. Women and children, whose kin had died of the fever, got stoned out of the villages. Some were even herded over the cliffs and made to jump to their deaths, in case they spread the sickness to others. If panic takes hold, there's no knowing what even decent folk will do.

Safer for you to stay inside. Just till we know for sure. But we'll not see you starve. Bald John here has a sack of food for you. You stand back, he'll pass it through the casement on a cord.'

The shutters flew open. Torchlight flickered over the dried fish bladders that were stretched across the opening to keep out wind and flies. They split with a crackle as a stick was thrust through them and a sack dangling on the end of a cord spun rapidly down to thump on to the floor. Almost before it reached the ground, the end of the rope slithered down behind it. The shutters were slammed and the torchlight vanished. We heard the sound of hammering as they nailed planks across the shutters.

Aldith barged me aside and thumped on the door.

'Now you listen to me, Cador. You've no right to lock us up as if we were common felons. We've chillern in here. My Kitto's only a babby and my sister about to whelp hers any day now. I swear on the milk of the Blessed Virgin we'll stay right away from the village. Camp out in the forest if needs be, till you're satisfied we've not taken sick.'

'And suppose you drink from the brook upstream and poison carries down?' Bald John shouted. 'Or your chillern wander back to the village 'cause you're too sick to mind them?'

'Whole village is agreed on it,' Cador said. ''Tis safest for all of us. And I warn you, Elis, don't even think of trying to break out. I'll not stay any man's hand, if you do.'

It's night in the cottage, though I think it must be day outside. Steel-bright slivers of light pierce the cracks between the planks they have nailed across the windows and the door, but they reach no more than a hand's breadth inside.

We're trying to save what rush candles we have, burning them only when we cook and eat, extinguishing them as soon as we can, for who knows how long they may have to last. When they're gone and the firewood is used up, we shall have no light at all.

Elis wrenched the door open as soon as he was sure Cador and the villagers had gone, but the gap had been boarded up with stout planks and nails, and stones piled against them. Elis was certain he could work the boards loose, but Daveth said if they saw we'd tried to break out, they might refuse to bring us food or, worse, set fire to the cottage with us inside.

'You heard him. Even if we pushed the chillern out through a gap, they'd more than likely stone them.'

Even as they were arguing a thought struck me like a blow from a fist. 'Little Hob! He's still out there!'

The shock of the mob arriving had driven out all remembrance of why I had been listening so hard only moments before I heard them.

'He went out to the midden . . . They must have surrounded the cottage afore he could get back!'

I stumbled to the window, pressing my mouth to the crack in the shutter and yelling his name, but Aldith pulled me back, shaking me.

'Stop that! If any hear you they'll know he's out there and start hunting him. I dare say he ran off as soon as he saw that crowd coming. He'll have hidden in the trees.'

'All alone in that forest!' I yelled at her. 'How's he supposed to fend for himself? Where's he going to find food? He'd only a shirt on when he ran out. He'll freeze! This is your Col's fault. If your little heller hadn't tormented Hob so, the boy would've used the pisspot inside.'

'All boys tease each other, 'tis only natural,' Aldith retorted. 'If you didn't coddle the lad so, he'd be able to stand up for himself.'

Daveth laid an arm on his wife's shoulders. 'We can't be falling out, not now. Might be a blessing your lad did run out, Sara. At least he'll be spared—'

He broke off and I knew he couldn't bring himself to say it. I didn't even want to think it. Being walled up was bad enough, but what if we were not shut in here alone? Suppose there was another with us, invisible, standing in the shadows, crawling over the walls, slithering between us. Who would it reach out and touch first?

We eat a little of what the villagers gave us. The bread first, since it's already a day old, and growing hard. We use it as a sop for the fish stew left from last night. Besides that, there is dried fish and conger eel in the sack, with some dried beans and peas. Not much for so many mouths, but I know few have anything to spare in the village after the storm. How long is this intended to last us? We have a little water, which I collected yesterday, but will they remember to bring more? I dare not waste any to soak the fish. We will need every precious drop to drink.

On the other side of the thin wattle wall that separates our living space from the animals, my two goats and their kids bleat fretfully, unable to understand why I have not let them out to graze. I stir myself, light one of the tallow candles in the embers of the fire and clamber through the wicker door into the byre.

I drag the stool over to where the she-goats are tethered and try to milk them, but they're restless. They are used to being given fresh fodder to keep them occupied while they're

110

milked. They know something is wrong and will not stand still, keeping back their milk and kicking out at the pail until I am forced to call Aldith and Luke to hold both goat and bucket.

Aldith won't look at me. She grips the horns, muttering, 'Whist, whist,' as the cantankerous beast twists its head and tries to back away. I see her staring at the manger. It's empty and there's precious little of last year's hay left in the loft. Their stone trough is barely half filled with water. I know what she's thinking, what we're both thinking. Will they let us out before we're forced to slaughter them?

Even in the mustard light of the tallow candle, I can see Luke's face is wan, his eyes swollen. He's been crying, smothering the sound in the darkness, so as not to betray himself. Does he blame me? I want to hug him, hold him close, but I know he'd push me away.

I want to hold Hob too, smell the sweat in his hair and feel the warmth of his soft cheek. He's somewhere out there, alone and terrified. Is he hungry? What will he find to eat? A sob rises that I cannot suppress. Before I even know what I'm doing, I'm at the byre door, shaking it, trying to tear it open with my bare hands. Aldith seizes my wrist, and jerks me backwards.

'Let me go!' I shriek at her. 'I have to find Hob. I must get to him!'

Aldith holds me tightly. 'Don't you go fretting about him. Nights are getting warmer and he's built dens often enough with the boys to make hisself a shelter to creep into.'

Luke slams his fist into the byre wall. '*I* should have gone out last night, too, then I'd not be shut up in here with you. I could have found food easy.'

'By stealing it!' I snap. 'And how long would it have been

before you were caught and chased over the cliff by the dogs? Be thankful you've got a full belly. Your brother hasn't.'

Tears spring into his eyes again. I know this is harder on him than any of us. The boy's out from morn to night even in the foulest weathers. Keeping him in the cottage is like locking a wild creature in a cage. I feel like those men Elis once told me of, tied between wild horses to be ripped apart. Part of me desperately wants both my boys to be out there, away from the sickness, but I want them in here with me where I can keep them safe.

Aldith shares out the warm goat's milk among the chillern, all except baby Kitto for she's still nursing him.

'Give what's left to Goda,' I urge. 'She's scarce eaten a bite.'

Goda lies on the bed, turned on her side, her legs bent and her arm clutching her belly. She has stopped wailing. Now she stares blankly at the wall, as if her soul is travelling far off.

She pushes the beaker away, but Aldith insists, holding her head with one hand and pushing the beaker to her lips as if she is teaching a child to drink.

'Sup it! Else you'll lose this babby an' all.'

Goda snatches the beaker and swallows it in one draught, flinging the empty cup at the wall.

'My babby wasn't dead. He wasn't. I could feel him moving inside me. *You* killed him with your birthwort and dittany. Now you want this one to die, too, just to spite me. I shouldn't be in here. I never went near those corpses. Why didn't you tell them, make them let me out? You just want to keep me from my Jory. But Jory's coming back for me, do you hear?'

Aldith snorts impatiently. 'Course he is. I told you that.

Try the patience of the Blessed Virgin herself, you would.'
She rolls her eyes at me.

The babe was rotting when Aldith and I pulled it out of her, but she still refuses to believe it died days before in her belly. Father Cuthbert didn't help, telling her that she lost him 'cause of her sin. Up in the hayloft, baby Kitto starts wailing.

Aldith sighs. 'Wanting *his* milk now.'

We've blown out all the tallow-candles. The red glow of the embers in the hearth lights up only the stones around it. Daveth is asleep. Elis whittles a piece of wood. He never looks at what he is whittling even when the lamps are lit. Col is playing with knuckle bones, testing himself as if the darkness is just another element of the game, another skill to be learned. It is strange sitting in this eternal night, hearing the sounds of daylight outside. Gulls shrieking, dogs barking, the goats still bleating to be let out. I keep remembering the morning the sun turned black and twilight came at noon. All the birds fell silent then. They sing now. It's us who are silent.

Where is my little Hob? Is he close by, hiding, watching the cottage? If only he would creep back and call out to us. I could talk to him, tell him what to do, how to keep himself safe. A word, one word, is all I ask, just so as I know they haven't hurt him.

'Luke?'

He doesn't answer me.

'That box that you took from the sea, did you throw it back?'

The dead chillern came from the sea, a curse that the sea threw at us. First the storm and Janiveer, then the pestilence – they all three came out of the sea. She wants the box.

Whatever is in it, the sea wants us to give it back.

Luke says nothing. He jiggles his leg up and down. It irritates me. Why does he do it?

'Where is the box, Luke? Answer me.'

'You blame me for this, don't you?' he demands. 'You think it's my fault – the storm . . . everything.'

'Where is the box?'

'Hid it. Knew you'd take it off me. Just wanted to see inside, that's all.'

'And did you?'

'Couldn't get it open. But I will! Soon as I get out of here, I will. Then I'll throw it back . . . then . . .' His voice trails from defiance to defeat, as if he knows it is already too late.

He scrambles to his feet, knocking into his father as he passes. Elis yelps and curses. 'Stop charging about, boy! You nearly had my finger off.' I hear him sucking the wound.

Luke blunders through the wicker door into the byre, hammering and kicking the door on the far side, shouting and screaming, venting all his impotent rage on the wood. He will panic the goats. I yell at him to come back. But in the semi-darkness I feel Elis's broad hand on my knee.

'Leave the lad. He has to let it out. Can't say as I blame him.'

'The cut, is it deep?' I ask him.

He grunts. 'More to worry about than a little scratch,' he says, and he wraps the bottom of his tunic around his finger.

Chapter 14

Will

Riddle me this: What brings ill fortune to him who rides and good fortune to him who flies?

The lights of torches in the darkness marked each villager's progress through the village. A scarlet flicker halfway up the hill, an orange one weaving along the shoreline until they converged in front of the brew-house, like sparks flying down into a fire.

I knew that night would be my best chance of making another attempt on those piglets. I'd take two this time, three if I could. Eat some, smoke the rest. Something told me that every man and woman in the village was going to be snatching food like starving gulls before the month was out, so better I took those juicy little piglets before someone else did. I was most obliged to Cador for telling everyone he hadn't selected for his walling-in army to stay inside with their doors firmly shut. If the Holy Hag heard anything outside, with luck she'd think it was Cador's rabble and ignore it.

If I was forced to flee the village, I'd need all the food I could carry, for the towns would soon be barring their gates to strangers, as they did the last time the pestilence struck.

But I'd still not decided if it was safer to stay or go. Porlock Weir was the first village I'd come to when I'd found myself a vagabond. I stayed, though I hadn't planned to, because at least I could take refuge in a cave, and forage for food along the shore. And, believe me, I was in dire need of free food and shelter. I even found myself envying the lepers. At least they could beg for alms. I couldn't even do that to keep from starving without risking another whipping.

The day Master Wallace, Sir Nigel's steward, finally threw me out of Porlock Manor, having decided that even banishment to such a remote estate from the bustling life I'd enjoyed at Chalgrave Manor was not sufficient punishment for my heinous crimes, I waddled off down the road on my bandy legs, owning absolutely nothing in the world but a bruised and lacerated back. I had no home, no work, not even so much as a crooked farthing to buy a bite to eat, but of all the thoughts and fears that clamoured for attention in my head, the one that shouted loudest was that I no longer possessed a name.

The day I'd been given to Sir Nigel – presented riding on the back of a hairy black pig and dressed like a little knight complete with a child-size lance – he informed me, after he and the company had stopped laughing, that from then on I was to be known as Gaubert. It was the name of the dwarf I'd been bought to replace. Of course, it probably wasn't that fellow's real name either.

An ancient servant who'd been in my lord's employ all his life remembered the old dwarf well and insisted he was the same little man who'd been jester there in the time of his own grandfather, but then the old servant's wits often wandered off to Faery Land, so I didn't set much store by that tale. Just how many Gauberts there'd been in that manor house through the years the other servants couldn't recall, but it didn't much matter for we were all one to my lord and his household. It was the same with his hounds: his best pair of lymers were always called Holdfast and Sturdy, had been for generations. It was more convenient that way.

Of course, Gaubert wasn't the first name that had been thrust upon me. Before I'd been sold, my master had called me Courtney, his little joke for it means 'short nose'. He liked a good laugh, did my master. But if my mother or father had ever given me a name before that, I'll never know it.

My master reckoned I'd been dumped on the steps of a monastery while I was still bloody from my birth. 'Should be grateful,' he used to say. 'If I hadn't stumbled over you first, you'd have spent the rest of your life eating naught but herbs, and freezing your cods off in a chapel all night, instead of sleeping by a warm fire in a lord's hall, your belly stuffed full of venison and roast goose.'

Maybe he was telling the truth and I had been abandoned by parents who couldn't afford to fill another hungry mouth or by a mother frightened because she'd given birth to a bastard. But I know my master paid for other babies. Infants snatched from cradles or careless nursemaids and brought to him at night, half smothered in blankets. I'd seen the coins slipped into dirty hands.

When I was a lad, I used to tell myself I had been stolen and some day my parents would find me, or else that I was the bastard son of some wealthy noble, who would at last claim me for his own. But that fantasy died as soon as I found myself cavorting and grimacing at my lord's banquets for the entertainment of his guests. I was popular, a favourite even. The men laughed drunkenly at my jokes and the women petted me, like a winsome puppy, but I knew that even if my own father and mother had been among the guests and had recognised me as their own, they'd no more want to name me son than they would claim kin to a clothed monkey.

So walking away from my erstwhile lord's manor on that bitter day in winter, I made the first real choice I'd ever be granted in my forty-two years of life. I'd choose my own name. I'd called myself William, after that other great bastard, the Conqueror. Made me feel I could do as I pleased now, just like him, even took the sting from my whipped back, and I swaggered down that road, feeling bolder than any longshanks popinjay at the king's court.

It didn't last long. I soon discovered I could call myself whatever I liked: it made not a pig's fart worth of difference to the rest of the world. The moment I uttered my new name in Porlock Weir, the villagers shortened it to Will. A short man needs a short name, they said. And who was I to argue? There are far worse names a manikin like me can be called.

I edged along the dark track, hoping I wouldn't run into any stragglers coming the other way to join Cador's house-sealing party. Just as I'd hoped, the Holy Hag's door was firmly shut. We dwarfs, even fake ones, are trained to be light on our feet. We caper and prance. We learn how to creep up behind the unsuspecting guest to pull the chair out from under their backside or slip a live toad on to their platter for the amusement of others, so I easily got past Matilda's casement in the dark and into the pigpen without stepping on any of her vicious caltrops or cracking a single twig.

It was a mild night and the old sow – the pig, that is, not Matilda – was grunting and snuffling as she lay outside her hut, her piglets heaped upon each other for warmth. I knew I'd have only one chance, for the moment the piglets started squealing the sow would be on her feet. A pig can chew your hand off as easily as you can bite through a piece of roast crackling. I've seen a sow and her brood devour half the carcass of a dead horse in a single night. So I made a lunge for the piglets, grabbed a little wriggler in each hand and was bounding down the slope before the sow had lumbered to her feet.

I stopped at a safe distance from the cottage to stuff the two piglets into my sack. They were screaming shrilly enough to raise the dead from the deep. But the unholy din up at Elis's cottage would have drowned out a whole herd of shrieking swine. I couldn't see the cottage itself, but I saw the flickering orange and red glow of the burning torches above it in the night sky. It sounded as if a dozen blacksmiths and a score of carpenters were hard at work. Banging and hammering mingled with the shouts and bellows. I pitied the prey who found themselves caught in that trap.

But I still had to get my little piggies safely home before I found myself locked up. The little wrigglers were shrieking louder than ever and I couldn't risk carrying them past the cottages on the shore. The noise from Elis's cottage wouldn't mask the squeals down there. So I squatted down and hauled each out of the sack in turn, swiftly cutting their throats. Scalding blood gushed over my hands and breeches, splashing on to the dry grass. The bloodstains on the ground might be spotted in the morning, especially if the dogs started licking them, but who would be able to prove what had been slaughtered there and whether the killer was human or beast?

I thrust the steaming carcasses back into my sack, and

was just about to clamber to my feet when something came hurtling towards me out of the darkness. A small boy tumbled over me, knocking me backwards. He quickly scrambled to his feet, but I was faster. Grabbing him by his bare leg, I jerked him down again, and held on to him. He struggled to escape from my grasp, but I was having none of that. For all I knew, he'd seen me kill those piglets. I wasn't about to let him go squealing to Matilda.

'Stay still, you little brat, or I'll sit on your head!'

The boy gave a few feeble twists, then sat panting hard, his body taut as a stringed bow, while he considered his next move. It was too dark to see the features of his face.

'So, what are you in such a hurry for? Shouldn't go running like that at night when you can't see what's under your feet. Knew a lad once who fell straight on to a ploughshare, chopped himself clean in two. Your mam know you're out, does she?'

He said nothing, but I felt a sob shudder through his little body.

'You in trouble, lad? Someone catch you thieving? That it?'

A louder burst of hammering and shouting gusted down from the hillside above, and the boy gave a frightened yelp, turning his head towards the flickering red glow that hung over the cottage. Tears glistened on his cheeks and his body heaved with sobs. I suddenly realised he was half naked.

'Ah, it's young Hob, isn't it? Now I understand.'

I scrambled to my feet, hauling him up with me, by the back of his shirt. I could feel him shivering in the chill night air. 'Right, we'd best get you out of sight before anyone realises that one of their birds has escaped the trap. No one comes near my cave at night. You'll be safe enough there.'

At once, the lad started punching and kicking me in an effort to get away, though since his feet were bare, he must have hurt himself more than me.

'Let me go!' he squealed. 'You drag chillern into the cave and gobble them up.'

I chuckled. 'Now, who told you that, lad? Your brother, I suppose.'

When I'd first taken up residence in the cave, Luke and his cousin Col, along with a few other boys from the village, had amused themselves by finding ways to annoy me, hurling stones and dung into the cave or hiding rotten fish or sharpened sticks under the bracken I used as a bed. I played a few tricks of my own on them, which mostly kept them away, but I still occasionally heard them dragging some child they were tormenting towards the cave, threatening to toss them to the man-eating dwarf.

Hob, redoubling his efforts to tear himself away, began to scream. I clamped my bloody paw over his mouth.

'Stop that, boy.' I turned him so that he could see the light from the flickering torches. 'See what they're doing. Want them to do it to you too?' I spun him to face me. 'There's two plump little piglets in this sack. I'm going to cook one of them for my supper tonight. So why would I want to eat a scrawny little runt like you? And I'd wager my own beard you like roasted pork, don't you? Nice wedge of juicy crackling to go with it?'

I sat in the mouth of the cave, staring down at the sea rocking in the arms of the bay. I'd become used to the constant hiss and slither of the waves as they broke over the rocks, could even sleep through their pounding and crashing when the sea was in a raging temper. But tonight she was in good humour, the waves rolling in as soft as a lullaby. A broad path of bright moonlight shivered across the black water. The great dome of stars stretched from the cliffs on one side of the bay to the dark forested hills on the other and far out across the sea. Sometimes I imagined that if I could only sail far enough, I could reach the place where the glittering stars touched the horizon and pluck them like silver sprats from a net. Maybe that was what I should do. Sail and keep sailing until I found one of those strange isles the sailors tell of, one where every man and beast is a dwarf. But even there I'd be a fraud, an imposter.

Behind me the boy was asleep on my bed of bracken, having stuffed himself with so much pork, he could barely stand. When I'd first hauled him in, still wailing that I was going to eat him, he'd crouched in the furthest corner of the cave, wary as a trapped rabbit, watching me eviscerate a piglet. As I cut it into pieces, I kept up a stream of riddles and mindless chatter, as I used to do to amuse the children in the manor, until the need for warmth overcame his fear and he began to edge closer and closer to the fire. Finally, I even persuaded him to turn some pieces of the skewered pork over the flames. He was almost dribbling as the smell of roasting meat filled the cave.

'Why – did they shut my mam in the cottage?' he blurted out. 'She wanted to come out. I heard her shouting.'

I wiped my greasy fingers down my bloodstained tunic. How do you explain the Great Mortality to a boy who's never known the terror of it, never seen the corpses lying unburied in the fields or looked into the dead eyes of living children who sit rocking themselves in the doorways of empty houses, when even their pet dog has deserted them?

'They'll let her out in time,' I said cheerily, 'soon as they know she hasn't got the fever.'

'Is she sick?' The boy scrambled up in alarm. 'I – I want to see her!'

I grabbed his arm, pulling him down. 'Your mam doesn't want you getting sick and worrying her.'

But suppose young Hob already was? I tried to resist the urge to move away from the child.

'They won't let you back into the cottage. And if Cador or others in the village see you near it, they'll lock you up all by yourself in the dark. You'd not want that, would you?'

Hob's eyes widened in fear. It was a harsh thing to say to him, but I had to make him so afraid that he'd not dare risk trying to return to the cottage. And, in truth, locking him up might be the very least they would do. But just how long could I keep him hidden in the cave, and if he did fall sick, would I be able to conceal it from the villagers? I'd have no choice. There were men and women, too, in Porlock Weir, who wouldn't hesitate to hurl us both into the sea, like those two children, if they thought it would save their own.

Chapter 15

Sara

*If you count the fish you have caught, you will catch
no more that day.*

We sleep and wake, not knowing how many hours have passed. I should be washing the clothes in the tub outside, tending my beans or sitting in the doorway cleaning fish. My neighbours would be passing by on the path, chattering to each other, calling out a greeting to me. I listen for those voices now, but there are none. Not a soul comes near the cottage. Only the gulls wheeling above and cockerels in distant gardens call out to us.

The pisspot is overflowing again. Elis tips it into the gully that runs down the middle of the byre, but there is not enough liquid to wash the shit from the pail out through the tiny gap in the wall. It lies there stinking. Elis covers it with straw as best he can, but that, too, is sodden and soiled by the goats. The air in the cottage is thick and heavy, and when I sleep, I dream that I am being sucked down into quicksand in the bay, gasping and choking as my mouth fills with liquid mud.

I wake with a jolt as someone bangs on the shutter. 'Elis, Daveth . . . how goes it in there? Any sick?' Cador calls.

The men rush to the window bumping against the table and overturning stools in their haste. Col and Luke are not far behind. Aldith tries to scramble down the ladder so quickly I fear she will overturn it.

'No one's sick,' Elis shouts back. 'We're all fit as fleas. You can let us out now.'

'Only been three days. A week more, then maybe . . .'

'A week!' Daveth bellows. 'You can't keep us in here that long. What about my weirs, Elis's widgebeasts?'

'Don't you fret, they're being cared for. But if you swear there's none of you ailing, we'll open these shutters and pass water and food in. I dare say you could do with some tallows too.'

'And firewood,' I remind them.

'Firewood,' Elis yells through the shutters, 'and fodder for goats 'n' all.'

There are mutterings outside, as if some hasty discussion is taking place.

'Next time . . . maybe,' Cador calls. 'Now keep far back from the casement, you hear?'

Planks are prised away with iron crows, and after another warning, as if the bailiff fears we've turned into demons and will come flying out of the window, the shutters open. We blink in the sudden rush of light and stand gulping in the blessed fresh air, heavy with the salt tang of the sea and crushed thyme from the bushes I planted beneath the window.

A face appears, only the eyes showing. The mouth and nose are masked by a piece of sacking tied round the head, which, judging by the smell, has been soaked in herbs and vinegar. After the fetid stench of the cottage I drink in the sharp scent of it, like the perfume of a sweet rose.

A sack is lowered in on a cord, then a water barrel is

raised to the window. But it will not pass through the narrow gap. It vanishes.

Goda suddenly rouses herself and pushes past us, stretching her arm through the hole in the fish bladders, trying to catch hold of someone or something outside. 'Let me out! I shouldn't be in here. I never touched those dead chillern, never, never!'

She shrieks, as a plank is struck against her hand, beating her back.

'Get away from the casement!' Bald John yells. 'Else we'll not come again.'

Aldith pulls her sister aside and yells through the gap. 'If you don't give us water, we'll perish of thirst, and I swear to you, Cador, and you 'n' all, Bald John, if we die, my spirit will haunt you to your grave and beyond for the murderers you are.'

There are more whispers outside, but it seems the threat of Aldith haunting them is enough. After an age, a cord descends through the window with several old water skins and seal bladders tied down the length of it, like fish caught on a long line.

No sooner than Elis has caught it and lowered it to the ground than the shutters are slammed and once more comes the sound of hammering as the planks are nailed back. I have to bite my knuckle to stop myself calling out, begging to know if they have seen Hob, if they have hurt him. All too soon, the last plank is laid across the shutters and the cottage is in darkness again.

The groaning wakes me. I can't tell where it is coming from. I ease myself from the bed, trying not to wake Goda. One of the men is sitting up, a blanket pulled over his head and shoulders, trying to shuffle so close to the glowing embers of the fire that I fear he means to clamber on top of them. His teeth are chattering, as he rocks back and forward. Blessed Virgin, let it not be my Elis! Dropping to my knees on the floor, I crawl over and pull the blanket from his face. The dim red glow from the dying fire is scarcely bright enough to distinguish maid from man, but you cannot share a bed with a man for twelve years without knowing his features even in that hell-light.

He's shivering, yet his skin is burning, drenched with sweat. I grope for one of the water-skins and pour a little into a beaker. He grabs it, almost upturning it in his haste, gulping it frantically, draining every drop.

'More,' he begs. 'So thirsty.'

I glance over at the others. They're still sleeping. We had all agreed only to drink together to make sure none was taking more than his share, but I can't refuse Elis.

I pour another small measure.

Daveth stirs, propping himself up on one elbow. He watches us. 'Sick?'

'A little fever is all,' I whisper. 'It's being cooped up in here . . . and the stench from the pisspots. Foul air is enough to sicken anyone's stomach.'

'A woman's maybe, but he's slept in worse on the pack trail.'

Daveth scrambles up, gropes for one of the tallow candles and lights it in the embers. A dim yellowish-brown glow fills the room and the stench of burning fat grows with it. He holds the flame close to Elis's face. He squints, turning his face away as if the light hurts his eyes. The sweat on his skin glistens.

'What ails you?' Daveth demands.

Goda is sitting up now and Aldith, gingerly climbing down the ladder, turns to peer at Elis. 'Is it the . . .' She will not utter the word.

Snatching the tallow from her husband's hand, Aldith pulls open Elis's blanket, peering at what little skin she can see on his chest. Elis struggles to pull the blanket round himself again, but his movements are weak, clumsy.

'He's not coughing blood,' Aldith pronounces. 'You got any black spots?' She tugs at the blanket again as if she would see for herself, but I push her away.

'It's only a summer ague. Anyone can see that. Day or so, he'll be fit again. Go back to sleep. I'll tend him.'

Aldith and Daveth look at each other, frowning.

'I reckon he should sleep in the byre till we're sure,' Daveth says.

'So you want to start walling people up now, do you?' I snap. 'You're as bad as Cador. The air in the byre is foul. That's what's given him the fever. It's heat he needs, any luggins can see that.'

'There'll not be a fire by morning,' Daveth says. 'Wood's finished.'

'Then we'll burn goat dung or the table if we have to.'

Elis sinks down into the bracken and curls around the fire. As I pull the blanket over him, I brush his hand and he cries out. It is swollen, the skin tight and shiny in the candlelight. Was that the hand he cut? At any other time I would be worried, but now I am flooded with relief. A cut that's gone foul, that is all. It can be healed. We can draw the poison and all will be well. He will be well!

Chapter 16

Will

Riddle me this: How many straws go to make a goose's nest?

Hob looked more cheerful after a night's sleep and another bellyful of the pork. I even managed to make him smile. I'd never seen such a small lad eat so much. Several times I had to take it from him and force him to slow down for fear he'd vomit. I guessed meat was a rare treat for him, and when it did come his way, his portion would have been small, when there were working men to be fed first.

Now that even he was finally satiated, he began to poke about the cave, not that there was much to explore. It was six or seven feet above the sea when the tide was in. A waterfall of rocks and boulders spilled from its lip down on the shore, so it was easy enough to scramble up and down at low tide, and I knew the safest route over those rocks as well as I knew the staircase of my old lord's manor. At high water, the sea lapped round the base of the rocks, cutting off the cave from all but those prepared to swim.

The cave itself was like the inside of a winkle shell, broad at the front, but narrowing and sloping sharply upwards, round a curve at the back. It might once have been a tunnel leading who knew where, but the back was blocked by a fall of huge boulders as young Hob soon discovered, much to his disappointment, although his attention was briefly captured by what appeared to be the ribs of some gigantic animal embedded in the wall.

'Those,' I told him, 'are the bones of a ferocious dragon, which used to terrify passing fishermen with its roaring by day. At night it sent great jets of fire into the dark sky, luring ships to the shore where they'd smash into the rocks below. The dragon used to snatch the sailors off the deck in his huge claws and devour them head first, like you'd crunch an apple. Everyone was terrified of the beast, and not even the bravest knight in the land could slay it, for before they even came close enough to thrust in their lance, the dragon would see them and shoot out a blast of fire, which roasted them to ashes.

'Then one day a fearless dwarf crept into the cave under the very nose of the dragon, and because he was so short the dragon didn't see him. The dwarf tickled the dragon under the armpits till it rose up, bellowing with laughter. Then he ran under its belly and thrust a sword up into its heart. The dragon gave a mighty roar that made the whole hillside tremble and the beast came crashing down on to the floor of this cave. It would have squashed the dwarf flat if he hadn't managed to roll away just in time.'

Hob stared at the giant bones and back at me, clearly uncertain what to believe. Then he giggled.

The rest of the cave held nothing more exciting than driftwood drying for the fire and a jumble of flotsam I'd gleaned from the seashore, which I thought might one day prove useful – lengths of old rope, pieces of sea-bleached sailcloth, empty kegs, lumps of tar, even shells and dried starfish I thought I might fashion into something I could sell, if only I had the skill. But there was nothing among those poor treasures to capture the interest of a boy who had lived all his short life by the sea.

Hob kept wandering back to the mouth of the cave. The tide was receding and before long the fishermen would follow it out, pushing themselves over the soft sand on the sledges they called mud-horses to harvest the eels, fish and crabs from their traps. If one should happen to glance our way and recognise him, or if Hob took it into his head to wave at someone he knew . . .

I tried to distract him, and lure him deeper into the shadows, by getting him to help me disembowel the other piglet. We had to singe the hair off the skin strip by strip, with glowing sticks pulled from the fire, before I could cut it up and hang the pieces in the smoke. I'd smoked fish before, but had little idea how long it would take to cure the meat. Dwarfs, thankfully, are seldom set to work in the kitchens, for we can't reach the tables or shelves, although I did hear of one dwarf who fell out of favour with his lord and, in place of the dog, was locked inside a tread-wheel that turned the great spit on the fire. He was made to walk all day and half the night in the heat of the roaring flames and stinging smoke, turning the wheel to roast the boars and oxen. I shuddered, just thinking about it. I'd been fortunate there had been no such wheel in Sir Nigel's manor, or I might have suffered the same fate.

As we dismembered the piglet, the boy kept gazing at me. I could tell there was something he wanted to ask. Finally, he blurted it out: 'You're no bigger than me, but you're very old. My head only comes up to my father's belt. If you had a son would he only come up to your belt? If he did he'd be as small as a chicken.' He chuckled. 'People would keep treading on him . . . He'd be small as a cat. Small as . . . cat's shit. Small as . . .' Hob cast around to find some other insignificant thing to which he could compare my imagined offspring.

I pretended to lunge at him. 'I'm going to catch you and tickle you to death like that dragon.' It was a foolish mistake.

Squealing in delight, the boy leaped up and dashed across the cave towards the opening, turning his head to see if I was chasing him.

'No, Hob, come away from the entrance. Someone might see.'

But it was too late! I heard someone, a way off, give a cry. I rushed to the mouth of the cave, grabbed the boy and dragged him back into the shadows.

'Stay down,' I whispered. 'Don't move!'

Cautiously I peered out. The tide was still ebbing, but I could tell from the wet boulders that only a foot or so of water still surrounded my rocky staircase. Cador and old Abel were splashing their way around the base of the cliff, making straight for me.

My thoughts were spinning. I could hide the boy behind the curve at the back of the cave, but it was too shallow to conceal him for long if they started to search for him. I had only moments to decide. I seized the lad and hurried him to the far side near the entrance, keeping him pressed between me and the wall of the cave. With the tide not yet fully out, if Cador and Abel were to walk around to the front of the outfall of rocks they'd have to wade out into much deeper water. An old fisherman like Abel knew better than to attempt that if he couldn't see what was under his feet. So I wagered they'd start to climb up from the side they were approaching, where the water was much shallower. There would be a few moments when they'd be so close to the base of the rocks that the mouth of the cave above them would be hidden from their view.

'Listen, Hob,' I whispered. 'Cador is searching for you. If he finds you he'll lock you up in a dark hut all alone.' I quickly pressed my hand over his mouth to stop him squealing in fear. 'When I tell you to, you must climb out of the cave on that side and duck down so they can't see you as they come up. Wait until you see Cador and Abel step into the cave then, quick as you can, scramble over the rocks to the other side where the water is shallow and work your way round till you reach the goat path that leads up on to the cliff. Don't make any sound. If you see anyone at all, you must hide. Then you run for the forest. Don't go near your cottage. I'll come and find you tonight, bring you food. But you mustn't let them catch you? Understand?'

He nodded, though I could see the fear in his eyes. 'Good lad. Don't you worry, I'll come as soon as it's dark.' I glanced out again. I couldn't see the men, which meant they couldn't see us. 'Now, Hob,' I whispered. 'Over the side and keep low.'

Like most boys raised on the shore, Hob was as surefooted on the rocks as the goats that came to nibble the seaweed. He vanished. I slipped back into the cave, rapidly gazing round for any signs that might betray he'd been there. Moments later, the shadow of Cador fell across the entrance, followed by that of Abel, who was wheezing badly after the climb. Would Hob remember what I'd said? I retreated further inside, hoping to draw Cador and Abel away from the cave mouth and, like dogs on a leash, they followed.

Cador looked down at me, a grin spreading across his

ugly face. 'At least we'll not have to search far for the evidence of this crime. Matilda swore blind it was you stole two of her grunters last night and what do we find here? That's one.' He pointed to the dismembered piglet still lying on the floor.

I can curse a man for being seven kinds of fool in three different languages and I used every one on myself at that moment. I'd been so sure they were searching for the boy, I'd entirely forgotten about the piglets.

Cador dipped his knife blade into the stew pot and skewered a large piece of pork. 'And I reckon the second must have thrown hisself in here. I'd better taste it, though, just to be sure. Wouldn't want to go accusing a man without proof, now, would we?'

He chewed the meat with undisguised relish, before fishing out two more pieces, one of which he handed to Abel before devouring the second himself. 'What you think, Abel? That taste like grunter to you?'

'Hard to be sure,' Abel said. 'Need another chunk, maybe two, afore I could tell for certain.'

'Seems to me, Abel,' Cador said thickly, through a mouthful of pork, 'we caught our thief, plain as a fox with a hen in its mouth. And since he's no money to pay a fine, I reckon they'll have to hang him.'

Chapter 17

Sara

St Columba trod on a flounder one day and slipped in the water, so the saint cursed the fish and for ever more the flounder's face will be lopsided as a mark of the saint's curse.

All is not well. We have moved Elis into the byre. We had no choice. His stench is making us all vomit. I tethered the goats as far away from him as I could. They are weak, bleating incessantly day and night from hunger and thirst. One kid is already dead. Aldith cut it up and added it to the pot. The others are dying.

Elis lies in the fouled straw. His head is forced sideways, almost touching his shoulder, by the great swelling on his neck. There is another in his groin. The pain is terrible. The slightest movement or brush of a blanket makes him cry out, and sweat breaks in great beads over his body. Black marks have appeared on his limbs, like huge bruises. Blood pours out when he shits and his piss is scarlet. Both stink, like his breath, worse than a rotting seal putrefying in the sun. I gag whenever I go near him, then feel so ashamed, for I shouldn't be revolted by my own husband. I feel again the guilt I knew when I ran from my mam all those years ago. Is God punishing me for leaving her by sending the same foul sickness to my husband? Blessed Virgin, forgive me, forgive me. I will not leave Elis. I swear I will not!

But he no longer knows me as his wife. Sometimes he thinks I am his mam, though she has been in her grave these many years. Other times he shrinks from me, screaming that I am a demon come to pull him down to Hell. How can he not know me after twelve years' sharing my bed? It hurts to see the fear and hatred in his face when he looks at me. He babbles incoherently and, in spite of the pain and his weakness, tries to crawl to the door, crying out that there are wolves attacking his beasts and he must drive them off. He shouts at us to let him out and fights with what feeble strength he has, lashing out wildly until he collapses again and we can drag him back to his corner.

It is Luke and I who must drag him back. For Daveth, too, lies in the byre, coughing blood, gasping, his belly swollen, eyes bulging as he gurgles and gasps for breath, like a drowning man.

The water is all but finished. The villagers have not returned. Can they smell the stench even through the walls, hear the screams of pain, the mad ravings? Maybe they are afraid of what they might find next time they open those shutters. But I am terrified they will never open them again.

Chapter 18

Porlock Manor

A friend is never known till a man have need.
Medieval proverb

Christina's eyes ached from staring out of the slit window of the turret. Wait, she told herself. Go too soon and someone would see her. Leave it too late and she'd be caught returning. She had to judge the moment exactly right. But how could she, when she could barely see anything more than a sliver of the courtyard through the narrow slit? She slapped the cold wall in frustration.

A few days ago she'd been gazing from that window and thought she saw her beloved crossing the courtyard, just a glimpse, enough to make her heart pound and her stomach leap, as it used to when her eyes searched for him in her uncle's great hall at Chalgrave Manor, or when she walked in the shade of the orchard there. And though she knew it was impossible that he could be here in Porlock, still she could not tear herself from that casement. He had been everything that Randel was not.

While they had all been guests of Sir Nigel at Chalgrave, Christina's mother and Randel had been often in each other's company, whispering and laughing together as if it was they who were betrothed. They flirted, tossing mocking jibes about Christina back and forth before the company, like young lovers sharing private jokes. But her gallant defender had seen her humiliation and he'd interrupt with some word, drawing the mockery on to himself to spare her.

One night her beloved began to talk loudly of having seen a loathsome darnel in the meadow, but that the daisies flourished and would choke it out. She knew he was telling her that Randel was nothing but a noxious weed and of the strength of his own silent love for her. She had adored him for that and loved him the more for knowing she would understand his message, but when she glanced up and saw her uncle watching, her stomach had contracted in fear. If he guessed . . . if he knew . . . *Take care, my love, take care!*

A crash echoed across the courtyard, followed moments later by a sharp crack and a yelp of pain. Christina pressed her face against the gap in the stones, but all she could see was a servant trying to balance a huge platter of meats as he craned round to stare behind him. She imagined that one of the scullions must have slipped on some goose dung as he left the kitchens, dropped a dish of food and felt the smart of the cook's calloused hand for it.

For the third time in as many hours Christina drew back slightly from the slit, but she kept her gaze fixed on the fragment of the courtyard as she eased her hand down the front of her gown and gingerly pressed the linen strips bound cruelly tightly about her breasts. The soggy green poultice of pounded colewort and sage leaves beneath oozed through the bandages, but her breasts felt just as swollen and tender as they had yesterday, perhaps even more so. Christina did not know whether to smile or sob.

Eda had slapped the mess on to her hot, aching breasts,

138

threatening to tie her wrists to the bedposts if she did not stand still.

'Be grateful Master Wallace dismissed the stillroom maid, Rosa, this very morning, else I would not have been able to make this without her demanding to know who it was for.'

Her fingers jabbed the green mash on to Christina's tender nipples.

'You've no cause to be pulling faces, m'lady. If the cup is bitter it is you who made it so and you who must swallow what you have brewed. If you had convinced Lady Pavia that you need rest, she would not now be insisting you be moved to the solar. How do you imagine you can hide the wet patches on the front of your gown or mask the stench of milk? Do you think I can smuggle the bastard to the solar for you to give suck? Your milk must be dried up. I've told Lady Pavia that you've a bad headache and cannot endure noise just now. But that will hold her off for only a day or so, so pray that your milk dries quickly. That's if your prayers don't sink straight down to Hell. You'd best try lighting a candle to Mary Magdalene for she's the only saint in heaven who's likely to hear the prayers of a harlot.'

If her milk dried she'd be free to leave her turret prison. But if it did, Eda would never again bring little Oswin to her. She had made that quite clear. 'There'll be no reason for you to see it,' she'd said, with a malicious smile that made her look even more like a snarling ferret than usual.

'But he'll starve,' Christina had protested tearfully.

'I dare say the little bastard will thrive well enough on goat's milk. Plenty do, more's the pity. It won't care whether 'tis a whore's teat it's sucking or a bit of rag stuffed in an old cow's horn, so long as it gets its fill. Takes after its father, that one.'

139

A voice whispered in Christina's head, urging her to stay silent, for she knew Eda was trying to goad her into betrayal, but her anger and hatred of the old witch would not heed the warning. 'You don't know anything—'

Fortunately, Eda chose that moment to give a particularly vicious tug on the linen strips she was winding so tightly about her chest. The shock of the pain had brought tears to Christina's already swollen eyes, but it snapped her into sense. She pressed her hand to her mouth to keep from crying out and, no matter how much Eda jabbed with spiteful tongue and cruel fingers, the girl refused to allow another sound to escape her, until finally the old woman gave up and retreated from the chamber.

Christina pressed her face to the cold stones again. The trail of servants carrying dishes towards the great hall had slowed and none was coming out. It meant that, having served their master's guests, they would be sliding on to their own benches at the bottom table to devour their own meal before the next courses needed fetching. She must go now and quickly.

She ran across the room and clattered down the spiral staircase, wincing as every step jolted her bruised and tender breasts, but she could not afford to slow. She struggled to lift the latch and pull open the heavy door. Had Eda locked her in? She tugged harder and, to her immense relief, the door creaked open. Keeping to the shadow of the doorway, her gaze darted around the courtyard. She blinked in the bright evening sunshine, unaccustomed to light after weeks confined to the gloomy chamber.

The courtyard was empty, except for a few chickens scratching at the dung and a couple of hairy young pigs trying to roll in the water-splashed weeds that were struggling to grow between the cobbles around the well. A clamour of chatter, laughter and the clatter of knives against pots drifted out from the casement of the great hall, almost drowning the faltering notes of the lute played by some servant, who made up for his lack of skill with his heavy-fisted twanging of the strings.

Christina, holding her skirts out of the dust and dung, scurried along the wall towards the archway that led into the wider yard beyond. It, too, was empty of people. A few horses tethered in the stables turned their heads to watch her and nickered to each other. A hound scrambled up and ambled towards her, its chain clanging over the stones, but it was used to servants coming and going at this hour and did not bark.

Christina ignored it and darted towards a cluster of wattle and daub buildings that huddled against each other at the far end of the courtyard. She hesitated. The smell from one of the small huts suggested it was the brew-house for ale, but which of the others was the stillroom? Servants might be asleep behind those doors or else tending fires, and what explanation would she give if she went blundering in?

Then she heard it: the cry of a baby, her baby. The wail died away almost at once. Was Eda in there? Had she picked up Oswin to comfort him? Rosa had been sent packing. Who else would be minding him? Her nerve almost failed her and she might have retreated to the turret had not a worse fear suddenly seized her. Suppose it was Eda who had stopped him crying – stopped him for ever! She might be on the other side of that door, pressing a cloth over his mouth, smothering the life out of him. Christina flung the door open and rushed in, 'Stop! Don't you . . .'

But it was Christina who stopped. A woman she did not

recognise was sitting on a stool, cradling Oswin in her arms. He was sucking contentedly on a bladder tied around the tip of a hollow horn half filled with creamy-white milk.

The woman glanced up, frowning. 'Draught from the door makes the fire gutter. I need a steady flame for my pot.'

Christina was staring at her son, watching his tiny mouth suck, the muscles flex in his throat as he gulped the milk. His wide blue eyes were not gazing up into her face, but the face of the woman who held him in her arms, and she felt a pang of jealousy. She ached to snatch him back, but she knew he'd cry.

'Close the door, m'lady,' the woman said sharply. 'The smoke . . .'

Christina jerked, swiftly pushing the door closed as she realised that anyone passing the hut might see her. The room was bathed in the soft red-yellow glow of the firelight and a single rush candle that flickered on an iron prick on the wall.

'I . . . was looking for Eda.'

'She will be eating in the great hall at this hour. Did you not see her there, m'lady?'

'I have my meals in my chamber. I am unwell.'

'You are the Lady Christina. Eda told me she waits on you there. Shall I fetch her?'

'No!' The word burst from Christina's mouth more vehemently than she intended.

Startled, Oswin turned his little head and the bladder slipped from his mouth. His face crumpled. But the woman gently rubbed his plump soft lips with it, until he fastened on it again. As soon as he was sucking once more, the woman raised her head.

'I am Rosa, m'lady. If you do not want Eda, can I fetch something for you?'

'The stillroom maid? Eda said you were dismissed.'

'I am the new Rosa.' She pronounced the name slowly as if she was trying out an unfamiliar word. 'You want to hold the baby?'

She rose, and before Christina could reply, she'd laid him in her arms, and guided Christina to the stool, steadying her as she sat. Christina winced as Oswin wriggled against her breasts, but she took the cow's horn and let him suck the last spoonful. Then tipping the child across her shoulder, she rubbed his back and snuggled the soft down of hair as she rested her chin on his warm head.

'See, he is content. A lamb always knows its dam,' Rosa murmured, smiling.

For a moment Christina paid no heed to the words, revelling in the weight and warmth of her son in her arms. Then she realised what the woman had said and her cheeks flushed hot. 'I'm not his mother,' she said, standing up and thrusting Oswin back into Rosa's arms. 'Why would you think such a thing? Didn't Eda tell you? This is her dead niece's child.'

Rosa laid Oswin on a sheepskin that lined a small wicker crib. As she drew a coverlet over the sleeping child, she said softly, 'If that is what you wish me to believe, then I will say it is so, as I say I am Rosa.' She swung round, her eyes bright in the firelight. 'But your dugs pain you. Let me see them.'

Christina backed towards the door. 'You're mistaken. I have no pain. Why would I?'

Rosa made no move to stop her, but as Christina put her hand to the latch she said quietly, 'Women die of milk fever. It is an agonising death, almost as bad as the Great Pestilence. You are already sickening. Your eyes are feverish. Daylight hurts them. Your head aches. You feel hot and dizzy. Your dugs throb and burn. Come, sit.'

Even as she said it, Christina felt the beads of sweat trickling down her forehead. The pain in her breasts seemed to grow more intense, more unbearable. She fumbled with the laces on her gown, but only succeeded in making herself hotter and more exhausted, till she was almost crying with pain and frustration.

Rosa unlaced her gown and began to unwrap the linen. The relief as the tightness eased was swiftly followed by a wave of pain from the movement. Rosa dipped a cloth in water and gently wiped away the green mess of poultice. Though the slightest touch hurt her, Christina was grateful for the blessed coldness on her burning skin.

Rosa gave an animal growl in the back of her throat. 'Was it that foolish woman Eda who did this? Was she trying to kill you?'

'I think . . . she would be glad if I died. Oswin, too. That's why I came. I was so afraid she'd hurt him.'

Christina knew there was little point now in trying to deny that he was her child. Rosa was too shrewd to believe her; besides she found herself trusting the woman. She'd seen the tenderness in Rosa's face as she looked at the baby, watched how gently she had laid him in the wicker cradle. If anyone could protect her child from Eda, it was this woman. 'I thought if I could give him suck . . . when Eda wasn't here . . .'

'Your milk's soured. Besides, you'd not bear the pain of it.'

Laying the cloth aside, the woman inspected the shelves of the stillroom, finally lifting down a jar and examining the fragments of dried plants tied to the lid. She untied the parchment covering the top and sniffed the contents, giving

144

a grunt of satisfaction. She dipped her fingers into the jar and gently anointed Christina's breasts with a thick layer of a bitter-smelling unguent, then loosely bound fresh linen strips over them. Then she studied the shelves again, selecting clay jars of herbs and standing them in a neat row on the rough wooden table.

She muttered to herself as she sprinkled pinches of each herb into a small iron pot of water that steamed over the fire. 'Herb robert, sage, chickenwort, devil's eye, yarrow . . .'

Stirring it carefully, she drained the liquid through muslin into a jar, keeping a little back, which she tipped into a beaker and handed to Christina. 'Drink it. It will dry your milk and soothe your fever.'

Christina's gaze darted towards the sleeping baby.

As if she understood the unspoken question, Rosa said, 'You cannot suckle him again. But I will see that he is well fed. He shall come to no harm, so long as I remain here. Drink.'

She watched Christina drain the green liquid to the last foul drop. Then she handed her the jar. 'Drink half tonight before you sleep and the rest in the morning when you wake. Return tomorrow evening when Eda goes to the great hall and I will have more ready for you. Two, maybe three days and your dugs will be dry and no longer paining you. But go now. Eda will be back soon.'

Christina bent and kissed Oswin, breathing in the scent of his skin. His eyelids, as translucent as mother-of-pearl, fluttered at her touch, but did not open.

Christina paused at the door. She should give the maid something for her care of Oswin and for her silence. She dug her fingers into the small leather purse that hung from the belt about her hips, and proffered a coin.

But Rosa did not take it. 'I do not ask for payment in coin.' A whisper of a smile played about her mouth before she turned away, her hands busy with her herbs.

For the first time since Christina had discovered she was with child, the dark, chill cloud of misery and loneliness that had enveloped her parted just a hand's breadth and she found herself beaming as she closed the door of the stillroom behind her.

It was twilight outside and the burning torches were already being set in their brackets on the walls. Servants were lumbering down the steps that led from the great hall, bearing platters of dismembered birds and beasts, their white bones poking up through the remains of the sauce, like the half-submerged wrecks of old ships. Several hounds, three cats, a squabble of chickens and the two hairy pigs ran around their legs as they tried to hold the remains of the food high out of their reach.

One of the scullions, who'd almost been sent sprawling by the cats, flung the contents of his platter across the yard so that it splashed on the cobbles on the far side, narrowly missing Christina as she picked her way across. The pack of animals rushed towards the mess, snarling, spitting and clucking as they snatched the fragments of meat and bones and lapped the thick gravy from the stones. The boy, who had plainly not noticed Lady Christina in the half-light, realised too late that he'd almost befouled one of his master's guests. He gave a cry and fled, as if expecting to be dragged back and flogged on the spot.

Christina glanced up the steps towards the great hall. She knew that inside cloths were being drawn from the tables and the final wines of the meal being poured for the guests, sweet and heavily spiced, to settle the stomach for sleep. At any moment Eda would be descending those steps to return to the stillroom or, worse still, climbing to the turret to check on her. She might already be there, waiting.

Panicked, Christina ran to the door, but was almost dashed against the wall as someone emerging from the dark corner bumped her shoulder.

'You clumsy ox!' she snapped. Not content with trying to drench her in sauce, now the servants were intent on knocking her to the ground.

The man bowed low. 'Indeed I am become an ox in your presence, Lady Christina, struck dumb by your beauty and yoked to your command.'

Christina peered through the fading light and gasped. Her stomach lurched as she recognised the features of the one man she had never expected to see in Porlock. The very last time they had been in each other's company had been at Chalgrave on her wedding day, when he had been forced to escort the drunken bridegroom to the nuptial bed. How could *he* be here? Had he followed her?

'Sir Harry? But . . . but Eda didn't tell me . . .'

He chuckled. 'I can hardly wonder at that. The old hen would have had me driven from the farmyard the hour I arrived if she were the cock of it. No doubt she's already dispatched word to your mother, but since I am here at your uncle's request, they may both cackle as much as they like for they will not banish me.'

He edged closer, and she caught the smell of powdered myrtle leaves and damask roses that always perfumed his clothing. He took her hand and raised it to his mouth. She felt the long, hot pressure of his lips, and the brush of his beard against her wrist. Conscious of the curious glances of the servants, she tried to pull away, but he was reluctant to let her go.

147

'My poor sweeting, they tell me you have been ill since we were parted. And without you, I, too, sickened, like grass deprived of the sun.' He smoothed his glossy beard with his elegantly shaped fingernails as he studied her. 'But I confess, after such alarming rumours about your health, I am relieved, if not a little wounded, to see that you appear quite radiant despite my absence. You have grown from cygnet to swan in these last few months. What has brought about this miracle? Did you not miss me?'

Christina dropped her gaze to stare down at the great blood-red stone on his ring, but she could feel his eyes searching every inch of her face. Someone else was studying Christina too, though she did not know it. A barefoot woman was standing in the dark shadow of the archway. Rosa's sea-grey eyes were fixed unblinkingly on the couple, like those of a wolf in a thicket waiting for its prey to run.

Chapter 19

Matilda

St Coloman of Stockerau is the patron saint of hanged men and protects against the pestilence. He was an Irish pilgrim travelling to the Holy Land, who was hanged as a spy on account of his strange appearance. But after his death, the scaffold took root and sprouted green leaves.

The horse's hoofs clattered down the stony path as the shadow on the sundial crept towards the eleventh hour. I knew he would be here on time. Father Cuthbert never permits himself to be late.

'Hurry, toll the bell,' I scolded, cuffing the boy to his feet. 'The congregation must be assembled as soon as Father Cuthbert is ready to begin. Last month they were still trailing in when Mass was half over.'

Father Cuthbert came trotting up the path on a brown and white gelding. He always looked immaculate, even after a long ride. There was not a mote of dust on his russet gypon or pied hose. His freshly shaven tonsure gleamed in the sun, while the black fringe of hair around it was clipped as neatly as a halo crowning a saint. He dismounted and waited, tapping his whip in impatience, for his acolyte,

Harold, to come ambling into the churchyard on his ancient donkey.

I hurried up to him. 'Father Cuthbert, have you had a good journey?'

He smiled graciously, his head jerking up as the chapel bell above us began to ring. I confess I had not noticed it before, but in that moment he was the very image of my statue of the young St Sebastian with his thin nose and seraphic eyes. I found myself blushing, as he turned those brown eyes once more towards me.

'The Lord preserved our steps, I am thankful to say, Mistress Matilda. Though the road was uncommonly hard and dusty.'

He frowned as Harold awkwardly slid off his wooden saddle and heaved the pack over his shoulder, coughing and beating his tunic to remove the dust that Father Cuthbert's horse had kicked back at him. The lank, mousy hair round his tonsure flopped across the livid pustules that always covered his forehead. Though he could have been no more than fifteen, he shuffled like an old man.

He was an indolent youth, never meeting my eyes when he spoke, as if he was trying to hide something, which I don't doubt he was. I devoutly hoped he had no ambitions to be ordained into Major Orders, for I shuddered to think how he might serve a congregation as a priest. I couldn't think of any trade he would be fit for, save a kitchen scullion.

Father Cuthbert flapped a hand at him. 'Stir yourself, you idle boy. The bell is tolling. I will not have my parishioners kept waiting.'

Harold jerked his head in what might have been a nod, and sidled inside to prepare the altar for Mass.

Down at the shore, I could see the men, women and children still sorting their catch from the weirs. They would not come to Mass until that was done, however long it took. But for once I was relieved. The path leading up to St Olaf's chapel was, as yet, deserted.

'Father Cuthbert, I must speak with you.'

He gave a faint smile. 'I cannot hear confessions directly before Mass, Mistress Matilda. Besides, I am sure that you can have committed no sin since your last confession so great that it would prevent your attendance at the service.'

'It is not a sin *I* have committed, Father Cuthbert.' I flushed, annoyed that he should accuse me of not knowing the proper time to confess. 'The bailiff and the villagers are trying to conceal—'

'Now, Matilda, don't you go telling the priest we've been catching more fish than we're letting on. He'll start asking for more tithes.' Abel came stomping up the path, his arms still slimy with fish guts and scales. 'Always reckons we don't give enough to the Church, she do.' Abel batted at the cloud of flies that buzzed round him. 'But, like I say to her, we'll give him our dues, when the Good Lord gives us ours.'

Father Cuthbert drew back slightly, wrinkling his nose at the pungent odour of sweat and stale fish blood. 'Give to God even when you have little, Master Abel, and he will prosper your work. Remember how Our Lord multiplied the loaves and the fishes. The people gave what they had and it was returned many times over.'

'Putting honest fishermen and bakers out of work,' Abel muttered.

I crossed myself, expecting Father Cuthbert to take him to task at once, but he merely shook his head sadly.

151

'Your catches are small, so you blame Our Lord, when in truth the cause is that you have neglected Him. By good fortune that is the subject of my sermon today, and I can see it is much needed. I will see you inside.'

'But, Father, I must speak—' I began.

'Later, Mistress Matilda, later. I cannot keep God waiting.' He put his hand to the iron ring in the chapel door, then paused, wrinkling his nose again. 'And, Master Abel, be so good as to wash those fish guts from your arms before you enter the holy chapel. It is the sweet smell of incense that is pleasing to God, not the stench of dead fish.'

Abel scowled. '*Be so good as to wash yerself,*' he mimicked, as soon as the door had closed behind Father Cuthbert. 'I reckon God ought to be used to the smell b'now. Jesus'd have been stinking of fish, if He were out in a boat with those disciples of His.'

He took several paces towards me, thrusting his grimy weather-beaten face into mine. 'Guessed you'd be tattling to the priest. That's why I came hurrying up here soon as I heard the bell. You were warned to say naught. This stays in the village. Keep that flapping tongue of yours still. Remember, not everything that washes up dead in the sea gets there by accident.'

'You can't keep this quiet, Abel. I won't be silenced.'

He made to grab my arm, but before he could do or say more, we heard voices and footsteps approaching on the stony path. He turned away and, with a curt nod to the women strolling towards the chapel, he lurched around the corner and out of sight.

As I stepped aside to let the women pass, I found I was trembling. I was furious with myself for my weakness. I wouldn't be threatened into silence. Father Cuthbert had a right to know what deadly secret the villagers were concealing in Sara's cottage. He should also be told that two children had been buried in the corner of the graveyard without the offices of any priest or even the poor services of an acolyte such as Harold. I would show Father Cuthbert the graves myself just as soon as Mass was concluded and tell him all.

I slipped out quickly, as soon as Mass was ended, and waited in the shadow of the yew tree while the villagers filed out. Father Cuthbert stood at the door dutifully blessing children as they were dragged past him and asking after absent relatives. As usual, few of the villagers met his gaze, mumbling replies he plainly could not understand.

A gaggle of fishwives lingered by the wall, gossiping. They ignored me, as they usually did. 'Didn't see your husband at the weirs this morning, Katharine,' one was saying. 'Too much ale last night, was it?'

Katharine flushed and avoided her questioner's gaze by rebraiding the end of her long flaxen plait. 'You know Skiener.'

Indeed we all did. He was one of several men in the village who if he'd a coin to spare, or even if he hadn't, chose to spend it on ale at Sybil's brew-house instead of bread, and Sybil did nothing to discourage him. At least Katharine's face did not bear the usual marks of his drinking, but if he had missed a morning's catch, it would be the family who would suffer. But the women were making light of it, as if it was something to boast of to have such drunken husbands. I tried to ignore their chatter and strained to hear what Father Cuthbert might be saying, waiting my chance.

'. . . congregation seems smaller than usual, Cador,' he said.

'Some of the packmen are away about their work. Not due back for a day or two.'

'But their women and children?' Father Cuthbert frowned as if he was trying to remember who might be missing. 'The unwed woman, the one who's with child *again*.' He wrinkled his nose as if even to utter the words left a foul taste in his mouth. 'Last time she came to Mass she was crying and wailing so loudly I could barely remember the words.'

'Goda?' Cador ventured.

'I believe that was the name. Where is she? Has she been delivered?'

Cador shrugged, turning his hood in his hand. 'Some women take to their beds afore their time . . . vomiting and the like.'

'Perhaps I should call on her before I depart. Childbirth is a dangerous time for women. If she should die, I would not like it on my conscience that I did not offer her a chance to confess her many sins.'

Cador shook his head firmly. 'You'll not get any sense out of her at a time like this. Best leave it to the womenfolk. They know what they're about. Don't want to go getting mixed up with all that screaming and blood and the like. When my Isobel were pushing out our first, I just put my head round the door to ask what she'd made me for my supper and I got a pisspot thrown at my head for my pains. And it weren't an empty one neither.'

Father Cuthbert shuddered. 'Perhaps you're right. Besides, I've several parishioners who have urgent need of me back in Porlock town, respectable and devout women, who merit God's comfort . . . Harold!' he shouted. 'You idler, aren't you finished yet? Come at once, we're leaving.'

Harold stumbled out through the door, still hastily stuffing

154

chasuble, amice and stole back into the priest's pack, as carelessly as if they were old rags instead of holy garments.

As Father Cuthbert swung up into the saddle, I hurried over and grasped the reins. 'I have a meal prepared, Father. Will you not take some refreshment before you ride back?'

If I could get him alone in my cottage, away from the many straining ears, I could relate all the details of what had transpired since the night of the storm, but he merely patted my hand.

'You are a good and charitable soul, goodwife Matilda, and Our Lord will bless you for the thought. But have no fear that I shall go hungry, for I dine with Sir Nigel's steward at the manor and he always keeps a rich table. I am hopeful we may enjoy a little hunting too.'

With that, he pulled on the reins and trotted off down the path without waiting for Harold, who was still trying to fasten the straps of the pack around the belly of the donkey.

As soon as Father Cuthbert was nothing more than a ball of dust in the distance, the women sauntered back down the path. They paused at the fork, looking up the rise to where the ridge of the thatched roof of Sara's cottage could just be seen behind the hillock. No smoke from the hearth rose into the blue sky. Were Sara and her family sick? Dead? Or merely still abed, having no work to do? No one would venture there to find out.

I followed the women at a distance down the path, making my way back round to my own cottage. Katharine peeled off from the others, hastened up to her own door and slipped in, shutting it firmly behind her. Skiener was evidently too drunk to stir himself, for the shutters were fastened and the door, in spite of the warmth of the day.

As I pushed open the door of my little cottage, a streak of black fur shot out, slithering between my legs and the door frame. I had unwittingly trapped Gatty inside and she was plainly annoyed that I had been away so long. I knew she would stay out for hours now just to punish me.

Still angry that Abel had prevented me from speaking to Father Cuthbert, I crossed to the table in the corner of my cottage on which I had placed all the statues of the saints. I had rescued them from those shrines where I could plainly see they were not being given proper reverence. The nuns in the convent where I had been raised as a child had taught me that neglect of a saint's statue was as grave a sin as failing to pray to the saints themselves. And Our Blessed Lord would never have occasion to reproach me with that.

There was St Amphibalus bound to a tree by his eviscerated bowels, while he was scourged bloody; St Laurence roasting on a gridiron; St Edmund, his decapitated head borne in the mouth of a wolf. And the one I was most devoted to – St Sebastian, his naked flesh pierced with a dozen arrows, his sweet mouth lifted up as if he was begging Christ to lean down from Heaven to kiss his lips.

Each morning I bathed them carefully in turn, rubbing clean each sinew and muscle, foot and nose. I stitched little cloaks to cover them, red for when it was their saint's day, black for Lent and Advent, and white for all other days. Above the table I hung my bloody scourge, my discipline, as nuns have to mortify the flesh, and at the feet of the saints I laid the sharp stones I used to press into my intimate parts to mortify them. My saints watched over both.

I took a taper from the fire and used it to light a candle. I always made the candles for my shrine from the finest beeswax, perfumed with oil of roses or lavender, and moulded them in human vertebrae. The spines on the bones made useful handles and it pleased me to think that I could mark my devotions by the time it took for the wick to burn to nothing in a man's backbone. It was a fitting sacred light for my holy saints.

But that day nothing pleased me. I had lain awake half the night before, planning what I would say to Father Cuthbert, imagining his outrage when I showed him the new graves, his gratitude when he finally realised that I was the only person in the village he could trust. I'd risen early to bake new bread and prepare the dish of pumpes, which I made from the last of the salt pork, mixed with cloves and currants, which are not cheap. I had fried them in pig's fat, till they were golden and crisp and I planned to serve them dusted with sugar and decorated with ramson flowers from the forest. Father Cuthbert always says pork is the most wholesome and Christian of meats. And it was meat I could ill afford since that little vermin had stolen so many of my piglets. Now that he was caught, I would see that he was hanged, but that would not restore my pigs.

I knelt before the flickering candles and stared up into the painted face of St Sebastian, but his eyes seemed not to be turned to Heaven but turned away from me. Again I saw the uncanny resemblance between the saint and the priest as if their faces were one. The saint's lips moved with Father Cuthbert's.

'You have failed us,' they were saying. 'You have failed us and you will be punished.'

Chapter 20

Sara

If a child has the whooping cough, put the head of a live fish in the child's mouth and let him breathe into the fish's mouth. After, release the fish and it shall carry the cough away with it down into the sea.

The corpse-birds are screeching on the roof again. Goda shrieks as if their call is ripping her soul from her body. Ever since we've been walled up in the cottage, she's been sitting in the corner pressed to the wall, as if she wants to melt into it. She whimpers constantly, asleep and awake, as if she doesn't know which is the prison and which the nightmare. But, then, neither can I tell if I'm still among the living or have been dragged down to torment in Purgatory.

Even when my Elis died, Goda barely noticed, but he was not her husband. Elis gripped my hand as fiercely as a woman in labour, but all he gave birth to was blood. He pissed it, shit it, coughed it and vomited it, till I was certain there could be not a drop left in his body, for the straw in the byre was soaked with it. They say bleeding cures a man of all ills, from winter ague to summer flux. If that were so, my Elis should have been the fittest man in all England.

I'd known him boy and man all the days of his life, played

with him in the dirt when we were both babbies ourselves. My first kiss I gave to him, joined hands with him in the chapel door, bore him two sons, and yet those last days he stared at me as if I was a stranger to him. He constantly begged for water, but vomited as soon as he swallowed it.

I made a little meat broth from one of the dead goats and what little water we had left, though my own throat was raw from thirst. I tried to help Elis swallow it, but he swore I was one of the faery folk who'd imprisoned him inside a hill and was trying to make him eat enchanted food. He dashed the bowl from my hand. The precious liquid vanished into the fouled straw. I wept then. I cried over a bowl of spilled broth.

Soon after, he fell to a violent fit of coughing, gasping and choking on his own blood, like a man drowning in the sea. He fell back lifeless, his eyes rolling up into his head. But I was all dried up. I couldn't find a single tear to shed, not for my husband or for Daveth, who followed him into death so soon after that it was as if he was hanging tight to his heels. I could only marvel at the silence that flooded the stinking byre, feel only relief that the screaming, which had split my head in two, had ended. Their pain, which I could do nothing, nothing to ease, was finally over.

I sit on the floor of the cottage now, staring at the thin red veins of fire that zigzag through the grey ash in the hearth, too numb, too exhausted even to wipe away the bead of sweat that crawls, like a spider, down my face. Luke is hunched in the corner, his legs drawn up, crying like an infant. I should try to comfort him, but if I try, he will only push me away.

Aldith rocks Kitto and Ibb, keeping up a tuneless hum as if she is trying to drown voices only she can hear. She did not sit with Daveth as he died. She's not gone near him, since Luke and I dragged him into the byre.

'The chillern . . . I have to take care of the chillern. Can't do nothing for him.'

I can just make out the grey smudge of her Col lying near the door, his mouth pressed against the thin gap at the bottom trying to suck in splinters of air and light. He didn't even turn his head when the coughing and the screaming stopped. Does he realise what the silence means?

I stagger to my feet. The ground seems to rock beneath me as if I'm standing on a boat. I have to hold my own wrist to keep my hand steady enough to light one of the two remaining tallow candles. I drag myself back into the byre. The last goat lies on the stinking straw, her neck stretched out, her tongue lolling. She feebly lifts her head, bleating. Her pale-yellow eyes fix on mine as if she is pleading with me, one mother to another. But even if we had so much as a mouthful of water to spare, it won't save her.

I watch the goat because I don't want to look at the bodies of the men. But I can smell them. You stop noticing most smells after a while, but this stench grows and grows, as if it is coming from inside you. I can't bear it. I must get rid of it. I must bury it.

I snatch up a spade and scrape away at the straw until I reach the beaten-earth floor into which pebbles from the beach have been hammered, edge on, to cobble it. I try to dig them out, but they are set too close, too deep. Even with the end of a mattock, I can only prise a few loose. Thirst claws at my throat. I will never be able to dig a hole deep enough in that floor to bury two big men. There is nothing to be done except leave them and seal the flimsy wicker door between the byre and the house as best I can.

160

If we had given Janiveer what she demanded, if we had even promised . . . if *I* had promised, would Elis be alive? Would I be sitting outside in the sun, watching my little Hob racing up the hill towards me, bubbling over with some wild new tale? I should have listened to her. I should have believed, begged her to save us, even if no one else in the village would. What Janiveer asked then does not seem so great a price now. If I had given my life, she would not have taken Elis. And Hob: has she taken my little Hob too?

The goat stares up at me as I cut her throat. She doesn't struggle, barely even twitches as the blood splashes hot on my hand. I drag the carcass into the cottage. The lights and liver, still steaming, I drop in the pot. We've no firewood or dried salt-weed to cook them, but what else can I do with them? The bloody limbs, carcass and head I hang from the beams of the cottage. I don't want ever to return to the byre. Blood drips on to the bracken. I see it everywhere I look, a great surging tide of it.

Goda gives a sharp, sudden cry as if she's been slapped. She is staring up at the skinned goat's head. The eyes stare down at her. She grips her belly and a shudder runs through her. Her birth pangs have started! But a tomb is no place to birth a babby. The fire is almost gone and the tallow light nearly burned away. We will need both light and heat before the child is delivered.

'Luke, chop the table and the stools into logs to burn on the fire.'

He doesn't even raise his head. I shake him. 'The table! Shift yourself, boy! Goda's baby is coming.'

He shoves me away. 'Leave me alone! My father's dead! Don't you remember? Don't you even care?'

'My *husband* is dead . . . mine!' I shout at him. 'You're

the man now. You think your father would just have sat there and let a babe freeze to death? He'd be ashamed of you.'

Luke glowers up at me. Even in that dim light I can see the resentment glittering in his eyes. He wishes I'd died, not his father.

He struggles to his feet. 'So what am I supposed to chop it with? We've no axe in the cottage. Father left it outside on the wood pile, afore they shut us . . . Why didn't he bring it in? Why?'

He is sobbing and I cannot look at him. We have nothing left in here except time, but we can spare none of it for tears.

'Find something to smash the table then. In the byre . . .' But I can't make him go in there.

Goda howls for Aldith as another wave of pain sweeps over her. Aldith sets Ibb down on the bracken, and dumps little Kitto in Ibb's lap where she can watch them both as she rubs her sister's belly. Who does she fear will snatch them in here? Ibb gazes up, wide-eyed, as Goda writhes and moans. We lift her shift to see how close the baby is to coming. Ibb watches it all, just as she watched the goats and the horses give birth. Goda's gaze keeps straying back to the bloody goat's head dangling above her. Its eyes, blackened now, stare down at her.

The tallow light gutters and dies. We are plunged into darkness. Luke gropes towards the faint glow of the embers of the fire. He has smashed the legs from the table and thrusts them into the embers. I blow on them, willing the wood to catch, and finally it does. Flames lick up, bathing the cottage in blood-red light. But four legs will not burn for long.

162

'Top won't break,' Luke mutters.

'Good solid wood that is, my maid,' Elis had said, slapping the table he had just completed and beaming his pride. 'See us both through till we're in our graves, our grandchillern too, God willing.'

But even as I see his hand caressing that table, I see the same hand clawing in agony. And God was willing, only too willing, for the table to outlive the man. Suddenly I want it smashed to splinters, burned to ashes, destroyed not for warmth but because it should not be allowed to survive when he was not.

'For pity's sake, Luke,' I snap, 'you're not even trying. You're no more use than a babby in clouts!'

They are cruel words to utter. I know it even as I speak them, but I don't stop myself.

Chapter 21

Matilda

'St Anthony, please look around; something is lost and must be found.' When St Anthony was a monk, a novice once borrowed his psalter without asking permission, but after being haunted by a terrifying spectre of the monk, he returned it at once.

A scream half roused me from my sleep. A vixen in the forest, that was all. The devil's creature often shrieks like a terrified woman. Many have been deceived by the cry and led into danger. I turned over and tried to burrow back into sleep. But the shriek echoed again, and as I was jerked awake, I heard a muffled banging as if those lying in coffins up in the graveyard were hammering with their bones on the stone lids, trying to break out. I groaned and sat up in bed. I was sure the noise was emanating from Sara's cottage. The clamour had haunted half the village these past nights. Mostly it had been the sound of men shouting, but the new voice was so shrill it set my teeth on edge.

So Sara and her family weren't dead, after all, or perhaps they were and it was their ghosts rattling the shutters and crying curses on the village. But no one would venture out in the dark to investigate. How long would Cador wait before he had the cottage reopened, or would he simply leave the bodies to rot in there? He wasn't willing to discuss the matter, and tried to pretend that he couldn't even hear the screams, though I could see by his haggard face, and that of his wife Isobel too, that neither was getting any more sleep than the rest of us.

I had given my word I would say nothing to Father Cuthbert, but I would find a way of bringing him to a place in the village where he could see and hear the evidence for himself. He'd ask questions then, of that you could be certain. And when he did, Cador would not remain bailiff for a single day more.

I turned over and tried to blot out the cries, but swiftly sat up again. There was another sound that had gained my attention, one that was much softer, but much closer – a scratching on the door, a strange little squeaking. Gatty! My naughty little cat had finally returned and was clawing and mewing to coax me to open the door and let her in to her supper and the warmth of the fire.

I was almost tempted to make her stay out in the cold a few minutes more, just to teach her not to stay away so long. But the scrabbling became ever more frantic and I thought I heard something else moving around outside in the dark as well. Suppose a fox was chasing her and she had come running to me for protection.

I struggled from the narrow bed and pulled my cloak about my shoulders, for I certainly did not want to face danger clad only in my shift. I snatched up the billhook that I always kept sharp and ready by the door. Easing the door open, just a hand's breadth, I peered out into the darkness.

I expected to feel Gatty's soft fur against my leg as she squeezed through the gap. She would scratch frantically on the door whenever she wanted to come in, as if she was being pursued by a pack of slavering wolves, yet whenever I opened it, the cat would saunter in with a little grunt to make in plain she was bestowing a great favour on me by returning at all. But tonight there was no grunt, no warm body rubbing against my leg. Had someone chased her off?

I fumbled to light the lantern and lifted it to the gap, trying to see if anything was moving outside. Only the currant bushes stirred in the breeze, the shadows of their twigs clawing across the ground.

'Gatty! Here, little gyb! Don't you want your supper?'

But there was no answering miaow, no sign of any creature running towards me. If she was crouching beside the wood pile on the trail of a mouse or had taken shelter beneath a bush, I would see her green eyes glowing in the candlelight to show where she was hiding. But nothing shone back at me.

It was only when I pulled the door a few inches wider to thrust the lantern out that I felt a dull thump on the wood and glimpsed something swinging at the level of my face. At first I thought someone had tied a dead ferret to my door. But as the light shone full on the fur, I saw exactly what it was, though my mind would not make sense of it.

I stared, unable to move, as it swung limply back and forwards, rocked by the motion of the door. The furry body hung from a noose tied tightly around the slender neck. The glazed eyes bulged wide. The mouth was drawn back in a snarl. The little tongue hung purple between tiny needle-sharp teeth. I thought my little Gatty had been scratching for me to let her in, but she had been clawing in agony as she fought for her last breath.

Chapter 22

Will

Riddle me this: Which man killed a quarter of all the people in the world?

Shouts and howls of pain drifted up on the wind. It was worse listening to them in the dead of night, when all else was quiet. You couldn't pretend to yourself that it was just the gulls screeching then. It was hard to tell where the cries were coming from, but it wasn't the sound of sailors getting drunk at Sybil's brew-house, that was for certain. I shuffled along the stone wall as far as the chains round my ankles would allow, trying to find a place that was less draughty. I swear whichever bastard had built that tower had deliberately made it so that, no matter where you lay, the wind whining through the grille in the door would freeze your cods off.

I'll grant you that a cave is none too warm, summer or winter, but at least I'd always had a fire to toast my toes and a belly full of hot food. The pigpen Cador had chained me up in didn't even have those comforts. I'd been thrown, none too gently, I might add, into the chamber at the base of the village's beacon. It was a small round stone tower with a flat roof on which the iron brazier stood ready to be

167

lit whenever there was trouble. The room beneath, if you can call it that, had a cold earth floor and no windows, except for the grille in the door. The tower was sometimes used to store valuable cargoes from the ships until they could be taken over the moor, and judging by the stench of piss and dried droppings, Cador had kept the odd stray animal in there too.

It was the Holy Hag who had insisted I be locked up till the next manor court. I think most of the villagers, maybe even Cador too, would have let me go on living in the cave until the trial, but that spiteful witch insisted I'd run off if they let me loose. The old cat was right. I certainly wouldn't have hung around waiting to be branded with a hot iron or to have my crippled back whipped bloody again. My hide still bore the scars of my last flogging at Master Wallace's hands and I was in no hurry to repeat it.

But I think I'd have risked even that for the boy. Each time another howl shattered the silence I imagined Hob crouching somewhere alone out there in the darkness, listening to those cries. Did he recognise the voices? Did he know who was screaming? If he did, each cry must have cut him like a scourge I would have stayed, if only to see him hidden safely somewhere, ensured that he had food to eat each day, but stuck in that tower, I could do nothing to help him. My growling belly reminded me I couldn't even help myself.

Prisoners only get fed if they've money to pay for food or someone has the charity to feed them. Cador came once a day with half a loaf of stale bread and some water. The bread I could barely chew it was so hard and the water tasted like piss, and probably was, though I tried not to think about that. Even a strip of dried fish would have been a banquet in there and I'd have given my right hand for a mouthful of pork. I winced. Don't even think it! They could cut off my hand for theft, for it certainly wasn't the first time I had stolen. I didn't want to dwell on that prospect.

My head jerked up as I heard the faint, but unmistakable, sound of a long drawn-out scream, a woman this time, poor creature. I shivered. The last time the pestilence struck, prisoners were left to die and rot, still chained to the walls, when their gaolers fell ill or fled. *Riddle me this — Who dies faster from thirst and starvation? A dwarf or a longshanks?* There are some answers even a wise fool doesn't want to learn.

Chapter 23

Sara

The sucking-fish, though tiny, can fasten itself to the hull of a mighty ship and drag it backwards. But if it is placed on the belly of a pregnant woman it can hold the baby in the womb and prevent it being expelled before its time.

I don't know how many hours have passed. If the cocks crowed the dawn or the rooks cawed as they settled in their evening roosts, I didn't hear them. They belong to another kingdom, one that lies far beyond our blood-bathed cottage. Every living thing in the outside world seems no more than the grey wraiths of drowned men circling about our walls. Only we three women are solid and alive in our sweat and pain.

A tiny head burrows out between Goda's legs. I can scarce see anything save for the roundness of it, yet I know there's something strange about what I am watching. The flames of the fire make the blob of a head glisten, a hundred tiny flames reflected on it like sunlight on a bubble of water.

I draw a piece of burning wood from the fire and hold it closer. Aldith peers in too, her head touching mine.

'That's not right,' she whispers, glancing anxiously at Goda. But her sister doesn't make any sign she's heard. She has sunk back against the wall, her head lolling, her arms limp. She's even stopped moaning. I touch her forehead. It's cold with sweat. Her breath is shallow and rapid, like that of an old woman approaching the grave. We must get the child out or we will lose them both.

'One push is all, Goda, the head is already born. One last big push and then you can sleep.'

She murmurs something and tries to shove me away but she's too weak. Two of my kin already lie dead in my byre. I cannot let there be a third.

'Make her push, Aldith. Make her!'

I try to wriggle my fingers either side of the half-born babby, like I do for the goats if a kid's leg is twisted backwards.

Aldith shakes Goda to rouse her, and her scream of pain, when it finally comes, would shatter a boulder. The babby slithers into my hands like a blowfly maggot bursting from a horse's hide. It doesn't cry. Its face is pressed flat, distorted by a glistening film, as fine and transparent as a fish bladder. The tiny hand lifts as if it is struggling to free itself, but still it makes no sound, takes no breath. Only now do I understand what I am seeing.

'She's a caul-bearer,' I whisper. I've heard such tales from the old women, but I only half believed them. I struggle to remember what they said must be done.

My hands are shaking with tiredness and thirst as I cut a piece from my shift and wrap it quickly around the babby's head.

'Dead?' Aldith says sharply.

Goda wails, a strange, high-pitched animal sound, like a snared rabbit.

The caul comes away with the cloth as I peel it back. Almost at once, the babby makes a feeble, mewing cry.

Aldith takes her from me, wraps her in one of the bed coverings and thrusts her into Goda's arms, smiling in relief. 'Blessed Virgin be praised. Here she is, sister, your own fine daughter. See you give her suck now. She'll be needing it.'

She turns from the bed and bends her head close to mine. 'You'd best be putting that caul somewhere safe till Goda's stronger. 'Tis said that if the caul's lost, the caul-bearer will be too.'

I stumble across to a shelf, lifting down jars and boxes, which are all empty, until I have space to stretch the cloth, with the caul still sticking to it, and leave it to dry. The last water skin is almost empty. I'm so desperately thirsty I can barely move my tongue. It feels like a lump of leather in my mouth, gagging me, choking me. Just one mouthful, just one tiny sip . . .

Goda reaches out. 'Water!'

I push the skin into her hands and turn away, unable to bear the torment of watching her drink. They will come with water today. They must! They are plodding up the path towards us even now. I'm sure I can hear their footsteps. They've heard Goda's cries. They know we have a new life. At any moment, they'll be prising the shutters open.

Blessed Virgin, let them come. Let them come now . . . I beg you.

Luke is crouching near the door. The light from the fire is too dim for me to see the expression on his face, but his shoulders are shaking. His breath comes in jerking sobs.

'Don't take on so, Luke, not yet. We cannot grieve yet . . . When we are let out, then . . . Now we must take care of the living. Goda, the baby, the chillern . . . Then we'll bury your father.'

'And Col,' he snarls.

'Yes, Col. He's lost his father too. You can help each other.'

Luke scrambles to his feet. 'Col's dead and you didn't even notice. You were . . . Col is dead!'

'No!' Aldith gasps. 'Why would you play such a cruel joke? He's my son. He's not even sick . . . He said he wasn't sick.'

Pushing me aside she falls to her knees, shaking the boy, who still lies with his mouth pressed to the tiny gap beneath the door. 'Lazy little heller! You get up now, boy, if you know what's good for you. Get up when I tell you!'

Grabbing his arms she hauls him into a sitting position, but his head lolls backwards. She pulls him away from the door, cradling him in her arms, her eyes glittering in the firelight. 'Always been a sound sleeper,' she murmurs. 'Sometimes he sleeps that deep even young Ibb jumping on him doesn't waken him. Daveth says . . . Daveth . . .' Her face crumples and she lets out a howl of pain and rage. Col's head snaps back and forth as she rocks him with all the violence of raw grief.

Luke stares down at her. He strides to the door, wrenching it open. But behind it, the planks are still nailed across the opening. He shakes them in a frenzy, but they will not budge. Gazing wildly around him, he hefts up the top of the legless table. He charges towards us. I cringe, fearing he's going to smash it over our heads. But he barges past us. Using the wooden slab like a battering ram, he runs at the planks, yelling as if he is charging at an enemy. Again and again he slams the edge of the table top into the planks until they begin to splinter and the nails work loose.

I try to grab him. 'Stop it! Stop it! They'll kill us if we break out.'

But he is in such a fury, not even his own father could

173

restrain him. The nails holding one of the planks are torn loose. It crashes down on to the stone threshold outside. Light and wind rush in through the gap, almost snatching my breath. Luke is suddenly still, gazing transfixed at the oblong of light as if he has never seen daylight before.

But the demon of rage rises in him again. Using the corner of the table top as a hammer, he pounds on the other planks until they snap and fall away, the broken ends dangling from solitary nails. Throwing the wood aside, Luke clambers out through the hole. I try to grab him, but his shirt slips through my fingers. He doesn't hesitate, doesn't speak, doesn't look back. He simply runs.

June 1361

Trust not a new friend, nor an old enemy.

Medieval Proverb

Chapter 24

Porlock Manor

Words serve to hide a man's character as well as reveal it.
Medieval Proverb

'Master Wallace asks that you attend him in the great hall, m'lady,' the maid said, bending her knee for the second time since she'd entered the solar.

'A steward asks *me* to attend *him?*' Lady Pavia echoed incredulously.

The girl flushed to the shade of a ripe strawberry and bobbed even lower by way of answer.

'Stop dancing around me, girl. I am not a maypole. If the steward wishes to ask my advice he will wait on me here, in the solar.'

'He begs . . . he . . . Not just you, m'lady, but Sir Harry and Lady Margery too.'

Little escaped Lady Pavia even when she was vexed by impudent demands from servants. Her sharp eyes registered the jerk of Christina's head at the mention of Sir Harry's name and not for the first time. Though Sir Harry appeared to pay no more court to Christina than he did to any of the pretty young wards, she had noticed how a flush always stained the girl's cheeks whenever he addressed her and how tensely she held herself whenever he was close by. *Love and a cough cannot be hid*, Lady Pavia recited grimly to herself. It would not be uncommon for a young girl to be attracted to such a honey-tongued man, though it was very far from desirable. She would have to keep a close watch on Christina.

The maid was still babbling: '. . . but he says it's best the young ladies do not attend.'

The three young wards glowered at her from their seats in the casement where they were supposed to be occupied with their stitching, but were in fact playing knuckle bones, their elderly chaperon, Lady Margery, having nodded off as usual.

'Then the girls will walk in the gardens and Master Wallace may attend us in here. And when he does, you may be sure I will have words with him about what is expected of a steward in my cousin's household.' She flapped her fingers at the maid in an impatient gesture of dismissal.

The maid rocked miserably on the balls of her feet, her expression that of a martyr praying that an angel might suddenly appear to deliver her from the jaws of this lioness. 'Beg pardon, m'lady, but Master Wallace is also summoning the servants – farmhands, grooms and dairymaids too. It wouldn't be right, them all coming in here, straight from the fields, rubbing up against the fine hangings and the like.'

'You foolish girl, why didn't you say so?' Lady Pavia exclaimed. 'That is a dish of a different meat entirely.' She waved an arm at the maid, as she tried, but failed, to heave her ample buttocks from the chair. 'Help me up and rouse Lady Margery, but do it gently. Any sudden alarms at her age and her poor wits might take fright and depart for good.'

The three young wards sniggered. Lady Pavia turned a

baleful eye upon them. 'You will remain here with Lady Christina, and I expect to see a deal of progress made on those flowers you're stitching when I return. What is that supposed to be, Helen? A daisy?'

The girl pouted. 'A white rose.'

Lady Pavia snorted. 'It appears to have been gnawed by a worm. I suggest you fashion a bird to catch the culprit.'

The great hall was crowded. Rarely did field hands, dairy-maids and stable boys come to dine with the indoor servants except for the great Christmas and Easter feasts, and now, ill at ease, they kept to the back of the long hall near the huge doors, pulling off hoods and caps, then hastily replacing them, uncertain which was more fitting. The indoor servants, more confident in the presence of their betters, had gathered in small groups in front of the dais, on which high-backed chairs had been placed for Sir Nigel's guests as befitted their rank.

From the snatches that drifted up to Lady Pavia from the babble below, it was clear that the servants knew no more than she did about why they had been summoned. Were Sir Nigel and his retinue about to descend on Porlock? Maybe even the Black Prince himself?

A side door opened. Lady Pavia could not see who had entered over the throng of burly men, but it was evidently someone of importance for the mass of servants parted down the middle like a seam tearing up a pair of breeches until finally Master Wallace emerged, striding towards the front, a stout stave clutched in his hand.

Wallace gave the impression of being a giant of a man, though he was not overly tall. But every part of him was brawny, from his tree-trunk thighs straining the fabric of his green hose to his great bulbous purple nose. The man following closely on his heels, whom Lady Pavia recognised as Father Cuthbert, appeared even more slender and willowy than usual by comparison, like a greyhound trotting delicately behind a mastiff.

As he drew close Wallace at least remembered his manners enough to make a perfunctory bow to the guests, though his awkwardness suggested he was not well practised at it. As Lady Pavia's first husband, Hubert, had been known to remark many times, *The mouse sits boldly on the throne when he knows the cat's away.* Sir Nigel had been absent far too long, she thought, and it was high time that this particular mouse had its tail and whiskers cropped before he forgot who was master of this manor.

The two men stepped up on to the dais. Lady Pavia was gratified to observe that Father Cuthbert at least remembered the duty he owed to his patron's guests and had the grace to kiss her hand, though she couldn't help shuddering a little: his lips and fingers were as cold and limp as a plucked chicken.

Wallace thumped the end of his stave on the wooden boards of the dais to quell the murmuring.

'I know you'll not be thanking me for fetching you here,' he announced, not endearing himself to Lady Pavia by addressing the crowd of servants rather than her. 'But I've been steward of this manor for nigh on twenty years and many a time I've heard wagging tongues fan a spark of gossip into a roaring blaze in less time than it takes to say a paternoster. So I thought it best you all hear the truth straight from the priest's mouth afore the devil makes more mischief.'

He nodded curtly to Father Cuthbert, who took a pace forward. 'You've no doubt heard that the Great Mortality has these past months been raging in London.'

A muttering broke out and someone jeered, 'That news is such old fish not even a starving cat'll sniff at it.'

Wallace banged his stave on the boards again. 'Kennel that tongue of yours, Jackin, 'less you want me to toss it to the hounds.'

'I have *fresh* tidings,' Father Cuthbert resumed, glaring pointedly at Jackin. 'Many good men believed that the pestilence would not again spread as far as this corner of our fair land. While it ravaged France, it seemed that here in England it was confined within the seething masses and foul ditches of London.' He glanced towards Lady Pavia and Sir Harry. 'Indeed, Sir Nigel has sent some of those souls who are most dear to him to take shelter here in the belief that they would be safe.'

Lady Pavia inclined her head, graciously acknowledging the compliment. But though she would never have betrayed her alarm in front of servants, she nevertheless felt her heart quicken. Was she not safe here, after all?

'But I have just this day learned,' Father Cuthbert continued, 'that for some weeks now this deadly enemy, unseen by us, has crept upon us in stealth and has been besieging our very gates. Would that I had been appraised of these grave tidings sooner.'

Muttering again broke out in the hall, but from the servants' bemused expressions, Lady Pavia could see that their priest might as well have been speaking in Latin.

She coughed pointedly. 'Father Cuthbert, unless you are telling us that the French are laying siege to this manor, I suggest you speak plainly. Otherwise I fear these men will rush out armed with bows and pikestaffs to engage the invisible enemy.'

'The French?' For a moment, the priest looked as confused

as the servants. 'No, no, m'lady, it is the Great Mortality. It has broken out in Porlock Weir and the—'

But he got no further. A howl arose from the crowd of men and women. Some were wailing and clutching each other, others angrily demanded to know *When? How many are stricken? Are any dead?*

It took several hard thumps of Wallace's staff on the dais and repeated bellowed orders to 'Hold your noise', before the great hall fell silent once more. Even then the steward could not silence the sobs of some of the women.

Father Cuthbert held up his hands. 'The people of Porlock Weir have sought to conceal the plague that has struck them, as a leper tries to hide his sores or a harlot her shorn head. They are ashamed—'

'And so they should be,' Lady Pavia snapped.

'*But,*' Father Cuthbert shouted, struggling to be heard over the hubbub that was once again rising, 'those who are faithful in their prayers and tithes need have no fear. The Angel of Death will pass over this manor for, as it says in the holy scriptures, two shall be gleaning together in the field, one shall be taken and the other left.'

Wallace took a pace forward. 'There'll be no gleaning in the fields with any of them from Porlock Weir, I'll make certain of that. And I've sent a rider to find Sir Nigel to tell him all that's afoot. Porlock Weir is his property and he must rule on what's to be done. Soon as he learns of it, I warrant Sir Nigel'll send a physician straight here to tend his kin and all who serve in the manor. So you can hush your noise, Maud. There's no cause for you to keep wailing like a cat with its tail afire.'

Sir Harry leaned across to Lady Pavia. 'And I'll wager my

best horse the only physician Sir Nigel will spare for this manor will be a dead one.'

He pushed himself to his feet. Laying his hand on Wallace's shoulder, he tugged him round to face him. 'See that you start provisioning this manor at once, Master Wallace. Dispatch every man and boy who can be spared to hunt down whatever wild beast and bird they can that's fit for eating and set the women to smoke, salt and pickle them. Send every wagon you've got to buy what stores of flour there are to be had and—'

Wallace brushed off the hand as if it was an irritating fly. 'I know my duty as steward, Sir Harry. I'd not have been trusted with the keeping of this place for twenty years if I didn't. And I was just on the point of giving those self-same orders, if you'd let me finish.'

Father Cuthbert leaned in, almost shouting to make Wallace hear over the tumult that was growing ever louder in the hall. 'I must insist that I be allowed to lead the servants in prayer before you send them about their work. Tell them to kneel.'

Sir Harry gave a mocking laugh. 'It would take the Angel Gabriel himself to drive them to their knees. And even though our steward here plainly thinks he's Moses, surely even he does not claim to have angelic powers.'

With a great effort Lady Pavia heaved herself from the chair and snatching the staff from the startled steward's hand she rapped sharply upon the floor. Those at the front turned at once and while it took longer for those at the back to fall silent, eventually they all did, most from sheer amazement that a woman was calling for their attention.

'Father Cuthbert wishes you to kneel and receive his

blessing, which only a fool would refuse with Death knocking at our door.' She rapped the staff impatiently again. 'Quickly now, kneel, and then you may be about your duties.'

Using the staff to balance herself, Lady Pavia sank painfully to her knees. She wasn't at all convinced she would be able to rise again without assistance, but as her husband, Hubert, had always said, *Example is better than precept.*

As it transpired, the Angel Gabriel could take many guises, even that of a redoubtable matron upholstered in pea-green velvet for, one by one, the servants pulled off caps and hoods and knelt. The last to kneel were Sir Harry and Master Wallace, though from the poisonous glances they were darting at each other and at Father Cuthbert, it seemed neither was entertaining spiritual or contrite thoughts.

Lady Pavia barely registered the Latin invocations Father Cuthbert was intoning, for she was offering her own prayers with as much fervency as any angel. Though she was determined not to show it, she was as frightened as any of the women sobbing in the hall. Had it been only thirteen years?

Hubert had been carried home on a bier by men with their faces masked in vinegar-soaked cloths. They had dumped him in the courtyard and lumbered wearily away, abandoning him to his pain as he lay shivering and coughing in the rain. Most of the servants had run off weeks before and those who remained had taken one look at the blue-black marks on their master's face and backed away, crossing themselves and muttering wild incantations. So it had been left to Lady Pavia and an ancient maid to haul her husband into the great hall. Lady Pavia had hurried to the stables and was thankful to find two servants who had not fled, drinking from a flagon of wine and playing dice. She'd ordered them to saddle the fastest horses and fetch a physician and a priest. But though she had waited and prayed, neither man ever returned.

Alone in the manor, Lady Pavia and the maid had soothed Hubert's fever as best they could, with cloths soaked in thyme water, and trickled syrups into the corner of his mouth to ease his cough. She'd held the basin and rubbed her husband's back as he vomited blackened blood. He'd fallen back exhausted and stared up at her from bloodshot eyes, his lips drawn back in a terrible grimace. '*No herb . . . in the garden can prevail . . . against the power of death,*' he'd rasped. If her throat had not been choked with tears, she would have smiled. It was so like Hubert that his final words should not be whispers of love, or even a prayer, but one of his favourite old saws. Doubtless he'd be ready with another for the Archangel Michael at the gates of Purgatory. But perhaps, if the Archangel thought the proverb wise enough, it would shorten Hubert's days of torment. She hoped it would be so.

All through that long night, Lady Pavia had sat beside her husband's corpse in the vastness of the cold, echoing hall, praying for his soul. Even the maid had, at the last, deserted her. And when the candles finally guttered out, Lady Pavia had sat on alone in the impenetrable darkness, listening to the rain splashing down into the empty hearth and dripping from the eaves on to the flagstones outside. Somewhere a dog was howling. It howled all night.

Finally, when dawn broke and a chill grey light seeped into the hall, she called out for someone, anyone, to come and help her bury her husband. But not even the birds answered her. It was only then, when she rose, stiff with cold, and staggered out into the rain, that she saw a heap of sodden clothes lying across the threshold. Only when she

185

prodded them with the tip of her shoe and felt the dull weight of cold flesh, did she understand. The maid had withdrawn to die discreetly and alone, outside in the rain-soaked night, so as not to disturb her mistress in her grief. Tears had caught in Lady Pavia's throat as she crouched down beside the old woman to cover her face, but even then she had not permitted them to fall.

'I distinctly instructed that mulled ale be brought,' Eda scolded. 'This – this pagan brew is fit only for cottagers.'

Rosa merely gazed at her, her expression unchanging and unfathomable.

'Answer me, Rosa!' Eda demanded. 'Are you so stupid that you cannot tell mead from ale? That hardly augurs well for a stillroom maid.'

But Rosa, unmoved, continued to gaze at her until finally it was Eda who was forced to look away. 'I can see I shall just have to fetch it myself,' she said, tottering out of the solar.

Rosa waited until the door closed behind her, then lifted the steaming jug and glanced enquiringly at Lady Pavia. The sweet aroma of hot honey and thyme wafted across Lady Pavia's nostrils.

'My lady, warm metheglin is soothing to the spirits and wards off fevers. It is better than wine for the stomach.'

Sir Harry grunted. 'Nothing soothes the spirits or the stomach like wine.'

'Wine gives me wind,' Lady Margery grumbled, from her chair by the fire. The young wards giggled. Lady Margery's farts, especially when she was dozing, were a source of constant amusement to them.

Lady Pavia glared them into silence. 'I will try a little.'

Rosa poured the warm metheglin into a goblet. Lady Pavia sipped it warily. The herbed mead had not been drunk in court circles for years; nor was it served in any of the manors she visited. Indeed, she could not recall tasting it since she was a child, but she had to admit that it warmed the body right down to the toes.

She nodded. 'I will take some more and you may pour some for the Lady Christina. It will do her good, and the girls too. Lady Margery, I do urge you to try some.'

Rosa inclined her head by way of acknowledgement and, padding softly across the solar on the thick yellow skin of her bare feet, she handed a goblet to Christina, briefly raising her grey-blue eyes to meet the girl's with a steady gaze. Lady Pavia caught Christina's hesitant, almost furtive, smile but, seeing no reason why there should be any secrets between a lady and a stillroom maid, looked around for another source and immediately found it in Sir Harry, who was gazing at the pair with a wolfish expression that made the dowager most uneasy.

'Sir Harry,' Lady Pavia said sharply, 'now that the Great Mortality has crept so close, I think you would be well advised to return to my cousin. It would appear no corner of this land can be hid from this deadly cloud.'

Lady Margery gave a deep moan, crossing herself more fervently than a nun. Lady Pavia ignored her.

'I have no intention of leaving, Lady Pavia,' Sir Harry said. 'With this present danger threatening, Sir Nigel will be relying on me to guard his interests here. Indeed, I expect to receive word from him as soon as the messenger returns. Rest assured, I have dispatched my own rider to Sir Nigel. I would not trust any message the steward sent to be other than a hound's dinner of rumour, boasts and half-truths.'

'We should all depart at once,' Lady Margery wailed, taking another large gulp from her goblet. 'It is not myself I fear for, but those dear, innocent girls. If any sickness should befall his wards, Sir Nigel would never forgive me.'

'Take another sip of metheglin, Lady Margery. It will calm you,' Lady Pavia said, not unkindly. 'You speak of interests, Sir Harry. What would those be exactly?' Her gaze slipped sideways to Christina. 'You appear to have taken very little interest in the running of the manor. I have not observed you examining the books or inspecting the barns. Indeed, you seem to spend an uncommon amount of time riding off alone.'

'Hunting, Lady Pavia,' he said. His gaze also darted towards Christina. 'The chase quickens the blood and wards off sickness. But, alas, since you will not grace me with your delightful company, I am forced to hunt in wretched solitude.' He gave a courtly bow of the head to Lady Pavia, but she was under no illusion it was her company he sought.

'Your wretchedness has clearly affected your skill with a bow, Sir Harry, for I have not seen you return with any kill.'

'Alas, I am too tender-hearted.' He gazed directly at Christina. 'I see the gentle hind or the graceful bird and I cannot bring myself to pierce its poor, trembling heart.'

Although he had not asked for any, Rosa padded across the boards and held out a gently steaming goblet. He was motioning her to take it away when he froze mid-gesture, staring at the string of blue glass beads hanging about the woman's neck. He caught hold of it, pulling it up so that the concealed portion slid out from beneath the top of her kirtle. It flashed like a silver dagger in the firelight. Dangling from the necklace was a curved tusk or tooth of some kind, the tip sheathed with silver.

Rosa did not try to pull it back but stood patiently while he examined it.

'What is this?' Sir Harry demanded.

'A bear's tooth. Very sharp.'

'Since when did bears have silver teeth? Take it off. I want to see it properly.'

He barely released his hold on the necklace long enough for Rosa to pull it over her head and snatched it the moment she held it out.

The three young wards abandoned their sewing, and came rushing over, pawing at the beads, like a pack of excited puppies.

'If a bear had a head full of teeth as big as that, he could bite your arm off,' Helen squealed.

'It would bite your whole head off, silly,' Anne said, trying to snatch at the beads. 'Can I try it on?'

'Girls!' Lady Margery squawked. 'Return to your sewing this instant.' The three wards, scowling, slunk back to their seats. 'The very idea of putting something round your delicate necks that has been worn by a base-born maid, much less the tooth of some savage beast!'

The elderly aunt was still scolding and fretting in equal measure, but Lady Pavia was no longer listening, bemused by Sir Harry's fascination with the amulet.

He held it close to the candle. 'Something is carved on the tooth . . . a snake and . . . a bird.' He lowered the amulet, frowning. 'Where did you get this? The silver cap alone is worth far more than any maid could earn in a year.' He dug his fingers into her arm, but though it must have pained her, she did not cry out. 'You stole this!'

Rosa's grey-blue eyes hardened to flint, but she said nothing.

Christina jumped up. 'She isn't a thief!'

She flushed as both Lady Pavia and Sir Harry stared at her in surprise.

'The Lady Christina is a trifle impetuous,' Lady Pavia snapped, 'but nevertheless I, too, see no reason to accuse the maid of theft. If the beast's tooth were the property of any noblewoman or -man, the amulet would have hung on a costly chain of silver or gold, not on a tawdry necklace of the sort pedlars sell to ploughboys to give to their sweethearts. I think you had best return it to her, Sir Harry. And you would do well to keep it hidden, Rosa. I doubt Father Cuthbert would approve of a woman employed in Sir Nigel's household wearing such an amulet.'

Sir Harry hesitated. He tipped the necklace from one hand to the other, watching the blue beads cascade into his palm, before tossing it on to the table. Rosa scooped it up and hung it around her neck again, dropping the tooth down the neck of gown to lie between her breasts.

Sir Harry suddenly smiled. 'Forgive me. I was merely curious. I have seen the carving on that tooth before, but I can't quite remember . . .'

'On a stone, my lord?' Rosa replied with equal sweetness. 'There is one such on the mound towards Porlock Weir.'

'A cairn!' Sir Harry's gaze flicked towards Lady Pavia, who was still watching him. But, as if he could not stop himself, he reached out once more and caressed the beads round Rosa's throat. 'And is this ancient mound where you found that beast's tooth?'

'The bear's tooth was not found for it was never lost, my lord,' Rosa said. 'Much *is* lost and some found, but there is more, my lord. Much more, if you know where to look.'

'There! You see, Sir Harry?' Lady Pavia said. 'If you are

190

desirous of having a bear's tooth yourself, there are plenty more to be discovered, without depriving this poor woman.' She glanced out of the casement towards the dense, dark tangle of trees covering the steep hillside beyond the wall of the manor. 'But I suggest you make sure the bear is quite dead before you pull out its teeth. If wild bears still exist anywhere in this realm, I would not be surprised if this desolate corner is their last hiding place.'

But when she turned her head, she saw that Sir Harry was not listening to her: he was gazing intently at the retreating back of the stillroom maid, his eyes glittering with excitement. Lady Pavia permitted herself a self-satisfied smile. If Sir Harry was here to hunt for a hind, far better he should harbour a stillroom maid than Randel's wife. And, besides, Lady Pavia had glimpsed enough spirit in Rosa to suspect she was more than capable of drawing the teeth and claws of any bear that attempted to pursue her, even a noble one.

Chapter 25

And he shall gather them together into a place which is called Armageddon.

The Apocalypse of St John

Luke jerked awake in the darkness and, for one terrible moment, thought he was still in the suffocating cottage, hearing those shrieks that went on and on, like a knife slashing in his head. *Make them stop! Make them . . .* Gasping and choking on his own panic, he flung out his arms and felt the crunch of dried leaves beneath his hands. He lay still, panting, drenched in sweat. Somewhere a vixen was screaming, then fell silent, and there was only the rustling of the trees around him.

The boy sat up, banging his head on the dead branches that held up the low roof of his shelter. It was a poxy den. Last summer, he, Col and Hob had collected these branches and lashed them together to build a hideout in the forest. Luke had told them they ought to make it bigger, higher, but the only really long branches they found on the ground were rotten and crumbled as soon as they started dragging them out from the undergrowth.

It was Col's lame idea, anyway. They'd only come to the forest 'cause he wanted to go hunting with the spear he'd made from a broken fishing pole. Even though it wouldn't fly straight enough to hit the trunk of a hollow oak, he'd still reckoned he could kill a deer or a hare and cook a feast for them. Hob had started whining that he was hungry as soon as they'd got there, but when they'd told him to run home to his mam, he wouldn't go, because Col had shown him a paw print and told him it was a wolf's, so he'd not walk back through the forest alone.

Now Col . . . Col was dead. Luke knew he was. He'd seen his body lying by the door, yet he'd still half expected to find him here peering out from the den, pulling his mouth into a gormless grin to look like Crabfish. And Hob . . . Luke had been so sure Hob would be waiting here. Where else would he have gone? It was the place they always came to when they wanted to hide. Why wasn't he here?

Luke felt his eyes welling again and rubbed them savagely. Stupid little nisseler! Well, Hob needn't think his brother was going to waste any more time looking for him. Why should Luke give a beggar's arse-rag if the idiot had got himself lost? He had enough to do taking care of himself now, without looking after some snotty-nosed babby.

Luke lifted his head and sniffed. Smoke! He could smell wood-smoke and something else, something that drew him like a wolf to blood: the sweet smell of roasting meat. His stomach growled with hunger. But he didn't move. Suppose Cador and the villagers had discovered he'd escaped and come hunting for him. They might be sweeping the forest under cover of darkness. He shrank down on his belly, straining to listen for voices or footsteps in the dry leaves. But he could hear nothing except the hiss of the breeze in the branches above.

He wriggled forward, straining to catch a glimmer of movement between black trunks or the flames of lanterns and torches in the darkness. But the breeze was teasing him with the aroma of roasting meat, drawing across his nose, till he thought his stomach would burst from his belly and chase after it. Was that chicken he could smell? Hunger overcame fear. He no longer cared if they did catch him just so long as he could stuff his mouth with that meat.

Luke crawled out of the shelter, scrambled to his feet and darted towards the cover of the nearest trunk. He ran as lightly as he could from tree to tree, pausing each time to sniff the air and peering into the blackness to find the source of the luscious smell.

In the end, he almost fell on top of it before he spotted where it was coming from. Only a curl of smoke, glowing red in the darkness, betrayed the fire burning beneath which had been lit in a shallow pit, hidden behind the massive trunk of a fallen tree.

Luke crouched. Edging towards the end of the trunk, he peeped between the torn-up roots. An old man, his face as wrinkled as the tree bark, squatted on a low stone, warming his knobbly hands over the small fire pit. A great pack rested against his thigh as if he was afraid to move so much as an inch from it in case it should be snatched. Luke had no doubt that he had found the place his belly was seeking: suspended above the glowing wood, a row of plucked pigeons was skewered on a long stick, balanced between the forks of two branches thrust into the ground on either side. The birds' skins sizzled and bubbled.

The man reached out and snapped off one of the pigeon's legs. He chewed it thoughtfully, before spitting out a bone. ''Bout done, I reckon. Hungry, are you, boy?'

Luke ducked down behind the trunk, sure he'd been seen, but someone else answered the old man.

'I could eat six pigeons all to myself – no . . . a dozen.'

The old man chuckled. 'I can see I'll have to teach you to count, boy. There's only five birds a-roasting. I'll be having one of them and I reckon that lad hiding behind the tree trunk has his eye on another, so how many will that leave you, eh?'

He raised his voice. 'As for you, my young spy, you'd best show yourself if you want a bite before all this meat vanishes. This little 'un may be no bigger than a robin, but he's got the belly of a gannet.'

Luke cautiously straightened up and peered over the fallen tree, just as another boy raised his head on the other side. For a moment they stared at each other in disbelief. Then Luke was knocked flat on his back as Hob flung himself over the trunk, with a shriek of delight, and clung to Luke, hugging and pummelling him in equal measure.

'Where've you been, Luke? I waited and waited, but the dwarf didn't come like he promised and then I waited for you and you didn't come neither. Where were you?'

'Get off me, you stupid luggins.' His older brother finally succeeded in prising the little boy's arms from around his neck and tumbled him over into a heap of dried leaves.

Luke sat up, raking the dirt and twigs from his hair. 'Where have *I* been? Me? Where've you been, Nug-head? Why didn't you stay put in the den? You knew I'd come looking for you there.'

'Nug-head yourself,' Hob retorted, but he was beaming so broadly he looked as if his face might split in two.

He threw himself once more at Luke, giving him another hug, before darting out of reach of the cuff his exasperated brother aimed at him, chuckling as he ran. Luke followed him cautiously round the end of the fallen tree and edged towards the fire.

The old man was still squatting on his stone seat by the roasting birds. 'So you must be this Luke the boy's always chattering about. Way he's been talking these past weeks, I expected a giant with strength enough to carry a horse on his shoulders.'

Luke stared at his brother, but Hob wasn't listening. He was peering anxiously around him into the dark tangle of trees beyond the firelight. 'Where's Mam and Father? Are they here too, Luke? Can we go home now?'

Luke said nothing, but he was aware the old man was watching him intently and turned away, hiding his face.

'Best you two put something in your bellies first 'fore you think about going anywhere,' the old man said briskly. 'Don't want these plump birds to burn to cinders now, do we?' He wrapped a filthy rag about his hand, then slid one of the carcasses off the stick.

He held the roasted pigeon up towards Hob. 'Mind! It's hot. Blow on it good and hard.'

Hob, all other concerns evidently forgotten, ran over and, puffing up his cheeks, blew wetly on the bird, before he snatched it and scurried back to the shelter of the tree-trunk to eat.

But Luke, ravenous though he was, hung back. What if the old man expected money for the food? The pie-sellers who came to Porlock Weir always did. And they were quick to turn nasty if a boy bit into one before confessing he'd no money to pay for it, as he and Col had discovered more than once.

But the old man had already pulled another bird from the stick and waved it in Luke's direction. 'Here, take it. I'd not see any lad go hungry when there's food enough to share. Not afraid of an old pedlar, are you? Never so much

as hurt a flea, I haven't, save for the odd pigeon, of course.'
He chuckled, waving the carcass in his grimy paw. 'There's
plen—'

Luke heard the swoosh and then the sickening thud. The
pedlar arched backwards, eyes bulging. As his jaw dropped
open a thin trickle of blood ran from the corner of his
mouth. For a moment, he sat bolt upright, a look of agony
and shock on his face. Then, with a terrible gurgle, he
pitched face forward into the fire pit. Only then did Luke
see the shaft of the arrow sticking out from between his
shoulder blades.

Before Luke could move, a man with a bow still grasped
in his hand, leaped from between the trees and kicked the
body. It rolled away from the fire into the darkness. Luke
had taken only a single step, before he felt a brawny arm
lock around his waist from behind. He was lifted off his
feet and carried fighting and yelling to be dumped on the
ground next to the fallen tree.

'No cause for you to go screeching, like a ruffled hen.
We mean you no harm, lad.'

His captor vaulted on to the trunk above him, and sat
down. His heavy legs dangled down over Luke's shoulders
pinning him back against the rough bark.

The man with the bow had grabbed Hob with his free arm
and pushed him down to sit on the ground. He hardly needed
to restrain him, for Hob was rigid with shock and sat where
he'd been put, gasping for breath like a beached fish.

The man gestured with his bow towards the dim outline of
the corpse beyond the fire's glow. 'That old rogue was one
of the most evil cutthroats ever to breathe God's good air.'

'Cutthroat?' The single word pierced the fog of fear and
panic in Luke's brain.

'Aye, if we hadn't smelt the smoke and come to investigate that would be you, my lad, lying there instead of him, with your throat slit so wide you could have stuffed a whole chicken in it, feathers an' all.'

In case Luke hadn't understood, the man sitting above him leaned down and made a slicing movement with his forefinger around Luke's throat from ear to ear.

The first man laid down his bow and crossed to where the pedlar's pack lay abandoned. He crouched and untied the top, peering inside, though he took nothing from it.

He glanced up at his companion and nodded. 'He'll have stolen that from some poor traveller and left them dead in a ditch somewhere. Same as he would you.'

'But I've got nothing to steal,' Luke protested, struggling to make sense of what had just happened.

The old man had seemed kindly enough, not like some of those scar-faced seamen with their long knives who put in at Porlock Weir. Luke couldn't believe he was a robber and murderer.

'He's . . . been taking care of my brother . . . feeding him. That's right, isn't it, Hob?'

But the boy just stared blankly into mid-air, his thin chest heaving.

The two men exchanged knowing glances. 'Favourite trick of that evil old butcher, wasn't it, Brother David?' the man on the tree trunk above him said. 'See, he knew if he had a child with him people would let down their guard around him, specially a boy with the face of a cherub, like young Hob here. Draws others in like a tethered bird calls wild birds to the net.'

'"The devil walks abroad in innocent guise,"' Brother David said. 'The Prophet warns us to beware his cunning ways.'

'See, that old butcher killed most men just to rob them, but when he found any pretty-looking lads like you two . . .' Luke felt a hand patting his hair. 'Well, let's just say he did things to them that made them want to cut their own throats from the shame of it. Then he'd sell the boys on to the stew-houses in the towns for other fornicators and sodomites to commit their foul sins with.'

David nodded grimly, and tugged at the eelskin cap he wore, settling it more tightly over his head. 'God and the Prophet were watching over you, lads. God sent Brother Noll and me to save you. And that means you've been chosen.'

Lifting the stick of roasted pigeons from the ground, where it had been knocked as the old pedlar fell, he brushed the leaf mould from the carcasses. Pulling the remaining birds off the stick, he tossed one each to Luke and Noll before sinking his teeth into the third. Hob was still clutching his meat, staring sightlessly at the stone where the old pedlar had been sitting.

Luke's mind would not make sense of anything the men were saying. Even the death of the old man didn't seem real to him. It was like the strange, nonsensical things you see somewhere between sleeping and waking. All he knew was how hungry he was and how good that pigeon smelt. He couldn't think. He had to eat. He tore off a leg and bit into it. Never had anything in his life tasted so good, but his belly was roaring to be filled. He could barely chew it before his stomach demanded that he swallow.

None of them spoke again until the meat had been pulled from the birds. Even Hob ate his pigeon in the end. When they had stripped most of the flesh from theirs, David and Noll tossed the skeletons on to the fire, but Luke clung to his, gnawing and sucking each bone until it was nothing but a splinter.

David wiped greasy fingers on his jerkin. 'So, lad, what you doing out here in the forest? Have you kin in these parts?'

Luke hesitated. He kept his face turned away from the old man's body, trying not to see other corpses lying on the floor of a cottage in the fire's glow. Yet even when he closed his eyes, he could not stop seeing those. If these two men discovered what he and Hob had escaped from, they'd likely kill them both. And he knew he couldn't run faster than the arrow that had come singing out of the darkness.

'Got no kin,' he muttered.

He shivered even as he said it, frightened that his denial had made the words come true. His mam might be lying back there in agony, crying for him, for anyone to help her. Cador had threatened they would bring no more food if any of them tried to break out. What if the bailiff let his mam starve to death to punish her because her son had escaped? The hard ball of meat churned in his stomach and he had to clench his jaw and dig his nails into his arm to keep from vomiting. He hadn't meant . . . He wished he'd told her . . .

David stood up. Pulling out his cock, he pissed copiously on the embers of the dying fire, sending up a hiss of steam. He stamped on the wood, scattering the damp ashes.

'There's a deep hollow over yonder. We'll throw that stinking wretch into it. No one'll spot him, unless they fall into it themselves. Beasts'll soon pick him clean.'

He bent down, patting over the corpse until he found a small leather money bag concealed beneath the shirt. He cut the strings, stuffing it beneath his own tunic.

He peered upwards into the starry sky. 'If we keep up a good pace we'll be home before dawn.' He jerked his chin towards the pedlar's pack. 'God has blessed our work, Brother Noll. Brother Praeco's prayers have been answered again.'

Noll grinned. 'And the lads? You reckon the Prophet will want them?'

David put his head on one side and studied Hob. 'He'll want this one right enough.' He laughed. 'As the Lord said, "Suffer the little children."'

Chapter 26

Matilda

Shake her, good Devil, shake her once well. Then shake her no more till you shake her in hell.
A local charm to cure St Vitus's Dance

Another died yesterday. A fisherman, a strapping young man, went out to tend his nets at low tide, stretched forward over his mud-horse, pushing himself across the wet sand, until he was far out in the bay. It was such a familiar sight that no one gave him a second glance until they saw the sea flowing back and him still out there, in the middle of the bay, bent over the mud-horse, his legs trailing limp, lifting like seaweed on the tide. No one went out to fetch him.

We stood on the shore watching the tide rise higher and higher, until eventually it lifted his body off the wooden frame. He floated, in and out, in and out. Then the corpse turned over in the water as if it wanted one last look at the sky before the sea closed over it and it was gone. At the next low tide his mud-horse was revealed, still standing where he'd left it, garlanded with strands of broken seaweed, but of the man there was no sign. He was fortunate to be taken so swiftly. It took some many days to die, writhing in agony.

There were no cats left in Porlock Weir. Every single one had been caught in snares, poisoned or hanged. Some of their little bodies were dried in the smoke of fires, then hidden among the rafters. Cats bring the pestilence so their corpses will ward it off, or so the villagers believe. Gatty was the first. I thought that evil little dwarf had done it, except he was locked in the beacon tower. But when I saw other cats hanging, I knew it must have been Katharine.

She'd told no one that her husband was ill, though I'd suspected, for not even Skiener could be drunk for a week. Afterwards, she swore my poor Gatty had cursed him for she'd seen the cat rubbing herself against his nets. That's why I'm certain it was her who hanged Gatty, thinking that if the cat was dead it would lift the curse and her husband would live. But Skiener died anyway.

Even then she would not admit the pestilence was in her home, tried to bury the body herself at night, but she was seen. Some of the women wanted her walled up in her cottage – I would have seen her locked up without food or water for what she'd done to Gatty – but Cador refused to do anything, for he said it was already too late. By the time Skiener, Daveth, Elis and Col had been buried, a half-dozen more in the village were already groaning in their beds.

The bell tolled in St Olaf's chapel. Father Cuthbert had arrived for Mass. These past weeks since the pestilence struck he could no longer be relied upon to appear on a Sunday, but came on any day when he was not detained elsewhere. I hastened out at once and laboured up the hill. A scatter of women hurried up the path ahead of me. Just a few weeks ago, they would have been walking in groups, gossiping and prattling their nonsense, but now they were each walking alone, giving only furtive glances at the others as if they feared there was poison or worse in the others' eyes. Katharine was not among them. She daren't venture out for fear of being spat at or having backs turned upon her. The women would not forgive or forget in a hurry, and no more would I.

Father Cuthbert pressed a stuffed cloth bag to his mouth and nose. It had been soaked in strong vinegar and filled with spices, thyme and lavender. He always held it close even at Mass when it dangled from a short cord around his neck so that it hung just below his chin. Now he lowered it an inch or two, gasping with the effort of trying to breathe through it. In spite of the heat of the day, his face was pale, his eyes sunk into dark hollows, and for a moment I feared he himself had been stricken.

He edged to the far side of the graveyard and, pressing the bag tightly against his face, flung holy water at the long burial pit on the other side of the wall. He was standing so far away that few of the drops could have reached the raw earth. That done, he scuttled towards the chapel without even glancing my way.

The dead had been buried without a priest as soon as they could be dragged from the cottages or wherever they had fallen. The packhorses had been pressed into service, hauling each corpse up the hill, tied to a wooden sledge, like the corpses of executed felons, to be laid side by side in a common grave, for there were not men enough willing to carry them on a bier. The far end of the pit was as yet empty. The women turned their faces away as they hurried by, afraid they might see the apparitions of their own bodies lying in that hole.

I scurried ahead of them into the chapel, ignoring Meryn

who lay by the door, his crutches beside him, eyes half closed, listlessly holding up a cracked wooden bowl for alms; there was nothing in it.

A shaft of bright sunshine filtered through the casement and illuminated the new hanging cloth covering the reliquary niche in the wall. The reliquary was in the form of a silver right arm with a gold and garnet ring encircling the first joint of the third finger. It encased the hand of the blessed St Cadeyrn. I had embroidered the cloth, using fine needles I had fashioned with my own hands from splinters of rib bones, and decorated it with symbols of St Cadeyrn's life and death: his royal crown; the raven that had saved him from the serpent's poison; the axe that had severed his holy head and hand; the spring of water that gushed from his bloody wrist; and the bear that had borne his martyred remains to their resting place. Father Cuthbert would surely notice the new cloth and enquire who had stitched it so exquisitely. As he said, in our present tribulations it was more important than ever to offer our talents to God, for who knew when death might strike?

I regret to say that, though his holy relic consecrated our chapel, Father Cuthbert did not hold St Cadeyrn in high regard; indeed he seldom mentioned him, preferring to invoke St Olaf for whom the chapel was named. He said St Cadeyrn was a saint of the Celtic Church, not the Holy Catholic Church. I knew Father Cuthbert dearly desired a relic of the great St Olaf himself, but the saint's body lay in Norway, and Porlock Weir could never have afforded so much as a snippet of cloth from such an important saint. So Father Cuthbert had to be content with St Cadeyrn's hand for a church must have a relic and, besides, the people of Porlock would have deemed it ill luck to remove it. But perhaps my cloth would remind Father Cuthbert that no saint is to be neglected, especially in such perilous times.

Up at the altar Father Cuthbert, standing with his back to us, turned his head briefly to nod at the squint window where the boy outside was supposed to be watching for the signal to toll the sanctus bell. But no bell sounded. The wretched child had let his attention wander again or even fallen asleep. Father Cuthbert gave the signal again, but still there was no answering bell. He glowered at his acolyte.

With a long-suffering sigh, Harold set down the little censer he was waving and ambled out through the door. Finally, we heard the dull clang of the bell over our heads. The congregation fell silent as they sank to their knees, waiting for the moment when, by the priest's words, the bread would become the blessed flesh of Christ. But Harold did not return. Darting a furious glance at the closed door, Father Cuthbert had no choice but to continue alone with the Mass.

'. . . *accepit panem in sanctas manus* . . .' The words of consecration trailed away as he turned his head towards the small window.

Now that the gossips' tongues were briefly stilled, a new sound invaded the chapel. No doubt the cries of another widow or bereaved mother, whose husband or child was being dragged up to the churchyard for burial. The wails of mourners were becoming as commonplace as the gulls' screeching.

'*Benedixit, fregit, deditque discipulis* . . .' Again Father Cuthbert faltered.

The noise was growing closer. I thought I could hear a drum, but it wasn't the solemn measured beating of a death drum. I could hear wild shrieks too, but they were more like screams of uncontrolled laughter than despair. The priest replaced the Host on the paten and the tiny congregation scrambled to its feet.

'Did they not hear the Mass bell ring?' Father Cuthbert demanded furiously, though since Harold had still not returned it was hard to tell whom he was addressing. He strode to the door, almost knocking an old woman off her feet, and dragged it open.

For a moment he stood transfixed as the sound of drumming and the cackle of laughter filled the chapel. He ran forward, shouting something, but his words were drowned by the noise. We all crowded out behind him.

Six or seven women were prancing and cavorting round the chapel, threading in and out of the graves as if they were weaving round maypoles. They'd hitched up their skirts to their bare thighs and were dancing wildly, kicking up their heels and flinging their limbs about, their loose hair whipping around them as they jerked their heads. One, evidently their leader, was using a deer horn to beat out a crazed rhythm on a tabor strapped to her arm. I could not make out who she was for she whisked round the back of the chapel as I emerged.

Several overexcited dogs were rushing back and forth, barking and howling. Meryn, wide awake now, was leaning on the graveyard wall, chortling with glee, and pounding one of his crutches up and down on the hard earth, keeping time with the rhythm of the tabor. Father Cuthbert shouted at the women to stop, but could hardly make himself heard over the barks, mad laughter and shrieks as the women leaped and twisted.

In the end he was forced to seize one by the arm. 'Are you drunk or has a demon taken possession of you? Stop this at once!'

The girl, unable to wrest herself from his grasp, continued to prance up and down on the spot, lashing her head back and forth to the pounding beat of the tabor, and giggling madly.

'St Vitus's Day,' she panted, between gales of laughter. 'Must dance . . . for St Vitus . . . He can . . . stop the pestilence. Must dance . . . Come and dance!'

She seized the front of Father Cuthbert's robes, and another woman caught his hand, while a third pushed him from behind. They began dragging and shoving the poor man round the graveyard, jerking his arms up and down as if he was a puppet.

'Let go of me! I command you to cease,' he yelled, trying to break free. But as soon as he managed to shake off one of the grasping hands, the women would grab him somewhere else as if he was in the grasp of one of those eight-armed polypus-fish.

'Harold!' he shouted. 'Stop them.'

Father Cuthbert's acolyte had evidently not moved from the spot where he'd first seen the women. His hand still grasped the bell rope and his mouth gaped, like a stranded herring's.

'Help your priest, boy,' I snapped. 'Don't just stand there.'

Harold, dropping the bell rope, made some vague gesture as Father Cuthbert was danced past him, but he made no attempt to stop anyone, either from fear of being dragged into the dance or because he was afraid to lay hands on a woman. Just as it seemed that Father Cuthbert might be danced to death, he tripped over one of the grave mounds and sprawled face down on the grave.

Before he could struggle up, the leader of the women emerged round the side of the chapel still beating out her frenzied rhythm on the tabor. It was Aldith, her long tangle of sandy hair whipping back and forth as she swung her head in time with her own drumbeat. The others fell into line behind her, still prancing, and began to fling off their own clothes and to tear the garments from the women in front, till all were bare-breasted, their dugs jiggling as they pounded their bare feet on the hard earth. Three or four women who'd come out of the chapel ran forward and joined in the mad dance, ripping off their gowns, and tearing the bindings from their hair. One was even grasping her baby, which first laughed then howled as his mother spun him high and low in the clear blue sky. But though the child was plainly terrified, the mother could not seem to stop.

I ran to Father Cuthbert and helped him to his feet, trying to brush the dirt and dust from his red chasuble, which he was still wearing over his robes. But he pushed my hand brusquely aside, bellowing for Harold, who sidled across and stood out of arm's reach of his priest, cringing as if he expected a blow.

Father Cuthbert began to strip himself of amice, chasuble and stole, flinging them one by one at the boy's head without so much as a kiss on the cloth or any reverence for the holy nature of the garments he was discarding.

'The Mass, Father? It's not yet concluded,' I reminded him, fearing that the fall might have shaken his wits. I had to shout to make myself heard over the thumping tabor and the shrieks.

'Nor will it be, Mistress Matilda. Do you imagine I would continue while they . . . they . . .' he spluttered, gesturing towards the frenzied women, as if he could not find words dark enough for their depravity. 'I had thought to come here one last time to bring comfort and hope. Instead I am subjected to this spectacle.'

The women had danced round behind the chapel and,

though we could still hear them, the walls deadened the sound a little.

Father Cuthbert glowered at Harold, who stood clutching the heap of garments. 'Pack those, boy, and the holy vessels, then load the bag on my horse. Quickly now.'

'Your horse?' Harold repeated.

'*Mine*. I will be returning to Porlock alone. You will remain here. Have you forgotten you are exorcist to this parish as well as acolyte? It is your duty to deal with these women. They are clearly possessed by foul spirits – exorcise them! Do not return to Porlock until you have. And I advise you to work quickly. The steward has received orders from Sir Nigel to block the road between Porlock Weir and Porlock to prevent any carts bringing the sick or dead into the town. He intends to seal off his manor to protect it. So if you do not make haste you will find yourself shut out.'

He dragged off the white linen alb, which covered his riding clothes, and added that to the towering pile in Harold's arms. 'Don't stand there gawping like a halfwit, boy. My robes and vessels – get them packed!'

I stared at Father Cuthbert, struggling to make sense of his words. 'Block the road? But where will you be, Father?'

'Naturally Sir Nigel insists I should reside in the manor. I have a duty to tend the members of his family. He waits on the Black Prince, but some of his relatives have taken refuge in Porlock Manor – an aunt, niece, cousin and several of his young wards. But you need have no fear for us, Mistress Matilda. Master Wallace has done an admirable job of ensuring the cellars and stores are well stocked. He has seen to it that plenty of game and meat has been salted down and stored in case there should be need of it.

'As the prophet Isaiah wrote, Mistress Matilda, "*Comedite*

bonum et delectabitur in crassitudine anima vestra – eat that which is good, and your soul shall be delighted in fatness." You would do well to heed that. To deny ourselves the pleasures of food and wine, Mistress Matilda, is to throw God's bounty in His face and invoke His wrath. If we delight in His gifts, the pestilence will not touch us.'

I stared at him, certain that I had misunderstood. 'But, Father, you will come back to hear our confessions, celebrate Mass? With so many in the village mortally sick, they must be shriven.'

'You would not have me neglect my duty and leave Sir Nigel's household bereft of the comfort of the Church? Surely you would not put your own needs above theirs.'

Harold emerged from the chapel and began strapping the leather bag to Father Cuthbert's horse. The priest started towards the beast, then stopped and ran back into the chapel, returning a few minutes later with a linen cloth tied up like a sack.

'But, Father Cuthbert, you cannot neglect your duty here,' I pleaded. 'Sir Nigel can surely send a chaplain to attend to his kin at the manor.'

He ignored me. Snapping at his acolyte to hold the beast steady, he heaved himself into the saddle. I picked up my skirts and hurried towards him, determined to block his path. But the women burst around the side of the chapel again, forcing themselves between us and spinning me round so that I was obliged to run to the far side of the graveyard to avoid being dragged into their dance. They looked exhausted, their faces slack and dripping with sweat, their eyes unfocused as if they were drunk, but still they danced on as if the drumbeat had trapped them in an enchantment and would dance them into their graves.

211

Chapter 27

Porlock Manor

Trust is the mother of deceit.

Medieval Proverb

The shouting outside grew louder. Unable to contain her curiosity, Lady Pavia stepped out of the great hall and on to the short flight of steps leading down into the courtyard. Sir Harry was standing with his back to her, bellowing at a groom. The servant was as tall as he was, and burly, but even so he was edging further and further away from the riding whip Sir Harry was brandishing. Servants peered out from doorways and open casements, or suddenly found the need to re-lace their shoes as they crossed the courtyard.

'Steward says no one's to take the horses out. No exceptions, m'lord. Says he'll not risk any getting sick or being stolen.'

'Do you dare to call me a thief, you worthless piece of goat shit?' Sir Harry lunged forward and lashed the whip at the man's head. Already on his guard, the groom raised his arm and leaped backwards, narrowly saving his face and eye. He cursed, rubbing the purple welt rapidly swelling on his hairy forearm, smearing a thin film of scarlet blood across his skin.

Sir Harry raised the whip again, but before he could bring it down, he found himself spinning round as a hand grabbed it from behind and jerked it from his grasp. 'You got a quarrel with my orders,' Master Wallace growled, 'you take it up with me. And you,' he yelled, brandishing the whip handle at the gawping servants, 'get about your work, else you'll find yourselves taking your chances in Porlock Weir.'

The servants melted away, like snowflakes in a fire.

'How dare you lay hands on me?' Sir Harry roared. 'This flea-bitten dog was calling me a thief. I insist you dismiss him.'

The groom began to babble an explanation, but both men ignored him.

'I heard what he said. He's only repeating what I told him, though he's the wits of a dung beetle.' Wallace jerked his head at the groom. 'Back to your horses.'

The hapless groom opened his mouth to protest, but seemed to think better of it and slouched away, still rubbing his lacerated arm.

Lady Pavia descended a couple of steps, and as both men caught sight of her, they made sullen bows in her direction. 'I hope there are not more bad tidings, Master Wallace.'

'Merely bad servants, Lady Pavia,' Sir Harry said, before the steward could answer. 'When his master's guest asks for his own horse to be saddled, it is customary for a groom to obey without question.'

'They say, *A good servant must have the back of an ass and the tongue of a sheep.* Is that not so, Master Wallace?'

'I've heard *some* say it, m'lady,' Wallace muttered darkly. 'But not when that servant's been given his orders. Last time the Great Pestilence came to these parts we lost a great many horses to the sickness, but we lost just as many to thieves. The bastards knew they could get away with it 'cause there was no sheriff to catch them, nor any judge to hang them.'

213

'But that is *my* horse,' Harry protested. 'I've every right to take it.'

'That's as maybe, Sir Harry,' Wallace said. 'But, like I say, horses fall to the pestilence just as easily as any man, and that fever is already at our gates. If your horse carries the contagion in here, it could spread to every beast and man in the manor.'

Lady Pavia nodded. 'I fear he's right, Sir Harry. Besides, we can't have you putting yourself in danger by venturing abroad.' She arched an eyebrow. 'Unless, of course, you were thinking of abandoning us poor women.'

'I would sooner fall upon my own sword than neglect my duty,' he said, giving a courtly bow. 'No, I merely wished to indulge in a little hunting. Pleasure is good for the health.'

Lady Pavia smiled as if she believed every word. True, there were no signs Sir Harry intended to run away. He was not carrying blankets or travelling bags, just an empty leather sack, the kind a huntsman might fill with small game. But she couldn't help observing that for a man going hunting he seemed singularly ill-equipped. He had no bow and arrows, or bird of prey on his arm, not even a hound at his heel. Perhaps he intended to creep up on his prey and strangle it. And just what was his quarry? She found herself glancing up at the solar, where Christina sat with the three wards and Lady Margery. Would the groom have been asked to saddle another horse, a lady's palfrey, perhaps?

Chapter 28

Sara

*The mouth of a flounder falls to one side for it froze that
way when the flounder pulled a face in jealousy when the
herring was crowned King of the Sea.*

Shielding my eyes from the early-morning sun, I squinted
up and down the beach. There was scarcely a boy to be seen
in either direction, but still I hoped and prayed that this
time . . . *Blessed Virgin, let it be today.*

Every morning I looked for my sons along the shore.
Every evening I stood on the edge of the forest calling to
them. Each time I heard footsteps outside the cottage in
the day or woke in the night thinking I'd heard voices, I
ran outside, certain it was them coming home. But neither
Hob nor Luke had returned.

Once I thought I saw Hob with another boy out on the
rocks in the bay. I tried to pick my way over the slippery
stones, yelling his name, terrified he'd vanish before I could
reach him. I must have sounded like an angry gull swooping
down. But as soon as the lad turned I could see it wasn't Hob,
nothing like him. How could I ever have thought he was?

I cursed myself a hundred times a day that I hadn't run
after Luke when he broke out, but I couldn't cross that

threshold. It was as if the boards were still nailed across the door keeping me in. How long had it been since we'd felt the sun, smelt the salt air? There had been no days in that cottage, only one everlasting night, and I couldn't make myself walk out into the light. It didn't seem real. If I stepped into it, I would vanish.

Panic seized me. Cador and the villagers would see the broken boards. I had to replace them. My hands trembling, I tried to hang the planks back from the inside, but the wood was smashed and they wouldn't stay up. Flies buzzed in, hundreds of them, swarming over the goat's head and the birth blood on the bed. I couldn't keep them out. If the villagers discovered we'd corpses in the cottage, they'd burn it down with us inside.

I tried to calm myself. We had to leave the cottage now. I must get Aldith and Goda out before anyone noticed the broken wood. I needed Aldith to help me with Goda and her babby, for Goda was too weak to stand, but Aldith wouldn't let go of Col's body. She just clung to him, rocking and moaning. I think we'd have been there still if little Ibb hadn't suddenly scrambled out through the hole and, before I'd a chance to think, I was chasing after the little heller to catch her afore she went running down to the village.

We hid among the trees for the rest of that day, but no one went near my cottage except the flies. At nightfall, I crept into the village searching for food and water. That's when I realised the villagers no longer cared if we were shut in the cottage or not, for by then it was too late.

I stood in the dark, deserted street, listening to the cries of agony, the wails of fear and grief behind the closed doors. A tide of helplessness and rage flooded over me. All that we had suffered, all that I had lost, had been for nothing.

I wanted to be with my Elis, to feel his arms about me. I couldn't face this alone again. I stumbled down to the shore and waded out into the dark, icy water. I wanted to go on walking deeper and deeper into the waves, till the sea closed over me and all the misery was ended.

I think I would have done it too, but for the cry. I don't know if it was the cry of a child in the village I heard or a bird on the cliff, but it was the sound Luke had made when he was first laid in my arms. I knew then I had to live. I had to stay alive until I found my sons and brought them home.

Not a soul in the village had laid eyes on my chillern since the day we were shut into the cottage, but I wouldn't give up. They'd come back to me, I knew it. Some of the women tried to tell me that, like Col, they must be dead, but I'd not believe it. I'd never believe it. I was their mam. I'd know if they were gone from this world. I'd feel them leave it, just as I'd felt them stir in my belly before they'd come into it. I prayed my boys had found each other. Together they could survive.

Hooking my fingers under the fishes' gills, I trudged back up the path that ran along the shoreline. I'd sent Goda to fetch what water she could from the stream, but I'd no real hope that she'd go there, much less wait till it was her turn to dip her pail into the trickle. She had to be watching the sea all the time, couldn't bear to be out of sight of it, as if she was the beacon that must keep burning to guide the ship to safety. She was convinced only she could call Jory home.

Most days, Goda wandered up to the cliffs, clutching that babby of hers as if it was a rare jewel someone might try to steal. But the poor little cheal still had no name.

Goda refused to give her one in case the faery folk learned it and stole her afore she could be christened. Said her father must name her when he stood for her in the chapel. I kept telling her that when Jory returned, it would not be to her, but to his wife. He'd never dare stand and admit before the whole village that Goda's by-blow was of his getting. And I warned her, for her own sake, she'd best not be making it common knowledge either. But Goda would give that far-off smile of hers and say he'd be so proud that he had a babby, he'd shout the news from the ship's mast. Goda had always been moon-kissed, not daft exactly, but not right either.

I found myself drawing close to Aldith's cottage. I'd no mind to call on her. She'd been strange since Daveth died, cold. She'd not been near my home since the day we'd escaped from it and would turn from me if we passed on the track, as if she thought I had the evil eye. Yet I'd seen her laughing with some of the other women, as if she was a giddy maid not a grieving widow, and I feared she was becoming as fey as her sister.

But though I meant to pass by her cottage, I could see at once something was wrong. The door and shutters were closed and there wasn't a wisp of smoke rising from the thatch. Even through the door, I could hear little Ibb bellering, as if she'd been left to sob for hours.

'Aldith, you there?'

My heart was thumping. *Blessed Virgin, not her fallen sick too, not Aldith.* I pushed open the door of the cottage, steeling myself to enter. Death could strike so suddenly, prowling through the village like a great black cat, snatching one here, another there before anyone even glimpsed its shadow.

But I breathed easier as soon as I saw little Ibb was alone. She was sitting on the bare earth floor, her face covered with snot and the sticky remains of dried pottage. She gazed up at me with big wet eyes, her wails giving way to hiccuping mewls that jerked her little body.

I made to pick her up, but she drew back from me. 'You sick, Ibb? Got a pain?' Even as I said it, I was ashamed of myself. When a little one is ill, they need cuddling, but fear was more easily caught than the pestilence. I crouched down and laid a hand on her forehead. She flinched away, as if she thought I might hit her, but she wasn't burning up. If anything she was too cold. How long had she been sitting there?

'Where's your mam, Ibb?'

She only stared at me.

'How long has she been gone? She give you any breakfast?'

The fire had not been stirred into life, and the charred embers beneath the thick grey ash were barely warm. No wonder the little 'un was shivering. An empty cooking pot lay on its side on the floor. By the state of Ibb's face and hands, she had given up waiting for Aldith and dug her own fists into whatever had remained in the cold pot.

I bent again to her, and again she flinched away from me, her gaze darting sideways to the corner of the room. 'What's wrong, cheal? Don't fret, your mam'll not scold you for eating food from the pot.'

I pulled her to her feet. She'd messed herself, her shift was soiled and stinking. 'Best fetch you home with me, till we can find your mam.'

I gnawed my lip. Was that wise, though? Aldith had been acting so oddly that she might take it amiss if she found I'd taken Ibb. But Aldith would never let her hearth fire go out if she was close by. Something must have happened to keep her from home.

I took Ibb's hand. But she resisted me, craning around to stare at the bundle in the corner, wrapped in the cloth she always used as a blanket for her rag doll.

'What do you want? Your poppet, is it? Fetch it then.'

She'd fret for it, if we left without it. But she didn't move. So I bent and picked it up, expecting to lift the rag doll easily in one hand, but it was unexpectedly heavy. Before I could grasp it properly, it thudded down on to the hard earth floor.

'Won't wake up,' a plaintive little voice said behind me. 'Won't play with me. I wrapped him to make him warm.'

My hands shaking, I gingerly peeled back the wrapping. The face under the cloth was grey and waxen, the eyes sunk beneath the half-closed lids. I didn't need to touch the bare skin to know that babby Kitto was dead and had been for many hours.

I had washed Ibb in the sea and wrapped her in Aldith's old cloak before hurrying the shivering cheal up the path towards my cottage. Whatever Aldith might think of me, I'd not leave a mite like her alone with that corpse. And for all I knew Aldith herself might be lying dead somewhere, struck down when she went to fetch water or wood.

Ibb suddenly shrank into my side, refusing to take another step. She was staring ahead at Cador's cottage. Bangs and shouts were coming from inside, though not cries of sickness or pain but of anger. Sybil and Bald John's wife, Cecily, were standing outside, trying to peer in through the casements, though the door was shut. The boy, Crabfish, was there too, shuffling from side to side, chuntering away to himself as always. I could hear Cador's wife, Isobel, bellowing in fury and his gruffer tones answering.

I wanted to box Isobel's ears. Everyone was exhausted, irritable, but didn't she realise how lucky she was, that she still had a husband living, and a child too? Two of Aldith's children now lay dead, and mine . . . Where were my boys?

'Cador can't be drunk,' I muttered, as I dragged little Ibb past. 'There's not a drop of ale in the village.'

Cecily snorted. 'It's not drink has got her rampin. It's that whore—'

But her words were cut short as the door burst open. Aldith came tumbling out and fell sprawling on the sun-baked path. Her hair was loose and the laces on the front of her kirtle were undone, so that her breasts flopped out. Isobel stood glaring in the doorway, her cheeks scarlet and her own hair half pulled from its bindings.

'If I so much as see your face near my cottage again, I'll scratch it off your skull. You stay away from my Cador, do you hear?'

Aldith clambered to her feet, brushing the dust from her skirt, but made little attempt to straighten her kirtle. 'I'll go where I please and *with* whoever I please. Your man owes me. My Daveth wouldn't have got sick if Cador hadn't shut us up in there, nor my boy. My husband, my brother and my two sons taken from me 'cause of *your* husband, so let him get me with more sons. That's only fair, isn't it?'

'Two sons?' Sybil frowned. 'But I thought it was only Col you'd lost. Don't tell me little Kitto . . . When? It can't be more than a day or so 'cause I saw—'

Isobel's eyes flashed wide with fear. 'You telling me her babe's newly dead and she comes into my cottage and throws

221

herself all over my husband? And her still befouled with her brat's sickness!'

'We share everything in Porlock Weir,' Aldith said. 'Fish, pestilence, graves. You'll soon be sharing that 'n' all. Or do you want a grave all to yourself? Common grave not good enough for the bailiff's wife?'

Appalled, I shoved little Ibb towards Aldith, hoping the sight of the shivering cheal might bring my sister-in-law to her senses. 'Aldith . . . you've a daughter still living, have you forgotten?'

'What good's a daughter with no men to care for us? And who'll put a babby in her belly when she's grown?'

Crabfish suddenly began to giggle, though he looked scared. He often gave that cackling magpie laugh of his when he was anxious. Usually no one paid much heed to it, but Aldith rounded on the moon-faced boy, pulling open her kirtle and thrusting her pendulous breasts so close to his face they almost took his ears off. 'Reckon you can give me a son, do you? Come on, then, get your breeches down. I'll take a babby from any mumper that can get it up.'

Crabfish, who never looked at anything straight on, tried to back away, turning his head, but his eyes seemed glued to the mounds of swinging flesh and his giggling rose to a near scream of terror.

Cecily bustled forward, dragging the lad away. 'Be off with you now, boy. Go on, shoo! And as for you,' she scolded, grabbing the laces on the front of Aldith's kirtle and jerking them together, 'you stop this! You're behaving worse than a tavern whore.'

Aldith tried to pull away from her, but Cecily slapped her hard. 'Stand still,' she ordered, trying to lace up her kirtle. 'What would your Daveth say if he could see you disgracing his good name like this? He'd be shamed he ever called you wife.'

Aldith pushed Cecily away. 'What good is any name to a man when he's rotting in his grave? It was her husband and yours that put him there. And your husband and hers that'll pay for it. She always thought she were better than the rest of us, could give us orders just 'cause her man's the bailiff. But worms can't tell the difference between a bailiff and a beggar. Cador and Bald John will be lying in that grave pit afore the week is out, do you hear me? And you and her will be crawling into any man's bed you can find left alive, even Crabfish's or that crook-backed dwarf's.'

Chapter 29

I heard one of the four living beasts say in a voice of thunder, 'Come'.

The Apocalypse of St John

The girl they called Raguel crouched down and pushed a steaming bowl of pottage into Hob's hands and held a second out to Luke, which he seized eagerly. But instead of moving away, Raguel leaned towards him, pressing her mouth so close to Luke's ear that the tickle of her hot breath made his groin throb. Her tangle of long hair brushed against his face. It smelt of damp sheep and wood-smoke.

'I put more meat in yours, handsome, so you'll grow tall and strong. You want to be strong for me, don't you?' Her fingers ran spider-like up the inside of his thigh, making his leg jerk so that the gravy in the bowl slopped on to the cave floor. She stifled a giggle. 'Don't you be telling anyone now, or you'll get me into trouble with the Prophet.' Her gaze darted towards the back of the cave, where Brother Praeco sat, but he was too intent on fishing the chunks of goat's meat from his own bowl to glance in his pretty young wife's direction.

Raguel rose, padding softly on bare feet back towards the fire, edging between the twenty or so men and women hunkered down on heaps of bracken and ancient sheep-skins, gobbling their share of the fragrant stew. They were a raggle-taggle band. There was one man who hobbled on crutches, his leg as withered and scaly as a bird's; a blind woman given to visions that left her writhing on the ground; several men who boasted of having been hardened cutthroats before Brother Praeco saved their souls; and a young woman who claimed she'd been a nun, but who, old Friar Tom whispered to Luke, was really a witch. But, then, Friar Tom swore that when he was a hermit, a naked girl had appeared to him while he was praying and tried to tempt him into lustful sin. When he'd resisted, she'd turned into a fiery black goat. Luke was never sure if the old man was teasing him, but compared to the tales Brother Praeco told, girls turning into burning goats seemed as common-place as hens laying eggs.

Friar Tom said he'd walked all the way from Winchester following the Prophet. His watery eyes always took on a dreamy look when he told the story, like the old seamen in Porlock when they spoke of the lands across the sea.

'I'd been begging for alms from the pilgrims queuing to pray at St Swithun's shrine, but the monks from the cath-edral drove me off, said I'd no right begging on their land and the pilgrims should give their money to the shrine. Beat me, they did, with their staves. Real savage they were. Then they pitched me into a stinking ditch. But Brother Praeco saw what they did and pulled me out of the filth with his own hand. He got his disciples to push a wagon loaded with kegs of wine hard up against the door of the shrine to block it and climbed on top of the kegs. He shouted to all how God was going to send wind, fire and pestilence to sweep away the putrid corruption of the Church and the Pope. Said God would destroy the bishops and the nobles and even the King of England himself.

'The pilgrims drew close to listen. Some were jeering, but the Prophet told them how the last time God sent the Great Pestilence three popes were struck down by it and they all died, one right after another, certain proof of their corruption. That was God's warning for the Church to mend her sinful ways, but she hadn't and now the Day of Wrath was coming when God would destroy them all. Brother Praeco looked like Our Blessed Lord Himself standing up there. This blinding glow shone behind his head as if his very hair were afire, but 'twasn't burning. I knew then that he was a holy prophet sent to save us.

'Some of the pilgrims and clergy began hurling dung and stones at him, but those of the Chosen that were already with him fought back, giving as good as they got till the men-at-arms arrived with whips, dogs and swords. Brother Praeco and his disciples were thrown out of the city, but I followed them. Been walking from town to town with him ever since. That's how it always is. He preaches the Word and warns the people of the wrath to come and most mock him, but there's always some who have ears to hear and follows him to be saved.'

Little Hob was coughing again. He was always coughing. It was worse when he lay down to sleep. The air in the cave was choked with smoke and the fumes of fishy oil from the dead gannets burning in place of candles. The wicks plaited from rags and thrust deep into their throats smouldered with a muddy flame that turned everything in the cave to the colour of dung. Grotesque shadows crawled over the walls, and crept around the rocks, as if the dead were still there watching, waiting.

The cave was shaped like a giant egg, except for a short tunnel to one side leading to a shallow recess, just big enough to squat over a bucket and shit. The only way in or out was through a hole high above in the ceiling, reached by a single stout pole with rungs poking out from either side, like the branches of a tree from a trunk. No one entered or left by that ladder without permission from Brother Praeco, and that was only granted to his most trusted disciples.

On the floor of the cave, covered now with bracken and bodies, the outline of an ancient labyrinth was picked out in white pebbles hammered in edgeways. Sometimes the Prophet walked this labyrinth, while the others pressed themselves against the wall and watched in silence so as not to disturb their leader's prayers. He said the labyrinth was a holy mystery, a sign left there by God to show His Chosen Ones the way in the Last Days. But when the leader was out of hearing, his little band grumbled that the pebbles only made it harder to sleep, another petty torment sent to test the faith of the Chosen.

Those disciples who had proved their worthiness had been elevated from the cave floor and allowed to spread their bedding in long, smooth niches carved into the walls. Once, the dead had rested there, but their ancient and desiccated corpses had been burned to ashes on the cooking fire. Maybe that was why their ghosts still slithered about the cave, restlessly searching for their lost bodies. Luke took care always to lie down on his belly, his mouth pressed into the bracken. If you slept with your mouth open, the spirits could creep in.

There were other caves beyond the one they all lived and slept in, reached by a long, low tunnel. Luke had watched Raguel emerge from that tunnel with buckets of water, clear and sweet, but as cold as the sea in winter, so he guessed there must be a spring or even a stream back there.

What else lay in the caves further down the tunnel, Luke had not discovered, for the Prophet permitted only his trusted disciples and his three wives to follow him there. But Luke had heard muttered stories about what lay beyond. The cave was always humming with whispers. And he'd heard the distant cries of despair and pain echoing from that tunnel too. He'd seen the Chosen Ones glance nervously behind them, shuddering and lowering their heads, as if even to be caught listening might be a transgression. Not Uriel, though, Brother Praeco's first wife: whenever she heard those wails of misery, she smiled in satisfaction. It was the only time Luke ever saw her smile.

Luke had never dreamed a man could have three wives. No one in Porlock Weir had ever had more than one at a time, but Brother Praeco was not like any man in the village. He was tall and thin, with a great nose, as hooked and shiny as a falcon's beak, jutting over a wild black beard that hung halfway down his chest. His arms and chest, too, were covered with dense mats of black hair, but his pate was completely bald except for a long fringe at the back straggling below his shoulders.

He wore a coarse russet robe, tied by a knotted scourge at the waist. But whenever he left the cave to climb up to the world above, he would don a heavy cloak stitched from a ragbag of animal pelts – grey rabbit, red fox, dappled deer, nut-brown stoat and the black-and-white stripes of the badger. The badger's head, with glittering red stones in place of its eyes, flopped over Brother Praeco's shoulder, its sharp white teeth constantly bared at any who might approach him. Whatever Friar Tom said, Brother Praeco certainly did not resemble the picture of Jesus on His throne in Heaven, which was painted on the wall of the

228

chapel in Porlock, but maybe you looked different when you got to Heaven.

Uriel, the oldest of the Prophet's wives, was sour and pinch-mouthed, her faded eyes constantly darting about in search of the smallest speck of sin. His second wife, Phanuel, was a pale, anxious creature who, in contrast, barely looked anywhere except the ground and fluttered like a wild bird in a cage whenever her husband's voice rang out. Raguel, Praeco's third wife, could scarcely have been more than three or four years older than Luke, but her breasts rose, like two newly baked loaves of bread, over the top of her kirtle and her skirts strained tight over her rounded buttocks whenever she bent over the cooking pots. More than once as he watched her, Luke had imagined that gown splitting in two and falling away like the husk of a seed and her naked white body . . .

He felt a sharp elbow in his ribs. 'Put your eyes back in their cages, lad,' Friar Tom muttered. 'Just you remember his wives are named for the seven angels of destruction and with good reason. That Raguel could suck the life from a dozen blacksmiths if she had her way with them, let alone a skinny little runt like you.'

'Wasn't even looking at her,' Luke said, flushing scarlet. ''Sides it's daft naming them after seven angels when he's only got three.'

Friar Tom gave one of his twisted grins and tapped the side of his nose with the stumps of his fingers. 'Maybe he reckons to take another four. Don't want to run out of names.'

Having finished his bowl of pottage, Hob was staring covetously at the large chunk of meat Luke had speared on the tip of his knife and was raising to his mouth. In spite of Tom's warning, Luke's attention had been dragged back to Raguel's breasts as she bent over the steaming cooking pot. She gave a little jiggle, tossing her hair back from her eyes. Luke seemed to forget what he was holding, but Hob didn't. He snatched the meat and, in one swift movement, stuffed it into his mouth, grinning at the outrage on his brother's face.

'You little sneak thief!' Luke yelled. 'You wait—' He broke off as all eyes turned to him.

The Prophet raised his head, peering through the mustard haze of smoke and fumes towards the sound. Luke shrank down, stuffing his mouth with pottage as if to prove it couldn't possibly have been him who'd spoken.

'Did someone say we have a thief among the Chosen?' Brother Praeco rose to his feet.

In a flash Hob's expression had changed from glee to terror. He grabbed at Luke's jerkin, holding on to him as if he expected to be dragged from his side.

'Let the one who spoke come to me!'

Friar Tom poked Luke in the back. 'Best do as he says. Not a man you want to keep waiting.'

Hob stared up at Luke, his eyes wide with apprehension. Luke saw Uriel's horny feet picking their way through the crowd of disciples. She was coming towards him. She was going to pounce and drag him out in front of everyone.

Somewhere above, a bell tolled. Everyone froze, staring upwards as stone grated over stone and a faint shaft of grey light and a sudden draught of chill air penetrated the stifling gloom of the cave. The smoke from the cooking fire and the tongues of flames in the dead gannets' beaks guttered wildly. No one moved. No one uttered a sound.

Chapter 30

Will

Riddle me this: How many hoof prints does an ox leave in the last furrow when it has ploughed all the day?

I was asleep when the door at the base of the watchtower crashed open. There isn't much else to do except sleep when you're locked up. You soon get tired of juggling pebbles and balancing them on your nose and elbow when there is no audience to applaud. I could hear the voice of my first master, the one who created me. *Practise every hour of your scrawny little life, Courtney, even practise in your sleep. I made the dwarf, but only you can make the jester.*

We practised all right, he saw to that, every skill our future masters might ever require of us for their amusement – tumbling, inventing riddles, simpering in the parody of a coquettish lady or mimicking a boisterous hound by cocking our legs. He had us conjuring one day, and the next swinging from a minstrels' gallery, like drunken squirrels.

'Which is worth more – an ass or fool?' my master used to say. 'The ass, of course, for when he fails to carry his burden, he makes good meat for his lord's hounds, but when a fool fails to entertain, he is good for nothing save food for the worms.'

231

So we always had to be ready to divert our lords and their guests with something new the moment the fancy took them – plucking eggs from the ears of their sulky children; teasing a bashful bridegroom with bawdy jokes; coaxing an old man from his melancholy humour . . .

. . . And falling in love? No, that was not a trick our master taught us. We invented riddles about love. We made the ladies cry with laughter as we sighed and swooned in wicked impersonation of their swains. We carried love tokens and kisses from man to maid, but we could never fall in love. We were the imitation, the parody, the mockery of love, but we must never be *in love*. The very idea was an outrage, a blasphemy against God and man, like a dirty little imp lusting after a holy angel. When God created man in His own image, it was a longshanks He created and set above all the beasts that crawl and creep and cavort. Dwarfs, real or fake, are not made in the image of their creators. I should know. For, unlike most men, I have seen the one who formed me, though, believe me, my master was no god.

Yet the imp did fall in love with the angel, though I tried to conceal it, like a murderer conceals a bloody knife. I took care never to look at her directly in the great hall, and if my gaze strayed unbidden to her, I would set myself a penance. I would prance across to another woman and conjure a rose for her, or play at being a smitten lover insanely jealous of her knight. There were more beautiful, sophisticated ladies in that hall, made so by nature or by the skill of their tiring maids, and every man from aged knight to callow stable boy declared himself infatuated with those creatures, but none of those women possessed her mind. As an iron shoe is made to fit the hoof of only one horse, so our minds fitted each other's as perfectly as if we had been crafted for one another before even the world itself was fashioned.

'What is it that grows in a pouch, swells and stands up, lifting its covering? A proud bride grasps that boneless wonder. The daughter of a knight covers that swollen thing.'

It was the same every time I asked it. All the women blushed and giggled behind their hands. All the men raucously yelled out the crudest answer. But that night, the first night I ever laid eyes on her, a woman's voice rang out bold as a jester and sharp as an arrow: 'The answer is bread dough, of course.'

Of course it is, my love, my wonderful, enchanting love.

And from then on when I was forced to look at every woman but her, kiss every breast but hers, then we proclaimed our love, our fears, our secret to the whole world in our language.

'I have no feet, but open my mouth to a flood of salt tears. With the point of his knife, a man will open me and swallow me. What am I?' she asked

'An oyster,' I called, and the guests, blind and deaf, applauded us for our quick wit.

She was not an oyster. She was a rare pearl of great price, *my* pearl, and they prised my treasure from me as she knew they would.

But in my dreams I can still find her, hold her, look again into those gentle eyes. Hear her soft voice whisper her own name for me, *Josse, Josse.* Sleep is a wondrous eagle, which can carry you back to where you long to be. And I resented being torn from its grasp.

I squinted up to see Cador filling the doorway, though not quite as snugly as he had done a few weeks ago. His belly was less rotund. The skin of his double chin was as scrawny as a chicken's wattle, and as he drew off his hood to wipe the sweat from his head, the sunlight bounced off a pate that I swear was balder than before. He had a black eye too.

I clambered painfully to my feet, wincing as the iron fetters on my ankles bit into the sores. My twisted back and neck have always ached. But my master's whip taught me to ignore it, as a dancing bear must learn not to snarl at the smart of the chain through its nose. But since I had left my lord's employ, my back had stiffened, and sleeping on the cold, hard floor of that watchtower had not improved it.

I expected to see a pail of water in Cador's hands, with my meagre ration of stale bread, but he carried nothing except his stave. My belly lurched. Was the day finally come? Was he here to take me to the manor court? I could expect no mercy there. I had dreaded a whipping, or branding with a hot iron. Agonising though they were, I knew the pain and humiliation would pass and I had convinced myself that that was the very worst that could befall me. But as I saw Cador standing there I knew, with a sudden churning of my bowels, I had been deceiving myself, like the fool I was. Before the sun set that day, I could be choking at the end of a rope. Master Wallace would delight in watching me dance on the manor's gallows, instead of in its great hall.

Like any pet dog, I've been forced to spend my life appeasing those who owned me. Cador was not my master, but I'd swallowed so much pride over the years that gulping down another cupful wasn't going to kill me. On the other hand if I didn't . . .

'Master Bailiff, you're a fair man. And you and I both know Sir Nigel's steward is a greedy, malicious fellow. A good many coins that should be lying chastely in my lord's coffers have been led astray and ended up in Master Wallace's purse. I may have stolen a piglet or two, but if any man should be tried as a thief, it's him.'

Cador grunted. 'He's skimmed the cream from my wages more times than I can count and left me with the whey. *Fines*, he calls them, for neglecting my duty, when you'd not find any bailiff in England more diligent than me. If the wind blows contrary, Wallace finds a way to make me pay for it. But who's to stand against him? He's the only man in these parts that has the ear of Sir Nigel.'

'I know it better than most,' I told him. 'When I threatened to expose what he did, he had me flogged and kicked out into a ditch.'

That was only half the truth, of course. But half a mug of ale is still ale, so half a truth must still be truth.

'Master Bailiff, if you deliver me into the hands of that man, I swear he'll see me hanged just to silence me.' It is hard to beg a man earnestly for your life when you know that your mouth is grinning. I turned my face to the wall, hoping my voice alone would move him to pity. 'And how will my death serve Mistress Matilda? It won't put flesh on the bones of those piglets again. But if I live, I swear I'll find a way to pay what I owe her in time.'

I thought I heard Cador chuckling and my fear turned to fury. Thought it was funny to see a dwarf hanged, did he, just another entertainment for the longshanks? I suppose he fancied he could just stuff me in a sack and carry me to the manor all by himself. Well, just let him take one pace inside that door—

'Don't fret, sprat, you'll not be going to Porlock.'

I was convinced I must have misheard him. 'Where's the manor court sitting, then?'

'It'll not be sitting anywhere, least not till the pestilence is over. Not a court in the land'll be in session now, I reckon. 'Sides, I couldn't fetch you there, even if I'd a mind to. Porlock Manor's sealed its gates and they've blocked the cart track 'twixt us and the town with trees and rocks. Won't let so much as a fart out or in. So there's no sense me keeping you in here, wasting good food on you.'

I was tempted to tell him that half a loaf of stale horse bread barely warranted the title of *food*, let alone *good*, but I was not out of irons yet.

Cador tossed a key at me. 'Go on, unfasten the chain.' He sighed. 'Matilda'll be a wasp in my ear, wanting you arrested again soon as this is over. But I reckon many a tide'll ebb and flow afore that day comes and you could both be dead by then, so you may as well go where you please for now. Though after a day out there, you'll more than likely wish you'd stayed locked safe inside.' He gingerly pressed his blackened eye and winced. 'Womenfolk are running mad,' he muttered. 'A man's not safe from any of 'em.'

He vanished from my sight and re-emerged leading a string of three shaggy packhorses. 'Going to head up over the hill and across the moors to villages on the other side. They're far enough away that news of our troubles will not have reached them and, please God, neither has the pestilence.' He crossed himself fervently. 'I've a small purse and a stick or two of dried eel and fish to trade. I'll fetch back any grain they've for sale and ask what news they've heard from London. I dare say the fever's already over in the city and ships'll be sailing again back into our bay before the next new moon.' He gave a lopsided grin, but the fear in his eyes told me he couldn't convince even himself of that.

*

236

Once, when I was in Sir Nigel's employ, a mad old beggar had come knocking for alms on the feast of St Stephen, claiming he was the true King of England and King Edward was an imposter. The young men, bored and in need of sport, made him a cloak of straw, pulled a fouled stick from the midden and stuck it into his hand for a sceptre, then sat him on a dung heap for a throne. They bowed and taunted that mockery of a king, though the old man's wits had so far fled from him, he thought they were honouring him. I remembered him, as I waddled down through the village, for that was what Porlock Weir had become, a cruel mockery of itself.

The lanes and small square in front of the bake-house were deserted. Those who ventured out looked warily up and down the track and hesitated if they saw someone approaching, looking for any sign of sickness. All the doors were shut, but none was marked. It was impossible to tell the households that had been touched by the pestilence from those that were trying to keep it out. The bay was empty. No mud-horses skimmed across the wet sand. Only three women collected fish from the shallow trenches of the closest weirs, while the fish trapped behind the walls further out or caught in the wicker traps were left to flap and die unharvested. The women kept stopping, leaning against the dripping stones as if the small effort of picking the fish exhausted them. On the shore, a pack of hungry dogs snarled and snapped over the carcass of something that might have been a rotting seal.

My belly rumbled as I approached the bake-house. While I was grateful to Cador for releasing me, he might at least have brought me my breakfast first. The tide was out and my stomach was not prepared to wait for it to come back in, then for the hours it might take me to catch some fish and cook them. I stared out at the weirs where the fish lay ready for the taking, but I daren't risk snatching one from there, not so soon after being let out, even if I could walk across the mud without getting stuck.

But the smell of the steam rising from the bake-house yard was not that of new bread or even roasting meat, but boiling fish. I found Sybil hunkered on the ground beside a fire in the yard, staring listlessly into the flames. I don't think I'd ever seen her sitting before. She was always pounding dough, chopping meat, scrubbing pots with sand or pushing driftwood into the fire hole to stoke the oven. But the yard was unswept. Empty barrels lay abandoned, rolling back and forth on their sides in the sea breeze, like men with a bellyache. The oven was cold. Ash and charred fragments of wood spilled from the stoke hole.

Sybil glanced up as my squat shadow fell across her face, but she didn't rise. 'Let you out, did they, runt? You needn't bother going back to Matilda's pigsty. All her piglets have been took. I guess you're not the only thief in this village. She's only got the old sow left now, and I reckon she'll not have her much longer, 'less she slaughters her quick.'

I decided to ignore this. 'Not baking today?'

I'd lost count of how long I'd been in the tower. It could well have been a Sunday or feast day, not that Sybil ever took much notice of either. But I hadn't heard the chapel bell tolling. Come to think of it, I couldn't recall when I last had.

'What am I to bake with? Fish bones?' she said, gesturing to the small pot that hung over the smouldering fire. 'There's not a barrel of flour or sack of grain left in Porlock Weir. Even the dried beans are used up. What acorns and beech-nuts fell in the forest the swine and beasts feasted on over the winter. You were a jester, weren't you? Good at conjuring. You try conjuring this fish into bread and ale, then. 'Cause if you can't, fish is all you'll be eating and water is all you'll be drinking and there's precious little of that left in the river too.'

'Cador told me that the track to Porlock's been blocked, but there are other towns and this village has still got boats. Can't men sail down to buy—'

Sybil cut me off with a crackle of laughter. 'What men would those be – pixies, ghosts? Those are the only kind of men we got left round here. Go you up to the graveyard and see for yourself. It's the men and young ones that are lying up in there, while their wives and the old folks dig the graves, least those that have still got the strength.'

It was only as she said it I realised that, apart from Cador, I hadn't seen a single man so far that morning, or any children out playing or fetching wood or water, only women.

Sybil let me share her fish and a mouthful or two of the boiled salty slime they called laver. After the dried horse bread I'd been enduring, it was almost a feast. But there'd been many weeks in the sea cave when I'd lived on little else but fish and I knew it didn't fill the belly in the way bread or beans did. It gave you the flux and left you exhausted. None of us could survive long on fish and seaweed alone and it was plain to see that the beans and onions, which had been planted for this year's harvest, had already withered into dust in the scorched earth.

I left Sybil still sitting and clambered around the base of the cliffs towards my cave. It was good to feel the sun hot on my head, taste the salt on the wind and see the gulls bobbing, like little ships, on the clear blue-green waves. I stood watching the white-fringed wavelets roll in over the glistening wet sand, and the terns picking over pebbles in the wet mud. After the brown earth and grey stone of the watchtower prison, the colours of sea and sky danced and cavorted as gaudily as any painting on the walls of my lord's manor. As I stared out at the rolling waves, it was as if nothing had changed for a thousand years. Yet, the sea had thrown something on to the land that was destroying all, changing everything.

I felt a woman's head resting on my shoulder, her hair against my neck, the weight of her soft body in my arms. But the hair was wet, the body cold, and the eyes that stared up at me were as grey as the ocean in winter. Was I the cause of all this? Was this the sea's revenge, because I had stolen a corpse she had claimed? Or was this Janiveer's revenge and the sea merely her poor jester?

I shivered. Hastily scrambling over the sharp wet rocks, I hauled myself up into the cave, suddenly afraid that all I possessed would have vanished. I owned precious little, but that made what poor things I had the more valuable to me. Besides, the treasures I had rescued from the seashore were the things I depended upon to survive – nets I had cobbled together from bits of rope and old cloth, fish hooks, needles and spoons made from animal bones, shells I used as scoops or trenchers and my cooking pots. Yes, I'll admit I'd stolen those, likewise the sheepskins, which I now called my own, but that didn't stop me feeling indignant at the thought they might have been snatched from me.

But, to my relief, I saw they were all still there, except they were not where I had left them. I always kept my tools where I needed them. The fishing nets, hooks and rope together by the mouth of the cave; the cooking pot and scoops near the ring of stones that marked my fire, the sheepskins and my supplies of dried food at the far back of the cave where they'd be protected from wind and water. But all had been moved. The empty shells I had collected, even those I had wedged into handles to use as ladles, were now laid in piles: razor shells had been separated from scallops, oysters from mussels. Needles, marrow-spoons and spikes that I had fashioned from bone were piled in another heap. Rope had been separated from cloth, lumps of tar from driftwood. And all my stores of food were gone.

Hob? Had he crept back and hidden here? I wouldn't have blamed the lad if he had. It was a good place to camp provided he could stay out of sight. The fire was cold, though. Either he'd let it go out and had not been able to relight it or he had not returned for some days.

But perhaps someone else had entered, searching for something. Yet people searching usually left possessions in complete disarray, not neatly stacked, unless someone had been planning to take this flotsam to sell. But I couldn't imagine anyone in these parts who'd want to buy it.

One thing was certain: I would need to find food, since my visitor had not left me so much as a scrap of dried cod. But the tide was still too far out to attempt to fish and I should fetch fresh water first. If Sybil was to be believed, that was even harder to obtain and I'd not survive long without it.

I hunted around until I found the two water-skins I'd fashioned out of a dead seal. They were hanging from a rocky projection near the back of the cave. They too were empty and I was about to hook them down when I caught sight of something lying on the floor immediately below them. It was a thin branch of sweet briar, which had been twisted round itself to form a hoop. The leaves had long since dried and the rose petals had withered and fallen, lying scattered on the rock around the thorny stem. But the briar hoop was not really what attracted my attention, it was what it encircled: a dead bird, flattened, dried, the flesh eaten away, so that only the bones and pale feathers remained. It was no seabird, though, a pigeon or a dove, perhaps.

I crouched, staring at the thing, strangely unnerved by the sight. Birds often took shelter in caves. One could easily have flown in and died. If I'd simply discovered it lying on the floor, I would have tossed it out without another thought, though the Holy Hag would doubtless have told me it was an evil omen. A dove dropping dead where you sleep is hardly likely to be a good one. But if I believed every dead bird was a sign of death, I'd have hanged myself long ago. No, it was the ring of roses around it that made me certain the bird had not simply been blown in by a storm.

Maybe Hob had brought it in. Young lads have a morbid curiosity for dead creatures, collecting them as treasures and watching in fascination as they decay. Perhaps he had tried to care for an injured bird, but it had died and the rose garland was his attempt to give the poor creature a funeral, as he'd seen adults do. That must be it. The dead roses and the bird had no more significance than the game of a lonely little boy. All the same, I didn't want to sleep with them.

I hooked up the briar hoop, trying not to impale myself on the thorns, and picked up the bird by one of its twig legs, but the leg came apart from the body as I lifted it, and the little pile of feathers and bones settled back on the rock. Something small and hard bounced out of its beak and rolled across the floor with a clatter. I groped for it, though it proved to be nothing more than a dried cherry stone. Maybe the bird had choked on its last meal. But I couldn't imagine where either the dove or Hob had found a ripe cherry in these parts and at this season. I hadn't tasted cherries since I left my lord's employ and, come to think of it, I couldn't recall seeing a cherry tree anywhere in the village.

The snatch of a troubadour's song suddenly rose up from deep in my memory:

> *. . . have a young sister across the sea,*
> *Many be the dowries that she sent to me.*
> *She sent me a cherry without any stone . . .*

I could hear the lad now, trying to make himself heard above the chatter of the guests, squabbling dogs and the clatter of dishes in my lord's hall. I could feel the heat of that roaring fire, smell the venison simmering in the rich blood sauce, see the skin on that roasted suckling pig glistening honey-red in the candlelight. My belly growled, reminding me that I didn't have even a sprat for my supper.

I scraped up the remains of the bird, with the fallen blossoms, and flung them from the mouth of the cave. The wind caught the dried petals, bones and feathers, scattering them and sending them swirling, like a flock of tiny birds, up into the blue sky and out across the bay. The notes of that troubadour's song buzzed in my head, like a trapped fly. I'd be humming it all day now . . . *She sent me a dove without any bone . . .* What *was* the next line? I couldn't recall it. That banqueting hall was a lifetime away.

Chapter 31

Matilda

St Anne is the patron saint of all who sew, for she taught her daughter, the infant Virgin Mary, to sew cloths for the Temple.

'Harold, I have already removed all the holy oil and water from the chapel.'

The young acolyte stared at me in alarm, opening his mouth to protest, but I would suffer no argument.

'There are some women in this village who would try to steal oil and water to anoint their dead in a wicked mockery of the extreme unction, even when their husbands and sons died in sin. They think it will stop the devil taking their souls, but God has given Satan leave to punish the wicked and these women are damning their own souls with such practices.'

'But I – I am the one in Holy Orders,' Harold protested. 'I should take care of the holy water and chrism.'

'Indeed you should, but you don't,' I snapped. 'Left to you, any witch or cunning woman could take them to use in their dark spells and you wouldn't raise a hand to stop them.' I pushed past him to reach the reliquary niche. 'And this we must also put in a place of safety before thieves steal it. The casket is extremely valuable.'

I drew back the embroidered hanging cloth, which I had stitched with my own hands. The niche behind it was in deep shadow, for Harold, of course, had neglected to light the candles that should burn perpetually before the relic of a holy saint. It was so dark, I couldn't even see the reliquary. I reached up to lift the casket out, but my fingers touched nothing except empty space.

I stared in disbelief. 'It's gone!'

Harold, holding a cloth pressed firmly over his nose and mouth against the grave pit stench, squeezed between me and the back of the stone altar and peered into the recess where the reliquary, in the form of a silver arm, had always stood. He thrust his fingers inside, groping around as if he expected to feel what he couldn't see.

'It hasn't suddenly become invisible, you blockhead! Where is the hand of St Cadeyrn? What have you done with it?'

'I've not touched it,' he said indignantly. His gaze darted back towards the niche as if he thought it might miraculously have reappeared when he wasn't looking.

'It was here on the Eve of St Vitus,' I told him, 'for I hung the new cloth then, and there have been no services since St Vitus's Day. You were supposed to be guarding this place and now a costly reliquary has gone missing, not to mention the sacred relic of a saint. So unless you want to find yourself standing trial for the theft, boy, you had better think carefully. Who else have you let in here?'

Alarm and panic filled his eyes. Harold was clumsy and idle, but I didn't really believe him to be a thief – at least, not of anything more than an apple or the stub of a candle. He was far too timid to take anything as valuable as a reliquary. Nor would he have had the wit to know where or how to sell it.

Harold's pimpled forehead wrinkled in concentration, as if trying to recall the names of a whole multitude of visitors. 'But there's not been anyone save you, Mistress Matilda.'

'Nonsense! Of course there have been others. They bring the bodies to the corpse pit at all times of the day and night. And anyone could slip in here, especially that thieving dwarf,' I said tartly. 'You should be here on your knees keeping vigil in prayer. Look at this holy place! It's a desolation, an abomination. Birds flying in, leaving their droppings all over the holy altar. Stray dogs pissing up the walls outside and digging up the bones of the dead.'

Furiously, I strode over to the far wall where the church chest stood. I held out my hand. 'The key, Harold.'

'I've not got it. Father Cuthbert took it from me when he bade me load the chalice and vestments on to his mount.'

'Then,' I said grimly, 'I will have to use this.' I unfastened the sack I had brought with me and removed an iron twibill.

Above the rag mask he was holding over his nose, Harold's pale eyes flashed wide. 'But you can't break into the chest, Mistress Matilda! Stealing from the Church, it's the worst sin. And Father Cuthbert will blame me if—'

'Father Cuthbert has abandoned his duty to his parishioners and to this chapel,' I reminded his acolyte sternly. 'The reliquary has already been stolen and that makes it all the more urgent that I remove the linens to prevent them being taken too. If you'd continued to sleep in the chapel and kept watch, this would not be necessary.'

'Kept retching,' Harold mumbled, through the cloth. 'It's the stink.'

I had to admit that, even though I, too, had taken the precaution of bringing a cloth soaked in strong vinegar, I was finding it hard not to gag at the stench.

246

The lad stared miserably at the floor. 'And at night, when it's dark, I keep thinking about those corpses outside, not even buried. I hear them clambering out of the pit and slithering round the walls of the chapel, scratching at the door, trying to find their way in.'

'You were trained as an exorcist,' I snapped.

'They just gave me a book,' he wailed. 'Father Cuthbert said I only had to sprinkle the newborn babies with holy water before they were brought into the chapel. He never said anything about driving off armies of the dead.'

I always itched to give the lad a good shaking whenever I spoke to him, but I suppose he deserved some credit. At least he made an attempt at a burial service for those who were dropped into the pit, though being in Minor Orders he could not say Mass for them.

The grave pit could not be sealed. No one had the energy to dig fresh graves each time. What charcoal the village had had was finished and the lime too, so they covered the bodies with layers of seaweed to try to counter the smell and keep the sun from them. But the rotting seaweed baking under the sun did nothing to mask the reek of bloated corpses. It merely added a new sickly stench of its own and drew yet more flies.

But at least the dead of Porlock Weir had a grave of sorts. The bodies of strangers that were washed up from time to time were left on the shore for the next tide to pick up again. Some vanished. Others returned again and again, sprawled on the rocks or washed up behind the fish weirs as if they were determined to claw their way back to the land. Crabs crawled over them, brazenly plucking at their flesh. Living fish flapped against them. Gulls stabbed their bellies open. But we barely glanced at them now.

Harold kept staring at the heavy oak chest, shuffling awkwardly from foot to foot, as if he couldn't decide whether or not to throw himself across it to defend it. But I was determined to have my way. There was no linen left in the village to make winding sheets. The corpses were being wrapped in sacks, old sheepskins or the soiled, bloody blankets in which they had died, and bound tightly with straw rope. But sooner or later someone would remember the linens stored in the chest. Since no Masses could be said, the sanctity of the altar cloths would make them even more desirable coverings in which to wrap the dead, for then neither evil spirits nor the devil himself would be able to touch them. But I had sewn a great many of the fine linens with my own hands. I would not see them defiled, or used to keep wicked sinners from their just punishment.

'Stand aside, Harold,' I ordered.

He took a determined pace towards me as if he intended to lay hands on me to prevent me by force, but I raised the iron twibill menacingly and he stumbled backwards out of reach of its swing. The twibill belonged to my husband, George. He always kept the two chiselled ends finely ground, so I knew they'd be sharp. When he was home from sea, George lavished all his attention on his tools, grinding and polishing them half the night while I lay alone in our bed waiting for him. He insisted he couldn't rest until he'd oiled the wooden shafts and wrapped the iron blades in unwashed wool so that they wouldn't rust, though he never put a single one of his tools to work in my cottage.

Sliding one of the honed ends of the twibill into the crack between the lid and the hinged side of the chest box, I pumped up and down on the handle. Harold was chewing his nails in agitation. He kept begging me to stop, but I ignored him. Finally, with a cracking and splintering, the wooden lid of the chest was torn from the hinges, and clattered on to the floor.

Harold darted forward, and peered at the lid. 'Look, it wasn't locked after all! But I locked it on St Vitus's Day. I know I did! And no one's been nigh it since.'

I snorted. 'Just as you were certain no one had been in the chapel, but the reliquary vanished all the same. Next you'll tell me the corpses you heard scrabbling at the church door were responsible. You will have much to answer for, boy, when the church court next sits. And I suggest you use the time wisely between now and that day to think of a better excuse for this desecration than the walking dead. I can see I have not come to rescue these precious linens a moment too soon.'

I lifted the cloths out carefully, one at a time. First the fair linen that covered the altar, rolled not folded, in accordance with church rule. Next the chalice veil, linen towel and the first of the two heavier cloths that were laid beneath the altar covering. But the second cloth was not lying flat. I growled. That was Harold again, stuffing them in any old way in his haste to leave. Everything beneath would be crumpled. There was even a danger of the delicate threads being broken. I pulled out the second cloth and, just as I'd feared, the baptismal cloth underneath was twisted around something. I tugged at it and stumbled backwards. I think from the squeal I must have trodden on Harold's foot, or maybe he cried out because of what he saw.

In the dim light of the chapel, I thought a giant black spider was crouching on the white linen. I almost struck at it with the twibill, fearing it would scuttle out. But it didn't move. A few moments passed before I realised I was staring down at a mummified human hand, the fingers long and thin. It had been roughly severed at the wrist.

'Where did this come from?' I demanded. 'Did you hide it in here? Was this why you were trying to stop me opening the chest?'

Harold had let the rag drop from his nose and mouth and from his dumbfounded expression, I could see he had had no more idea than I that the hand was hidden in the chest.

'Hand of glory,' he breathed. 'I've heard about those. Thieves cut them from a man on the gallows and use them to open locks.'

'And what would such an evil thing be doing in here?' I asked. 'No . . . this must be . . . It must be the hand of the Blessed St Cadeyrn. But who would dare to remove such a holy relic from its reliquary?'

I peered into the linen chest, hoping that the hand might simply have tumbled out of its silver reliquary as I tugged at the linens. But even as I searched, I knew the casket was not in the chest. I would have seen it glinting. The reliquary was gone and the blessed saint's hand had been hidden in the chest by whoever had stolen it. Whoever? No: I knew exactly who had done this. There was only one thief in Porlock Weir brazen and wicked enough to commit such sacrilege. That evil dwarf would think nothing of casting aside a holy relic. I'd wager he'd come here the first chance he'd had, after Cador was foolish enough to release him from the tower. I'd see him hanged for this, if it was the last thing I did.

Chapter 32

And I looked and beheld a white horse and he that sat on him had a bow.

The Apocalypse of St John

A sacking bag descended on a rope from the black hole in the cave roof. Several hands grabbed for it and steadied it until it reached the ground. The rope vanished to reappear twice more, depositing first a small wooden chest, then a skinned and eviscerated hind, which showered drops of blood, like holy water, as it spun to the floor. Finally, a pair of worn leather boots appeared on the rungs of the ladder straddling the central pole. Brother David descended, clutching his bow, his quiver, almost empty of arrows, slung across his back. He was dressed in the same homespun brown as his master, Brother Praeco, but whenever he left the cave he wore his eelskin cap over his long hair for, as Luke had since discovered, it disguised the puckered holes that were all that remained of his lopped-off ears.

Men and women drew aside as best they could in the crowded cave as Brother Praeco strode towards him. 'Our Lord has blessed your hunting, Brother David,' he said, staring down at the plunder.

David grinned, stroking his bow as if it was a favourite hound. 'As you taught us, Master, *I will heap evils upon them and fire my arrows among them.*'

The Prophet's black beard waggled as he waved a reproving finger. 'The Lord's words. I am merely his mouthpiece.' But he did not look displeased. 'Come!'

He led the way to the back of the cave without troubling to glance round to see if his order would be obeyed. David followed him into the tunnel as closely as a hound at heel. No one moved until the sound of their footsteps had faded. Then everyone turned expectantly to Brother Praeco's oldest wife, Uriel, who was plucking at the tightly knotted cord at the neck of the sack. She emptied the contents on to the floor of the cave: a small bag of dried beans; another of peas; strips of dried meat; a bundle of dried fish, stiff and sharp as flakes of flint; a few onions and bulbs of garlic; some withered beets; sprigs of potherbs and a jar of salt.

Luke caught sight of his brother Hob creeping through the forest of legs towards the dried meat. He seized the back of the boy's shirt, yanking him away. Hob scowled and wrested himself free, but was wise enough not to attempt it again. His eyes hungrily followed the bundle of meat strips as the leader's other two wives, Phanuel and Raguel, gathered up the meagre haul of food and vanished into the tunnel with it.

By the time they emerged again, Uriel and one of the men were prising open the wooden chest with an iron crow. The lid crashed backwards and the crowd of men and women shuffled closer. On the top were several sealed rolls of parchment and a small leather-bound book. But Luke barely registered these, as he caught the glitter of silver beneath the scrolls. The contents of the chest must have been packed with haste for although there were wrappings of woollen cloth they had been loosened by the jolts and bumps of the journey, exposing silver goblets and plates shining crimson

252

in the firelight. Uriel lifted these out, then a box with a lid shaped like a miniature house and embellished with blue enamel, and finally a cross on a gilded stand. The cross itself was fashioned from wood, shiny and black as ship's tar, studded with five blood-red stones, mounted in gold and polished till they shone like liquid fire.

At the sight of the cross, Friar Tom fell to his knees, pressing the stumps of his fingers together in prayer, but he had barely begun before a voice thundered from behind, 'Like Moses, I leave my children for a short time and return to find them worshipping graven images.'

The Prophet pushed his way through the crowd, seized old Tom's arm and hauled him to his feet.

'But it is a cross . . . the holy cross,' the old friar protested.

'It is a tawdry made by man,' Brother Praeco roared. 'God smote the Israelites with pestilence and slaughtered them with the sword for no less.'

Friar Tom began to shake. His old legs buckled and he sank to his knees at his master's feet.

Raguel sidled up to her husband. 'Forgive him, Holy One. He's long set in his ways. He's yet to grasp all the wonders you teach him. The old need time to learn.'

She ran a finger lightly down the thick pelt of black hair on her husband's arm, gazing up at him from under long lashes. Brother Praeco's free hand strayed towards the twin creamy pillows of her breasts thrusting up over the top of her kirtle, as if he was about to plunge his fingers deep between them. For a moment, all that could be heard was the sound of laboured breathing, though whether it was the Prophet's or the quaking friar's, Luke couldn't be certain.

'Idolaters must be punished,' Uriel declared suddenly.

'I am the anointed of the Lord,' Brother Praeco snapped,

abruptly averting his gaze from his young wife's breasts. 'I alone will decide who is punished and who shown mercy. Women should keep silent in the presence of men. Clear these baubles away quickly, before anyone else is corrupted by them. The parchments and book, take to my cell.'

All three of his wives bowed their heads and bent to gather up the valuables, stuffing them back into the chest. All the while Uriel darted venomous glances at Raguel, who grinned back when she thought her husband wasn't watching, her eyes dancing in triumph.

As his wives carried the chest awkwardly down the low, narrow tunnel, Brother Praeco strode over to an outcrop of rock covered with a wolf's pelt, which formed the semblance of a bishop's throne. The Chosen, taking this as a signal, settled themselves down on the heaps of bracken and sheepskins, gazing up at him expectantly. Luke grabbed Hob, who was wriggling to the front, and dragged him as far back as he could get within the confines of the cave, squatting behind a beefy man with ears like pitcher handles. He was afraid of Brother Praeco, in a way he had never been afraid of any man in the village, including his own father.

The Prophet held up his hands. 'In addition to the fresh venison and other food Brother David has brought us, for which we give thanks to God, he also brings grave news of the world above.'

He paused, gazing around the Chosen Ones, as if he wanted to be sure of their attention, though that was hardly in doubt. They were as hungry for news as they were for meat.

'Brother David has seen with his own eyes the rotting corpses lying heaped in the villages, unshriven and unburied, for those few who remain alive have run mad with grief and despair. It is the living who are to be pitied now, for what they have suffered thus far is as nothing to the horrors that are yet to come. Soon they will gnash their teeth and weep that the pale horseman did not strike them, too, with the mercy of death.'

Luke glanced down at Hob who was staring miserably at his fingers. He had told his little brother over and over that their father was dead, Col and Uncle Daveth too, but he wasn't sure Hob really believed him, even though he'd said he did after Luke had threatened to punch his head.

'Men, driven mad by hunger, roast their own infants and devour them,' the Prophet was saying.

Luke thought of Goda's baby. Had that been spitted over a fire? When he tried to recall what the baby had looked like, all he could see was the bloody head of the skinned goat cradled in Goda's arms. Maybe she'd whelped a goat instead of a baby. Sometimes he couldn't tell what had really happened and what he had dreamed.

'Women have made a giant phallus to worship as a god and they copulate before it with their own fathers and sons, as they did in the days of Sodom.'

Hob tugged on Luke's jerkin. 'What's that mean?' the boy whispered.

Luke dimly recalled Father Cuthbert once preaching about a village called Sodom. It was a place where fire rained down, destroying everyone except one family who'd escaped, like he and Hob had done.

'He means they're . . . they're dead, all dead.'

'Even Mam?' Hob's eyes were brimming with tears.

'I told you, don't you remember?' Luke growled. 'You and me are the only ones left. That's why we got to stay down here. Else we'll die too. And there's no use in your skritching,' he added fiercely, punching his brother's arm.

'But,' the Prophet bellowed, 'you, my brothers and sisters, need have no fear. We are the Chosen Ones, the elect, who will be saved in the Last Days. Even as we sit here the pale horseman gallops back and forth across the face of the earth above us, crushing kings and bishops beneath his hoofs, slaying the wicked and cleansing the world of their iniquities. The sun shall become as black as charcoal, the moon shall turn to blood, the stars fall from the heavens and a great wind shall blow across the face of the earth.'

His voice grew exultant. 'But the Lord will hide His Chosen Ones in His secret dwelling inside the mountains till His wrath is past and when that day comes we shall walk out into a new world, purged and pure as the Garden of Eden on the day it was planted, and we shall take up our golden crowns and live for ever as the rulers of the new earth, His paradise.'

A sigh like a summer's breeze ran round the huddled group.

'Will you follow me to that garden? Will you prove yourself worthy of that golden crown?'

A chorus of affirmation rose up, like a flight of starlings.

Brother Praeco stood up and stared down at the people sitting at his feet. In the shadowy cave, his deep-set eyes had become black tunnels and Luke, gazing up at him, felt himself being sucked towards them, as if he might vanish inside the Prophet's skull.

'But the Lord says if anyone among you sins, if anyone does not hearken to the word of the Prophet, if any sets himself against God's will, you are to cast him out from among you. And we obeyed our righteous Lord, for Alfred set himself against us and we cast him out. Cast him out to face God's terrible wrath alone and unprotected. Cast him out into the darkness of that world.' The Prophet raised his arm, jabbing his long, thin finger towards the hole in the roof of the cave now covered once more by the slab of stone.

A muttering broke out, as the disciples gazed fearfully upwards. Luke had heard them whispering about Alfred before. They said he'd argued with the Prophet and had been banished from the Chosen to take his chances above.

'Are there other unbelievers hiding among us? Is there any man or woman here who foolishly believes he can abandon God's Chosen Ones and survive in a world where pestilence prowls the land like a devouring lion, where villages lie empty and desolate, and men are so hungry they would strike your arm from its shoulder with an axe and devour it before your very eyes? And there is worse to come, for the horseman who rides upon the red horse is yet to be released. Would you face his terrible sword alone?'

Friar Tom gave a great cry and crawled on his hands and knees towards his master clasping the hem of his coarse robe, wailing for forgiveness. Brother Praeco gazed down at him, then, bending, laid his hand upon the grizzled head.

'God will show you mercy and forgive you. He will not cast you out, but you must submit yourself to His burning light. You must be cleansed of your sin.'

Friar Tom gazed rapturously up at him. 'Cleanse me, I want to be cleansed!'

The Prophet nodded to Uriel, who seized the old man's arm and, none too gently, hauled him to his feet, bustling him towards the tunnel.

Brother Praeco watched until they were out of sight, then ran his fingers through his wild black beard. 'Where is the newest disciple who seeks to become one of us?' He peered around the band. 'The boy who called out there was a thief among us . . . Bring him here.'

257

Before Luke could fully grasp that the Prophet was asking for him, he felt hands grasping him and dragging him forward. Behind him he heard Hob cry out, alarmed by the separation, but he was struggling too hard in the hands of his captors to be able to turn. He found himself staring up at the tangle of black beard. He'd never been as close to Brother Praeco as this, and the strange musky scent of his robe reminded Luke of the polecat he'd once caught and had planned to keep in a cage till it sank its teeth into his hand. Although Luke knew he couldn't break free – and where could he run to even if he did? – it didn't stop him giving another violent squirm to show he would not submit easily.

To his surprise, the Prophet smiled at his struggles. 'A fierce young warrior. The Lord has need of those.'

He flicked his hand at the two men who held Luke tight. 'Let him stand alone.' They released Luke and took a pace back.

'You accused someone of theft. That is a grave charge.'

Luke dare not turn his head, but he could feel his little brother's terror as if a wave of water was breaking on his back.

'Just a game,' Luke muttered. 'I was only teasing . . .'

'Only teasing, yes,' Brother Praeco said softly. 'I remember how much pleasure young boys take in taunting others.' He raised his voice. 'But the Chosen Ones have only the words of God on their lips. Were you not taught you shall not bear false witness?'

The crowd of people in the cave were motionless as if they were holding their breath, waiting. Luke's throat tightened. He wanted to protest that it meant no more than Hob calling him a nug-head, but he didn't know how to explain.

To his surprise, though, the stern expression on the Prophet's face softened a little and he caressed Luke's hair.

Brother Praeco raised his head, gazing out over the disciples. 'God saved this boy from a cutthroat's knife. We must trust He will cleanse Him of all sin, if he is chosen.'

Everyone in the cave seemed to start breathing again.

Brother Praeco glanced down. 'But let us see if you are as wise as your namesake, Luke. Your brother is a child, too young to understand the choices he faces, though we will see to it that he learns in time. But you are a man, old enough to decide your own future. You have seen God's wrath fall upon your own village. You have heard me speak of the fate that, even now, awaits the godless in the world above. So, I set before you this day life and death. Will you choose death and be cast out, as Alfred was, to take your chances alone up there, or will you choose life and join us?'

Luke opened his mouth to speak, though his brain did not yet know what would come out of it, but the leader's sweaty fingers shot out and covered his lips.

'Not so hasty. Words are easy. It is not enough for you to choose God. God must choose you, and God's elected must be tested in the furnace of His judgment. Will you submit to that test, Luke?'

The Holy Prophet lowered his head and his deep-set eyes stared down into Luke's. 'Will you prove yourself worthy?'

For a moment, Luke was paralysed by his piercing gaze. He knew he must answer, but he seemed to have forgotten how to say a single word. Then his head jerked round as, from somewhere deep in that tunnel, he heard an old man screaming.

Chapter 33

Sara

If the blood of a man is shed on the coast, the fish will desert that place and come no more till that place is cleansed with fire.

'Hob! Luke! Come home. Please . . . come home.'

Shading my eyes, I stared up at the distant moorland track where it emerged from between the trees. I glimpsed a movement on the path and my heart jolted. The small figure vanished, hidden by the branches, then reappeared further down the track. Someone was leading a packhorse slowly down the hillside. It was the track my Elis always took and for a moment I thought . . . I really thought . . . But he was not gone away, he was gone for ever. Tears burned my eyes, but I angrily scrubbed at them with my sleeve. I must give over crying.

I made myself look up at that track again. I hadn't imagined it. Someone was definitely coming. And they were leading a well-laden widgebeast too. I couldn't get a clear view on account of the trees, though I could tell the figure was far too small to be Cador. Maybe he'd sent a boy back with whatever he'd been able to buy at the first village, while he travelled on to see what else he could find. From the way the load was hanging either side of the beast, it looked like a couple of sacks of grain. It was welcome, whatever it was, but it wouldn't go far among the villagers. I'd best stir myself.

I ran into the cottage, snatching up empty sacks and a pot. When I came out the boy and beast had vanished. They must have taken the other track that led straight down into the village. I hurried towards the sea. I'd not walked more than a few yards before sweat was running down my back and my legs were trembling with tiredness. Before the pestilence came, I could've run all the way from the sea up to my cottage. Now I was breathless even walking down. But I couldn't afford to rest, else all the grain would be gone.

Goda needed bread if her milk was to keep flowing, and when Luke and Hob returned, they'd be starving, they always were, and I must have food to give them. At least, that was what I told myself, but truth was, I had such hunger myself for bread or beans or any solid mouthful, I'd have waded through a bay of stinging jellyfish to get it.

Cecily came hurrying hard on my heels and that bitter-weed, Matilda. News had plainly spread that a widgebeast was coming into the village, for a small crowd was beginning to gather in the square before Sybil's bake-house. Katharine hovered in the shadow of one of the cottages. Cecily, catching sight of her, spat at her and the rest turned their backs, but Katharine didn't retreat. I don't know why she lingered. She must surely have realised that no one would let her have so much as a single grain, even if it fell in the dirt. They'd not forgiven her for hiding her husband's sickness and brazenly walking about the village when she knew there was pestilence in her house.

Isobel, Cador's wife, bustled along from her cottage,

shouting orders before she'd even reached us. 'It's no use you all crowding round. As his wife, the bailiff would want me to take charge. I'll inspect what he has sent and decide what measure each goodwife can buy.'

Sybil folded her great meaty arms. 'If it's flour or grain then it should all come to me to bake. I know better than any here how to stretch it and I'll see bread's shared out fairly.'

'If there's grain to be had, then it's good strong ale we should be brewing with it,' Abel grumbled. 'Half the village has got flux from drinking nowt but water.'

'All the more reason to put solid bread in your belly,' Sybil retorted.

'Only way bread'll cure it is if I shove it up—' He broke off, a look of fear spreading across his wrinkled face.

Alarmed, I turned to see what he was staring at. The shaggy widgebeast was ambling round the side of the cottage, led not by a boy but by the grinning dwarf. But it was not who was guiding the horse that caused the cries and gasps, but the load it was carrying. Slung over the beast's low back, his arms and feet almost grazing the ground, was the body of a man. Flies buzzed over a large rusty stain where his tunic covered his thigh.

Isobel gave a shriek and stood swaying back and forth for a moment, before she rushed forward to lift the man's head. The features were swollen and dark, but we all recognised them.

'Cador . . . Cador,' Isobel sobbed, trying to cradle his face.

'Don't just stand there!' Sybil shouted. 'Get him down.'

But no one in the small crowd seemed able to move. The dwarf pulled a knife from his belt and, trying to hold the beast still with one hand, attempted to saw through the straw rope that bound Cador's body to the wooden cradle on the horse's back. Alarmed by Isobel's wailing, the horse tried to pull away. It kicked out, catching the dwarf on his shin, making him drop both rope and knife. Only Isobel, her arms still wrapped about her husband's dangling head, prevented the horse from bolting and the corpse became a macabre prize in a tug-of-war between woman and beast. Sybil and I rushed forward to catch the animal and cut Cador's body down.

It wasn't until Cador was slumped on the ground, being rocked in Isobel's arms, and the widgebeast was safely tethered some distance away, that a babble of angry questions started flying. Bald John came hurrying up and pushed his way through the women, staring in disbelief at the body lying across Isobel's lap. 'What happened?' he demanded. 'Where was he found?'

Everyone started talking and yelling at once.

The dwarf, who was sitting on the ground, rubbing his bruised shin, clambered awkwardly to his feet. 'Now hold fast. I'll tell you what I can if you'll whip your tongues back into their kennels.' With that queer rocking motion, he waddled a few paces to an upturned boat and clambered on to the top, sitting there, grinning, like he was a bishop on his throne.

'I was up in the forest—'

'Hunting boar, was you?' Abel said. 'What do you do? Run under their bellies and swing on their cods?'

'I heard a horse whinnying, and crashing about,' the dwarf continued. 'I thought it might be caught in a snare or a bush. So I followed the sound.'

'Thought you might steal the horse, more likely, just like you stole the precious reliquary,' Matilda snarled. 'On your way to sell it, were you, dwarf?'

We all stared at her. I could see from the other women's expressions they'd no more notion of what she was chuntering about than I had, but we'd more to concern ourselves with than her ravings.

'If you keep interrupting him, woman, he'll never get his story told,' Bald John said. 'Out with it, runt. What happened?'

'I found Cador lying face down on the ground, the lead rein of the packhorse still tied to his belt. That was why the horse was fighting. She must have dragged him a few yards, judging by the marks in the leaf litter, but the body had caught behind a tree and she'd tangled the rein around the trunk trying to break free. I couldn't see any sign of the other horses.'

'But that doesn't explain what killed him,' Bald John said gruffly.

The dwarf reached into a sack tied over his shoulder. 'I found this lying where he must have fallen, before the horse dragged him.'

It was a knife, set into a white bone handle, the kind any man, woman or child would carry to cut their meat at table or for a dozen different tasks in the fields, though most blades in those parts were set in wood. That was the one thing we had aplenty. The rusty-red stain on the blade and smears on the handle left little doubt that the last time it had been used was to cut the flesh of some creature, but whether man or beast, it was impossible to tell.

Bald John took it from the dwarf and, holding it gingerly by the end of the handle, crouched beside Isobel.

'No, don't touch him.' She jerked Cador's head closer, flinging her other arm out protectively over his back as if he was still living and she feared Bald John meant to stab him. All her fury at her husband over Aldith had dissolved in her grief.

'Whist, woman, nothing can hurt him now. I just want to see if the blade fits.'

He pulled up the bloodstained tunic, ripped the hole in the hose wider, then laid the blade flat against the livid wound beneath.

'Wound's a mite wider than the knife, but if the blade was pulled out at an angle that'd make sense. I reckon this is what he were stabbed with, right enough.'

He lifted Cador's right hand and turned it, examining the horny palm. 'Blood. Probably dragged the knife out himself. But that wound couldn't have killed him, unless . . .'

Dropping the stained knife, he pulled out his own from his belt and cut through the laces holding up the dun-coloured hose, peeling it down till the hairy thigh was exposed. The skin was blue-black, the flesh so swollen round the wound that it seemed the slightest touch might burst it.

'Pestilence,' Cecily shrieked. 'He died of the pestilence.'

'Tried to burst the swelling with his own knife to ease the pain,' Abel said.

Everyone backed away, but Bald John shook his head. 'There's no stench and no pus in that wound. It wasn't the pestilence that killed him.'

Meryn hopped forward on his crutches, dragging his withered leg. Balancing awkwardly he peered at the wound on Cador's thigh. 'That there flesh looks same as my foot, day I stepped on a viperfish out there in the bay. Whole leg swelled up. Pain were worse than fires of hell. 'Tis useless now.' He rapped his lame leg with one of his crutches.

A woman nodded. 'That's viperfish, right enough, seen

265

it many a time, but Cador didn't go stepping on no fish, not up there in the forest.'

Bald John picked up the bone-handled knife once again, holding the handle gingerly between thumb and forefinger. 'But he got a knife stuck in him right enough, so I reckon as someone must have coated this blade with poison.'

Chapter 34

Will

Riddle me this: Which craftsman builds the house that will stand the longest?

There are some words you can be certain will unleash a hail of arrows just as surely as the order to 'loose' on a battlefield. *Poison* is one of those. Toss that single word into the air and it will be answered by a volley of accusations flying thick and fast. Before I could slide off the upturned boat, I was surrounded by a crowd of women screaming like gulls that I was the murderer. The most vehement of my accusers was, of course, the Holy Hag.

'Cador should have taken him straight to Porlock to be hanged when he was caught with my piglets. Now he's stolen the reliquary from the chapel. With Father Cuthbert being away I dare say he thought he could sell it before anyone noticed it was gone. The bailiff probably caught him with it, that's why the dwarf killed him.'

'He's a proved thief,' Isobel screeched, 'and he knew my Cador was taking money to buy grain. Lay in wait to rob him. Why else would a dwarf be lurking around in the forest?'

'Cador locked him up, so this is his revenge.'

'The wound's just at the height where a dwarf would strike. A proper man would stab his victim in the heart.'

'Knew he couldn't reach the heart so he used poison.'

'Just the kind of evil trick you'd expect from a dwarf. Must have been planning it all along.'

'Dwarfs are supposed to dance, aren't they? Let's see him dance on a rope. No sense waiting. We all know he's guilty.'

Several hands grabbed my arms and legs. I fought, kicking and struggling, but a rope halter was thrown over my shoulders, pinning my arms to my sides. Another loop was twisted round my ankles. I knew the next one would be round my neck. A surge of panic engulfed me. Ever since I can remember I've been terrified of being tied up, unable to move. I suppose it was all those years strapped inside that box. Somehow finding my arms trapped was a greater terror than the death I knew was coming. I couldn't breathe. They started to drag me by the rope about my feet, my back scraping against the sharp stones. All I could see was the filthy skirts of the women and the yellowed soles of their feet as they pranced inches from my face. I was choking in a cloud of dust and dried dung. The rope went slack.

'Which way up shall we hang him, by the neck or heels?'

'Heels is what he deserves. Die slower then. Could take hours.'

'Days more like.'

The rope jerked upwards, crushing my ankle bones as they slowly hauled me up. My head cracked against a stone as I was swung into the air. A searing pain shot through my back and legs. The rope twisted and swayed, creaking over the beam above. I closed my eyes, trying not to vomit.

'Hold hard!' Bald John called. 'There's naught in the dwarf's sack but a few snares. And Cador's purse is still on his own belt. If the little runt killed Cador to steal from him, why didn't he take the money? And there's summat else don't make sense. If you'd killed a man, you'd not go to the trouble of fetching his body back. You'd get as far away as you could before the corpse was discovered. Could have been days, weeks even, before we realised anything was amiss and went looking for Cador, that's if we ever did. Why would the runt come back here and draw attention to murder, specially if he'd stolen summat from the chapel?'

My head felt as if it was going to burst open. 'I didn't kill him! I swear by every saint in Christendom.'

'Well, if he didn't, who did?' someone asked. 'You just said it couldn't have been robbers who attacked him 'cause the money is still there.'

Everyone began arguing again.

Blood pounded in my ears. My legs felt as if they were being torn from their sockets. I was so sick and dizzy, I daren't open my eyes. 'Let me down!' I yelled.

I felt a blade sawing at the rope and I plummeted down on to the hard stones with a crash that drove the breath from my body. I gasped and coughed, trying to get the air back into my lungs, waiting for the waves of pain and sickness to pass.

But no one took any notice of me. They were all too busy blaming each other, Isobel yelling that we'd all heard that harlot, Aldith, threaten to kill Cador, Sara shouting that Isobel had murdered her own husband in a rage because he'd lain with Aldith. Others pointed out that as bailiff Cador had been in charge of collecting taxes and fines so anyone in the village might have harboured a grudge against him.

I struggled to pull myself into a sitting position. The rope around my chest and arms had shifted upwards while I was being dragged, so with some effort I was able to wriggle out of it and free my ankles from the loop wrapped around them. Grazed and bruised, I staggered to my feet, wincing against the sharp pains that were shooting up my crooked spine.

'What's the use of arguing? Cador's dead,' Sara shouted. 'And we'll all be following him unless we find a way to stop this sickness.'

Everyone fell silent, turning to look at her.

'If we fast and pray,' Matilda said primly, 'God will spare those who deserve to live.'

'My Elis deserved to live,' Sara snapped. 'He was a good man. But God didn't spare him. Or those innocent chillern that lie up there.'

'Rest their souls,' old Abel muttered. 'But what's to be done, save wait for the pestilence to pass over, like it did afore?'

'We can't wait for it to pass!' Sara said. 'Some of us'll escape the sickness, but by then we'll be dead of starvation. Look around you. Half the working men are dead. Weirs are beginning to break. Land's not been tilled or nets mended because we can't do our work and theirs. It's all we can do to care for the old folk and the sick and the chillern that still live. What we planted in the spring has died for lack of water. So there'll be no harvest, nothing to see us through the winter, save fish. And we'll not even have fish when the weirs breach in the next storm. Most of us are as weak as whey already from the flux, so we'll not have strength to repair them.'

'You think we don't know that,' Sybil barked. 'But road to Porlock's sealed. Cador was to fetch grain from the moor villages, but see how that's ended. Waste of time anyway. If any village still has grain, they'd have more sense than to sell it to outlanders knowing they'll have need of it themselves afore the year is out. I reckon Cador knew it was hopeless and he had no intention of coming back to this village or to her.' She gestured towards Isobel, who was still sitting on the ground.

Cador's widow let out a howl of misery and outrage. Cecily patted her shoulder, glowering at her own husband, Bald John, as if to warn him not even to think about doing the same.

'When the men get back from the sea, they'll know what to do,' one old woman said timidly. 'My son and Matilda's husband, too, they'll be back and a half-dozen more from this village. Ship could sail round that point tomorrow.'

'And it could be weeks or months more,' Sara said. 'That's if they come at all. For all we know the ship could be lost or stricken with the pestilence itself, like the ship that brought those chillern.'

Several of the women wailed, spitting on their fingers and crossing themselves feverishly to stop Sara's words coming true. Though I noticed the Holy Hag wasn't among them. Maybe she wasn't in any hurry to see her husband return. And I wouldn't have blamed George if he stayed away for another year. If I'd been married to Matilda I'd have asked the captain to put me ashore a hundred leagues away.

'Crying won't stop it,' Sara said. 'I should know – I've shed enough tears – but there's one who could. She knew the pestilence was coming. She swore she could end it too.'

The Holy Hag snorted. 'She knew because it was her who summoned it. Janiveer cursed this village. I saw her do it on the track to Kitnor. That very same hour those dead children were dragged out of the weir and carried into the heart of this village by your own brother-in-law.'

271

'All the more reason to find her,' Sara said. 'Make her lift the curse. If she can work such dark magic as call death to this village, then it stands to reason she's the skill and power to banish it too. And if it was her curse that's done this to us, the pestilence'll not pass like last time. It'll not end till every man, woman and child in Porlock Weir lies dead and rotting in that pit.'

'But Janiveer has long gone,' Matilda protested. 'You'll never find her.'

'Can't see why not.' I waddled forward, coughing to make them look down, not that I had to fake that, my lungs were still choked with dust and dung. 'You just told us she took the path to Kitnor so we know which way she went. Isn't there a village deep in the forest where they used to send the mad? I remember there was some talk of it when I was in my lord's employ. Sir Nigel joked about sending his elderly aunt there.'

'The village is deserted,' Matilda snapped, glaring down at me as if she'd gladly string me up again.

'But they reckon the ghosts of the madmen and sorcerers who were banished there still howl among its ruins,' Cecily said.

Old Abel nodded gravely. 'One terrible bad winter when I were a lad, my brother and me, we went foraging for firewood in the forest. Mam warned us to be home afore dark, but we didn't pay her no mind. Wandered too far, see, and it grew dark. We heard shrieks and cries coming from deep in the forest, like souls in the torment of Hell, they were. Took to our heels and ran, we did. Didn't stop till we were safe by our hearth.'

'Nobody with any sense would go there after dark,' Sara said uneasily. 'But my Elis went there once in summer, years back. Said the church was still standing and some of the old round stone huts. Hunters take shelter there and the charcoal-burners sometimes.'

'Then Janiveer might still be there,' I said. 'She seemed the kind of woman who would take to the life of a hermit, and if she knew the pestilence was coming, she might think herself safer there, living alone.'

'She'd likely know that we'd have to come looking for her,' Sara said. 'I reckon she'd not go far.'

'Aye,' Bald John said, 'but even if you found her, she said there was a price to be paid if she was to save the village. It was a cruel bargain she offered, a price that none of us would pay then. Are you saying you'd be willing to pay it now?'

All eyes were fastened on Sara. 'I . . .' She gnawed her lip. 'I've lost my husband, maybe my chillern too. I'd give anything, anything at all, to bring my boys home safe. What use is my life without them?'

The agonised expression in her eyes was one I'd once seen in the eyes of another woman. I understood Sara's misery only too well. I, too, had plunged to the bottom of that dark, cold pit of grief and hopelessness. Maybe that was why I said one of the most foolish things I've ever prattled in a lifetime of being a fool.

'You never know,' I said, as cheerily as any jester, 'if she's found no other village willing to pay her price, she might be open to a little haggling. Let's find this Janiveer first, then worry about payment. If Mistress Sara is willing to go, I'll travel with her.'

'You think we'd let a woman from this village go off alone with a creature like you?' the Holy Hag sneered. 'We all know what you intend. As soon as you get her alone, you'll force yourself on her, then cut her throat.'

Rage boiled up in me. Another had accused me of forcing myself on a woman, as if it was beyond the belief even of a saint that a woman could freely love such a hideous mockery of a man.

'It's your throat I'd like to cut,' I blurted out.

'You hear that?' she squawked. 'I told you *he* stabbed Cador. Now he's threatening to murder me as well.'

'Half the village would buy him an ale if he did,' Bald John muttered. 'But it's a fair point,' he added loudly. 'Will mayn't have killed Cador, but someone murdered him. And Cador was a strapping man. What kind of a fight could a woman put up if it came to it? That little runt's not going to be much use as a bodyguard unless he's going to nip their ankles.'

Cecily barged her way forward, planting herself squarely in front of her husband, arms folded. 'So that's what you're planning, is it? Going off with Sara into the forest to *protect* her. First it's that slut Aldith, and now you want her sister-in-law too. I warn you, John, you take so much as a step down that path and I'll be using your cods as bait for the crabs.'

'I told you, woman, I never touched Aldith, and as for going to search for this Janiveer, it'll be as much use as plaiting rope from sand. And, worse, it's dangerous. I'll not allow Sara or anyone else to go.'

'Not allow!' This time it was Sara who squared up to him. 'Who are you to be telling me where I can and can't go?'

'With Cador dead, someone's got to take charge of this village and act as bailiff and I reckon I'm the fittest man to do it, least till this is over and Sir Nigel's steward can appoint another.'

'Now, you listen to me, Bald John. You can crown

yourself king of the village, if you want, but you'll not be telling me what to do. I lost the only man who'd the right to order me. It's thanks to you and Cador my boys are missing and I'll not have them come back only to watch them die of pestilence or hunger. I'm going to find Janiveer and make her lift the curse. And if I get my throat cut in the forest at least it'll be quick. Any who wants to come with me and the dwarf are welcome. Rest of you can sit around here and wait for death to take you.'

Chapter 35

*And the third part of the waters became wormwood. And
many men died of the waters, because they were made bitter.*
The Apocalypse of St John

Luke's head rolled back, hitting the rock wall, and instantly
he was awake again, his heart thumping, as he tried to grab
anything to hold on to, but there was nothing to cling to
in the darkness, nothing to stop him falling down and down.

The Prophet's most trusted disciples, David and Noll,
had led him down the rocky tunnel. David lit the way with
a blazing torch held above Luke's head. They passed the
entrance to other caves or crypts, but he could see little of
what lay inside, save a glimpse of some boxes in one, and
in another a deep pile of skins and a glitter of silver. In the
distance, Luke became aware of a murmur, like the far-off
sound of the sea, but as he stumbled along the uneven
passage, the murmur grew to a roar that hurt his ears. Were
they dragging him off to fight a dragon or monster?
He tried to tear himself out of their grip, but the men held
him tightly, urging him on.

They had stopped by the entrance to what Luke had
thought to be another dark cave. The men had pushed him
forward, holding him by the shoulders, steadying him as
his foot almost slipped over the edge. For as the flames of
the torch flickered across the hard rock, Luke saw that this

was not really a cave at all but the entrance to a vertical shaft, reaching so high above his head that he couldn't see the roof and so far below the earth, it made him sick and dizzy to look down.

From somewhere high above in the darkness, water cascaded down in a raging torrent, tumbling over the rocks above him, then arching out into a void, falling, falling, until it smashed into the angry pool far below. The light from the red flames of the torch darted across the black water that seethed and boiled in the pool, as if he was staring down into his mother's cooking pot, except that this water was colder than the sea in winter. Luke could feel the icy blast of it rolling up to envelop him.

David bent close, bellowing in Luke's ear to make himself heard over the thundering waterfall. 'Devil's Cauldron they call that,' he said, with a malicious grin. 'You know why? Fall in and you'd be sucked under and tumbled over and over, battered against those rocks, like Satan's demons beating the sinners in Hell.'

Noll pointed to a plank of wood that formed a bridge between the tunnel and a narrow ledge that projected from the sheer rock wall on the opposite side of the shaft. 'You're to crawl across that. Off you go. Hurry now, less you want a pitchfork up the arse.'

Both men had laughed, then stopped abruptly as they heard the Prophet approaching behind them.

The Prophet had put his face so close to Luke's his beard almost smothered him. 'The Lord does not choose cowards, Luke. Show me that you and your brother deserve to be saved from the pestilence and not cast out to face the horror of God's wrath alone. Show me that you have faith. Cross to the other side.'

Luke had crawled across that void, his arms and legs trembling so hard they almost gave way beneath him. He had not dared to look down. He was almost grateful when he reached the ledge, for at least that felt more solid than the plank. The rock was cold and slippery with spray. It was just long enough to sit with his legs stretched out, but not to lie down. He pressed his back hard against the slimy wall, his fingers feeling around for any crevice or handhold he could grip, but there was none.

Noll dragged the plank away and David handed the torch to the Prophet. Then both disciples, bowing respectfully, retreated back down the tunnel.

'*Then the devil took Jesus into the holy city and set Him upon a pinnacle,*' Brother Praeco bellowed. 'This is your pinnacle, Luke. You must stay here alone and pray. Pray that you may be accepted as one of the Chosen of God. Jesus was left alone for forty days and in all that time He did not eat or sleep. You must stay awake too, though the devil will tempt you to sleep, for if you give in to that temptation, you will fall from the ledge into the water below and be swallowed up. You must pray, Luke, pray that God will give you the strength to resist that temptation. The more exhausted you become, the more you long to sleep, the harder you must pray.'

'You . . . won't leave me here for forty days?' Luke could hear the catch of terror in his voice, but he was powerless to control it. His clothes were already sodden from the icy spray, and his teeth were beginning to chatter in the freezing air.

'I will leave you here until God instructs me to call you forth.'

The Prophet lifted the burning torch high and walked

278

back down the tunnel. Luke watched the flickering red glow of the torchlight on the wall until it vanished and he was plunged into icy darkness, with nothing but the roar of the water filling his head.

Chapter 36

Porlock Manor

A thief knows a thief as a wolf knows a wolf.
Medieval Proverb

A shadow falls across the open doorway of the stillroom, but Rosa does not glance up from the ink-black root she is pounding. She knows who has come calling. She has been waiting for him. Sir Harry ducks beneath the low beam and steps inside, pulling the door closed behind him, blocking out her light. Still Rosa does not look at him. He comes close, bending over the stone mortar, reaching out as if he means to dip his finger into it.

'It is not wise to touch what you do not know,' she cautions.

'Is that so?' He catches her wrist, pulling her so close to him that she can feel the swelling of his pizzle as it rises against her belly. 'But how I am to know if I don't touch? If that is a love potion you're grinding, you little witch, you needn't trouble yourself. I am already won.'

'It is a poison for the mice and squirrels that gnaw the manor's stores.' She doesn't struggle or push him away. She doesn't need to. She raises the pestle stained with the black juice and brings it close to his lips. 'White hellebore.

280

Do you know it, my lord? A single sniff has been known to kill a man.'

He loosens his grip and takes a hasty pace back.

'Master Wallace has asked for large quantities of poison,' she says. 'The drought has driven swarms of mice into the barns – there is nothing for them to eat in the fields. He fears they will spoil all our stores.'

She resumes her grinding, though with him blocking the light she can barely see the root, but she does not need to see what she intends to crush.

A fretful wail rises from the corner. They both glance over. Sir Harry takes a pace or two towards the wicker cradle, nudging it with the tip of his boot.

'Yours? You give a man lusty sons, it seems.'

'Not mine. The tiring maid, Eda's.'

Sir Harry laughs. 'That crone? Now that I cannot believe. She's old enough to be my own mother, and even if she were not, her sour face would shrivel any man's desire. Unlike yours, sweet maid. Yours ignites the fire.' He moves towards her again, but the rhythm of her pounding does not falter.

'Was it poison you sought too, my lord?'

'I can think of two men I'd gladly feed it to,' he mutters sourly. 'The one keeps me prisoner. The other makes that prison Purgatory, for all that he is in Holy Orders.' He spreads his hands in a helpless gesture. 'So you see I have come to seek a little solace here, sweet angel. Won't you take pity on me?'

He takes care to stand behind her this time, trapping her against the table, slipping his hand around her waist and up towards her breasts.

'Are you searching again for my necklace, my lord? If that is what you seek it has told you all it can.'

281

'But you have not,' he whispers. His hands slide to her arms, gripping them so that she cannot raise the pestle again.

He pulls her away from the table and she allows herself to be turned, meeting his gaze steadily with her sea-grey eyes.

'You're no stillroom maid. You look at your masters too boldly.' He seizes the blue beads around her neck, dragging them up till the bear's claw dangles in front of her face. 'I think you know full well what that bird and snake signify. Is that why you've come here? Searching for the king's grave on the pretence of picking herbs?'

'As you pretend to go hunting?'

He raises his hand to strike her, but she doesn't flinch away. Fear flashes across his face.

'What you seek, my lord, has already been taken. The king's mound is empty. His treasure is gone, stolen.'

He stares at her, then shakes his head violently as if trying to fling her words from his brain. 'Don't lie to me! Whoever you are outside the manor, inside these walls you are nothing more than a worthless maid. I could break your neck and not even Wallace would protest. And even if he did, he could do nothing about it with the manor sealed. So I want the truth. You know where the grave is and you've found what's buried there.' His eyes dart around the boxes and jars ranged along the shelves of the dark stillroom. 'Where have you hidden it?'

She smiles. 'If I had found a king's treasure, would I still be labouring here, sleeping on rags, taking orders from Master Wallace?'

'Then if you know for certain it is gone, why do you stay?' He gnaws at his lip. 'You stay because you know who has taken it . . . You stay because it's close by. That's it, isn't it? You're waiting your chance to steal it.' He takes a pace towards her. 'Tell me—'

Sunlight suddenly floods the cool dark room, making Sir Harry whip round.

Christina is standing in the doorway. Her face betrays more than surprise – alarm, fear, even.

They stare at each other, as if they have realised they need to offer some explanation for being there, but it is Sir Harry who recovers quicker. He makes an extravagant bow.

'I pray it is not sickness that brings you to seek the offices of a stillroom maid, Lady Christina, but I do believe my prayers have been answered already, for you look radiant. If Sir Nigel's physician could glimpse your beauty, he would surely advise all men to gaze upon you to keep them from the pestilence.'

Christina's gaze darts towards the cradle, where little Oswin, hearing her voice, is lifting his head and making gurgling sounds of pleasure. She glances back at Sir Harry and there is no mistaking the panic in her eyes.

Sir Harry excuses himself with another bow and strides out of the open door.

Christina closes it behind him and hurries towards the cradle, scooping the child up and nuzzling his soft cheek, her eyes tightly closed as if she is offering a silent but desperate prayer. She has her back to the casement, so she doesn't see the shadow that passes across it and lingers there.

The rhythm of the stillroom maid never falters as she pounds the deadly root, but Rosa sees both watcher and watched. As Christina rocks Oswin in her arms, Rosa observes the cold smile that slowly spreads across the features of the man who watches. Sir Harry understands now, understands the nature of the malady that kept Randel's new bride in her turret. But only Rosa understands the game. And she will decide who wins.

Chapter 37

Sara

*If the first fish caught in a season is female, then the
fishing for the rest of the year will be good, but if it is a
male the catches will be poor.*

'*I* will walk with you, Sara,' Matilda announced firmly.
'Katharine can walk behind with the dwarf creature, if she
pleases.'

'I have a name,' the little man growled. 'To my friends I'm
Will, but I'll let you call me William. Though I'm surprised
you want me to walk behind you. Aren't you afraid I'll
poke you up the arse with my nasty little poisoned dagger?'

Matilda gave that affronted sniff of hers, and I had to
turn away for fear she'd see me smiling. When I'd first
clapped eyes on the man, I'd not trusted him one whit.
With that perpetual grin of his, like one of the gargoyles
on the chapel, he always seemed to be mocking you. You
could never tell what he was thinking. But I was beginning
to believe he might not be as evil as some in the village
made out. At least he could get the better of old Matilda.

I'd not expected him to stand up for me as he did: he'd
no cause to. There was a kindness in him, a gentleness
without him being nesh, for he certainly wasn't that. When

284

life treats a man hard from the day he's born, it turns most to bitterness and cruelty. They lash out first, afore someone hits them. But in some men it makes them kinder as if, feeling the sting of pain in their own souls, they want to shield others. Will was one of those, and you'd have to walk many a mile to find another. I never thought I'd say so, but that morning I felt safer setting out with him alongside.

I tugged the two widgebeasts forward. They were used to going up the moor track and stubbornly kept trying to turn in that direction. Harold, walking ahead of all of us, hunched his shoulders till they were almost touching his ears and stepped out a little quicker, as if he hoped to leave all of us behind. He was the only one of us five who'd not wanted to come. The old witch Matilda had forced him to, telling him it was his duty and, glaring at the dwarf, that we needed 'some sort of a man' to protect us. She said if we did find Janiveer, we'd need someone who knew the words that could defeat a witch's malice. Harold had turned as pale as if he'd been ordered to stop a charging boar by hauling on its tail and started to babble about how he had to stay and bury the dead. But it did him no good, poor lad.

What I couldn't fathom was why Matilda insisted on coming. Katharine, I could understand. She was grateful for any excuse to leave. The other women had treated her worse than a murderer. They'd not speak a single word to her, driving her away from the weir whenever she tried to pick fish. Even when she was trying to make amends by saying she'd come with me to find Janiveer, some had jeered that she shouldn't bother coming back.

But Matilda? Bald John looked as if a jellyfish had jumped up and poked him in the eye when she announced she was coming.

'What if your husband's ship returns while you're gone?' Cecily said. 'I wouldn't leave any man of mine alone in this village with a slut like Aldith prowling the streets, especially when he'd been months at sea.' She threw such a furious look at her own husband, it would have felled an oak tree. 'It's that sister-in-law of yours you want to be taking on this goose-brained journey, Sara. Get her away from decent women's menfolk.'

They all thought the trip was a foolish notion.

'Might as well put a worm on a line and fish for red herring,' Old Abel said.

Deep down, I knew it, too. I'd not planned to go looking for the woman from the sea. I don't know what made me say it, but when I saw how many faces were missing from that square, how exhausted the women were, I felt as helpless as that goat of mine shut up in the byre watching me walk towards her with the knife. Even so, I don't think I'd have gone, if Bald John hadn't riled me so. *Won't allow it*, indeed!

Maybe Janiveer was the excuse I needed to go searching for my sons. I'd been to every place I thought they might be hiding near the village, every den they'd built under the trees, every secret cave. Chillern always believe they're first to find a hiding place, only to discover when they're grown that their fathers once played there when they were boys. Always I went looking with that mixture of hope and dread, hope that I'd find them, dread that I'd find them too late. But now I was sure they'd wandered much further than anywhere they'd been before, whether alone or together, I didn't know.

I'd never been right out of the village, save for a short way into the edge of the forest to collect herbs or wood or fodder for the goats. I'd not even trudged up on to the moors like Elis. 'Twas him who'd fetched anything we needed from Porlock or the other villages. What cause did I have to go anywhere, and what time was there for such journeys when beans wanted hoeing, goats milking and pottage cooking? That morning we set out my belly was churning, and not just from the flux.

It was cool under the trees, and a relief to be away from the stench of the grave. As long as we stayed on the fringe of the forest, following the path I knew, I felt almost peaceful. The path was lined with hart's tongues waving in the sea breeze, as if they were lapping up the air. The branches of the trees, shaggy with leaves, nodded in the wind, sending sunlight and shadows darting across the ground, like shoals of little fish. Long strands of silver-grey lichen and ferns, like tiny forests themselves, hung down from twisted trunks, and hillocks of pea-green moss covered the roots.

But as the path led us deeper in among the trees, further than I had ventured before, I became uneasy. It was darker here: the trees grew closer together. I kept thinking there were evil little faces peering out from holes in the banks. I'd glimpse a flash of movement as if spiteful eyes had been staring down at me and had whisked out of sight, as I turned. I felt trapped among all those trunks, only able to snatch glimpses of the sky between the branches or a flash of blue sea far below. You can't see what danger you're walking into in a forest, not like on the shore, and you can't see what's stalking you from behind. If I'd been alone, I'd have picked up my skirts and run back to the village. But I couldn't shame myself in front of young Harold: he looked more afeared than me.

'You're not reckoning to climb up there, are you?' Will

said, frowning, as we came to a halt on the bank of a rocky stream bed.

It was odd to see someone frown and grin at the same time. Him pulling his queer face into such shapes almost made me laugh, in spite of myself.

A scratch of a track led up the side of the stream towards the top of the steep hill, but it was hard to say if it was a way for travellers or just a trail that animals had made. There was no sign of the path we'd been following continuing on the opposite bank. If there was one, it was covered with last year's leaves and the summer's under-growth, which had sprung up wherever a shaft of light pierced the dense canopy above. The two widgebeasts, strung one behind the other, immediately started to nibble the grass.

I stared upwards. 'By the look of it, that path goes right over the top of the hill to the moors. Takes us too high up. My Elis said Kitnor was down in a valley, hidden till you're right on it. He used to point to the kites flying way off above the forest, reckoned they always circled over Kitnor.' I glanced up. But if there were any kites flying, we couldn't see them for the trees.

'I heard it can vanish,' Harold said. 'The sorcerers who lived there put the whole village under a spell so no strangers could find their way in or out. There's no path. Proves it doesn't want to be found. We may as well turn back,' he added hopefully.

'Porlock Weir vanishes whenever a sea fret rolls in,' I said. 'No mystery in that.'

'Haven't any of you been there?' Will asked impatiently. 'It's only the next village along.'

Matilda gestured to the tangle of twisted trees and ferns

ahead. 'Does it *look* as if anyone goes that way? I tell you there's nothing there but ruins.'

'There's ghosts,' Harold said. 'Ghosts of the madmen and sorcerers who were banished there long ago, and perished there too.'

'You are in Holy Orders,' Matilda snapped. 'Such spirits should hold no fears for you.'

Harold, scowling, muttered something none of us could quite catch, but I'm sure it wasn't a prayer.

Will sat on the bank and eased himself down on to the dry stones of the riverbed. He cupped his hands in the thread of water that still trickled through the pebbles in the centre. He slurped the water and rubbed his wet hands over his beard and face. Then something on the far bank seemed to capture his attention. He cocked his head to one side, like a puzzled hound, stood up, then crouched again, before scrambling over the far bank and heading towards one of the moss-covered hillocks beneath the trees.

He peered at it, then glanced back at us. 'Someone's been this way. Look at this!'

'I see nothing except mossy boulders,' Matilda said.

'I didn't see it either till I was crouched low. Then that shaft of light picks it out. It's an ancient marker. I'd wager a kestrel that if there ever was an old track to Kitnor this is it.'

'Do you expect us to go traipsing through trees and undergrowth?' Matilda snapped. 'Those trees could hide anything. We could plunge to our deaths in a ravine or walk straight into a pack of wild boar. We should take the path that runs up the hill alongside the stream.'

'That's nothing but a goat trail,' Katharine said. 'Like Sara says, it more than likely leads up to the moors. I think we should take whichever path Sara wants to follow.' She gave a defiant little tilt of her chin, then glanced at me with a timid smile.

Seeing Matilda bridling like an indignant hen, I snatched up the leading rein of the widgebeasts and tugged them towards the parched riverbed. I wasn't going to be told which way to walk by that bitterweed.

The banks were not steep, and the horses scrambled up the other side more easily than the dwarf had done. The others followed, even Matilda, though she was still grumbling. Pity, I'd hoped she might refuse and take herself home. We all crowded round the dwarf. It wasn't until I got up close that I saw the mossy stone was different from the surrounding rocks. It was flatter, taller and sticking upright out of the clump of ferns. But near the top someone had rubbed away the old moss to reveal a deep carving beneath. It was a simple thing – a circle with a cross over it. Two arms of the cross were longer than the others, one pointing straight down into the ground, like the cross on the chapel in Porlock Weir, the other sticking out over the edge of the circle, pointing directly away from the stream.

Katharine reached out, but drew her hand back before she touched it. 'My granddam had a holed stone with that sign carved on it. The sun, she said it was. Always hung over the door in her cottage to keep evil from entering. On her stone all the arms of the cross were the same length.'

'But it shows someone passed this way in the last few weeks,' Will said. 'I wouldn't have seen the sign if they hadn't rubbed the moss off it. They must have been searching for it.'

Katharine walked around the stone, peering warily as if it was a new grave. Then she suddenly bobbed down behind

290

it. 'Maybe whoever was here came to meet her lover.' She held out a withered garland of sweet briar. The roses were brown and most of the leaves had crumbled away, but the thorns still clung, sharp as ever. Thorns never fall.

At the sight of it, Will let out a startled cry, as if he'd been pricked, though the briar hadn't touched him. He scuttled round to the back of the stone, searching the ground.

'That mean something to you?' I asked.

He straightened up, shaking his misshapen head. 'No, not a thing, nothing. Why should it? Some foolish maid, prancing around, must have dropped it.' He stared again at the withered garland in Katharine's hand. 'Still, it proves one thing. Someone's been this way.'

We tried to make our way round the side of the steep hill, but without a path it was slow work. Brambles tore at our clothes, and branches scratched our faces. In places we were forced to trample a path through waist-high ferns and scramble over fallen mossy tree trunks. After what felt like hours of tripping over gnarled tree roots, stumbling over loose stones and falling headlong into holes hidden by drifts of leaves, I was beginning to think Harold was right, that Kitnor was under a sorcerer's spell and trying every trick it could to stop us finding it.

I fell and tripped more than most, for I couldn't help staring around, searching for any sign of my boys. Had they come this way? Had they left that garland? I couldn't imagine either of them making it, but still I searched for a scrap of torn clothing, the remains of a fire, a snare, anything that might give me hope. Far below I caught glimpses of the dazzle of sunlight glinting on waves. They'd more than likely make for an isolated cove to hide. Luke and Hob would know how to find food on the shore. But if there was a beach beneath us, it was hidden by the curve of the hill. Could they be down there, not knowing I was passing so close to them?

The leading widgebeast stopped abruptly, jerking its head and nearly snatching the rope from my hand. The ears of both animals were pricked and their lips curled back as if they were tasting the air. I glanced around uneasily. Something was vexing them, but I could hear nothing except the high-pitched mewing of a kite circling somewhere out of sight and the hissing of the sea far below.

'What's wrong with those creatures?' Matilda snapped. 'Are we to stand here all day?'

'I reckon they can smell water,' Katharine said.

She stared around, then pointed to a rock face deeper among the trees. It glistened, and at its foot, a patch of ferns and dark green moss showed where the ground was wet. Harold scrambled up the hill towards the rock and tried to cup the ooze running down it in his hands, but when that yielded little he pressed his face to the rock and slurped the water. He drew back, wiping his mouth, then stared at the ground. He gave a low whistle. 'What kind of beast made that?' Looking thoroughly alarmed, he stumbled back towards us, his eyes ranging around in every direction as if he expected some monster to spring out of the bushes or hurl itself down on him from the trees.

The dwarf waddled towards him. 'What is it, lad? What did you see?'

'A paw print.' Harold gestured towards the rock. 'In the wet ground over there.'

'What kind of print, you foolish boy?' Matilda asked,

though she, too, was staring anxiously around. 'A fox, a wildcat?'

Harold shook his head. 'Bigger, much bigger.' He held out his hands till the gap between them was the width of his own head.

Matilda clucked in exasperation. 'Men are incapable of answering a simple question without exaggerating, though a lad in Holy Orders should have learned to speak the truth by now. I dare say it was nothing more than a squirrel or a stoat. Sara, I have no wish to spend the night sleeping under the trees, so will you please make those horses of yours move, before Harold starts whimpering that the kite screeching above us is a monstrous griffin?'

It took Katharine switching them from behind and me dragging on the rope to make the horses move, though once we were safely past the rock they became calm again and followed me docilely enough. Ahead, I could see Harold creeping along as if he feared attack at any moment, jumping at the slightest sound, from the crack of a broken twig to a rustle in the trees above. Whatever he had seen had really alarmed him and his fear made my belly churn, too, not for myself, but for Luke and Hob. If there was some great beast prowling through the forest, a small boy would be easy prey.

We found ourselves turning inland round the curve of the hill into a deep gorge, its floor hidden by a thick mass of twisted trees, as if a pit of writhing snakes had been frozen by some spell.

'Down there!' Will called, stopping so suddenly that Harold almost pitched headfirst over him.

We all stared down to where the dwarf pointed through the canopy of trees. On a long narrow shelf, squeezed between the steep hills that rose sharply on three sides, a cluster of ruins was scattered around a slightly taller building, which, from its cross and the cock on the sagging roof, I took to be a chapel, though it was even smaller than our own. Here and there sunlight glinted off a stream that ran down the side of the narrow valley, almost hidden beneath a dense covering of reeds and bushes.

Above the desolate grey ruins, four or five scavenging kites circled high in the blinding blue-white sky, the sunlight turning their feathers to flame as they spiralled higher and higher, without so much as a beat of their wings. Nothing else stirred, save the leaves on the twisted branches.

'Only ghosts down there,' Harold whispered.

'Then clearly Janiveer is not here,' Matilda said. 'We should retrace our steps and take the path by the stream, as I advised from the beginning.'

'Mistress Matilda walks on the sand, but sees no foot-prints behind her,' the dwarf sang out. 'Tell me, fair mistress, how can such a thing be?'

Harold gave a nervous giggle.

Will made a great flourish of a bow. 'Because Mistress Matilda is walking backwards.'

Harold and I both laughed and even Katharine smiled.

'Stop babbling nonsense,' Matilda snapped.

'Ah, but you see I must, mistress, for I am a fool, but not so foolish as to try to find someone who is ahead of us by wasting time going back. If that stone marked a path that once led to the village, perhaps there is a track going out of it.' Without another word, the dwarf waddled a few paces round the bend of the hill and vanished.

With a whistling scream, one of the kites dived, catching a rock dove on the wing as it foolishly emerged from the

294

roof of the chapel ruins. It flapped upwards with its prey, plunging its sharp beak into the downy breast and tearing at the dove's flesh as it flew.

Katharine stared down at the forbidding grey ruins. 'They say if the living wander into a nest of vengeful ghosts, the ghosts keep them trapped there till they become of them. They can't ever find their way out, for the path keeps leading them back.'

I didn't trust myself to speak. I knew if I stopped to think, if I even hesitated, I'd turn back. I grasped the rein more tightly and dragged the two widgebeasts forward, into the village of ghosts.

Chapter 38

Will

Riddle me this: If you say my name, I vanish.

'Be off with ye!' a man's voice screeched. 'Mine, this is all mine.'

Katharine almost fell headlong over a heap of rubble in her haste to scramble through the briars and weeds to reach Sara and cowered behind her as if she was a child clinging to her mother's skirts. I stared about, trying to find the owner of the voice, but there was no sign of any living person among the ruins of the village.

All that remained of Kitnor was a scatter of half-ruined circular stone dwellings, shaped like large bee skeps. They clung to the steep sides of the hills, and ranged down the narrow sloping shelf that hung over the lower valley, keeping their distance from each other, as if those who had once occupied them were deeply suspicious of their neighbours.

Trees had grown up between the ruins. Saplings butted through the domed roofs. Poison-green ferns snaked out of the window slits, and brambles slithered over the rough stone walls. Peas that had once, no doubt, been carefully tended, had turned feral, their tendrils twisting around the throats of golden buttercups and throttling the white cow parsley. The tiny church stood apart, like a condemned heretic, while the green flames of ivy licked up its sides, trying to pull it down into dust and ashes.

It was a lonely place, all right, hidden from land and sea, as if it was a lost island set adrift from the world. A dozen kings might rise and fall and no one who lived in that place would have known of it. I tell you, if any banished to Kitnor had been sane when they'd gone there, they'd be as mad as the dog star before the year was out. And a man might drag out his existence there for centuries: even the angel of death would forget where to find him.

I caught a glimpse of movement in the small casement of the church and edged towards the door. A squirrel darted out of the window, scrambled over the sagging roof and vanished with an impudent flash of its rusty tail.

'Go away! Get!' the voice shrieked again.

There was a loud clatter, like the noise of a crow scarer. Then a figure appeared in the doorway of the church, half concealed in the shadows, save for a hand that was thrust out into the sunshine vigorously shaking a clapper made from two pieces of bone, such as lepers use to warn of their approach. From what little I could see, though, he did not appear to be wearing leper's garb and the skin of his hand was as brown as a beechnut, without any of the tell-tale white spots.

'I command you to depart, foul creatures,' he called, shaking the bones even harder.

'What can he see? Evil spirits?' Matilda demanded. She glanced anxiously behind her. 'Where's that wretched boy? If there are demons here, he should be defending us.'

'I think we are the foul creatures,' I said.

The look of indignation and outrage that crossed Matilda's sour face would have made me chuckle except that the figure in the doorway seemed to make up his mind that more was needed to drive us away than curses and rattles. He dropped the clapper and, howling, charged out of the church, brandishing a rusty pollax in both hands, swinging it wildly. All of us fled in different directions. I found my way blocked by the remains of a wall, which, try as I might, I couldn't scramble over. I heard a shriek of fear behind me and half turned to see Katharine crouching on the ground, her arms raised to shield her face. The hammer side of the pollax blade hung menacingly above her head, as the man shrieked at her to be gone. But Katharine seemed unable to move. The man's howls were growing ever more maniacal and the lethal iron swung closer and closer to her bent head.

Even had I not fallen into the hands of the dwarf-maker and had been allowed to grow to my natural stature, I doubt I would have been the kind of man gallantly to charge to the aid of any maiden, fair or otherwise. But I could see that if the stupid woman simply remained cringing on the ground, the madman would crack her skull, like a walnut. Taking a deep breath, I lolloped towards the pair of them, prancing, grimacing and jabbering, as if I was twice as moon-crazed as the man himself, while taking care to stay out of reach of the murderous weapon.

He stared at me, his jaw hanging slack, but the pollax was still hovering perilously over Katharine's head.

'Move, mistress,' I whispered, as I cavorted back and forth in front of him. 'Crawl away, as fast as you can, then get up and run.'

I danced away from them, hoping to distract the mad hermit, but though he turned his head, like a dog, to watch me, Katharine remained crouching on the ground, whimpering with fear.

I pranced a little closer and sang out, 'Pray tell me, my lord, if a black boar wallows in the mud, but has not a bristle to its back, what should we call it?'

He frowned, his head tilted to one side, repeating the riddle to himself, then a grin split his face. ''Tis a dung beetle, that's what it is.' His eyes suddenly narrowed. 'Who told you about me? Who told you what I know?'

I bowed low. 'Why, everyone, my lord. Word of your great wisdom and knowledge spreads far and wide.'

It's a dwarf's stock answer, that one. Flattery diverts a man more swiftly and easily than a horse may be turned aside by a tug on the reins. A dwarf doesn't survive long in this world if he doesn't learn that lesson. And I was relieved to see the pollax sink down to the man's side, where it swung loosely from one hand. But Katharine was still trembling on the ground, her eyes tight shut, as if she thought the blow would fall at any moment.

'I crave an audience, my lord.' I beckoned to him, jerking my head in the hope of drawing him away from her.

He preened, like a cockerel, each time I addressed him as *my lord* and where was the harm in that? Believe me, there are lesser men who demand far higher titles, and that does sour the tongue.

He took a couple of paces away from Katharine, still gripping the weapon. He was dressed in layers of rags. It appeared that he'd never troubled to remove his threadbare old clothes, but simply added the latest garment he'd acquired on top. I could even glimpse another pair of shoes peeping through the holes in his boots. His black hair and beard had grown into one matted and shaggy fleece around his face, leaving only his hooked nose and a pair of deep-set eyes visible.

299

'You can't stay here,' he repeated, his gaze darting towards the others, who I guessed had withdrawn to a safe distance behind me. 'No room.'

Considering the village was deserted except for him, there would have been ample room for twice our number, but I didn't argue. I couldn't imagine any in our band had the slightest desire to stay for a gnat's breath longer than we had to.

His gaze flicked back to me. 'Maybe I'll let you stay. I need a new servant. Can you bark? Need a dog too.'

I was tempted to show him I could bite, never mind bark, but he was still swinging that pollax, and I was armed only with a knife.

'We seek your wisdom, my lord, nothing more. There was a woman came this way, a few days after the sun turned black and the great storm. Maybe she is still here.'

'No woman here. No one here but me.'

'But do you remember one passing through? Janiveer, she called herself. Foreign way of speaking.'

He seemed on the verge of saying no again, but hesitated. 'Maybe.'

'Where did she go? That way?' I pointed towards the coast in the opposite direction to Porlock Weir. 'Or up?' I gestured towards the moors high above.

His lips parted, showing a glimpse of jagged teeth, though it was impossible to see if he was smiling or grimacing beneath his beard.

'Want me to find her for ye, that it? That why you come?' He thrust his dirt-crusted palm towards me. 'Well, don't expect me to read for naught, do ye?'

'I've nothing—'

'Then you'll learn nothing. Get!' He swung the pollax

300

up in both hands again, as if he meant to drive us from the village.

I scrambled backwards as fast as my bandy legs would move. 'Wait, I . . .'

'Will he take this?' Sara was beside me. She was tugging at a bronze ring on her finger. Bending down, she pressed it into my hand.

'Your wedding band?'

She gave a curt nod. 'Was Elis's granddam's. She give it him afore she died, for when he took a wife.'

I tried to thrust it back at her, but she shook her head, clamping her naked hand beneath her armpit as if it might be tempted to grab back what she had stolen from it. 'Not a wife any more, am I? Meant to keep it, give it to Luke when he was of an age to wed, but what's the use if I can't find him?' She closed her fingers around my fist. 'You ask him, will you? Ask him if he can see where my boys are?'

'What's she given ye?' The crazed hermit was staring intently at my fist. He edged closer and Sara retreated. I opened my hand and he grunted in disgust.

'Gold's what I want.' But he snatched the ring anyway and gestured to a fallen stone. 'Wait there till I collect what I need.'

He ambled, head bent, through the weeds and rubble, using the handle of the pollax to hold brambles aside and as a stick to balance himself whenever he bent to pick something up. I thought he was collecting stones to cast, though the diviners that came to my lord's hall always brought theirs with them, unwrapping them as carefully as if they were the rarest jewels of the east instead of worthless pebbles. But it was all part of the diviners' mummery, and I can hardly criticise any man for making a spectacle of his craft,

301

for where would be the magic in my tricks if I gave them no flummery and flourish?

The hermit eased himself down opposite me and spread out his treasures. Not stones or bones, but dung – goat's shit, mice droppings, a human turd, one of his own, I assumed, deer dung and several others of assorted sizes, colours and stenches that I gladly confess I couldn't name. I'd collected any amount of worthless jetsam since I'd lived in the cave but even I hadn't hoarded shit. Pulling out the bone rattle again, he shook it vigorously over the dung piles. Then, closing his eyes, he rocked back and forth, humming tunelessly to himself.

The sun beat down on the stones and my head. The hum of bees and rasp of crickets filled the air. Beads of sweat trickled down my forehead. I wished I'd ignored the place to which he'd pointed and sat myself in the shade of the church walls instead. The rock on which I was perched had a particularly sharp point that was pressed into my arse and my leg kept twitching towards a thistle, whose prickles stabbed right through my breeches. But I knew diviners of old: if you so much as coughed they'd declare you'd driven off the spirits and they could see nothing more – any excuse to flounce off with your payment safely in their purse and you left with nothing to show for it. But Sara was watching us anxiously. She needed hope as badly as a drowning man needs a rope.

The hermit stopped swaying and leaned forward, peering at the piles of dung. Flies had found them and were crawling over them in drunken circles, clearly favouring the shit of some beasts over others.

'Cleverest creatures in the world, flies,' the hermit grunted. 'Not like ants. Ants scurry about from morn to

302

night, hefting great seeds and marching in lines, while flies idle their time away, eating nothing but the best. They dine off the very finest dishes in royal palaces, sip sweet wine from lords' goblets and steal kisses from the queen's lips while she sleeps.'

'And with all those riches on offer they choose dung?'

'And what did ye choose, dwarf?' he said, gazing sharply at me. 'Flies may go wherever they fancy. Try stopping them.'

'And I suppose they tell you what they've seen,' I said tersely.

He flapped his hand, motioning me to silence as he peered at the stinking heaps of dung. 'You has to watch which beast they choose and how they move on it. See the way they crawl contrary over the brock's droppings.' His eyes darted back and forth as he watched the creatures buzzing between the mounds of shit, like goodwives at a fair wandering between the stalls.

Finally he straightened his back again, smoothing the layers of his rags, as if he was a bird preening its feathers. 'This Janiveer, the flies say she's come for the bones. Find the bones and you'll find her.'

'Whose bones?' I asked.

'Her bones, of course, else she'd not have come for them. I'm only the dung beetle, you're the dwarf, so ye riddle it.'

'Bones indeed!' Matilda said, behind me. 'What right has she, a foreigner, to any bones in these parts? Why are you even listening to such nonsense? I tell you, Janiveer has long gone and she won't be coming back.'

Sara, ignoring Matilda, moved a few paces closer. 'But my sons. Do you know where my sons are?'

'Flies know all. Flies are born in the deep slime and

quickened from carcasses of rotting beasts. They walk on the earth and ride in the air.'

'My boys . . .' Sara pleaded.

'Are not walking on the earth or riding in the air.'

'Not on the earth? . . . Then they're dead?' Sara let out a great howl of despair and slowly sank to the ground, her body quivering and jerking as if it was being pierced by a dozen arrows.

Dung Beetle eyed her curiously, then lumbered to his feet and vanished back inside the shadow of the ruined chapel. I cursed myself as seven kinds of fool for ever allowing the wretched man to speak. I'd wanted to give Sara hope, and all I'd done was extinguish any last spark she still possessed.

I squatted beside her. 'Come now, you'd not believe him, would you? He's a madman who talks to flies, and when have you last seen a fly with any sense? Crawl into a flagon then can't even remember how to get out again, though the opening's right above them.'

'He said they were not walking on the earth,' Sara said dully.

'You know us fools, always talking in riddles. *I can run, but never walk. I have a mouth, but cannot talk.*' I gestured to the stream that trickled down the side of the valley. 'So if they're not walking, they're running.' I caught a look of alarm on her face. 'I mean *riding*. Your two lads have probably found themselves a horse to carry them or hitched a ride on the back of a wagon.'

'I think,' Matilda said coldly, 'we've heard quite enough wisdom from fools this day.'

She pulled Sara to her feet. 'Come. I warned you from the beginning this was a ridiculous quest. This is an accursed

304

place and the sooner we leave it and return to our homes, the safer we shall be.'

'But what of Janiveer?' Katharine asked timidly. 'Aren't we going to—'

'Good question,' I said. 'We came here to find her. Nothing's changed. We still need to bring Janiveer back to lift the curse. Sara, do you want to go on?'

But Sara was staring sightlessly at the ground. I don't think she even heard what we were saying. She was numb with grief.

Matilda rounded on Katharine. 'You should be thankful you're not lying dead with an axe in your skull, Katharine. But if you insist on going to look for Janiveer, you're welcome to go off by yourself and try. I warn you though, that madman is certainly not the last you will run into, and there are men out there who will do far worse to a woman travelling alone than merely murder her.

'As for you, dwarf, haven't you already done enough damage by encouraging poor Sara to come on this fool's journey? You were all so sure that Janiveer would be here. Well, you've seen for yourselves she's not. She's miles away by now and she could have travelled in any direction from Kitnor. She came to Porlock Weir aboard a ship, so who's to say she hasn't found passage on another boat and set sail for wherever she was going before the shipwreck? You haven't garnered a single clue as to where to start looking for her, but if you want to wander around this forest for the rest of your life, dwarf, I, for one, would be delighted. You certainly won't hear me begging a thief and a freak to return to my village.'

Had the Holy Hag not uttered those last words, I might very well have offered to go on with Katharine to search for Janiveer, if only to make amends to Sara. But, though all the king's torturers working together couldn't have forced me to admit it, I knew that for once Matilda was right: we'd no idea where Janiveer had gone and if she had taken a boat, we had no hope of finding her. Besides, I certainly wasn't going to give the old hag the satisfaction of thinking she'd got rid of me from *her* village. I'd go back just to torment her.

Sara did not resist, but allowed Katharine and Matilda to guide her back towards the stepping stones across the stream, as if she no longer cared or even knew where they were leading her. She stumbled on blindly, not pausing to untangle the brambles that clawed at her skirts as she lumbered through them. The thorns lacerated her arms, but she seemed not to notice the smart of them or the flies that swarmed to the bloody scratches.

I've told stories of corpses who rise from their graves and walk among the living, but though they are fine tales to entertain a lord on a dark winter's night, I never believed in such things. But seeing that dead, sightless expression in Sara's eyes, I came close to believing that day.

Harold crept up behind me as we followed the women, staying tight on my heels as if he thought the mad hermit might suddenly reappear behind a rock or sitting astride one of the ruined walls. 'Bones?' he whispered. 'He said if we find Janiveer's bones, we'll find her. Well, course we will, 'cause they'll be in her body, so that makes not a whit of sense. Unless . . .' He jerked his chin towards Sara's back. 'Did he mean she's dead, like Luke and Hob?'

'These diviners talk more nonsense than a court of fools,' I barked, 'so they can always claim whatever they said came true.'

Yes, I know what you're thinking – I was the pot calling the pan burned-arse. But I was not in the most cheerful of humours. My thighbones felt as if they'd been wrenched out of their sockets from clambering through the forest and over that rubble. I was as hot and thirsty as a smoked herring, and if that wasn't enough to make any man sour, I knew that all I'd achieved was to lose Sara her precious ring, probably the only thing of any real value she had left. And for what? We were no closer to finding Janiveer or Sara's sons than we had been before we started.

Harold gave a little shriek, like a woman when a mouse has run up her leg. He was staring towards one of the ruined huts, almost the last at the edge of the village. An ancient tree grew close by a crumbling wall. I followed his gaze and thought I glimpsed something moving in the shadow between the tree and the hut. It was too tall for an animal – probably a beggar or another madman lurking there.

'Come on,' I urged Harold. 'I've had my fill of hermits for today.'

But Harold was still staring, shading his eyes against the glare of the sun. 'I think he's dead!'

'And still standing and moving, that would be a miracle,' I said tartly. 'You've been listening to too many tales of saints walking about with their own heads tucked under their arms.'

All the same, I edged closer, expecting whoever was hiding there to run off.

And it took me several moments to realise why he didn't. The man was dead all right, had been for some time, for the birds had long pecked out his eyes and torn lumps from the rotting flesh of his face. His hair and blood-soaked clothes, shredded by wind and sun, waved in the breeze. That must have been what I saw moving. But only then did I see why the dead man still stood. He'd been crucified to the tree with large iron nails through his wrists, fastening his arms behind him about the trunk. And two long iron spikes had been hammered through his shoulders impaling him to the wood. I don't know how long it takes a man to die of such savage wounds, but I prayed I would never find out.

A piercing scream rang out behind us, startling me so violently my heart almost stopped. Harold whipped round, feverishly crossing himself. Ahead of us on the track, Matilda, Katharine and even Sara clutched each other.

'What was that?' Harold whispered, pale as a moonstone in spite of the heat.

I flapped my hand skyward. 'Kites probably, or some prey they just killed,' I said airily, though I was as shaken as he looked.

'But it sounded human,' Harold said.

'So does a hare when a hawk swoops on it. Come on,' I urged. 'Let's at least get under the cool of the trees.'

The others hurried forward. But as I glanced uneasily behind me, I saw the hermit standing in the shadow of the church, watching me. He stood more upright than before and there was no sign of madness about him now. I shivered and hurried into the trees. Wherever that scream had come from, it was not the sky and it was not made by any beast – I would have wagered my cods on that. Nor had that poor devil crucified himself. Something told me that the hermit was not alone in Kitnor.

Chapter 39

Porlock Manor

One drop of poison infects a whole tun of wine.
Medieval Proverb

Lady Pavia was aware of the figure keeping pace with her on the other side of the hedge as she waddled down the path towards the herb garden, but she had no intention of stopping to converse. She had come outside with the intention of finding a quiet place where she could be alone, in the hope that an hour spent sitting among the fragrant lavender bushes and camomile might soothe her aching head and calm her. The young wards had been spitting and scratching at each other, like bad-tempered kittens, all morning, bored to distraction by their stitchwork, while Sir Harry, having failed in yet another attempt to smuggle his horse out past Master Wallace, was venting his ill-humour on Father Cuthbert, who was most certainly not turning the other cheek.

Lady Pavia wanted, no, she positively *demanded* peace and solitude, and she was in no mood to attend to servants grumbling about this spice running out or that scullion spoiling the meat or any of the hundred other petty grievances that were causing the trapped household to squabble and snarl at each other from morn to night. Let Wallace deal with them.

She eased herself down on to a wooden bench beneath a quince tree, which provided some dappled shade from the sun. The lavender bushes at either side of the seat hummed with the soothing buzz of furry bees. A scarlet butterfly alighted on her skirt. The four blue and black spots on its wings looked like four great eyes staring up at her. But Lady Pavia was in no mood to be examined by anything. Irritated, she flapped her hand at the impertinent little creature to drive it away, then closed her eyes. Heat and the sweet smell of lavender gently caressed her towards the edge of a comfortable doze. Her head flopped down on her many chins and she began to snore.

She jerked upright as a high-pitched wail severed her from sleep. Something was wriggling on the grass by her feet, but it took several moments before she could rouse herself sufficiently to recognise it as an infant. He was lying on his back on the grass, thrashing his clenched fists, his eyes screwed up against the sharp sunlight that flicked across his face whenever the leaves of the quince tree stirred. The outraged shrieks emanating from this small creature cut through Lady Pavia, like the squeals of pigs at slaughter time.

The stillroom maid slid out of the shadows and knelt beside the baby, catching his hands and pulling him up so that he was leaning against her thigh. His cries stopped at once and he stared around with evident interest.

'If you imagine I would be entertained by the sight of a baby, Rosa, then you are quite mistaken. Other women may melt at the sight of a drooling child, but I can assure you I have never done so, not even my own. I have no interest in them until they are old enough to hold a sensible conversation. Take the child back to wherever it came from and tell the other servants I am not to be disturbed.'

The maid, glancing about her to make certain they were alone, leaned forward, speaking softly and rapidly: 'Oswin is Lady Christina's son, Lady Pavia. And I dare not take him back to the stillroom. His life is in danger.'

If Lady Pavia had been told just one of those facts, she might have grasped the import of it at once, but even though her wits were sharp, it was a moment or two before all the threads untangled in her head.

'Lady Christina's . . .'

She studied the baby. While she had never breastfed any of her own sons, she had considered it her duty as a wife to see to it that her husband's heirs thrived, and had therefore duly inspected her offspring daily, just as she had the household accounts, to ensure that there were no irregularities. And having successfully reared five sons, she considered herself as good a judge of an infant's age as her husband had been of the age of a horse.

'What nonsense is this, Rosa? This child is plainly three, four months old. The Lady Christina was married only ten months ago, not even that . . .'

She suddenly saw what she had been missing. Of course! Hiding the girl away down in this remote manor, pretending she was sick when she was clearly in the rudest of health. But there had been a certain look about her, the new maturity to her figure that only comes with childbirth.

But why hide it? There was no cause for shame for a betrothed woman being got with child by her future husband before the wedding night. Some might even say it was desirable, for there was nothing more inconvenient for a man

311

to discover, too late, that he had tied himself to a woman who could not give him sons. Unless . . .

She glanced sharply at Rosa. 'You said his life was in danger. From whom? Who is it who wishes to harm this child?'

Lady Pavia perched awkwardly on the narrow bench in the stillroom. Her ankles, never slender, were heavily swollen in the heat and the skin of her calves felt tight. But her decision to sit came more from a determination not to be seen to sway or, God forbid, faint. Although the chamber was slightly cooler than the courtyard outside, the darkness and dustiness felt suffocating.

A burst of sunlight drenched the feeble flame of the single candle burning on the table as the steward flung open the door. He stood in the doorway, panting slightly. Damp patches stained the front and sides of his shirt, and his face dripped with perspiration. In spite of the heavy perfume from the bunches of dried thyme, rosemary, honeysuckle and other herbs that dangled above Lady Pavia's head, a powerful stench of raw onion, wild garlic and sour sweat assailed her senses. But being the woman of steel that she was, she did not betray her distaste by so much as the flicker of an eyelid.

'Close the door, Master Wallace.'

When he hesitated, she added, 'The tongues of servants are made of very loose leather. I will not give them cause to flap.'

Wallace scowled, but kicked the door shut. He took several paces towards her as if he was determined to press his stench upon her.

'Eda, the elderly maid who waits upon Lady Christina, you know her well?'

Wallace shrugged, cocking his head suspiciously to one

side as if unwilling to commit himself for fear he was being accused of something.

'I wish you to ensure that Eda leaves the manor this evening, but quietly, unobserved by anyone else. While everyone else is in the great hall occupied with dinner, find some excuse to draw her outside, then take her swiftly to the gates and put her out.'

Wallace snorted indignantly. 'Can't do that, Lady Pavia. Gates are sealed. Sir Nigel's orders. You heard me tell Sir Harry he couldn't go roaming about. I'll certainly not allow a mere tiring maid to flout Sir Nigel's orders.'

'Your orders were not to let any *in* who might return carrying the contagion, but Eda will not be returning to the manor. She is dismissed.'

'Dismissed!' Wallace echoed. Lady Pavia could not read his expression in the darkened room, but the light creeping under the door and through the cracks in the shutters was sufficient for her to see the man's body stiffen.

'She's a sour crab right enough, and I'd be the first to admit there's neither of us would waste a kind word on each other, but she's an old woman. Whatever she's done can't be so terrible as to warrant sending her to her death. 'Cause that's what you'll be doing if you drive her out there. If the pestilence doesn't take her, she'll end her days starving as a beggar in a ditch, for I doubt she's kin to take care of her.'

Lady Pavia lowered her voice still further. 'What she has done, Master Wallace, is attempt to murder a child. Mercifully she was prevented, but I do not doubt that she will try again if she remains here.'

'God's blood!' Wallace crossed himself. He shook his head in disbelief. 'Her? She's a tongue as bitter as bull's gall, but she'd not have the stomach to wring a chicken's neck, never mind harm a babe. Begging your pardon, m'lady, but are you sure you got this right?'

'I am told she tried to smother him and almost succeeded, for he had already stopped breathing. If someone had not arrived just in time to pull Eda away, and if they had not been able to revive the child, Father Cuthbert would be burying him even now.'

Though she calmly uttered these words, Lady Pavia reminded herself that Father Cuthbert might well have refused even this small mercy, for Oswin was not baptised and was likely to remain in that perilous state until Christina could be persuaded to tell the truth. But that was something she would have to deal with later.

Thankfully, it did not seem to occur to Wallace to ask which of several children belonging to servants within the manor Eda had tried to murder.

'A woman . . . killing a child. 'Tis against all nature,' he spluttered. 'Evil . . . downright wicked. To think I've sheltered such a witch . . . She must hang!'

He drew himself up, standing braced with his feet apart and his chest thrust out. 'As steward of this manor it is my duty to see her brought to trial. Father Cuthbert can administer the oaths and Sir Harry may sit as judge in Sir Nigel's place, put questions to the witness and such like. It'll all be done fair and legal, m'lady. You can be assured of that. And when it is done, I'll tie the noose myself, that I will.'

Lady Pavia was on the verge of rising, not least because her ample buttocks had gone numb on the hard wooden bench, but she made herself remain seated. If she stood, Wallace would have the advantage of height, but as long as she remained seated and he was forced to stand before her, he would be reminded that she was his master's kin.

'There will be no trial, Master Wallace. You said yourself she is an old woman who has given years of faithful service. Likely her poor wits have been turned by fear of the Great Mortality. I have heard of fathers slaying their children with their own hands, believing a swift end is more merciful than leaving them to starve or die alone in agony when they are gone. It may be that Eda thought she was doing the child a kindness. God shall be her judge, not you or I, Master Wallace. If she dies of pestilence out there then that is His judgment on her, and if she is spared to do penance, then that also.'

Lady Pavia spoke as firmly as she could. She dared not risk a trial. That malicious old woman would delight in spitting out to the whole manor that Oswin was Christina's child and that he was a bastard, whether it was proved or not. Lady Pavia knew that it mattered not one jot if Christina was as pure as the Virgin Mary, the tiniest seed of doubt, once sown, would grow into a tree in which every pecking crow in the land would take roost. The girl would lose everything, for a man like Randel, who was just beginning to rise in the Black Prince's favour, would crash to earth like a stone if those at court began whispering he was a cuckold raising another man's son.

Wallace shook his head fiercely. 'But there must be a trial. If Sir Nigel hears I let a murderer walk free out of those gates, he'd like as not have me hanged as the accomplice. 'Sides, if Eda's wits have addled, she might easily harm another child out there, and suppose there's no one around to stop her next time. She might murder a dozen afore any discovered who'd done it, and I couldn't have that on my conscience.'

'It will be on *my* conscience,' Lady Pavia said firmly, 'not yours. And I will explain *my* decision to my cousin. You have only just succeeded in making the servants feel they are safe in here. How do you think they will react if they learn you locked them in with a murderer? What confidence will they or any of Sir Nigel's guests have in you then, Master Wallace?'

He blustered and protested, but when he finally walked out into the hot afternoon, Lady Pavia knew he was won over. She eased herself from the bench and crossed to the doorway. Shielding her eyes, she peered up at the sun dipping behind the tops of the trees. Another hour before dinner. She only hoped Wallace could remove the old woman before she or anyone else realised what was happening.

She felt a slight twinge of conscience. Eda had doubtless thought she was doing what Christina's mother would have wanted, and if the child really was a bastard, maybe she was right. A man may sire as many by-blows as he pleases and receive nothing but admiration for his prowess, but a girl of noble birth may not give birth to them. Her life would be ruined.

Lady Pavia plucked at a sprig of rue hanging from the rafters just inside the door. She rubbed the drying leaves between her fingers and sniffed. The pungent bitter smell helped to clear her thoughts.

As soon as Eda was safely away from the manor she would have to take Christina aside and prise out of her exactly when Randel had first bedded her. If, God grant, he had consummated the union before he left for France, she would write a carefully worded and flattering letter to him with the glad tidings that he had a healthy son and heir, and dispatch it to him the moment Sir Nigel's messengers were free to travel.

Lady Pavia found herself offering up a silent prayer to the Blessed Virgin that Randel had taken Christina to his bed while they were still betrothed for then he would need no persuasion to acknowledge the boy as his. If it transpired that the pair had waited until their wedding night, it would be harder to manage, but by no means impossible.

She plucked at her lower lip. There was the question of the servants' wagging tongues, of course. But Christina and Randel had been married far from here at Chalgrave. No one from Porlock had been present and she doubted there had even been talk of it in this remote manor, for few had ever laid eyes on Sir Nigel, much less heard of his niece. The servants here would certainly not know and would not presume to ask, when the Lady Christina had first lain with her husband.

Lady Pavia gazed thoughtfully at the empty cradle. If she believed they could convince Randel the child was his, she would let it be known that Christina's baby had been sent away to be cared for by a wet-nurse while she was sick. Nothing could be more natural, and with the poor girl stricken with melancholy, she had not been able to bear any mention of her child. But now that Christina was recovered, her beloved son would be brought back to the manor to be reunited with her, just as soon as the gates were unsealed. Rosa had assured her that Eda had kept the child well away from the inquisitive eyes of the servants, so they were unlikely to recognise him, especially when he was presented in a sumptuous new gown and coif.

And when the gates were reopened, Rosa could spread the rumour that the motherless babe Eda had abandoned in the stillroom had been claimed by his drover father or else had been delivered to a monastery to be

317

raised by the monks. Lady Pavia nodded to herself. Yes, with Rosa's help it could all be managed satisfactorily without arousing any suspicions, but only if the marriage had been consummated.

If it had not – Lady Pavia shuddered at the thought – then Randel must never hear so much as a whisper about the baby. Few men in his position would forgive betrayal, especially by a woman, and Randel was most certainly not one of them. Lady Pavia had more than once observed how violently his temper flared at the slightest offence, real or imagined, which had been offered to him. He was a man who could plan revenge with exquisite cruelty. Lady Pavia was no fool. She would pray for the best, but she knew that often in life such prayers went unanswered. Christina's baby might yet have to be disposed of, one way or another. And, if she had to, she was resolved that she would do it – better that than expose mother and child to Randel's less-than-tender mercies. But all her schemes would come to nothing unless Eda was silenced.

A flash of red caught her eye as she stepped out of the doorway. It was one of the butterflies with the blue eyes on its wings that had been flying about the lavender. It had been impaled on the wooden doorframe of the stillroom by a silver pin, which had been stabbed through its body. Its stretched-out wings fluttered gently in the soft breeze, as if the butterfly hadn't yet realised it was dead.

Chapter 40

Matilda

A sweet-smelling liquid, known as the Manna of St Nicholas or myrrh, oozes from the bones of St Nicholas, which are entombed in St Nicholas's Basilica in Bari. Vials of this manna are much prized for, when it is drunk, it cures all maladies.

The fire started at night. The flames ran along the edge of the reed thatch, then clawed upwards over the tinder-dry roof, snakes of orange and scarlet twisting through the smoke into the starry sky. At first, no one in the village realised the cottage was on fire. We were all asleep in our own beds, our shutters and doors tightly shut. Only when Sara and Goda ran outside screaming were we roused. We all hurried up the rise as soon as we saw the bright orange glow in the darkness over the cottage, but there was nothing we could do to quench the fire, for the spring was dry and the cottage too far from the shore to haul seawater uphill. Yelling to each other above the roar and crackle of the flames, we raked the burning thatch to the ground, and beat out the flames with spades to try to save the walls at least.

Fortunately, Sara's cottage was far from the others in the village, so there was little danger of the fire spreading to other roofs as it would have done on the crowded quayside, but the dwarf creature was prancing about yelling that we must stop the sparks carrying to the forest, for if the trees caught alight, the whole hillside might be set ablaze. The women thrashed the thatch until their faces were black with smoke and sweat. We threw pails of dry earth from Sara's vegetable patch through the door on to those bits of furniture that were smouldering inside. Mercifully, she had no hay left in the byre to catch light.

Afterwards, when every spark had been extinguished, there was an eerie silence. Everyone was too exhausted to move and stood in the darkness staring up at the roofless cottage, with its charred timbers, the walls black with smoke, the door and shutters burned through. In the moonlight, the cottage looked like the ruins at Kitnor, as if it had been abandoned a hundred years ago. Even Sara and Goda were silent. No tears, nothing. Sara just stood there, arms wrapped tightly around her body, rocking back and forth.

'It's a mercy you didn't set the whole village aflame,' Isobel scolded. 'Everything is so dry. If my poor Cador had been alive, he'd have had you brought before the manor court for not damping down your hearth fire. You should be ashamed putting us all in harm's way like that, as if we don't have troubles enough.'

Naturally, I rallied to Sara's defence. 'She's lost her home,' I said. 'Isn't that punishment enough for her carelessness?'

'But I did damp it. I know I did. It was safe,' Sara protested feebly, though it was plain to hear from the muttering and whispering that no one believed her.

'Any of you taken a look at that thatch?' the dwarf asked.

Several people muttered furiously that of course they had looked – they'd been the ones to beat it out.

'Look again. The worst of the burning is down in this corner, and it's on the top of the thatch, not underneath. I reckon whatever spark set it alight came from outside the cottage, not from her hearth.'

Isobel gestured towards the mass of houses down in the darkness by the shore. 'Do you see the glow of a single fire burning there? Where would the spark have come from, if not from Sara's own hearth?'

The dwarf pointed through the doorway, which now stood black and empty, like the mouth of a cave. 'But see for yourselves, her fire's covered.'

'Naturally it is now,' I snapped. 'We've all been throwing earth inside for hours to keep it from smouldering. And we're all too tired to be standing around in the middle of the night listening to the babbling of a fool. I, for one, would like to return to my bed where I was so abruptly woken.'

I patted Sara firmly on the arm. 'My dear, you were exhausted after that ridiculous journey to Kitnor and you fell asleep with the fire still burning. We all understand that. If only you'd allowed yourself to be guided by older and wiser heads . . . but what's done is done. The walls still stand. Your cottage could be rethatched in time. At least it will give you something to work at, instead of wasting your time chasing after bones.'

Sara slowly turned her head and stared at me, her eyes glittering in her soot-blackened face. 'Bones? You know which bones that diviner meant, I know you do. I saw it in your face at Kitnor. But I'll find them and I'll find Janiveer. My boys may be dead, like that hermit said, but Janiveer can tell me where they lie. I'll see them buried properly, not like their father. I'm their mam. I brought them into this world and I'll find a way to protect my sons' bodies and souls from every demon in this realm and the next, even if it costs me my life. I'll not give up, Matilda. I'll find Janiveer. Whatever you do to try to stop me, I'll bring my chillern home.'

Sara allowed herself to be guided away by Aldith, who said she would take her into her own house, and that poor, simple woman, Goda, trailed after them. Everyone seemed to have forgotten that she and her child were now homeless too. But I lifted the baby from her weary arms and insisted she come to my own cottage, where she could rest comfortably.

'Aldith can't care for her own daughter,' I told her. 'She's never even troubled to clean the sand and slime from her cottage after the night of the storm. She just squats among the filth with that poor child of hers, like beasts in a stable. She's not blankets or bedding enough for herself, much less you, Goda. Your baby will die within days if you take her into that chill, damp place.'

I turned and began to walk back to my cottage, Goda's child cradled in my arms. I glanced back, expecting to see Goda following me. But she hadn't moved. She was just standing in her shift, staring at the backs of Aldith and Sara as they edged down the path in the darkness, as if she couldn't make up her mind who to follow. Then her child began to wail and, like a dog pulled back on its leash, she ran after me.

Chapter 41

And I heard a voice from Heaven, as the noise of many waters and as the voice of great thunder.

The Apocalypse of St John

The demons are clawing up out of the boiling pool below him, clambering up the bare rock face towards him. It is so dark that, at first, Luke thought his eyeballs would burst straining to peer through it, but now he sees shapes in the blackness, sees the creatures who are born of hell. Bright white sparks flash across the shaft, so fast he cannot mark their progress. They spin across his vision and are gone. Red streaks dart below him. Faces, with no bodies, float up towards him, their mouths twisted open as if they are screaming, but their lips make no sound. He knows them, he knows them all, but he cannot remember their names.

The waterfall roars in his ears, but he can still hear the creatures slithering towards him over the rocks. He can hear their hearts beating, a single beat, growing faster and louder, like the pulse of a drum. He hears the rasp of their breathing, their wet bodies, their leathery wings and long claws scraping over the stone.

Something touches his toe. He jerks his foot back, draws his knees up under his chin, wrapping his fish-cold arms around his legs. He whimpers in fear as something wet and rough brushes his skin. A mouth! It is creeping across his leg, trying to find a place to bite, to suck, to drag him down into the boiling maelstrom below. He slams his fist into it, but feels only the wet cloth of his sleeve. Is it gone? Was it ever there?

In his terror, he clambers to his feet, cringing against the wet rock. His feet are so numb, his legs so stiff from cramp and cold, he can barely stand. He shrinks as far back from the edge of the ledge as he can, covering his head with his arms as the phantasms ooze towards him, closer, closer.

Something moves above his head. He sees them now. They are hanging from the walls, like giant bats, staring down at him with their bulging eyes, skinless, bloody, waiting till he falls asleep. Then they will drop on him.

'Let me out! Don't let them take me!'

But he cannot make himself heard above the rushing water. Maybe there is no one out there to hear him. What if the demons have taken the others, drowned them, devoured them, and he is the only one left . . . left alone on this ledge, trapped in the darkness?

A voice roars out of the water, a torrent of words crash down on him: '"The beast which thou sawest was, and is not, and shall come up out of the bottomless pit and go into hell." Do you want to be saved from that beast, Luke? Do you want to be saved?'

Luke's jaw is rigid from fear and cold. He cannot open his mouth, and that sudden realisation frightens him more than the creatures that are slithering towards him. He can't breathe. He is choking.

The voice throbs in the air. 'Do you want to be saved, Luke?'

Yes, YES! He tries to force out the words, but his teeth are locked together. He cannot make himself heard.

'And who will save you?'

Luke tries to prise his jaws apart with his fingers, but they will not move. He cannot feel them. Maybe he has no fingers, no hands. The beast has swallowed them.

'Who will save you? Say it, Luke, only say the word and you will be saved.'

But the word will not be spoken. He falls to his knees, crashing on to the hard rock. He is crouching on all fours, whimpering like an animal. Then he is falling, falling down into darkness that is blacker even than death.

Chapter 42

Matilda

St Sebastian was shot full of arrows, but they did not kill him. The widow Irene nursed him back to health, and the saint upbraided the emperor Diocletian for his cruelties. The emperor ordered Sebastian to be beaten to death with cudgels and his body thrown into a sewer, but it was recovered by a woman called Lucina, who buried it in the catacombs where now the Basilica of St Sebastian stands.

Goda wiped her sweating brow and rocked back on her heels away from the heat of the hearth fire. Although the door and shutters were flung wide to catch any breeze from the sea, the cottage was still as hot as a baker's oven.

'Don't let the wax burn,' I warned her. 'That's the last of the oil of roses. This drought has withered all the blooms this year.'

Alarm flashed across her dull face and she seized the iron rod from which the pot was suspended, swivelling it away from the fire. Scrambling to her feet, she carried it to the table where the human vertebrae stood in a neat row, the wicks already in place. I had supervised her cleaning of each one, ensuring that she carefully scraped the old wax out of each

326

crevice with a sharp bone pick I had fashioned myself. At first, she had recoiled from even touching them, but I insisted. It is the only way with simple girls. You must be firm with them if they are to overcome their foolishness and learn.

'You would be glad to touch a saint's bones, wouldn't you?' She stared at them. 'Are these holy relics?'

'Relics, yes, you might call them that. Pour carefully now. Don't fill them to the top else the wax will spill over when the candles are lit.'

Her hand shook. She gripped the pot tighter.

'Clean the pot at once before the wax sets hard.'

I watched her step out into the blinding sunshine, and crouch down to scrub the pot with a few sprigs of knee holly. Behind me, the baby wailed, and she sprang up abandoning the dirty pot.

'I will tend the child,' I said. 'You will need to fetch water to rinse the pot.'

I never allowed her to take the baby with her when she left the house to fetch water. I knew if I had, she would simply have wandered off with her and neglected to return. The child always pulled her back.

I waited until her bare feet had padded over the rise, the two pails dangling from the yoke across her neck. Then I closed the door and, kneeling, drew a box from beneath my bed. Slowly, and with great reverence, I unwrapped the white linen, exposing the stiff, blackened hand I had taken from the chest in the chapel.

When that foul diviner spoke of bones, he had stared directly at me. He knew what I possessed and he wanted it. But it had been given into my care by God. I would protect it from them all, even from Father Cuthbert, who cared nothing for St Cadeyrn. No one cared for these saints as I did.

Even when I'd been a child in the nunnery, I'd been more devoted to their shrines than the nuns were. I loved to look up at their gentle smiles in the candlelight, to see them garlanded and dressed. On their feast days, a host of candles would be lit at their feet, the flames spreading in a sea of holy fire. I'd gaze up into their faces and their painted lips would part and smile in pleasure. I heard them whispering to me, telling me how they loved me because of my care of them. They were my friends, my only friends. And still now they protected me as fiercely as I guarded them. I would allow no one to desecrate my saints.

The clank of a pail outside jerked me from my thoughts. Goda was returning and only then did I realise the baby was howling. Its face was scarlet and wet with sweat and tears. I wrapped the hand hastily and had only just managed to push the box back under the bed when the door burst open and Goda rushed in, snatching up her daughter and pressing her so hard to her face that the baby screamed even louder. Goda was babbling nonsense and trying to calm the child, promising never to leave her again. She sank on to a stool, unlaced the front of her gown, dragged out a long skinny breast and rubbed her dark nipple across the baby's mouth. The little one's lips fastened greedily around it and her sobs subsided as she tugged on it, gripping Goda's dug with her fist, as a drunken sailor would grasp at the breasts of a tavern whore.

I reached for the soft pigskin bag that I wore always at my waist and pulled out the skull goblet, which I half filled from a small flagon of mead.

I offered the skull goblet to Goda. 'Here, drink this. Mead will help your milk to flow.'

She gazed at the polished cup, with its arm-bone stem

and scapula base, though I could see she did not recognise it for what it was.

'Drink,' I urged her. 'It is a special cup. A holy relic. It will keep you from harm and bring your beloved Jory close to you, so close you will imagine he has already returned to you and that you hold him in your arms.'

Goda smiled, her eyes unfocused as if she was already dreaming of her lover. She took the goblet from me and drank as greedily as her babe.

Chapter 43

And it was given him to give life to the image of the beast and that the image of the beast should speak.

The Apocalypse of St John

A blessed warmth swept over Luke, but almost at the same instant there was an explosion of pain as if knives had been stabbed into his limbs and twisted violently. He shrieked. Something was crawling over his legs, rasping the skin from his flesh. He tried to fling it off.

'Be still, boy.'

He felt a hand pressing hard on his forehead. He opened his eyes, moaning and jerking his limbs to ease the agony. He was lying in a small chamber on a heap of stinking sheep-skins. He was naked. The Prophet's pinch-faced wife, Uriel, was laying cloths soaked in hot water on his legs and body. As blood seeped back into his numb icy flesh, the pain flowed in with it. Her fingers were hard and hot. They burned his bare skin as she probed him, rubbed him, lifted his cock.

Outraged and shrivelling in humiliation, Luke tried to push her hand away, but she twisted his cock savagely, making him yelp.

'You wet yourself like a baby. You must be washed, boy, cleansed of all your filth. If you don't lie still, it will be my duty to tell the Prophet you have not yet learned obedience and you need another lesson, a sharper one this time.'

330

Luke swallowed hard. He didn't know if it was true that he had wet himself, but he couldn't go back into that shaft, he couldn't.

He didn't know how long it was before the pain began to give way to tingling and an unbearable itching of his swollen feet and hands that was almost worse than the cramp, but that, too, eventually subsided. Uriel thrust his shirt and breeches at him. They were still damp, but Luke said nothing as he clumsily dressed himself as rapidly as his fat fingers would allow. He would willingly have covered himself with ice-soaked rags, anything to hide himself from her.

Uriel turned her head, frowning. 'Up, boy, the Prophet is coming,' she announced.

Moments later, Luke heard Brother Praeco's boots slapping along the tunnel. His stomach lurched and he clambered shakily to his feet. Uriel shuffled a couple of paces to the edge of the chamber, hands folded and head bowed respectfully.

The Prophet ducked under the low archway. He seemed to fill the whole chamber as he stepped inside. He stood looking down at Luke for a long time before he spoke. Luke was murmuring a single prayer over and over in his head, more fervently than any saint: *Please don't let him send me back to the ledge! Don't let him send me back!*

'You must understand, Luke, the Lord tests all those He has chosen in the fire of His crucible. God does not choose rich and powerful men to deliver His Word, but the poor and the humble, like you and me. In my youth I was nothing more than a clerk in Holy Orders forced to record the droolings and deceit of bishops and prelates, whose wealthy families had bought them the means to rule over men who were far more worthy in intellect and faith than

331

they. But I studied the Blessed Word of God and I understood what those prelates in their blindness and corruption could not see.

'And God called me forth to be His prophet, to go out into the world and warn men of the terrors to come. He sent me to preach in the marketplaces and churches, to rebuke the rich and powerful. But I was tested in the fire. I was put in chains and left to starve in a bishop's dungeons, flogged like a common harlot in the marketplace. I was set in the stocks before a baying mob, pelted with filth, left there in the bitter wind and rain for days at a time so that I almost froze to death. But I did not falter in my preaching, however much they mocked and derided me. And God rewarded me for faithfulness for He revealed to me in a dream that I was to lead His Chosen Ones and bring them through the Day of Wrath into His glorious new kingdom. I had proved myself worthy of His trust by my suffering.'

The Prophet hooked his fingers under Luke's chin, tilting the boy's head back so that he was forced to look into those twin black pits. 'I see so much of myself as a boy in you. You could be my own son. But are you worthy to become one of His Chosen Ones, Luke? Are you willing to do without question whatever the Lord demands? Will you obey me as your father?'

With his head tilted back, the boy could barely swallow, much less talk, but the Prophet seemed to take his earnest gasp as a *yes*.

He released the boy's head, and smoothed his wet hair. 'Good, good,' he murmured. 'But words are easily spoken. Now we must put them to the test.'

Chapter 44

Porlock Manor

A calf should not play with an ox for it is outmatched in horns.

Medieval Proverb

Rosa walks barefoot across the brown grass. Even though each leaf and twig is crisp and dry, her feet make no sound. Her mother and aunts taught her to move noiselessly. They taught her how to mask her body scent with the smells of the earth and plants, so that she could sit within touching distance of a wild hare or fox, but those creatures are not her quarry now. He is.

Father Cuthbert stands by the manor's fish pool, staring dismally into what little water remains. It is black now, though it was as green and thick as pease pottage just a few days ago. The fish, gasping on the surface or floating belly up, have been dragged out. Those few that could be revived in pails of well water, now circle in tubs in the relative cool of the dairy. The rest were smoked or eaten, smothered beneath strong vinegar sauces masking the taste of flesh that was far from fresh.

Rosa glides towards the far side of the pond, loosening her thick dark hair and shaking it out across her shoulders.

The leaves on the tree above her tremble violently as if caught in a sudden gust of wind, though there is scarcely a breeze. She gives no sign that she has seen the priest, but unties the laces fastening her gown and pulls it off, then the linen shift beneath, arching her bare back as she draws the garment over her head. Only the bear tooth amulet dangles between her breasts. The sun glints on the silver-capped tip, transforming it into a bright star.

She knows he is watching her. On the very edge of her vision she sees his body half turn as if he would hurry away, but his head doesn't follow. She ambles towards the pond, and across the cracked baked mud towards the stagnant puddle in the centre, until she stands ankle-deep. She bends, scooping up handfuls of water and dashing them over her arms and legs. Even the drops of black water sparkle as long as they are in the sunlight and glitter on her bare skin until they run back to the earth and become darkness again.

The mud beneath her feet is slimy and slippery, as she'd known it would be. Another step, and then a fall, a splash, a sharp cry of pain. She does not rise, but sits, grasping her ankle. Father Cuthbert runs around the edge of the pool, and without pausing to remove his shoes, edges down to the water's edge.

'Are you hurt? Have you sprained your ankle?'

'It is jarred, nothing more,' she says, struggling to rise. She does not address him as *Father*. She does not want him to be reminded of his vows. Let his eye and groin remind him that he is a man, nothing more.

He offers his hand. Hers is cool in his sticky palm. Then, with only a moment's hesitation, his arm slips round her back, beneath her armpit and across her soft breast as he

334

lifts her and supports her as she hobbles back and sinks down on the withered grassy bank.

He has to release her then – he no longer has any pretext for holding her. But he runs both his hands down the muscles of her leg, checking, as he tells her, that the limb is not injured. He checks slowly, thoroughly. His voice has an odd high pitch to it.

He sits down next to her, staring at the dead pool, but his eyes steal secret glances at her breasts, her belly and her thighs, like a naughty child, afraid of being caught.

'It is filthy water to wash yourself in.'

'I had not remembered the pond has dried up. It was so hot. I longed to bathe and since we cannot go to the sea . . .'

He could walk away now. He could fetch her clothes to let her cover herself. But he does neither. Instead his hand creeps spider-like towards her thigh. She leans forward so that the bear's tooth necklace swings free from her damp skin. The glinting silver tip wrests his attention from the curve of her leg.

She smiles, twisting her body towards him and cupping the tooth in her hand, so that he can examine the carving on it. 'The snake and the bird. You know them, of course. The emblem of St Cadeyrn.'

'I do not venerate the saints of the Celtic Church. The Holy Catholic Church is the only true faith. Only she may lay claim to unbroken succession from St Peter.'

'I thought the chapel at Porlock Weir was dedicated to him.'

'It is dedicated to the Blessed St Olaf, King of Norway, who brought that country to Christ.' He glowers at the tooth and almost seems to forget that it hangs about the neck of a naked woman. 'You should wear a cross, not that heathen object. Now that the pestilence rages, death might strike at any time and that will not keep you from Satan's grasp.'

He reaches towards it as if he would tear it off, but instead his fingers linger over her skin.

She thrusts herself gently towards him, so that his grasping fingers flatten over her breast. 'But why do they say the chapel belongs to St Cadeyrn?' she murmurs. 'Is his symbol carved in there?'

He stares at the amulet, which dangles against the back of his hand, pinning his fingers to her flesh. 'There is a reliquary. It is valuable. It cannot simply be discarded,' he says irritably. 'If I could—'

But he is interrupted by a shout. 'What an edifying spectacle – the pious priest and his whore.'

Father Cuthbert jerks round, scrambling to his feet in undignified haste. Rosa does not move. Sir Harry is standing behind them, his face flushed and perspiring – his padded gypon is far too heavy for such a sweltering day. His hand is clenched tightly around the hilt of his long dagger in the sheath that dangles from his belt. Father Cuthbert's hand slides to his own knife.

'The maid slipped and fell while she was bathing. I was merely assisting her until she could stand again.'

'Bathing – in that?' Sir Harry sneers. 'I saw you. Pray tell me how exactly you assist a woman to stand by groping her breast.' He takes a pace towards Rosa, who still sits on the bank, legs drawn up. He grabs her by the hair, jerking her head back, but she makes no attempt to defend herself, though she could. Pulling his dagger from its sheath, he uses the point of the blade to hook the bear's claw necklace up in front of her face.

'This is what your holy swain is really interested in, Rosa, or

336

did you think it was you? Were you flattered that a priest should choose you over the pretty little creatures in the manor? He wants to know where King Cadeyrn's treasures are to be found, all the gold that was buried with him. That's what he wants from you and he's prepared to commit any sin to get it!'

'I know nothing of any treasure.' Father Cuthbert's face is pale with rage. 'I don't even believe Cadeyrn existed. It's a mere legend, a superstition for the gullible who would rather put their trust in pagan stories than in Christ.'

Sir Harry gives a slow, humourless laugh. 'And yet you have his reliquary hidden in your bag. How so, if the man is merely a fireside tale?'

'You searched my possessions!'

Father Cuthbert launches himself at Sir Harry, his knife in his hand. The suddenness of the attack catches the nobleman by surprise. Father Cuthbert strikes out wildly, his blade slashing across Sir Harry's chest. Woollen padding bursts from the tear in the velvet gypon. Sir Harry yells in outrage as if his guts have been spilled.

He tries to raise his own dagger, but the point is still hooked under the bear amulet hanging around Rosa's throat. She gasps as the necklace jerks against her neck. The string of blue beads snaps so suddenly that Sir Harry is thrown off balance. The knife lurches upwards, missing Father Cuthbert's nose by a hair. A shower of beads bounces on the baked earth. The priest lashes out to protect himself with a savage, but uncontrolled, blow. Where Father Cuthbert is aiming is hard to tell, but as Sir Harry twists to avoid the blade, he slips on the beads and the priest's knife catches his elbow. Carried by the force of his fall, the blade slices up his arm to his shoulder, ripping not only cloth this time, but flesh too. Blood gushes from the long wound.

337

Sir Harry lies gasping on the ground, clutching his arm, pressing the gash to staunch the flow. The bloody knife falls from Father Cuthbert's hand and he sinks to his knees, staring in horror at the wound he has inflicted. Rosa runs back to the pile of her clothes. Snatching up her shift, she rips the linen with her teeth, tearing a long strip from it. Pressing the rest of the garment to Sir Harry's arm, she ties it tightly in place with the strip. Father Cuthbert still kneels on the scorched grass, unable to move.

Rosa snatches up the bloody knife and, quicker than a cut-purse, conceals it beneath the heap of her gown. 'I will get rid of this, Father. You must go quickly to the water trough in the herb garden and wash the blood from your hand and sleeve. No one'll be there at this hour. Then return to the house. I'll take him to the stillroom and stitch the wound. It is only a flesh wound.'

'A flesh wound,' Sir Harry squeals. 'He nearly took my arm off. I'll see you dance on the gallows for this, priest!'

'You can move your fingers,' Rosa tells him. 'There is no lasting damage. The wound will heal well if you let me tend it. But it would be wise to say that you cut your arm in a fall. Sir Nigel and the Black Prince have fought valiantly in many great battles. They would despise any nobleman who couldn't defend himself against an untrained priest armed only with a knife.'

Sir Harry snatches his arm away from her, wincing at the pain. 'Don't think you'll escape unpunished, priest. You'll pay for this and pay dearly. I'll see to that myself. You too, woman. You're the cause of all this. You know where Cadeyrn's gold is hidden, and before I've finished, you'll be begging to tell me.'

Chapter 45

Will

Riddle me this: I saw a man who never was, who smiled and wept, and walked and talked, but uttered not a sound.

Saw another body float past my cave on the high tide, lying on his back, staring up at the dawn-pink sky, his face and hands blackened from the pestilence. His arms were moving gently up and down with the motion of the waves, as if he was simply enjoying a swim after a hard day's work. Maybe he'd been thrown off a ship or dumped in the sea further along the coast by villagers who'd hoped he'd wash up on someone else's beach. If he floated ashore, the women would just push him out again with long poles. They hadn't the strength to bury their own dead, let alone a stranger.

As soon as the tide receded I clambered down over the wet rocks and picked my way towards the cottages. I could hear Sara and Aldith yelling at each other from the other end of the beach. Sara was telling her to stop idling and find food or mind her daughter. Aldith, who no longer cared for anything, not even her own child, was shrieking back at Sara, taunting her for failing to find Janiveer.

Aldith had a point. The journey had been a waste of

time, but time was the only thing we had left to waste. We'd learned precious little except the mad hermit's prediction about Janiveer's bones, which I'll grant you sounded profound, but then so does a drunk jester and his words mean nothing either. I suspected the whole mummery had simply been a ruse to get rid of unwanted visitors to Kitnor, and if that had been all the harm it had done, it was no harm at all. But Sara had paid dearly, losing her ring and her hope that her sons were alive. And, if I was any judge, that journey had probably caused her to lose her cottage too.

The villagers stood by the notion that the blaze had been started by nothing more than a spark from the fire, not properly banked down for the night. Sara, they said, was half crazed with grief, and women like that forget to do the most basic things. Else she had fallen asleep before she could tend it, worn out by that foolish journey. But though Sara was grieving she had not fallen into the numb stupor that was gripping some of the other women in Porlock Weir. They just sat and stared at nothing for hours, not stirring even when they were shaken. No, Sara was more determined than ever to find Janiveer, for she had convinced herself that only she could tell her where to find the bodies of her sons. I knew the fire had not been started by her carelessness. I reckon someone had deliberately set the thatch alight from outside the cottage, and I had a shrewd idea who it was, though I had no proof and not a clue as to why.

A couple of women were picking their way across the wet sand towards the fish weirs. Once, only those who had the rights to the weirs could pick the fish, but no one cared about rights any more. Whoever got there first grabbed their fill, though there were fewer fish than before, for in several places the stones had fallen away and the ditches behind them were becoming ever shallower as the sand washed in. But even so, most of the women were reluctant to be the first to arrive for, as well as fish, the sea washed in things no one wanted to find.

I never wanted to see or smell another fish. Meat: that was what I craved. The Holy Hag had no piglets left to steal, so I'd been trying my hand at setting snares in the clearing at the edge of the forest. I'd not caught much so far. My old master had taught us many things, but setting snares was not a skill he'd ever imagined a jester would require. My catch so far had been a fox that had tried to savage me when I went to release it and a squirrel, which had been welcome enough, though there wasn't enough flesh on it to keep a pixie fed for a day, never mind a ravenous dwarf, but I had repositioned my snares and tried to convince myself that this time I'd find a plump pheasant or even a hare in one.

A rattling and rumbling made me glance back. Sybil, the brewer and baker, was pushing a wheelbarrow covered with an old blanket up the rough, sun-baked track. Although she'd twice the muscles of most men, she was struggling with her load, weakened, like everyone in the village, from the diet of little more than fish. I knew that, whatever she was trying to move, it was unlikely to be kegs of ale. She stopped to wipe her brow on the back of her hand, then bent to lift the handles again.

She shoved it hard, trying to get enough momentum to roll the wooden wheel up the steepest part of the rise but, as I watched, it hit a stone jutting up out of the track. The wheelbarrow tipped sideways and the contents and blanket slithered out. Sybil sank down helplessly on the side of the path, her head in her hands. Reluctantly, I edged towards her. The blanket still partly covered the bundle, but as I drew close, I saw something pale sticking out from beneath. The blue-mottled toes of a foot, the nails yellow and thick.

I hastily took a few paces back, but Sybil glanced up. 'Don't fret, sprat. It was the flux that took him, not the pestilence.' She waved a meaty red hand towards the huddled figure lying on the track. 'Old Abel's finally gone, the stubborn old goat. Complaining right up to the end that he wanted ale and bread. Took him fish and fetched him water, but he had such a thirst on him. Kept telling him the stream was almost dry, but he was always grumbling that I didn't bring him enough.'

'He should have been grateful,' I said. 'You didn't need to take him any at all. He was no kin to you, was he?'

She shrugged. 'He was a good customer, when I'd ale to brew.' She sighed. 'Couldn't leave his poor old body in his cottage to rot, but it doesn't seem right, laying him in that pit as if he'd got the pestilence like them.' She spoke as if there was shame in their deaths.

Between us we heaved the body back into the wheelbarrow and I helped her trundle it down to the shore. We dug a hole in the wet sand and mud, heaving stones over it to keep the corpse anchored down. He'd been a fisherman once. Lying between land and sea, where he could listen to the gulls and the waves, was as good a place as any to rest. Better than that foul, stinking pit, anyway. I left Sybil squatting on the sand, staring out at the sea.

She turned her head as I waddled away. 'Sara's right,' she called out. 'You may be a runt, but you got more kindness in your small frame than men three times your size. And its kindness means far more to a woman than any amount of fine looks or gold, for they'll not keep her warm or comforted.'

I must have looked alarmed, for she gave a roar of laughter. 'Don't you fret, sprat. I'm not looking for a husband. With my girth I'd likely squash you as flat as flounder if I took you to my bed.'

She stared at the rocks covering old Abel, and such an expression of grief swept across her face that I wanted to hug her.

'Besides,' she murmured, 'I don't reckon we'll ever see weddings or happiness again after this. Feels like the whole world is dying.'

When I finally reached my snares they were empty. They'd not even been disturbed. Either I was hopeless at setting them or even the game had deserted the forest. I shifted them again and carefully covered them. Maybe all the birds and beasts had moved on in search of water. There was one snare left to check. I'd set it further into the forest, hoping that, if nothing else, I'd at least trap another squirrel. I pushed and trampled through the dry undergrowth. The blackberries were wizened and shrivelled before they'd had a chance to ripen, and even under the deep shade of the trees, the ferns' fronds were brown and crumbling.

I'd tied an old length of cord around the tree trunk so that I could spot where I'd concealed the snare. I found the marker cord easily enough; after all, I'd only set it there the night before. But when I cleared away the fallen leaves I'd used to hide it, I discovered the pegs I'd hammered into the ground had been wrenched out and the snare-line snapped. Something had got caught in the trap, but it

343

had broken free. I cursed heartily as only a dwarf, fake or otherwise, can.

I was waddling away when a flash of red caught my attention among the brown undergrowth. I moved closer. It was the bloody leg of a fox. My snare was pulled tight about it, but the top of the leg had been ripped from the body at the hip. I have to confess to being a little sick at the sight. I felt a pang of guilt that the wretched creature should have been so desperate to get away that it had torn off its own leg. But was that even possible?

I searched about, wondering if the creature was lying injured somewhere close by. It took several minutes to find it, but eventually I did. The fox was lying beneath a tree – or, rather, what was left of it. The carcass had been chewed and mauled, the bones cracked and splintered. The head looked as if someone had attacked it with a pollax, smashing the skull and tearing off half of the face, ripping the bloody flesh down to the white bone beneath. Something had killed the fox and ripped it from the snare with tremendous force. A pack of feral dogs or even other foxes? *Foxes running in packs, swarming out of the forests into villages and towns.* I glanced anxiously about me, feeling pairs of eyes watching me from the shadows.

But the idea that this might have been dogs was not a comforting thought either. Even longshanks fear packs of wild dogs, especially when you see what they can do to a sheep, but at least most men stand head and shoulders above dogs and can run. When you're a dwarf, your face is pretty much on a level with a dog's, and light of foot we may be, but fleet of foot we are not.

I began to edge away as softly and rapidly as I could, trying not to break a twig or make a sound, though even I could hear the rasp of my breath and the thumping of my heart. I was so busy looking over my shoulder for fear that I was being stalked, that I stumbled over a loose stone and fell to my knees.

As I heaved myself up on the rough bark of a tree, I suddenly saw what had been too far above my head for me to notice before. There were long thick scratches on either side of the tree trunk, so deep that the naked flesh of the tree showed through the grey bark. Those marks were fresh and I knew not even the largest mastiff in my lord's kennels could have reached up to claw that high. I ran as fast as my bandy legs would carry me, and didn't stop until I'd reached the burned shell of Sara's home.

Gasping for breath and sweating like a whore in a stew-house, I crumpled down on the sun-scorched grass on top of the rise in front of the cottage. Even after a week, the stench of burned reeds and charred timbers still hung in the air, but that didn't seem to trouble the rooks that perched in a long line along the top of the blackened shell cawing loudly and pecking at the walls, as if they were determined to reduce those to rubble too.

My legs were trembling and vicious pains were shooting through my hips and knees, but I knew I'd have to stir myself soon. My bag was empty, and though I could hardly bear to think of the prospect, a fish in the pot was better than an empty snare. I hoped there'd still be some fish unclaimed at the weir.

I was just about to roll over and heave myself to my feet, when I glimpsed a woman picking her way between the houses below me. There was something about the way she moved, her clothes . . . It took me several moments to realise why she seemed so familiar yet so strange at the same

345

time. But it couldn't be her, not here! What would she be doing in Porlock Weir?

I found myself on my feet without even being aware that I was standing and scuttled down the rise towards the place where she'd disappeared, but I couldn't see anyone ahead of me. I shook myself. I'd imagined it. Comes of eating too much fish: like toasted cheese, it gives you bad dreams.

Then, just as I turned around the bend in the track, I saw her again, shuffling along on the path below me that ran by the shore. It was her. There was no mistaking it. Eda! I'd know her nasty, wizened rat face anywhere. Always so loyal – *I thought you ought to know, m'lady* – always so venomous. How many times had I dreamed of squeezing the breath from that scraggy throat, but she'd probably have changed into a snake and wriggled out of my hand.

But where had she sprung from? It could only be the manor. And if that poisonous creature was staying there she wouldn't have come alone. Her mistress and her daughter must be with her. Eda would never have abandoned them. A prickle ran up the length of my twisted spine. They were here! Lady Aliena and Lady Christina were in Porlock. I was certain of it. I had to get word to her – I must. The manor might be sealed off, but surely if Eda could get out, then I could get in. But one thing I knew for certain: if Eda discovered I was close by, I'd never get near her mistress. She must not see me.

Chapter 46

Porlock Manor

He that has a guilty conscience thinks every whisper is about him.

Medieval Proverb

Father Cuthbert heard the shrieks and wails coming from inside the manor while he was still crossing the courtyard. Before he reached the door, it was dragged open and a pageboy hurtled down the manor stairs so fast that he staggered and almost fell as he leaped from the last step. He stared around, and a look of profound relief crossed his face as his gaze fell upon the priest.

'Father! Father, I was sent to find you. Come at once . . . It's Sir Harry . . . You're needed.'

But, much to the boy's consternation, instead of hurrying up the steps, Father Cuthbert stopped mid-stride. 'What . . . does Sir Harry want with me?'

The lad glanced fearfully up at the open door. 'Your services, Father. Please hurry!' he squeaked in desperation, reaching out his hand to seize the sleeve of the priest's gypon. 'You're wet, Father.'

Father Cuthbert glanced down, fearful that the sleeve and front of his gypon might still bear traces of the splashed blood, but the cold water had done its work well and, apart from the dark wet patches, there was nothing to betray him. Equally there was nothing to stop Sir Harry telling his version of the story, except for the fear of looking foolish. Maybe he was even now recounting some exaggerated tale to Lady Pavia.

'Please, Father!' the boy said, tugging at him.

Father Cuthbert was sorely tempted to take to his heels and run, but where could he run to? The pestilence was raging beyond these walls. Even if he could have escaped through the gates, he dared not risk going out into that deadly contagion. He took a deep breath and tried to calm his thoughts. It was a slight flesh wound, a mere scratch. He hadn't murdered the man, more was the pity. Even if Sir Harry claimed he had been attacked while unarmed, no priest could be punished or even brought to trial except in the ecclesiastical courts and those would not sit again until after the pestilence had burned itself out. It could be months, years even, before any charges were laid against him, if indeed anyone bothered. Surely once they were away from here, Sir Harry would have more important things to occupy him than taking revenge for a trifling nick on his arm.

His composure recovered, Father Cuthbert took a deep breath. 'Lead on, boy.'

Now that his panic had subsided, he was aware once more of the wails drifting through the open door.

'What is that commotion?' he demanded.

But the lad had already bounded up the steps, and glanced back only briefly to assure himself that Father Cuthbert was following, before disappearing through the doorway.

The hall was crowded with servants huddled in little knots. Sir Nigel's three wards were clinging to each other,

348

outdoing each other with cries and sobs as if they were paid mourners at some wealthy merchant's funeral. The elderly Lady Margery was attempting to soothe them, her efforts rendered useless by her own sniffling. Lady Christina and Lady Pavia were standing by one of the long tables, deep in discussion with the steward, Master Wallace.

It was taking a while for Father Cuthbert's eyes to adjust to the dimness of the great hall after the blinding sunlight outside. He blinked foolishly at the scene, while the page ran across the thick mat of rushes and hovered at Lady Pavia's elbow, trying in vain to attract her attention. Young though he was, even he realised he couldn't tug on her sleeve. Wallace looked to where the boy was frantically gesturing and came hurrying across.

'God's arse, but this is a terrible business. Lad told you, then?'

As Lady Pavia sailed across the hall towards him, Father Cuthbert finally began to register that something large was lying on the long table behind her, and it wasn't dinner. Bundles of washing, a roll of tapestry? He couldn't think what it might be. He edged towards it. Whatever it was had been covered by a long tablecloth. Then the form beneath the cloth suddenly took shape in his mind. It was a body.

He crossed himself. 'Blessed Virgin, defend us! Has the pestilence struck?'

The steward glanced at the table. 'Nay, not that. But there's been a death, all right. You're too late to hear his confession, Father, but you'd best pray for him, for he was taken so sudden I doubt he'd time to prepare hisself.'

Two maids came hurrying up with four candles on spikes, which they placed at each corner of the table. Another, shielding the flame carefully, lit them with a taper from the fire. The servants fell silent and parted, leaving a respectful space around the long table. Lady Pavia swept out a plump arm and ushered the weeping girls back. All around him, servants and Sir Nigel's guests knelt on the rushes, looking up at the priest expectantly.

Father Cuthbert approached the head of the corpse lying on the table. He stared at the white linen that covered the face. If this was merely a servant who'd met with some accident, there would never have been such a gathering in the great hall. His fingers trembled as he plucked at the cloth, then slowly peeled it back. The face was pale, the eyes closed, the black beard neat. One might almost think that Sir Harry merely lay sleeping. He was unmarked, except for a scarlet stain, no bigger than a butterfly's wing, on the white cloth that covered his arm. Father Cuthbert sank to his knees, but it was not piety that drove him down.

Chapter 47

Whoever has a woman grasps a serpent by the tail.
Medieval Proverb

Rosa hears the door of the stillroom open and close. Baby Oswin is almost asleep, a dribble of milk running between his soft petal lips. His eyes flicker open again in the sudden draught from the door, but Rosa continues her steady, gentle rocking of the cradle. Putting her finger to her lips, she gestures to her visitor not to disturb the child. But Father Cuthbert is in no mood to be silenced, as well she knows.

'You told me it was nothing but a flesh wound!' he explodes.

Rosa stands. 'Softly, Father. The child is sleeping. Besides, many servants cross the courtyard at this hour and they may hear you.'

He glances towards the shuttered window and takes a pace closer, lowering his voice to a savage whisper. 'You assured me you would tend him.'

'And I did,' she says, wandering over to the table. 'You should be grateful. You need not fear now that he will take revenge.'

'But his spirit will!' Father Cuthbert's eyes are wide with fear. 'A man who has been slain, a man who departs this life weighed down with all his sins, will never rest until he has dragged his killer into the grave with him.'

'Then you must ensure his corpse cannot walk when he is buried tomorrow,' she says calmly. 'If your Christian signs and holy water will not hold him in the earth, I have an amulet that will.'

'I will have no part of your dark magic,' the priest growls. 'I do not take help from witches and sorcerers.'

She shrugs. 'As you please. But the creatures that stalk the night are masters of the dark. You cannot fight a raging storm armed only with a candle flame.'

'Was that what you used to kill him? Magic?' Father Cuthbert whispers fiercely. 'I will see you hanged.'

'But he died from the wound in his arm. Have you forgotten, Father Cuthbert? It must have been deeper than you thought. It was a wound you inflicted with your knife. And I have that knife, Father, marked with your sign and coated with his blood. You should always clean your own blade.'

Father Cuthbert glances wildly about him, but she holds up her hand. 'Do not trouble to search. Do you really think I am so foolish as to have hidden it here? I know full well that a priest may not be condemned to death by a church court, but for certain kinds of murder, he can first be stripped of Holy Orders, then tried in a lay court. A common man attacking and murdering a noble, and one who has been in service to the Black Prince? Such an act might be regarded as treason. Execution would not be swift.'

Even in the dimness of the chamber, she can see he is trembling. He grips the table to stop himself falling. 'I will see you dragged down to Hell!' His voice is quavering. 'You are the daughter of Satan himself and you will suffer the worst agonies that the demons can devise. I will pray day and night that you are shown no mercy.'

Rosa laughs. 'If Satan is my father, then surely I will be treated with honour in his kingdom.'

Father Cuthbert sinks on to the stool, his head in his

hands. Rosa watches him and waits. That is her weapon. She can see by the clenching of his fingers that he longs to put his hands around her throat and choke the life from her, but he doesn't dare, not yet anyway.

When she knows that he is ready to grasp at any rope she tosses, she says softly, 'I will return the knife to you.'

His head jerks up. 'When? Now? Tonight?'

It amuses her to watch the hope flare up in his eyes. 'When you return to me what you have taken from me. An exchange. That is fair, is it not?'

'I – I have nothing of *yours*.' He spits this last as if the very word is putrid meat in his mouth.

'The relic of Cadeyrn. You have that.'

'The reliquary? So, it's gold you want. I thought as much. Like all women, you lust after money and jewels. But I will not permit a witch to steal a sacred reliquary from the sanctuary of the Holy Church.'

'But it is not in the sanctuary of the Church,' she tells him. 'You have it. And you may keep it. I have no interest in a Christian's gaudy trinket. It is the hand inside it that I seek. Cadeyrn was my forefather, slain here by treachery. The spirits of my ancestors charged me with bringing his bones back to the land that drank his birth blood, and the river into which his mother's birth water flowed. But your reliquary is empty. The hand is gone. Only tell me where I may find it. That is all I ask.'

She reaches into the little purse at her belt and pulls out the bear's tooth, which had hung from the blue beads. She clasps it in her fist and presses her lips to it. 'I swear by the Great Bear that guards my life and guides my spirit, your knife shall be returned to you, the very hour I hold Cadeyrn's hand in mine.'

Chapter 48

Will

Riddle me this: What is the widest stretch of water, yet the safest to cross?

I crept along the narrow track that slithered around the base of the steep rocky cliff. In the moonlight the wind-blown tangle of trees far above me looked like the fur on the back of a great slumbering beast. I stopped, listening for voices or any sound of movement that would warn me that the road which led from Porlock Weir to Porlock was guarded. But the only sounds were the lapping of distant waves and the whisper of last year's dry rushes. The moon was bright enough to pick out the stones on the path, for which I was thankful: one false step would have seen me plunge off the winding track into the great tidal salt marsh that stretched across the bay in front of Porlock.

Why had it taken me so long to understand? I was supposed to be the master of riddles. The briar garland, the dead bird, the cherry stone – someone had left a message in my cave, warning me that she was in Porlock. *She sent me a briar without any rind. She sent me a bird without any bone. She sent me a cherry without any stone.* Had Christina sent me those signs weeks ago, begging me to come to her?

I'd sat half the day in the mouth of my cave, watching the gulls rocking on the waves and trying to work out how to get into the manor. The cart track between Porlock Weir and Porlock had been blocked: tree-trunks and huge rocks had been dragged across it to stop horses, stray live-stock and wagons passing in either direction. They had set up the barricade at a place where the track was squeezed between the base of the sheer face of the cliff on one side and the treacherous marsh on the other so that no cattle or corpse-bearers could pass around it. But after months of clambering up rocks to my cave, I was sure I could scramble over it, so long as they'd left no one on watch.

But, as any gallant knight will tell you, walking up to a castle is one thing, storming inside is not so easy. I might be able to reach the manor unseen, but the gates would be firmly locked and Master Wallace would have posted men to watch the walls. Those walls had been built to fend off any attack. Even a longshanks with a ladder would have had a hard time scaling them, never mind a short-arse like me. And, unlike a siege army, I had to get in without being seen.

Master Wallace was never told why Sir Nigel had banished me to Porlock, only that I had become too bold and impu-dent, and he thought a few months in Porlock might mend my manners. But that was enough to damn any servant in Wallace's eyes. He'd loathed me from the first; a sentiment I freely admit was mutual. I vented my anger and resent-ment at being sent away by making Wallace the butt of my wit at table to the delight of the servants who'd felt the lash of his tongue. It was a foolish thing to do, I know, but I was so miserable, I couldn't seem to stop myself.

Wallace was itching to have me dismissed, and when the

butler and cook both complained that stores were missing, he accused me of stealing them and selling them on, though he and I both knew who the real thief was. When he had me whipped out of the gates he told me I was lucky to escape with my life, but my luck, he warned me, would not hold a second time and I'd known he meant it.

By the time I reached the outskirts of Porlock, the sun's first light was already gilding the distant sea with flakes of gold. Smoke was starting to rise into the grey-pink dawn from cottages dotted up the valley. I'd no idea what orders Master Wallace might have given to its inhabitants, but anyone entering the village brought the threat of pestilence and I'd no wish to be shot full of arrows before I got close enough to explain.

I slid down a sticky bank of mud at the side of the track and dropped into one of the river channels that cut through the salt marsh in front of the village. The incoming tide was beginning to inch back up the channel, but very little river water was coming downstream to swell it.

Voices! Women. I couldn't see where they were, but I flung myself down below the level of the bank, praying they would pass by quickly. Although which deity was likely to hear my prayers down there, I didn't know – Beelzebub probably, lord of the flyblown swamps. The voices died away and I peered over the edge of the bank. The place I was looking for must be somewhere to my right and above me.

Back in the cave, I'd suddenly recalled that when I'd lived at the manor I'd stumbled across a stream that ran from its fishponds through a low arch in the wall and emptied into the river outside. There was a grid over the hole, mainly to stop the larger fish escaping if the ponds flooded, but the iron bars were rusty. I couldn't imagine that Master Wallace had troubled to replace it, for it was in a neglected corner of the grounds and no army would attack by that route.

It took me a while, creeping around the manor walls, to find the low archway, for it was well hidden behind a mass of overgrown weeds. The water trickling out beneath was thick with brown-green slime and swarming with flies. From the outside the hole looked even smaller than I remembered.

I crouched in stagnant water, and peered through the grating. I could see the base of a tree some feet away but no people. They clearly didn't think this corner worth guarding. Unless – a cold hand gripped my guts – unless the pestilence had struck the manor. Suppose, instead of shutting it out, Wallace had shut it in with them. It had happened before: beggars creeping to the doors of great castles had found the bodies of lords and servants alike rotting in the hall and the kitchens. I sniffed hard. The stench from the grave pit at Porlock Weir carried all through the village, so if pestilence had reached here, I'd smell it.

I heaved at the iron grid. It was so rusty, I thought one sharp tug might snap it, but the metal was stronger than it looked. I searched around for a stone and, wrapping it in my mud-caked jerkin to muffle the sound, pounded it against the bars until they were bent enough for me to wriggle them out of the holes in the stone into which they'd been set. Clouds of flies crawled over my face and hands. I pressed my lips hard together to stop them creeping into my mouth, but gave up trying to bat them away.

Though my hands had grown as horny as the soles of my feet since that bastard Wallace had thrown me out, they were still ripped and bleeding before I wrested the final bar

357

from its socket. I paused, listening again. Far off, towards the manor house, I could hear clanging and banging, distant voices – the reassuring sounds of daily life as the servants busied themselves. At least I knew they were alive.

Even with the bars gone, fitting through the hole was not going to be easy. I lay flat on the rough stones of the stream bed and wriggled forward through the stinking green water. I tried not to think about what might be in it, though I could hardly ignore the turd that floated an inch from my mouth. What would old Dung Beetle, the hermit, predict from that? Good fortune, I hoped.

When I was far enough in to get my fingers round the lip of the arch on the other side, I dragged myself through. For a moment or two, I continued to lie flat in the stinking water in case the movement had been spotted. I was just about to raise my head when something splashed into the stream beside me. I heard panting, then a soft wet nose pressed into the back of my neck. The manor hounds!

'Go away. Get!' I whispered fiercely. The creature continued to sniff at me, apparently finding the aroma of stagnant water and excrement as alluring as the flies did. I sat up, and tried to push the hound away, but that was a mistake: it gave a great bark, then bared its teeth and growled. Snatching up a stone, I threw it at its flank, in the hope of driving it off. I leaped to my feet and ran the yard or so to the nearest tree. With a howl it bounded after me. I swung on to a low branch and hauled myself up, for once blessing my master for making us swing from pillars and galleries.

The hound jumped up, and I had to kick out to stop it sinking its teeth into my calf. I climbed higher still as it repeatedly leaped up at me, until I was out of reach of its snapping jaws. The hound fell back exhausted. It circled the tree, staring up, mouth open, pink tongue lolling over sharp white fangs. Then it sat on its haunches, threw back its head and began to bark loudly enough to bring every man in the manor running.

Chapter 49

And in her was found the blood of prophets and of saints
and of all that were slain upon the earth.

The Apocalypse of St John

Luke sat cross-legged at the Prophet's feet on the labyrinth of cold, sharp pebbles. The other disciples squatted on the piles of skins and heaps of bracken, wiping the last of their supper from their mouths and draining the icy water from their beakers. Brother Praeco's first two wives sat on either side of him, handing him food and drink as he required. Uriel's eyes constantly scanned the cave, searching for any sign of trouble, like a watchman on a castle wall. Phanuel stared fixedly at the floor, darting only fleeting sideways glances at her husband in case he should be in need of anything she must supply.

That evening Luke, though usually ravenous, had little appetite. He tried not to look at Hob, leaning against the wall across the far side of the cave, though his gaze kept being drawn back to him. The Prophet had told Luke what must be done. He said it would be his reward, but he knew it was a test. In spite of the suffocating heat and fug of the cave, Luke shivered. He'd not been able to get near to Hob to warn him.

You need only have faith, Luke. That was what the Prophet had said. But what if he didn't have faith enough, if he couldn't make it happen? What if he failed in front of all the Chosen? Would they take him back down that tunnel again, force him on to the ledge in the darkness? Maybe there were even worse things in other chambers, though he couldn't imagine what might be worse than that howling darkness and the demons that slithered over those wet, icy walls.

Above their heads the stone trapdoor grated open, swirling smoke from the fire around the room. Little Hob was seized by a spasm of coughing, his thin chest heaving with the effort to draw breath. Luke peered upwards, trying to see if it was daylight or dark outside. But it was always dark, always night. The Prophet had warned them that all was desolation up there. The sun had turned black just as it had that day, before the pestilence had come. Luke would never have believed that such things could happen had he not seen it for himself that day on the shore. But this time the sun had not returned, would never return until the world had been cleansed of all its iniquity. The stars and moon had fallen from the sky, just as the Prophet had foretold. Luke knew that too, for there was never a glimmer of moon-light in the darkness above that hole.

Noll, shovelling the last spoonful of stewed goat down his throat, dragged a ragged cloak around his shoulders over his torn shirt and climbed laboriously up the pole ladder to take his turn on watch. The Prophet constantly reminded the Chosen that Brother Noll and Brother David were true warriors of God, who would be rewarded through all eternity for venturing out into the terrible desolation of the over-world, to stand guard over His Chosen Ones.

As soon as Noll had reached the top and clambered out, the stone was pushed back into place from above. The swirling flames of the fire settled once more to a steady blaze.

The Prophet held up his hands and at once silence descended in the chamber. '"And ancients said to me – *Hii qui amicti sunt stolis albis qui sunt et unde venerunt.* These that are clothed in white robes, who are they? And whence came they?"'

Brother Praeco clapped his hand on Luke's shoulder. 'And what answer was given to the ancients, boy? Tell us?'

All eyes turned to Luke. Most of the faces were friendly, nodding and smiling encouragement, but Luke's gaze kept being drawn back to Uriel. Her eyes were narrowed, her mouth wrinkled and pinched, like a pig's arsehole. He knew she was waiting for him to fail.

He closed his eyes and swallowed hard. '"These are they who are come out of great . . . of great . . . tribulation and have washed their robes and have made them white in the blood of the Lamb,"' he finished in a rush.

He felt a squeeze of the fingers on his shoulder and glanced up to see the Prophet nodding approvingly at him. Luke beamed up at him. A warm glow of pride and belonging seeped through him. He was at last one of the Chosen Ones and he was sitting in the honoured place right next to the Prophet, just where the two warriors sat when they were whispering to him. He was almost a warrior himself.

Luke realised with a start that Brother Praeco was addressing the disciples again, and he tried to look attentive. '". . . wash in the blood and he shall not feel the heat of the sun, nor the thirst of the day, nor shall he suffer any pain or sickness." Faith is our shield and our test, brothers and sisters. Faith will save us.'

He paused and nodded towards Raguel, crouching by the fire. 'Bring the boy to me.'

Raguel rose gracefully. Stepping over legs and blankets,

she crossed to the wall, took Hob's hands in both of hers and pulled him to his feet. For the first few paces, Hob followed her docilely enough. He liked her. She was always kind to him. But then he suddenly seemed to realise where he was being taken and tried to pull his hand from hers.

She bent, murmuring something and pointing to Luke, who tried to smile encouragingly, but his face felt stiff and he knew he was probably grimacing.

Raguel tugged the little boy to the open space in front of the Prophet and pushed him down so that he was kneeling on the floor. He tried to struggle up again. Seeing Uriel reaching out her claws to grab him, Raguel hastily pushed Hob back to the floor, crouching beside him with her arm firmly round his shoulders, so that he could not wriggle away.

Phanuel emerged from the tunnel, though Luke had not even noticed her leave. She was carrying a small stone basin, holding it in both hands, and treading carefully, plainly terrified of spilling the contents. The bowl looked ancient, the carvings almost worn away, so that Luke could see little of what they had once been except for some lines that looked to him like the waves of the sea and a circle with a cross cutting through it. Phanuel set the basin in front of Hob. The dark red liquid in the bowl swirled from the jolt, like the water in the Devil's Cauldron, and the metallic stench of blood rose up from it. The child's eyes flashed wide in alarm and he tried once more to struggle away, but Raguel held him firmly.

Once more the Prophet's hand descended on Luke's shoulder, this time pulling him to his feet, as he himself rose. Hob shrank back from them both, trying to hide his face in Raguel's arms.

Brother Praeco lifted his hands, gazing around the silent disciples, fixing each in turn with his stare. 'This boy is afflicted with a coughing sickness, but he shall be healed. His brother will wash him in blood to cleanse him and he will pray for his brother's healing, and through Luke's faith, Hob will be cured. This innocent child was saved from the murderer's knife and given into our hands. He is our lamb. He shall be healed. He shall be perfected. He shall be presented spotless before God. We, the Chosen, shall pray with his brother Luke and God will hear us and he will heal the boy.'

He squeezed Luke's shoulder again. 'Only believe, Luke. If your faith is strong enough, if you are worthy to be counted among the Chosen, your brother shall be healed.'

Chapter 50

Will

Riddle me this: Little man clad all in red, with a stick up his backside and a stone in his belly.

'It's the dwarf! What you doing up there?' The young stable lad grinned at me, his eyes bright in his dung-streaked face. 'We all thought you was dead.'

'I will be if you don't stop that hound barking.'

The lad snapped his fingers close to the dog's ear. 'Quiet, Holdfast. Lay down!'

The hound, accustomed to keeping quarry at harbour, flopped on his belly under the tree and stared up at me fixedly, as if daring me to try to escape.

'Master Wallace'll have you flogged to death if he catches you,' the boy announced cheerfully, as if he'd been promised a great treat. 'Said if anyone spotted you hanging round the manor, we was to tell him straight away. He said you was a thief.'

The skin on my back smarted at the mere thought of what Master Wallace could do.

'Never mind my flogging, lad,' I said. 'Just you remember it was me who saw you put that weasel in the cook's basket, and if I were to tell the cook you'd done it, he'd beat you till you were nothing but a mash of beans.'

The boy giggled. 'He didn't half squeal when he put his hand in and thought he was going to pull out a dead rabbit and that weasel sank his teeth into his thumb instead. He was running round the kitchen, as mad as a wasp, with the weasel dangling from him. Couldn't shake it loose.' The lad cavorted round the tree, flinging his hand up and down in imitation.

'So you won't give me away, lad?'

'Course not, wouldn't anyway. Hate old Wallace. Never do him any favours.' He wrinkled his nose. 'But why you back? You come to rob from the manor again?'

I ignored this last. 'Have any guests been staying here, besides the wards and their companion?'

'That fat one, Lady Pavia. And Sir Harry, but he's dead. Old Wallace says he had a fall, cut his arm and bled to death. But Robert, the groom, says he reckons it wasn't a cut that killed him 'cause he helped carry Sir Harry into the hall and there weren't hardly any blood. But he said if he were to tell old Wallace that, he'd more than likely get the blame for it himself. Wallace'd say Robert killed him out of revenge for Sir Harry laying into him with a whip. But he—'

'Never mind that, lad,' I said. 'Have any other noble-women come to the manor recently? The Lady Aliena and her daughter?'

The boy looked sulky at having his story interrupted, but he shook his head. 'No . . . 'cept a girl, if you count her, but she came earlier with that sour-faced maid of hers, before Lady Pavia. None of us saw her at first 'cause she was sick, but she must be well enough now for I've seen her crossing the courtyard a fair few times. Lady . . . Lady Christina, they call her.'

My stomach lurched. 'And she's here now?'

He nodded.

'Do you think you could bring her to me without anyone else knowing?'

The lad frowned. 'Why? What's a dwarf want with her?'

'I need to speak with her.' I tried to think of some excuse that would intrigue him. 'I have a message . . . a *secret* message.'

His eyes danced in excitement. Then he grimaced. 'Can't fetch her from the manor house – they'd want to know why I was in there. But most days I see her in the courtyard when there's no one much about. I could catch her then.' He chewed his lip and squinted up through the branches at me. 'Might have to wait a bit, though.'

'I'll wait as long as it takes.' But seeing he was about to dash off, I added quickly, 'Take that hound with you, before he leads someone else here.'

The boy grinned, slipped his fingers through the hound's spiked collar and hauled him off, growling, in the direction of the stables.

I was pretty sure I could trust the lad not to tell Wallace, but whether luck would bless us both, I had no means of knowing. I waited until boy and dog were out of sight, then climbed down, retreating towards the hole in the wall, ready to duck down in the stream among the reeds if I spotted anyone wandering in my direction. It was going to be a long, hot morning.

Flies settled in a dense black crust on the stinking river mud, and a ball of gnats hovered in the air above. In the shimmering blue skies, gulls were mobbing a rust-coloured kite, shrieking and diving on the bird. It wheeled and dipped, trying to evade them.

I caught a flash of movement and leaped down into the stream, peering up through the reeds. My heart almost exploded in my chest. It was her, Christina, hurrying across the grass towards me, looking behind her anxiously as if she feared she might be observed. I had dreamed and daydreamed so often of seeing her again that now I couldn't believe she was here in the flesh and not in my fantasy. I shook my head, trying to wake myself if I was asleep.

I heaved myself out of the reeds and slid into the shadows behind the tree, suddenly all too aware of how I must look, not to mention smell. I'd been so desperate to get into the manor grounds, I hadn't given a thought to my appearance. The last time she'd seen me, I'd been dressed in a red-and-green gypon with gold trim, an exact replica of Sir Nigel's, hair curled, beard trimmed. Now I was clad in patched homespun, trimmed with mud, embroidered with green slime, and perfumed with shit and fish guts.

She looked more beautiful even than when I dreamed of her, her hair turned from tawny to burnished copper in the sunlight, her cheeks flushed, her breasts rising like soft dough over the top of her gown. I didn't remember them being so full, so perfect. She peered up at the tree. The boy must have told her I was there.

'Josse!' she called softly.

Josse, our private, intimate name. She told me once it meant *lord*. She wouldn't use the name my master gave me, for she said when she looked at me she saw a man not a dwarf.

'Josse!'

I had come all this way to find her, but now that I was there, I couldn't bring myself to face her. She was turning away! If I didn't show myself now, I might never get another chance.

I stepped from behind the trunk. Her expression turned to one of shock, and I almost fled. But then she smiled, though her eyes were brimming with tears.

'Christina, I . . .' I was desperate to tell her how much I had missed her. How long and lonely the nights had been without her words to fill them. But for once the jester had no words to juggle with.

'My house is not quiet,' she whispered. 'But I am not loud. I am the swifter, but my house endures longer. Even when I am still, my house still runs. Should we two be parted, my death is certain.'

'The fish and the river,' I answered softly. I gestured towards the stagnant stream. 'And when the fish was taken from the stream, the stream died too.'

'I didn't know where you'd gone!' she burst out. 'I didn't know if you were dead or alive. Or if you had *chosen* to leave . . . I couldn't bear it. I was so lonely. There was no one I could talk to, not like I could talk to you. Why didn't you send me word, just one word that I could have held on to?'

'Did Sir Nigel tell you nothing?' I asked her.

She shook her head, and one of the tears spilled over to run silently down her cheek. I wanted to kiss it away, as I had on the night she sobbed in fear in my arms when her betrothal to Randel was announced. But I sensed a barricade between us now that felt higher and wider even than the one on the road to Porlock, and I could find no way to cross it.

'I don't believe Sir Nigel knew anything for certain,' I said. 'He didn't even speak your name when he sent for me. But he's a shrewd man. He must have noticed a look or a gesture that made him smell danger. He said only that when a knight notices a beggar taking too much interest in his horse, he takes care to ensure the beggar is sent from the town before the sin of covetousness leads to a crime for which he would hang. That's why he sent me away from Chalgrave within the hour. I couldn't . . . I daren't get word to you.'

Crossing the gap between us, she took a few paces towards me. Horribly conscious of my wet, stinking carcass, I drew away, afraid of befouling her. She reached out a soft, pale hand, as if she would touch my face. But I turned my grotesque mask from her and she let her hand fall.

'I was so afraid they'd hurt you,' she whispered.

'Me? Never,' I lied. 'Us dwarfs are far too valuable.' I pranced around, pulling a face.

But she flinched. 'Don't do that. Don't perform for me.'

I could see I'd hurt her. I swallowed. 'And you, how came you to Porlock? Did you discover I'd been sent here? Was that why you came?'

I couldn't tell her of the love and fear and pain and all those thoughts that, for months, I'd been aching to share with her. Instead I found my mouth babbling inane questions as if a small boy had taken possession of my voice. 'I found your message in the cave. But I'm so stupid I didn't understand what it meant at first. I never dreamed you'd come to this manor.'

She frowned. 'Cave? I don't understand. I left no message. I didn't know where you were. You just vanished. Then Randel . . .'

She tugged at her finger as if she was trying to wrench it off, and I saw the thick, ugly ring weighing it down. His crest was incised into the bezel as if he had branded her, like a valuable horse, as his own property. An icy hand seemed to thrust itself deep inside my chest and clenched around my heart.

'It is done then,' I said dully. 'You are his wife now.'

Christina stared up at the burning blue sky. 'She is the bride of the sun, though sun would destroy her. She was made to comfort the night, but . . .'

'. . . she banishes it,' I finished for her. 'She weeps while she lives and when she is dying they cut off her head.'

'Poor little candle.' Christina shuddered. 'Every night I pray he might die in battle or that the pestilence will take him. Is that wicked?'

I couldn't answer, for a lump the size of a chicken's egg was caught in my throat. I hadn't just wished Randel dead; I'd lain awake at nights planning how to kill him, and if he'd shown himself at that moment, I would have done it, small as I was.

She stared down at the heavy gold ring. 'I have another reason now for being in terror of his return. You asked why I came to Porlock and I didn't answer. But the truth is my mother banished me here with Eda because . . . because I fell with child. I have a son, Josse, a beautiful little boy.'

I jerked backwards as if I'd been punched. Trying to recover myself, I bowed low.

'You . . . you are to be congratulated, m'lady. Sir Randel will no doubt be delighted when he returns.'

'But Randel is not the father,' Christina whispered.

'If you say so, m'lady.'

I quickly turned away, knowing that though my mouth, as always, would be grinning, I couldn't hide the tears of hurt, even as I angrily dashed them away. The thought of her in Randel's bed was agony enough, but knowing she had taken a lover . . . I'd thought I knew misery, but the pain and bitterness that engulfed me in that moment were made a thousand times worse by the knowledge that I had no more right to feel betrayed or hurt than a hunting hound when his master buys another dog.

'Riddle me this,' I sang out, in my high-pitched jester's voice. 'What does a wife give to her husband that he never sees? What does her husband wear that he never feels?'

I raised two fingers behind my head and waggled them, as I had done a thousand times for my master's guests. 'A handsome pair of horns you've given Randel as a wedding gift, m'lady. They suit him well. But, then, it is not for a poor fool to question who a noblewoman takes to her bed.'

'You are a fool indeed, if you cannot understand what the Lady Christina is telling you,' another voice said softly behind me.

'Rosa!' Christina breathed.

I spun round, staring up at the woman who stood in the shadows. It took me a few moments to realise who she was.

'Janiveer!'

Chapter 51

Love is full of fear.

Medieval Proverb

A slow smile creeps across Janiveer's face, but it does not reach her sea-cold eyes.

'The villagers have been searching for you,' the dwarf says. 'They journeyed to Kitnor.'

'So far!' she mocks. 'Yet a bold stride for Sara.'

'How did you know she was one of them?'

'Who else? She searches for her sons. She will not give them up for lost till they bury her, and even then she will rise from her grave and keep searching. Her spirit will never rest.'

Janiveer can see something approaching fear in Will's eyes. If he were a religious man, she knows he would be backing away from her, crossing himself. But instead he moves closer to the girl – how touching! Even though he thinks she has betrayed him, he still wants to protect her. A fool's love indeed.

Christina is staring from one to the other, bewilderment creasing her brow. 'Who is this woman you call Sara? What does she want with Rosa?'

'Calling yourself Rosa now?' Will says. 'A sweet flower that distracts the eye from its sharp thorns.'

Janiveer shrugs. 'Some call hemlock "devil's blossom", others call it "kex", but the plant brings death in answer to

373

any of these names, or none. So I carry whatever name others choose to lay upon me, as do you, dwarf.'

She jerks her chin at Christina. 'But you have still not put your lover out of his misery, m'lady. Why is that, I wonder? As much as you profess to love the dwarf, do you fear that your child will grow into the image of his father if you utter his name?'

Christina flushes. Her denial is hot, vehement, as if it is uttered in guilt.

'Josse . . .' She sinks to the ground, looking up at him. He is no gallant knight in gleaming armour. His matted hair hangs in long wet ropes about his shoulders. His clothes are torn and stinking, his beard tangled with slime and filth. Yet a seer's gifts are not needed to see plainly that the girl loves him and her voice trembles, as any woman's would if she feared the news she brings her beloved might not be welcome.

'Oswin is *your* son, Josse, *our* son.'

His eyes flash wide. 'Mine? Are you . . .'

He has sense enough not to finish that question. Can't he see the truth of it in her eyes? But men, even short ones, never look for truth, only for what they want to believe.

'He has never touched me, except . . .' she flinches '. . . except to punish me for angering him. On our wedding night he was so drunk he fell asleep the moment he crashed on to the bed. I lay awake all night, praying he would not wake. Before dawn I took a knife and cut myself inside my secret parts where he would not see. The next morning my mother showed his friends the bloodstain. They cheered him and each claimed a piece of the sheet for luck. They told him he had taken the castle and, still mazed from drink, he seemed to think he had, but if he should remember what

374

happened that night . . . Little Oswin was born six months later. He is yours, Josse. No other man has ever known me, save you. I swear it on our son's life.'

He reaches out, but his great, clumsy hand falls away before it touches her.

'Ask her then,' Janiveer says. 'Ask her if the child is twisted, like you. That is what you want to know, isn't it?'

Christina answers swiftly before he can. 'Your son is beautiful, perfect.'

There is both relief and pain in his face, and Christina realises too late what she has said. But words, once uttered, take flight and cannot be unspoken.

She rises to her knees, holding out her arms to him. 'Please, you must take us away now, Josse, today, before Randel returns. I don't care where we live or how. Sir Harry came here to Porlock! I was terrified he'd guess the truth and would tell Randel on his return. You cannot know the relief I felt when he died, though I know that is wicked. But Eda is alive out there somewhere and she's certain that Oswin is not Randel's son. If she gets word to my mother or uncle, it will be our death warrant, by their hands or by Randel's, for if he discovers I have borne a child that is not of his getting, he will kill us both, I know it. I want to be with you, Josse. I want *our* son to grow up knowing his father. We must go where they can never find us. Please, Josse, take us with you.'

He reaches out to her, holding her tightly, whispering words of love and wild promises that Janiveer is not intended to hear, but she does not need to hear the words to know them. Eventually, as if he is wrenching his own arm from its socket, he reluctantly pushes Christina away and holds her at arm's length, gazing into her face.

'Eda may still be in Porlock Weir. I saw her there yesterday. But we can make for Kitnor – it's well hidden. They'd never find us. There are stone huts. It wouldn't take much to make one into a good warm shelter for us. There's fresh water and I can set snares and fish.'

The words are dancing out of him, as if he was a child, breathless for adventure. Janiveer watches their shining eyes and waits.

'But first we have to get you and my son out of the manor.' The dwarf stares at the grating behind him and back at the girl standing there in her flowing grown, soiled now by his embraces. 'If you wore breeches . . .' he says.

Janiveer sees the doubt creeping into his face. He is ready to hear her now.

'Have you forgotten why this manor is sealed? Out there, the pestilence rages. You have seen the bodies thrown into the graves. Could you bear to watch your beloved Christina and your little son being tossed into those stinking pits? And what if you are the one who perishes, dwarf? How will a girl who has never even drawn a pail of water from the well, or lit a fire, or wrung a chicken's neck manage to survive alone out there with a baby? Her milk is dry. She cannot even feed her child. Would you see her huddled in some filthy hut, hungry and alone, miles from any who could help her, watching her baby starve before her eyes? She will be begging for the pestilence to take her to end her loneliness and pain. Is that love, dwarf, to condemn her to such a death?'

Janiveer sees the fear and misery in Will's eyes and knows that he recognises only too well the dark and dreadful maw opening before them, but Christina has never known the torment of hunger and she has been shielded from the terror that is the pestilence. She can only imagine. And, even now, there is still a flicker of hope in her eyes. She still believes. She has still not relinquished this foolish toy. Her chin juts out defying fear, defying the whole world.

She grips Will's hand tightly. 'But I must go. I don't care if we are cold and hungry. I would gladly suffer anything to be with him. And if we die, at least we will die together.'

Janiveer smiles. It is too easy to swear to death. The words drift from the tongue, like dandelion puffs floating on the wind. 'No one dies together, my lady,' Janiveer tells her. 'Even hand in hand, each man and woman dies alone. Company merely increases death's agony. You must watch as it wrenches those you most love from this world and know you are powerless to hold them in it.'

A shadow of fear darkens Christina's eyes, but Janiveer shows no mercy. The girl must be made to understand.

'The manor's bloodhounds have keen noses, and they can move far more swiftly than any dwarf and girl, even were that pair not laden with a baby. Those lymers could follow the faintest scent through forest and across streams, but together the three of you will lay such a reeking trail that they will have your lover by the backside of his breeches before the hour is out. And when they catch him, what do you imagine will happen to a dwarf who has abducted Sir Nigel's niece and his great-nephew, kidnapped Sir Randel's bride and son? You think Master Wallace would call off the hounds once they have sunk their teeth into that felon? He'll urge them to rip out his liver and devour it while he screams in agony, for it will save Wallace the trouble of doing it himself.'

Her words have found their mark. The pair stare up at

her, like frightened children, waiting for her to tell them how they may be saved. But Janiveer did not bring dwarf and girl together to reunite two lovers. Her nature is not to unite but to tear apart.

'You must leave Christina and the child here, under my protection, Will.'

'Yours! Sara is certain that you brought the pestilence to the village. Matilda saw you plant the curse stone. How can I be sure you won't bring it to the manor?'

'It was not me who brought the curse upon the village, but its own forefathers and mothers when they betrayed Cadeyrn, the warrior king. When his bones are reunited and laid to rest in the land that birthed him, and when the price for their treachery has been paid, the curse will be lifted. I have travelled the seas for many years to find what was taken from his grave. Only one thing more do I seek.'

She gazes down at Will and at Christina, who still kneels beside him. 'If you bring me the last of Cadeyrn's bones, I will ensure that Christina leaves this place safely with the child.'

'But I don't know where to find—' Will begins.

Janiveer silences him with her hand.

'The hand of Cadeyrn, which dealt death to his enemies and life to his friends, was stolen by the Church before the king was buried. Perhaps it is only justice then that one of their own priests should in turn steal the reliquary that encased the hand. Your priest brought the reliquary here to the manor, for such men covet silver and jewels, but the hand that lay within it he despised as worthless and discarded. But now he has revealed its hiding place to me. It was not a willing confession, I admit, but a truthful one. I made certain of that. He says he hid the hand in a chest inside the chapel at Porlock Weir.

'Bring me that hand, Will, and when I hold it, Christina and the child will come to you. I have protected the boy thus far. But he lives only because I want him to. You would do well to remember that, dwarf. Your son lives only as long as I wish it.'

Chapter 52

*For the great day of their wrath is come. And who shall
be able to stand?*

The Apocalypse of St John

Luke curled up on the floor of the cave as far from the
tunnel as he could crawl. All around him, in the dim red
glow of the fire's embers, the Chosen Ones lay sleeping,
some snoring like old hounds, others muttering and grunting
as they dreamed. On the walls, dark shadows stirred as if
the monsters of the sleepers' nightmares had escaped from
them and were slithering about the cave.

Brother Praeco had withdrawn to his private quarters with
his youngest wife, but Luke knew he could appear at any
time without warning, for the Prophet often climbed up
into the Great Desolation above while his disciples slept.
But Luke couldn't sleep. Every muscle in his body was tense,
waiting for the blow that he knew hung somewhere above
him in the darkness. But there was no knowing when it
would come crashing down upon him.

He had failed. He had failed in front of the Prophet and
all the disciples. He'd poured the stone basin of blood over
Hob's head as the boy, rigid with fear, sobbed. He had laid
his hands on his brother's wet, sticky hair and prayed with
increasing desperation, till he was shouting and screaming
for the boy to be healed. As Brother Praeco had urged him

to pray harder, the Chosen had moaned and wailed, biting their hands and beating their chests, urging Luke to believe. Luke had pressed down, gripping his brother's head till his fingers ached, as if he could squeeze the sickness from him. Hob cried, fighting like a wild cat to get away.

But when it was all over, when the Prophet had finally cried, 'Enough!' and Hob had been washed clean in the icy water, he was still coughing. If anything, the spasms were worse than before. Brother Praeco had turned away from Luke and addressed the disciples.

'You have prayed, but your faith is weak, my brethren, as is this boy's. That is why he has failed to heal the child. "Then came the disciples to Jesus and said, 'Why could not we cast him out?' Jesus said to them, 'Because of your unbelief. But this kind is not cast out except by prayer and fasting.'" My brothers and sisters, tomorrow we shall all fast and pray. God demands of you a greater faith, for tomorrow you will see a greater miracle.'

If Luke hadn't been too numb with humiliation and misery even to think about the Prophet's words, he would have imagined that by *fasting* Brother Praeco simply meant there would be no meat, like in the Lenten fast. Old Friar Tom and some of the other disciples clearly thought so too, until they woke the next morning and saw that no pot was bubbling on the fire. There had been a few resentful mutterings then. But as the day wore on and empty bellies began to rumble and ache in earnest, the grumbling grew vociferous and angry, though only when the Prophet and Uriel were out of hearing.

Many cast sour looks at Luke, and each time Hob coughed they glared at him, even kicked him, for they knew who to blame for their hunger. A few had tried to smile, praying and urging Luke to 'have faith'. Luke had prayed, too, but however much he intended to pray for Hob to stop coughing, he found himself instead begging any saint, whose name he could even dimly remember, to stop the Prophet taking him back to the Devil's Cauldron or banishing him for ever up there, in the terrors of the Great Desolation above.

Luke's head jerked up. He could hear the slap of boots approaching from the tunnel, and saw the yellow-orange glow from the flaming torch, which was still out of sight, creeping along the walls towards him. All the others in the cave seemed to have been cast into an enchanted sleep, for no one else stirred. His stomach tightening, the boy peered towards the tunnel mouth between the prone bodies.

The Prophet ducked under the low entrance then straightened up. He stood for a moment, filling the tunnel entrance, the torch raised. The flames clawed above his head, as wild and tangled as his own hair and beard. The sleeves of his robe were rolled up, revealing the black pelt of fur on his arms. In the writhing light and shadows that snaked about him, he seemed to swell until he filled the whole cave, like an ancient giant rising out of the mountain.

'Awake, you sleepers!' he roared. 'Gird your loins. I am come to drive out a foul demon from among you!'

Chapter 53

Will

Riddle me this: I never was. No one ever saw me, nor ever will. And yet that I will be is the hope of all men while they live.

The stench from the pit of bodies was more nauseating than ever. The smell of the pestilence rising up through the thin layers of earth and seaweed made worse as the bodies bloated and putrefied in the baking sun. If you glanced in you might be forgiven for thinking the pit had been covered in a layer of black earth, until you realised the earth was undulating, like waves, and what actually covered the grave was a thick blanket of flies.

Retching and gagging, I tried to turn the iron ring set in the chapel door, but it was locked, and the stout oak too thick even to attempt to smash it. I'd half expected that, and had brought a length of rope with me, thinking I could climb through one of the windows. But now that I examined them with a thief's eyes, I realised even a cat would be hard put to squeeze through that tracery, much less my crooked frame. I walked round and round, searching for a way in, finally sinking down in the shade of an overgrown yew tree to escape the heat while I tried to think.

Janiveer had fetched my son and laid him in my arms. I'd held him only a moment or two before she had taken him back and bustled Christina away for fear someone might see us. That witch could measure the torture she was inflicting better than the king's inquisitor. If I'd never seen Oswin, I might have convinced myself that he didn't exist, that he was nothing more than a whisper on the breeze or a snatch of a half-remembered dream. But, just as Janiveer had planned, once I'd seen him, felt the warm weight of him in my arms, I would have stolen the devil's own crown from the very depths of Hell if that had been the price she'd demanded to keep him safe.

I was so lost in reliving the precious moment when I had held my son – *my own son* – that had it not been for her coughing and muttering, I might not even have noticed the Holy Hag staggering up towards the chapel until she was at the door. She peered around her, wary as an old hen, the hem of her cloak clamped to her nose and mouth. Reaching into the leather bag at her waist, she extracted a large iron key. *Why hadn't I thought of that? If anyone possessed a key to that chapel it was bound to be her!* Gripping it in both hands, she wrestled to turn it in the salt-rusted lock. Finally, the door yielded and she shuffled inside.

I sidled forwards. She clearly didn't expect anyone to be around, for though she'd closed the door, she'd not locked it. I quietly lifted the latch, then crouched, pushing at the bottom of the door to open it just wide enough to scuttle through. Keeping as low as I could, I scurried to the far corner of the chapel. The Holy Hag was up by the altar, lighting a candle. She turned as the draught made the flame gutter but, as I'd wagered, her gaze was drawn towards the open door and away from the dark corner where I had rolled myself as tight as a prickly urchin.

'The wind brings only draughts, no rain,' she muttered to herself. '"And the Lord shall shut up the heavens against you and you shall perish from the good land that the Lord has given you!"'

She knelt and raised her head towards the light. 'Blessed St Sebastian and all you holy saints, hear my plea for justice. Let pestilence devour her and the dogs lick her blood as they licked the blood of Jezebel. Wipe the harlot from the face of the earth.'

As if she had been quietly reciting a *Pater Noster*, she humbly crossed herself and staggered to her feet. Bowing lower than any priest, she retreated, shuffling towards the door. It closed behind her with a great hollow bang, extinguishing the candle she had left burning on the altar. I climbed stiffly to my feet, staring dumbfounded at the closed door. I'd always known she was a spiteful and bitter old woman, but the vehemence of her curse had shaken even me. There was evidently someone she hated, even more than me, which I suppose should have given me some comfort, but at that moment Janiveer's threat concerned me more.

The chapel wasn't large, and although little light filtered through the high narrow casements, it was plain there were only two chests in the building. The small alms chest lay open and empty. Evidently Father Cuthbert had emptied that of any coins before he'd left, though I'd have wagered it had never contained much worth the stealing, for the villagers rarely had any coins, much less any to spare for charity. The other was a long, deep box that stood in a dark corner at the back.

I feared that, like the door, it would be locked. But the lid fell off as soon as I heaved at it for the wood around the hinges was splintered. The moment I saw the damage, I realised the chest had been ransacked, but even so, whoever had stolen the valuables from it would surely not bother to take the hand of a long-dead corpse.

It was so dark in the corner of the chapel that even a white dove could have hidden in the shadows of the deep chest undetected. I clambered inside and cautiously ran my hands over the bottom. Although I was desperate to find the hand, I still recoiled at the thought of touching dead flesh without warning. But eventually even I was forced to accept there was not so much as a mouldering fly inside that chest, much less a saint's bones.

I hauled myself out and wandered around the chapel, searching every nook and corner, hoping that the hand might have been cast aside or concealed somewhere. But the reliquary niche was empty and nothing had been hidden behind the stone altar. I stared around in the gloom trying to see if there was anywhere else a small object might be concealed, but it was a piss-poor place.

There was a crude and ugly wooden statue of the Virgin Mary, her garishly painted face cracked and flaking so that she more resembled an ancient stew-house whore than the holy maid. A crumbling wreath dangled like a noose about her neck. I groped under the Virgin's skirts, but nothing lay there, except dust and mouse droppings.

The only other decoration was the painted walls. Behind the altar, God sat in judgment while the sickly-looking righteous were hauled from their tombs, still trailing grave clothes, to be carried up to Heaven by tall, slender angels, while the sinners were pitchforked into the cauldrons of

Hell by squat, crooked demons who, from their grins, evidently relished their work.

The two side walls were painted with scenes from the life of St Olaf to whom the chapel was dedicated – the saint brandishing a pollax in the prow of a ship, that same pollax chopping the head off an enemy in battle, then being used to smash an idol while fat birds and corpulent rats fled from the mounds of food left by worshippers. The opposite wall showed St Olaf baptising men who looked terrified, as well they might, since he still clutched the menacing axe, and the last depicted him dying, with another bird hovering above him, presumably a white dove, though it looked more like an overfed goose.

I imagine the itinerant artist had been paid little for his work in such a remote village, which was only fair since he'd had little talent.

In one corner I discovered some gnawed straw-filled sacks, which I guessed Harold must have used for a bed. In desperation, I shook those out, but even the mice had vacated them. *Harold! I should have thought of him at once.* He must have taken the hand, thinking it would be eaten by vermin now that it no longer had a reliquary to protect it. As acolyte, he'd certainly get the blame if the relic was damaged, so he'd probably found another box to keep it in and another hiding place. I felt almost cheerful. He was a timid but kindly lad and I was certain I could make him give it to me if I could convince him it would save the life of a woman and her baby, though naturally I wouldn't tell him the whole truth.

I hurried towards the door, and reached up to twist the iron ring. The latch lifted, but when I pulled the door it didn't budge. I tried again. Nothing. I braced my foot against the wall and hauled. It didn't move. The Holy Hag had locked it behind her. Satan's arse! Why? It wasn't as if there was anything left in the chapel worth stealing, I could vouch for that. I pounded on the door, kicking and yelling, but I knew there wasn't a chance that she or anyone else would be hanging around that stinking graveyard.

As I ranged around the four walls looking for a way out, I realised it was hopeless. Even if I'd managed to swing myself up from the altar to the window behind it, I'd never be able to squeeze through the stone tracery. If I'd had a ladder I could have tried to break out through the thatch, but I didn't. Even the bell rope hung outside the chapel. I was trapped until either Matilda or Harold returned, but when would that be? I tried to convince myself that Harold must come at least once a day. It was his duty . . . Duty! I was beginning to sound like the Holy Hag. Why would the lad bother to come at all?

I kicked the door again and yelled till my throat was raw, but it was more out of frustration and fear than from any hope I'd be heard. Daylight was fading fast. There'd be no one passing the chapel that night. Maybe in the morning I could try to attract attention. In the meantime, there was nothing else to do but resign myself to spending the night there. I told myself it couldn't be any worse than the weeks I'd spent imprisoned in the watchtower, though at least there I'd had bread and water, and as that thought struck me I realised just how thirsty and hungry I was. I cursed the Holy Hag with every foul oath I knew and a few I invented just for her.

But it was no use wasting breath on her. There was nothing for it but to try to make myself as comfortable as I could. I retrieved the mouldy sacks and stuffed the straw back in them. Then as darkness crept upwards from the corners, like a cold tide, filling the church, I curled myself up on the straw bed and, pulling another sack over me for warmth, tried to sleep. But that isn't easy when your stomach is growling like a pack of hounds.

Riddle me this, m'lord, why do dogs come to church?

Because when they see the altar covered with a cloth they think their masters are about to dine.

I could hear the patter of mice feet as they fattened themselves on candle stubs. Fried mice . . . could spit roast them over a candle . . . trick is catching the little beasts . . .

Riddle me this, my fat lord, what has never happened and never will?

A mouse making a nest in a cat's ear.

You never guessed that one, Randel . . . not in all those months . . . Never guessed I was the sly little mouse in your ear . . .

I jerked awake. A strange odour filled my nostrils, not the stink of the grave pit, something that overpowered even that stench. It was as sweet as rotting fruit, but I could also smell blood, fresh blood. I sat up and stared around. The chapel was as dark as the devil's armpit, yet something even darker was moving towards me. I could see its huge bulk against the starlight in the window, hear the deep rasp of its breathing, the click of great claws on the stone flags. I shrank back against the solid wall. Two burning eyes turned in my direction, glowing like embers. Then came a deep rumbling growl.

The beast leaped forward and I rolled aside, curling up with my arms covering my head, expecting at any moment to feel the stab of teeth or talons. Its scalding breath scorched my neck. I daren't move even to reach for my knife. Its great paw smashed down beside my head. Its jaws snapped inches from my ear. Then I sensed it turn, charging back up the chapel towards the altar. It suddenly reared up, and as it stood there, silhouetted against the faint light from the casement, I realised it was a monstrous bear, bigger than I had ever seen in my life.

Its front paws crashed down on the altar, with such power that the whole building shook. Then it lumbered towards the wall and walked straight through it, as if it was made of water not stone. And it was gone.

For a long time I remained curled up on the floor, not daring to move or even breathe for fear that the beast might be waiting just outside the church. Finally, I slowly uncoiled, pulled out my knife and crept as noiselessly as I could towards the wall that the bear had barged through. At least I could escape and, once outside, I reckoned I'd have a better chance of hiding from the beast than if I was trapped in the chapel with it.

I groped along the stones in the darkness, trying to find the hole the bear must have made, but the wall was solid. I ran my hand over every inch I could reach, but there was no hole, no hidden door, nothing even a cat could have passed through, let alone a creature of that size. I stumbled back to the door through which I'd entered, but that remained as firmly locked as before. There was no breeze coming from anywhere to show how the bear had got in or out. And how could a beast of that size have forced its way into the chapel without me hearing? Even the roof had shaken when it had struck the altar.

I edged back towards the straw sacks, dragged them into the far corner and squashed myself into the space between the chest and the wall. I was trembling violently. I lay there in the darkness listening to every creak and rustle of the night. Even if I'd swallowed the juice from a whole field of poppies I wouldn't have fallen asleep. I wasn't sure I'd ever be able to sleep again.

Chapter 54

And on her forehead a name was written.
                        The Apocalypse of St John

Hob lay trussed up on the floor of the cave in front of the pelt-covered stone that was the Prophet's throne. His ankles had been tightly tied by Uriel on Brother Praeco's orders and his arms bound to his sides by a coil of rope, for demons do not leave easily.

'The demon of sickness will fight,' the Prophet warned. 'She will make Hob thrash around to injure himself and others, even try to fling the boy into the fire.'

The more timid of the Chosen, still trying to stifle yawns, having been dragged from their sleep, shuffled even further back, pressing against the walls and staring anxiously at Hob, as if they expected him to start vomiting flames.

Hob lay rigid but for his eyes, which darted fearfully from the Prophet to Uriel, trying to see where the danger might strike from first. The Prophet took a burning stick from the fire and advanced on the boy. Seeing the flames coming closer and closer to him, the child cried out and, as Brother Praeco had predicted, tried to flail and writhe against his bonds, but Uriel pressed his bony shoulders down hard against the pebbles stuck into the floor.

The Chosen held their breath. Hob, still shrieking, screwed his eyes shut against the burning brand. Luke's fists clenched and he pressed them hard against his mouth, trying to keep himself from yelling at the Prophet to stop. The flames guttered a few inches above Hob's chest. Great beads of sweat popped from the child's face as he tried to twist himself away from the heat scorching his bare skin, but Uriel pinned him to the floor.

'In the name of God, and by the might of His cleansing fire, I command you, demon, reveal your name. Speak!'

The brand swept lower and Hob screamed.

'Release the boy, wife,' Brother Praeco ordered, flicking his hand at Uriel. 'Else the demon may enter you when she leaves him.'

Uriel immediately sprang up and shuffled back, looking both alarmed and sulky.

The Prophet swept the burning brand through the air above Hob, ordering the demon to speak, but Hob was coughing and wheezing from the smoke. Lying flat on the ground, he was struggling even to breathe.

'See how the demon torments the child. Speak, demon. In the name of the Lamb, I command you to speak. Tell me your name,' Brother Praeco's voice boomed out.

Twice more he ordered the demon to reveal her name, sweeping the burning brand above Hob's writhing body, leaving great arcs of light and smoke suspended in the air. Closer and closer he whirled the stick, till Luke, certain that with the next pass the flames would touch Hob's skin, buried his face in his knees, unable to watch.

Then a woman's voice answered, rasping, as if it emanated from a throat that was burning with fire. 'I am Frica!' The voice echoed from the depths of the earth. 'I possess the boy. He is mine!'

Chapter 55

Will

Riddle me this: Put me in a bucket and I shall make your burden lighter.

Dawn, when it finally deigned to break, found me sitting stiff and cold in the far corner of the chapel, from which I had not moved all night, though I badly needed to piss. For there is only one thing more unnerving than a bear suddenly appearing beside you, and that's a bear looming over you when your naked cock is waving about in the dark. But now that it was light, I could contain myself not a minute longer. I turned my back on the altar and prayed that the Holy Hag would not choose that moment to unlock the door. Even I felt a slight twinge of guilt about pissing in a chapel.

A shaft of bright sunlight pierced the window, making the dust dance in the air, and although the rest of the chapel was still cold and gloomy, that ray of light was like a wand, transforming everything. Day and night are two different worlds and what is real in one is a phantasm in the other. By the time the rooks were cawing on the roof, I knew that what I had seen in the dark was nothing more than a nightmare, brought on by hunger and fear for Christina and my son. *My son!* Those words still felt strange on my tongue.

I wandered back to the wall again and thumped the massive stones, mocking myself for believing, even for a moment, that any creature could have passed through them. I was crossing back to the door to see if there was any way of loosening the lock from the inside when something on the altar caught my eye.

The body of a viper was lying on the edge of the stone table. The black zigzag that ran down the length of its back gleamed in the narrow strip of sunlight. I say *the body* but the head had been bitten off, leaving a ragged bloody stump and a long red smear of blood on the side of the pale stone. I saw something else too, now that I was up close. The thick granite slab had a crack running right through it, as if something heavy had crashed down upon it from above.

I stared back at the wall again. It was solid. Any fool could see that. I hurried back to the spot on the floor where I'd been sleeping before the dream had woken me. Just a foot away from where I'd lain, I saw another splash of blood and then the head of the viper, its mouth wide, its two poisonous fangs curving down, sharp as needles, as if it had been about to strike.

I was so stunned I didn't even hear the key turning in the lock, and it wasn't until I felt the breeze and heard my name called that I spun round.

'How did you get in here, Will?' Harold said, his voice muffled through the cloth he was holding over his face. He pushed the door shut and tentatively lowered the cloth.

'The Holy H—' My voice sounded shaky even to me. 'Matilda locked me in yesterday. Didn't realise I was in here . . . Did you know she has a key?'

Harold nodded glumly. 'She didn't have a key to the linen chest, though, not that it stopped her. Prised it open, she did. Expect she'd have done the same to the chapel door if it had been locked against her. She's stronger than she looks,' he added, gazing across at the shattered lid.

'So it was her who emptied the chest. Where did she take the linens?'

'Back to her cottage to stop the villagers using them to wrap their dead in.'

I nearly said they'd have given better service as shrouds than they ever did as altar cloths, but I stopped myself. Harold was a pious lad in his own way and I couldn't afford to offend him, not till I had some answers.

His gaze had been drawn to the red streak on the altar and, wearing a puzzled expression, he moved closer to peer at what was lying on it. As he realised what it was, he recoiled, his eyes wide with alarm.

'You kill this? We mostly get grass snakes in here. Come in after the mice. We only had a viper once before and it bit an old woman when she knelt for the elevation of the Host. She didn't die, not straight off anyways. But the wound never healed, whole leg turned black and stinki— Here, what's happened to the altar? There's a great crack across it. That wasn't there before. Did you smash it?'

I pranced a few paces in a fool's caper. 'A short-arse like me?'

He grinned, but his expression rapidly turned to one of puzzlement again and he stared down at the body of the viper. 'Then how did this . . . Suppose a cat must have dragged it in.'

Except that there aren't any cats left in Porlock Weir, I thought. I shuddered, thinking how close that viper's head had been to mine. If it hadn't been for the bear . . . But there was no bear! There couldn't have been. Yet something had killed that snake and it certainly hadn't been a blade. I tried to shake the night terror from my head. Never mind about bears and snakes: Christina and my son were all that mattered now.

'The chest, Harold, was there anything else in it besides the church linens?'

Harold's pimples seemed to become more livid as his pale face flushed. 'Nothing else is kept in there,' he muttered. 'Father Cuthbert took all the church plate . . . for safe keeping.'

But I saw his gaze slide over to the empty reliquary niche.

'He took the reliquary too,' I said.

Harold grimaced. 'Don't see who else could have but . . .'

'But not the relic that was inside,' I said. 'He left that in the linen chest.'

Harold's mouth fell open. 'How did you . . .'

I fixed him with my sternest glance. Not easy when you're looking up at a mere boy and your mouth is grinning. 'Who took the hand from the chest? You or Matilda?'

Harold's expression crumpled. 'I tried to stop her,' he wailed. 'But you've seen her when she's made up her mind to do something. Not even a ship full of bishops would be able to say no to her. I didn't even know the hand was in there! What will they do to me when they find out I lost the relic?'

He looked so scared that I drew closer and gave his arm a friendly squeeze. 'Nothing, boy, nothing. If we survive, I doubt anyone outside the village will even remember the chapel had a relic, and if they do, they'll blame Father Cuthbert since he took the reliquary, not you. But all the same, best not to say a word to Matilda or anyone else that I was asking about it. Our secret, yes?'

Harold nodded gratefully, and I left him brushing the remains of the viper off the altar while I set off in search of food and a place where I could keep watch on Matilda's cottage without being seen.

The moment I discovered Matilda had the relic I realised that asking her to give it to me, of all people, would be as much use as asking the pope to canonise a heretic. The hand was probably tucked away in her cottage somewhere, along with the church linens. If she even suspected I was after it, she'd make certain to hide it where I'd never be able to find it. But if she didn't know anyone was looking for it, she'd have no cause to move it. So the easiest thing was simply to wait until she went out and search for it myself. It would be more dangerous than raiding her pigsty at night, but Cador was dead, so even if she did catch me, there was no one to arrest me. Though I wouldn't put it past the Holy Hag to take matters into her own hands and act as judge and executioner. I hadn't forgotten those vicious caltrops she'd scattered about.

I found a spot above her house in what had been the herb patch of one of the cottages but was now a tangle of sickly yellow weeds and dead currant bushes. The door to the cottage had been pulled off either to use as a bier for the dead occupants, or to be chopped up as firewood by others in the village. Swallows had made a nest inside, and brambles were already wriggling over the threshold.

I settled down between the withered bushes and stared at the cottage below, trying to ignore my empty belly. Goda was the first to emerge, her baby cradled in one arm, and a pail swinging from the other. She set off towards what was left of the stream, but before she was out of sight of the cottage, the Holy Hag called her back, snatched the baby from her and carried the infant back into the cottage. The child's shrill wail rose from somewhere inside, and Goda rocked back and forth on her feet, plainly agitated, as if she wanted to go to her but was afraid to do so. Eventually the cries stilled and Goda, still casting anxious glances back at the cottage, ambled away. I waited, dozing in the heat, so that I nearly missed the door opening again. This time it was Matilda who emerged, with a basket on her arm, and hobbled down towards the shore. The baby must still be inside, but she couldn't tell any tales. I'd never get a better chance than this.

I crept up the path and gave the door a little push. It creaked open. With a quick glance round to ensure I was unobserved, I sidled in. It was dark and cool, plainly furnished, save for a table in one corner crowded with painted statues of martyred saints, their half-naked bodies covered with exquisitely stitched cloaks. How could the wife of a lowly ship's carpenter afford such figures?

I crept closer, peering at the objects that lay at the feet of the saints. They were pieces of bone, human backbone. Relics of some saint, I assumed, but where had she got them? Even a wealthy monastery or cathedral would have a hard time raising the money to buy so many holy bones. But it was little wonder she'd taken the hand of St Cadeyrn. She evidently collected holy bones the way some women collect jewels.

Cadeyrn's relic must be somewhere close by, though the table was so cluttered with statues, bones, vials of holy water and holy seals, it was hard to pick out anything in the dim light. I began lifting the objects one by one, searching for a box or a hollow inside one of the statues where she might have hidden it.

The slap of bare feet on the hard earth and a shadow falling across the open doorway made me wheel round. I don't know which of us was more startled, Goda or me. She jerked backwards, almost spilling the precious bucket of muddy water.

It had been some time since I'd seen her close to and she looked as if she'd aged twenty years. Her cheeks were hollow, her eyes sunk and rimmed with dark shadows, and her hair had noticeably thinned. Her arms were covered with green-yellow marks from fading bruises and fresh purple ones too. *The pestilence?* My heart began to pound. But she was blocking the doorway and I didn't want to risk touching her as I pushed past.

She set her pail down and gnawed her lip. 'You'd best not let Mistress see you in here,' she whispered. 'She said you're a thief.'

'You call her *Mistress?*'

'She says I must, now I've come to live here.'

'So she's made you her servant, has she?'

The girl shifted uncomfortably from one foot to the other. 'She says I'm to be grateful she took me in and feeds me. But when my Jory comes back from the sea, he'll take care of us.'

She spoke with the kind of desperation that the condemned cling to when they're standing in the gallows cart on their way to the scaffold, still hoping that someone will speak the one magical word – *pardon*. Even when the rope lies about their neck, still they believe they will hear the word, but they never do.

'Your baby,' I said, 'you'd do anything to protect her, wouldn't you?'

I edged deeper into the room, trying to draw her away from the doorway.

Her gaze darted to the heap of rags on the floor in the corner behind me. 'Don't take her!' She rushed past me and scooped up the sleeping child, turning to face me as I hastily backed out of the door. 'I won't let you have her! She's mine!'

I tried to reassure her, fearing she might start screaming for help. But it took several minutes before I could convince her I meant no harm to her child.

'Goda, I need your help. I have a baby son of my own, but someone will kill him if I cannot get him to safety. Like you, I'd do anything to protect him. You can understand how that feels, can't you?'

She nodded warily, still clutching her daughter to her chest.

'Matilda . . . *Mistress* Matilda took something from the church, a relic – the hand of St Cadeyrn. If I can deliver that hand to one of Cadeyrn's kin, they will help me get my child to safety. It's not stealing. Any court in the land would say the hand belongs to Cadeyrn's kin.'

That wasn't exactly true. Can you imagine the uproar if judges started ruling that abbots and bishops had to return all their stolen relics? There wouldn't be a single church in England that remained consecrated, but Goda was hardly going to argue that point.

'I'd merely be returning something that was lost to its rightful owner,' I told her. 'And I would be sparing Mistress Matilda the great trouble of having to do it herself. It's a long journey, far too long and wearisome for a delicate woman of her advancing years. So if you could just tell me where Matilda keeps it, I could remove it and be on my way, without having to bother her.'

An expression of horror crept over Goda's ravaged face.

'You want to take it behind her back? You can't . . . I won't let you . . . if the mistress found it had gone . . .'

'You could tell her you saw me fleeing from the house as you returned. She'd readily believe that I broke in and stole it.'

'She'd know it were a lie . . . she knows everything . . . she always knows.'

'I always know what, Goda?' Matilda pushed past me, her eyes blazing in fury. She grabbed the girl by the hair, dragging her out through the doorway. 'I took you, slut, and your bastard into my home out of Christian charity, shared what little food and shelter I have with you and this is how you repay me, conspiring with a thieving dwarf to rob me.'

She slapped Goda hard across her cheek. The girl cried out, but before she could move away, slaps and blows were raining down on her head, shoulders and back. Matilda, in a fury of rage, was punching and hitting her with both hands. Goda, her arms wrapped around her wailing baby, bent over the infant, trying to protect her from Matilda, but she could do nothing to protect herself.

'Don't!' I yelled. 'Goda was trying to defend your cottage. She was stopping me forcing my way in.'

But my words seemed only to infuriate her more, and she struck out with even greater force.

I grabbed the bucket of water and tossed it over Matilda. With a shriek, she turned towards me, and I thought she was going to start beating me, but the water had made the baked earth and her own shoes as slippery as butter. She took a single pace, slid and crashed down hard on her back, her legs flying up into the air. Goda took one look and fled into the cottage. I ran the other way, glancing back only once to see Matilda rocking on the ground, limbs flailing like those of an upturned beetle as she struggled to pull her wet skirts down to cover her scrawny legs.

Chapter 56

Matilda

St Edmund protects against pandemics. When he was martyred his severed head was tossed into the forest, but it was found by his men who followed the call of a wolf, which cried, 'Hic, hic, hic' – 'Here, here, here.'

'Answer me, Goda, and stop snivelling,' I snapped. 'I only gave you a little slap to bring you to your senses.'

The girl sat hunched on the stool in the far corner beside her sleeping baby, sniffing loudly and flinching away from me, like a whipped cur.

'What did that little piece of vermin want?'

She shook her head, bending her face even lower, trying to hide the truth. Goda was always a simple girl, with the temperament of a butterfly. When she was a child her poor mother would set her to stir a pot or spin wool and she'd return to find the pottage burned and the yarn blowing in the wind because Goda had wandered off, distracted by a flock of gulls or the sight of men gathered on the shore.

But what she lacked in brains she made up for in animal cunning. Before she was four summers old she'd already learned how to gaze up at men from under her long lashes and insinuate herself on to the lap of any adult who might feed her titbits or stroke her hair. Not even her mother could bring herself to scold her, much less punish her, however wayward she grew. That girl had never been corrected or made to do a day's work until she came to live with me, and it was left to me to teach her what she should have learned at her mother's knee or across it.

I ladled some hot broth into one of the wooden bowls and handed it to her. She took it warily, sniffing it. Then, tipping the bowl, she gobbled it down like a beggar's child.

'Goda,' I said, 'do you remember the painting on the chapel wall, where sinners are cast into Hell?'

Her eyes widening, she peeped at me over the rim of the bowl.

'Can you remember what those wicked demons looked like? Foul creatures, nasty little grinning dwarfs.'

She set the bowl down, staring at me. 'Is Will a demon? But he's got no tail. Those demons in the chapel, they got tails.'

'Have you ever seen him naked?' I asked her.

She shook her head.

'His clothes conceal his tail. It's curled up over his back. And you remember Father Cuthbert taught that you must not consort with demons. They lie and deceive you, so that they can drag you down to the flames of Hell. Think of the agony of burning in the fires and never being able to escape that pain. You don't want that to happen to you, do you, Goda? Hearing your baby shrieking and screaming as she burns and not being able to pull her from the flames because you are burning too.'

She stared at the burning wood on the hearth, and her hand edged over to clutch the cloth her baby was swaddled in, as if she feared the dwarf would burst through the door and drag them both through that fire and down into Hell below.

'So, you must be a good girl,' I said softly, 'and tell me exactly what the dwarf said to you. If you tell me the truth, he won't be able to take you.'

Wind shrieked around the cottage, rattling the dry wooden door and plucking at the shutters. Goda lay curled up around her child on a pile of moth-eaten sheepskins and blankets, but she was not asleep. I could see the red glow of the embers of the fire, shining in her eyes. But the baby slept on, oblivious to the wind's howls and the crash of waves down on the shore.

The candle flames burning in the bones around the little cluster of saints danced wildly in the icy draughts. Shadows darted across the painted faces and their tortured bodies writhed once more in the agony of martyrdom.

Goda gave a little shriek and sat up. Holding the blanket in front of her like a shield, she stared at the floor. I glimpsed the movement too. Something black was running across the bracken. In the dim light of the candle, I couldn't make out what it was – a mouse, a snake? I rose and, grasping the poker, edged warily towards it. It wriggled and I slammed the poker down, pinning it hard against the dried bracken, then bent closer. It was just a feather, a long black feather, blown under the door by the wind.

'It means death!' Goda moaned.

'It means a strong wind,' I snapped, hurling it on to the fire. It shrivelled, bursting into a tiny blaze of flame.

'It's bad luck to burn—' She broke off, turning her head towards the shuttered casement, listening. For a few moments I could hear nothing more than the wind and waves, then I heard it too, the sound of several pairs of feet scrabbling over the stones and the murmur of voices. Flickering orange light danced through the cracks in the wood and almost at once there was a heavy thumping on the door.

'Who is it?' I called, gripping the poker more tightly. 'What do you want at this hour?'

'It's me, Sara, and some of the village folk. We must speak with you. This'll not wait.'

'Are you sick?' I called. 'If it's food you want, I've none to spare.'

'There's none sick with us, and we'd not take a bite from you, but there's summat must be said. It'll not take long for we'd all sooner be in our beds than out in this wind.'

Goda had scrambled up from her corner and was already at the door. 'Is my sister with you? Is she come to take us home?'

She was already heaving the brace beam from its socket, and before I could stop her, she'd flung the door wide, staring out into the darkness. The wind roared into the house sending the smoke whirling, lifting the bracken from the floor and snatching away the candle flames. A half-dozen faces, lit by the guttering torch, crowded in front of my door.

'Aldith! That you?' Goda called out eagerly, standing on tiptoe to peer over their heads.

'Aldith's not with us,' Sara said quietly.

'With some man, no doubt,' I said.

Sara glanced down at little Ibb, who was balanced on her hip. The child's head flopped sleepily against her shoulder. 'Some days these dark humours come upon Aldith and she'll

407

not stir from where she sits. Next she's acting like she's a giddy maid again, laughing at naught and prancing round the village. Don't know what ails her. But it's not her we've come about.'

Without so much as a nod to manners, she marched in and deposited the sleeping child on my bed.

'Don't imagine for one moment you're going to leave that child at my door,' I said firmly. 'It's enough that I'm taking care of her sister and her babe. I'll not take in Aldith's brat as well. If she can't be bothered to look after—'

'Don't fret,' Sara growled. 'I'd not abandon a mad dog to your care, much less a helpless child!'

Sybil shoved her way through the door behind her. 'Bridle that tongue of yours, Sara. 'Tis honey not vinegar that's needed here.'

Sara muttered something I couldn't catch over the shriek of the wind.

I grabbed Goda's arm. 'Close the door, girl, before the wind lifts my thatch off.'

Goda and Sybil both pushed against the door and latched it, but not before the dwarf creature had slipped inside.

'Put him out!' I ordered. 'I'll not have that vermin in my cottage.'

Sybil glanced up from the fire where she was warming her great red hands. 'You want us to let that wind in again, do you? Just hold your peace and hear us out. Then we'll all be gone.'

They settled themselves on the floor, close to the fire. Goda had snatched up her baby and retreated to the furthest corner, her eyes fixed on the dwarf. I could see her mumbling as if she was reciting a prayer or, more likely, a charm to ward off evil.

Sybil and the dwarf caught Sara's eye and nodded. Evidently she was the one they'd chosen to speak for them.

'Will here has found Janiveer,' Sara announced.

'I might have known a dwarf could find a witch. Evil seeks out its own kind,' I said. 'And I suppose he's brought her back to the village to put us all in even greater danger.'

'I left her in Porlock Manor,' the dwarf said. 'Seems she's been working there all these weeks.'

'Then it is a blessing the road's been sealed between us and them. But how did you—'

'It doesn't matter how he came to be there,' Sara said. 'Point is, he's seen her and he reckons he can persuade her to come back here, if we give her what she seeks.'

'You want to bring that witch back to the village after what she did?' I glanced at Goda. 'Are you listening, girl? You see, I was right, wasn't I? This is what I warned you of – lies and deceit. He wants to bring her back so she can finish her evil work and kill those of us who by God's mercy have escaped her malice.'

Goda whimpered and pressed herself harder against the wall, holding her baby tightly against her.

'Will doesn't want her back here. I do!' Sara snapped.

'We all do,' Sybil said. 'We agreed. She put a curse on the village, so she has to be the one to lift it. You went looking for her, same as Will and Sara here. Why go unless you wanted to find her?'

I folded my lips. It should have been plain enough why I had gone, precisely to stop them bringing her back here.

'She may not even need to return,' Sybil said. 'If she's the power to bring such death, I reckon she could call it away from us without setting foot here again. But she'll do naught to help us, unless we give her what she wants—'

'What she wants is the hand of St Cadeyrn,' the dwarf interrupted. 'He was her forefather, and she means to take his bones back to the land of his birth. As soon as she has it, she'll be gone, not just from Porlock, but from England, too, which should please you.'

'The hand? To save us from the pestilence?' I said. 'But I seem to recall that what she said she wanted was a human life. Has she changed her price?'

For a moment, I thought I saw the dwarf's gaze flicker as if I had caught him out in a lie.

'Will says it's the hand she wants from us, that's all,' Sara said.

Sybil nodded firmly. 'Aye, it's that hand she's after. Maybe . . .' She glanced uncertainly at the dwarf as if she was suddenly puzzled too. 'Maybe what she said before was just to frighten us. Like the pedlars. They start with what they know you'd never pay to soften you up, then come down to the real price. Makes it seem a bargain then. After all, we'd have no more given her the relic than we would a life. There's none would've been willing to steal a holy relic from the church, not back then afore the sickness began. It would have meant a hanging or worse. Isn't that so, Will?'

He pulled one of his grotesque faces. 'How may a man dance without touching the ground? When he is hanged, poor fool.'

I ignored him. 'So what has this to do with me?'

The dwarf lifted his head, staring at me impudently as if we were equals. 'Because *you* have the hand,' he declared, his tone serious now. 'Harold told me you took it from the chapel.' He craned round to stare at the door. 'Where is Harold, anyway? He was right behind me when we were outside.'

Sybil gave a deep belly laugh. 'Taken to his heels, I'd wager. Exorcising a demon's one thing, but facing Matilda . . .' She turned her face away, trying to stifle another laugh.

'Father Cuthbert said he'd hidden Cadeyrn's hand in the linen chest,' the dwarf continued, 'but the chest is empty. Harold swears you both found it in there and you removed it along with the linens.'

Sara was staring pointedly at the altar cloth, which now covered the table on which my saints stood.

'Father Cuthbert!' I said. 'How dare you accuse a priest of such a sacrilege? It was you who stole the reliquary, dwarf, and when the road to Porlock is unblocked again, I intend to go straight to the manor and report your heinous crime. Even if you flee, they will pursue you till they have you hanging in a gibbet cage, you can be certain of that.'

The others were staring at the dwarf, but he still wore that foolish grin. He waggled his fingers at me.

'As Bald John pointed out the last time you tried to hang me, Matilda, would I really have returned to sit freezing my cods off in a cave if I had anything half as valuable as that lump of silver? Sorry to disappoint you, but Father Cuthbert has already admitted he took the reliquary for – well, let's be charitable, shall we? – for *safekeeping*, so he says. But he swears he left Cadeyrn's hand in the linen chest, and Harold is equally willing to swear he saw it there and you took it. So you have the oaths of two clergymen, Matilda. You going to call them both liars?'

'*If* it was Father Cuthbert who removed the reliquary,' I said, 'then he took it because he knew that it would be a sore temptation for thieves. He will naturally return it as soon as he is able to hold Mass in the chapel once more.'

'Your priest won't be in any hurry to return the reliquary,' the dwarf said. 'Far too valuable. And apparently he didn't care much for the relic, else he'd not have thrown it into the chest.'

Though I knew the dwarf was trying to provoke me, I kept my dignity. 'It is plain that Father Cuthbert did not want to deprive our village of the protection of her saint by removing the holy bones from Porlock Weir when we would most have need of them. But he knew if a thief like you stumbled across the hand when you were looting the chapel, you'd think nothing of tossing such a relic to the pigs.'

'I didn't know you had any pigs left to throw it to,' the dwarf sneered.

'So,' I said, ignoring his jibe, 'Father Cuthbert concealed the precious relic in the chapel's linen chest because he knows I mend the altar cloths and would be the one to discover it. He knew he could trust me to take it to a safe place and ensure that it was properly guarded until the reliquary can be returned to us.'

The dwarf looked as if he was about to make another vile remark, but Sybil held up her hand. 'No use arguing over what Father Cuthbert's done. He'll not be returning at all unless this curse is lifted. Bald John was stricken this very afternoon. If he dies, the village'll be without a black-smith – and who's going to shoe the packhorses and make the tools for tilling the land or mending the boats? We lose any more men, we'll all starve. We must give that hand to Janiveer, if that's her price.'

'Do you really imagine I am going to relinquish the relic of God's holy saint to a witch for her to use in some diabolic dark magic? St Cadeyrn's blessed hand will stay in my keeping, where it can protect this village.'

'A saint's hand it may be, but it didn't protect my Elis,' Sara said. She clambered to her feet and stood facing me, her fists clenched. 'If it'll make Janiveer lift that curse, if it'll make her tell me where I can find my sons, then she will get that hand.' She took a threatening pace towards me. 'You give it me, Matilda, right now, else we'll search every stick and pot in this cottage till we find it, even if we have to rip the thatch from the roof and tear down the walls stone by stone.'

Sybil and the dwarf scrambled to their feet and stood behind Sara, glaring at me.

The thought of that dwarf opening my chests, fingering my garments and desecrating my holy saints with his brutish hands made me shudder.

'Very well,' I said, drawing myself up, 'but when Janiveer uses St Cadeyrn's hand against you, to raise ghosts from their graves and summon the demons of Hell, don't say that you were not warned.'

I dragged a small box from under my bed, lifted out a bundle wrapped in oil cloth and thrust it towards Sara. 'There, take it. And may the blood of every living soul in this village be upon *your* head.'

Chapter 57

Sara

To cure whooping cough, catch a flatfish, even one as small as a dab, and lay it upon the bare chest of the sufferer till the fish dies.

The moon was fat, almost at full wax, so large and bright you could see the leaping hare in it. At least we'd have some light, though the trees were bending so low in the wind, I was afraid to enter the forest in case they came crashing down on us. Below us, the black sea roared in. The great white heads of the waves raced towards the shore, rearing up and pouncing down, like cats leaping on mice to break their backs.

'Need to go straight up the hillside, then along near the top as far as we can, before we drop down behind the manor,' Will said. 'But there's no need for you to come. It'll be a hard climb. The undergrowth is thick and there's no path.'

I took a firmer grasp of Elis's stave. 'If I can bell that old cat, Matilda, then a few bushes aren't going to stop me going,' I told him firmly. 'You just keep tight hold of that saint's hand.'

Will started to argue again, but I ignored him and, holding up the horn lantern that Sybil had lent us, began to edge in among the trees. I'd made up my mind to go with him before we ever reached Matilda. There was summat about his story that didn't seem right to me, like a fish covered with fur. It was queer the way he'd discovered Janiveer at the manor. I'd not have thought of looking for her there and I couldn't make out why he'd gone back to it in the first place, not when they'd thrown him out. Unless, like Matilda said, he was a thief. But I didn't want to believe that. I'd grown fond of Will these past months. I'd not put such trust in any man afore, save for my Elis. But now, suddenly, I felt uneasy, and angry because of it.

Once, years ago, when my Elis came back from carrying a cargo to one of the towns on the other side of the moor, he said that he'd seen a man hanged. They'd left him on the gallows long after he'd stopped dancing, just to make sure he was really dead. Only when they came to cut him down at sunset, his right hand was missing, sliced off at the wrist.

I'd shuddered when he told me. 'Whoever would want a dead man's hand?' I asked him.

'Thieves, that's who,' my Elis said, 'to make a hand of glory. The hand of a hanged felon'll open any lock and it'll put the whole household into a deep sleep, hounds too, so the thief could walk right in and pluck the hair from a man's nose without him waking.'

I stared at the crooked back of the little man waddling in front of me with his strange rocking gait. Was that why he wanted the hand? Because he meant to use it to steal from the manor? He'd stolen Matilda's piglets. Cador had caught him with the carcasses. And Cador was dead, murdered.

Maybe if I hadn't come to care for Will so much I'd not have felt so hurt, betrayed. But now I was sure he'd been gulling me with his kindness, laughing at us all, and I was the fool for not seeing it.

The dwarf stopped and snatched the lantern from my hand. Holding it up, he took a few paces forward, swinging the light around as he searched for some mark or tree he recognised. The bone-pale light threw a giant shadow of him against the trunk, so that he loomed over me, his great misshapen head and twisted back monstrous in the lamplight. Suddenly I was afraid, terrified. In a panic, I gripped the stave in both hands, and swung it high.

As if he sensed the movement, he half turned, and a look of shock and horror flooded his eyes. 'No!'

But even as that one word rang out, another rose above the howling wind – a woman's scream. Then a crashing and tearing of twigs and branches as if some huge beast was lumbering through the undergrowth.

Will caught my skirt and dragged me back, pushing me against the gnarled trunk of an oak.

'Keep still,' he whispered. 'Don't make a sound.'

He darted forward, taking the lantern with him, and the darkness closed around me. I pressed myself against the rough bark, but the wind was snatching at my skirts, tossing them around like the sails of a ship. I clamped them between my legs. Far off, I could just make out the faint glimmer of the lantern, but it kept vanishing as the branches and bushes whipped back and forth. I couldn't tell if it was still moving. Another scream split the night, and then something came crashing towards me through the bushes, snapping branches as if they were twigs. I gripped the stave so fiercely my hands ached. It was getting closer. I wanted to cry out, call Will back, but daren't, for fear of calling the monster to me.

The branches above me parted as a violent gust caught them. Moonlight flooded the forest floor. In that moment, I glimpsed a huge and shaggy creature lumbering towards me, taller and wider than any widgebeast. With a great roar, it reared up on its hind legs. Above me I could see a scarlet maw and great white fangs. It stretched up, clawing at the moon as if it would rake it from the sky. Then, as the darkness closed in again, it thumped back to the ground, bounded past me and was gone. I waited, my heart thumping, until the sound of its crashing died away and only the wind shrieked through the trees. Then I ran towards the faint glimmer of lantern light.

I was afeared I'd find Will lying bleeding on the ground, but he was standing with his back to me, the lantern at his feet casting a pool of yellow light across the ground. A thin, dishevelled woman stood facing him, her grey hair half tumbled, her skirts ripped and her hands bleeding from a dozen scratches as if she'd been tearing through brambles. The candlelight shining up from below made her face all sharpness and shadow like a skull.

'They should have hung you from the tower, dwarf. Instead, it's me they cast out. Me! Who was only trying to protect her.'

'Protect her? You tried to murder her son!' Will growled.

'That's a wicked lie! I told him – I told Wallace I've never harmed a child in my life! Nor would I! But he wouldn't listen. Dragged me to the gate as if I was a scullion. I'd not even the chance to pack my belongings or take so much as flint and iron with me to make a fire. It was me who kept m'lady's child alive. I fed it, tended it so it was warm and safe. I kept the whole manor from learning the truth – that she'd given birth to a bastard, *your* bastard. But I'll not keep silent now. I'll make sure Sir Randel knows his new bride is nothing but a whore. Worse than a whore, for she didn't betray him with another man, but with a beast. When he hears you laid your filthy hands on his niece, Sir Nigel'll have you hunted down and torn apart by the dogs.'

I glimpsed the flash of steel in the lantern light as Will drew his knife and sprang at her. She staggered backwards, crashing to the ground. As he lunged towards her, she scrambled back on her elbows to get away from him.

'Don't kill me,' she whimpered. 'I didn't mean—'

'You meant it!' Will raised the knife higher. 'It was your poisonous tongue that separated us. It was you who had me sent away. Let's see how many malicious tales you can tell when I've cut it out.'

He grabbed her by her straggly grey hair, hauling her head back so that she was forced to open her mouth. She was gasping, and struggling frantically to push him away, but her strength was no match for his. I could see the terror in her eyes. I darted forward and caught his arm trying to drag him away. 'No, Will. She's just an old woman. You'd never harm a woman.'

He tried to shake me off, but my weight on his arm unbalanced him. The old woman shoved him hard and rolled over. In a trice she was on her feet and running through the trees. The night swallowed her and the howls of the wind obliterated any sound.

Will sat in the dried leaves, his head in his hands, panting hard. Finally, he raised his head and glowered up at me. 'You should have let me kill her! She'll get word to Sir Nigel and that word will mean death for my son.'

'Your son?' I repeated, staring at him. 'You have chillern . . . a wife?'

'You heard Eda, what I have . . . *had* is another man's wife. But, yes, I have a son.' Will laughed bitterly. 'No need to gape at me like that. Even beasts breed.'

He struggled to his feet. 'I have to get my son and his mother away from the manor tonight before her husband learns of this. But I can't get her out without Janiveer's help and she won't give it unless she has the hand of Cadeyrn.'

'So that's why you wanted it, not to stop the pestilence but to save your son.'

He grimaced, then glanced slyly up at me. 'But you said you wanted to find Janiveer, and I found her for you, didn't I?'

He gave a comical little skip, pulling a face, like a small boy trying to coax his way out of trouble by making his mam smile, just like Hob used to do. A gust of wind ripped through the trees, making me shiver.

'No good'll come from standing here. We've a long night ahead of us,' I said.

He lifted the lantern, picked up my stave and handed it to me. 'Not sure it's safe to give you this. Are you intending to brain me with it again?'

I flushed. 'My Elis told me about the hand of glory that thieves use. I got to thinking maybe you'd another reason for wanting that hand.'

Will laughed. 'You'd best not let the Holy Hag hear you call her precious relic a glory hand.' He pursed his lips and flared his nostrils, looking so like Matilda when she was affronted that I laughed too.

Then, pulling his cloak tighter around him, he began pushing his way through the bushes again and I followed. We walked on in silence. Trees whipped round us in the darkness, and the wind dashed leaves and twigs against our skin, making it sting. I glanced behind me, remembering the huge creature that had lumbered out of the night. Where were my sons tonight? Will might fear for his son's life in the manor, but there was more to fear for a little boy lost out here and alone.

Chapter 58

The sea is a woman and her other name is Fate.
Medieval Proverb

Janiveer lifts the candle, moving the soft yellow flame towards baby Oswin to ensure that he sleeps, but she is careful to keep the light from falling full on his face and waking him. She watches his eyes flutter beneath the almost transparent lids. He is dreaming, an ancient dream, wandering the labyrinth of his ancestors, where water runs through fire, and fish swim in the red veins of the earth. It is a dream she could enter if she wished, but she has her own shadow lands to explore.

She settles herself in front of the fire, leaning forward and blowing the flames gently so that they flicker over the logs. She lights twigs of rowan, ash and flying thorn, letting the smoke wash over her, like running water, as her mother and aunts taught her.

She stares into the embers, marking the progress of the dwarf and the woman approaching ever closer through the forest of scarlet flame, blackened wood and white ash. She watches the other dark creatures of the forest too, beings that no dull-witted woodsman would ever see, but for once these spirits and phantasms do not interest her. Reluctantly, she pulls herself away from the fire, checking the child one last time, but she knows he will sleep for hours. She added dwale to his milk, not too much lest he sink into a sleep from which he would never wake, but enough to keep him silent until morning. The veil between sleep and death is thin and fragile, but Janiveer is mistress of it.

She steps outside, pulling the door closed behind her. The moonlight, as if by alchemy, has transmuted the dull stone of the high walls to quicksilver. But as soon as she moves from the shelter of the stillroom, the wind pounces, shrieking like a trapped animal, hurling itself around the courtyard, rolling and clattering the well buckets and a carelessly abandoned broom. But even above the din, the hounds hear the soft slap of Janiveer's bare feet. They smell her skin and raise their heads. With a gesture and an ancient word she bids them lie down and they do, without protest.

The watchman at the inner gate does not hear her. He was greedy for the flagon of strong cider she left for him and now his snores reverberate deep inside his hut. She slips through the wicket gate in the great door, gripping it tightly so it is not snatched from her hand.

Outside the shelter of the inner walls, the wind is even stronger. Every tree and blade of dry grass bends in obeisance before it. It tears at her gown, like an importunate lover, but she wraps her cloak tighter and barges against it, following the line of the stinking brook until she comes to the iron grating.

She hears the low voices almost at once, Will urging Sara to stay outside and not try to wriggle through the filth of the sewer. He emerges, kicking and wriggling, then turns to reach for something the woman hands to him through the arch. Janiveer motions him to sit close to the grating and she crouches on the opposite bank. She knows Sara is straining to hear every word that passes between her and the dwarf, just as she knows what Sara's heart is aching for, but she is not ready to give it to her, not yet. Sara must learn to wait, just as she has waited. Even time must be avenged.

'Have you brought the hand of Cadeyrn?'

Will holds up the small package but does not pass it across the filthy stream and Janiveer makes no attempt to snatch it.

The dwarf peers around in the darkness, staring over Janiveer's shoulder at the trees bending in the wind. 'Have you brought them, Christina and my son?'

'Out here, in the cold and the dark? Would you have them fall sick? She is not a packman's wife. I will bring them to you when it is time. Be patient.'

'But there is no more time,' the dwarf says urgently. 'They must leave the manor tonight. That evil old besom, Eda, saw me in the forest as we were coming here. I would have killed her, but she got away. She knows everything and she means to tell it. As soon as news reaches Lady Aliena or that fiend Randel, Christina's death warrant will be signed, and my son's too. I must get them away, far away from here.'

'And you shall, Will, but nothing has changed as yet. The pestilence still rages. You must wait.'

'Will,' Sara calls through the archway. 'Tell Janiveer . . . tell her I'm ready . . . I will pay the price she asks, if she'll only lift the curse and bring my lads back to me. Even if they're dead, I must know . . . I must look at them, one last time. See they're buried right.'

In the darkness, Janiveer smiles. And when a sea-witch smiles, men should tremble.

'Give me the hand of Cadeyrn,' she says quietly.

'You swear you will save Christina and my son?'

'And you'll come back to the village,' Sara adds swiftly.

'On the bones of my forefathers and -mothers, I swear it.'

Will stretches out his arm across the gurgling dark hole in the great wall. As he does so, a gust of wind finding the narrow gap, bursts through it with a great shriek, like the cry of a monstrous eagle.

Janiveer's fingers eagerly grasp the bundle that the dwarf holds out to her. She expects to feel the fire of Cadeyrn's bones run through her own, the power of that hand tingle in hers. When she touches his other bones, she can taste the blood, hear the screams of men and horses, feel her pulse throb with the weight of the pollax in her hand as it chops through living flesh and crushes skulls like birds' eggs. But now, holding this, she sees nothing, feels nothing.

Janiveer lays the small bundle in her lap, unwrapping it more by touch than sight, for clouds are racing across the moon. Her fingers explore the naked leathery skin, the cold dead nails, the smashed bone of severed wrist. She rises, towering above the dwarf.

She points the dead hand at him. 'You want me to save the woman you love yet you lie to me? Did you think me so easily deceived? You do not know me, dwarf.'

Will scrambles to his feet. 'But that's what you asked for, Cadeyrn's hand. Harold said the hand was hidden in the linen chest in the chapel, just where you told me the priest had left it. Matilda took it home and hid it. We went to her house and forced her to give it to us. I swear it's the saint's hand, the very one that was in the reliquary.'

'But it is not *Cadeyrn's* hand. The hand that was struck from him, the hand from which the spring flowed, was his right hand. His axe hand. This is a left hand.'

'But where would the old hag have got another hand?' the dwarf pleads. 'If this isn't Cadeyrn's hand, then it must have been substituted for the real one years ago . . . or maybe,' he adds desperately, 'your forefather was left-handed and fought with the other hand to fool the enemy.'

'I have his body, dwarf,' Janiveer says, her voice crackling with ice. 'A man, even a great man like the warrior king, does not possess two left hands. I ask you once more, where is the hand of Cadeyrn? Where is the hand of my bone and my blood?'

'I swear to you,' the dwarf says, 'this is the hand that was in that chapel.'

'And I know it is not!' Janiveer paces closer to the wall so that, even over the wind, Sara will hear her plainly. 'I asked the villagers to choose which life they would give me and you have offered me your life, Sara, your life to save the village. But you have both tried to deceive me. I will take a life, but now *I* will choose whose life it shall be.'

Chapter 59

Uriel cast another log on to the fire, though it was already hotter than Hades. Firelight flickered and twisted across the cave walls, undulating through the shadows. All the disciples were exhausted. Some flopped limply against the walls, heads drooping. Others dug their nails into their palms to keep themselves awake or shuffled on aching knees to find sharper pebbles to kneel on. They dared not rest. Uriel, though her own eyes were red-rimmed, stared down at them from her niche in the wall, like a buzzard searching for prey.

Only Hob was permitted to sleep. He lay curled on the ground while the Prophet prayed for guidance. The boy's naked body was covered with smudged signs, some black, inscribed with an end of a burned stick, others dark red, drawn in blood. All had been made to drive the succubus Frica, demon of sickness, from his small frame. But she would not depart.

The Prophet had commanded her, prayed over her, argued with her, but the boy was his, she said, and she would not come out of him. She had jeered and laughed. Her rasping cries had echoed up and down the tunnel, till the Chosen couldn't tell if she was mocking them from out of the boy's mouth or from the depths of Hell beneath. Sometimes one of her six demonic sisters, Restilia or Ignea, would taunt Brother Praeco from the rocks, threatening to enter the boy and lie with Frica, so he would be forced to drive them out too.

The Prophet had prayed at them in Latin and in a language that sounded to Luke like the drunken babbling of a madman, but which Friar Tom had whispered was the tongue of angels. But though sweat had poured down his face and soaked his shirt, neither earthly nor heavenly words would make Frica depart. Once, the Prophet had seized Hob and held him high above his head, threatening to dash him against the rocks if the demon would not leave him. Hob had screamed until he was rigid and blue. Luke heard himself screaming too, though neither could be heard over the shouts and exultations of the Chosen. But when Hob was set down again, the coughing returned so badly that he vomited, almost choking as he fought for breath.

When the Prophet rose from his knees and vanished into the darkness of the tunnel behind, Luke had felt the tension in his body ease just a little. Maybe Brother Praeco had given up and gone back to his own chamber to sleep. The disciples glanced furtively at one another – could they, too, rest now? Friar Tom's head sank back against the wall. David dipped a ladle several times into a bucket of water, pouring some over his own sweating face and slurping the rest. The Chosen watched enviously, licking dried lips. Only the Prophet's most trusted disciples would dare to take such licence.

'God has told me what must be done,' a deep voice announced.

Luke started violently, almost knocking himself out as his head banged against the rock. Brother Praeco was standing in front of the tunnel entrance. No one had heard him return. His tangled beard dragged over the mat of hair on his chest as he gazed slowly around the cave.

'A demon will remain in a human body only so long as it is in comfort there. If the body in which it resides feels pain, then the demon shall feel it also. We must drive this succubus from the child, punish her till she weeps and begs for mercy.'

He gazed down at the naked boy lying on the floor. Hob had fallen into a sleep of complete exhaustion, from which not even the Prophet's booming tones could wake him.

Brother Praeco raised his arm and pointed at Luke. 'Come!'

Shakily, Luke clambered to his feet. He was too numb, too scared to do anything but obey. He couldn't even seem to remember where he was any more. He was grateful to be told what to do. He stumbled forward, staring down at the body of his brother lying on the cave floor. The boy's ribs, like the spars of a wrecked ship, jutted out beneath the skin. Luke gazed uncomprehendingly at him as if he was an animal that had no connection to him at all.

Brother Praeco lifted Luke's hand and he felt something hard and smooth pressed against his palm. The Prophet closed Luke's fingers around a long springy stick.

'Now, Luke, God has given you another chance to prove your faith. You will thrash that demon who has been tormenting your brother. You will beat her without mercy. When Frica screams and cries, you will beat her all the harder. You will flog her, Luke, with all the strength in your arm. Beat her, Luke. Drive her out.'

'Beat her, Luke. Drive her out,' the chorus of the Chosen screamed. 'Beat out the devil! Beat out the devil!'

Luke was aware that his arm was rising. He heard the whistle as the stick rushed through the air and the thwack as it hit bare flesh. He heard the scream, a demon from Hell screaming in agony, and he was exalted.

Chapter 60

Matilda

St Laurence of Rome is the patron saint of cooks for it is said he was martyred on a gridiron. He took the Holy Grail from the Last Supper and sent it to be hidden in the monastery at Huesca, that it might give sustenance to the Kingdom of Aragon.

When I woke, it was the silence I noticed. There were no more cocks or hens to be heard in the village, for they'd long since been eaten, but the gulls always started to cry as soon as the thinnest rind of light showed itself over the hill. But that morning a pearly white light was already glowing through the fish skins that covered the narrow casement and yet there was still no sound from the gulls.

Goda was lying curled up around her baby in front of the hearth. I was tempted to kick her awake as I passed, for she should have been up mending the fire and heating what little we had in the pot. But I was glad of a moment or two of peace before her brat began bawling again.

I opened the door and stepped out into a white blanket of mist, the first sea fret of the closing year. I could just make out the posts of the pigsty appearing and vanishing again as the mist swirled around. Tiny beads of water clung to the spiders' webs, making them suddenly visible. There were webs all over the roof, more strung between the walls and the edge of the thatch, enveloping the shutters. The whole house seemed to be wrapped in these silvery-grey nets, each with a dark spider clinging to it, motionless, waiting in vain for its prey.

The damp air made my lungs and bones ache and there was nothing more likely to bring on the ague. I hurried back inside. Goda, woken by the draught from the door, was sitting cross-legged in front of the embers of the fire, trying to coax them into life with handfuls of dry grass and twigs. With her other hand she pressed her baby to her chest. Her shift was open and the child was pulling at her teat, grizzling. Goda's dugs were flat, just flaps of skin, like an old crone's. But she still insisted on trying to feed the baby.

'Put the child down and attend to that fire properly,' I snapped. 'You're just wasting what little strength she has. You can spoon a little from your bowl of pottage into her, when you can stir yourself to make it.'

'Naught to make pottage from, unless . . .' Her gaze flicked towards the barrel, where my last few pieces of pork swam in brine.

'Then you'd better take yourself down to the shore. See what you can gather.'

'There's a bad sea fret. 'Tisn't safe.'

'Nonsense, the tide will be out, and the mist can't harm you.' I hauled her to her feet. 'Winter's coming, so you'd better start doing something to earn your keep. Do you want to find yourself sleeping in the pigsty? How long do you think the child will survive that?'

Goda glanced down at the whimpering baby, gnawing

her lip. Then, with ill grace, she laid her back on the pile of skins, pressing an old pig's bone into her fist for her to suck. She hoisted the woven fish basket on to her back and, shivering, padded out into the mist, her broad bare feet pounding against the hard earth.

The baby was still whining, but I ignored her. I lifted down each of my saints and dusted them, running my fingers over the cold carved flesh and pressing my nails deep into the painted scarlet wounds – St Amphibalus bound to the tree by his intestines; St Laurence roasting on a gridiron; St Edmund with his severed head; and St Sebastian pierced with arrows. I dared not light candles to them, for I had precious little wax left and the winter nights were long and dark. But I took the skull goblet from its pouch and poured into it a few drops of the holy oil I had removed from the chapel. Dipping my fingers into it, I anointed each of the saints, touching heads, ears, eyes, lips, breast, hands, feet and the place where their private parts would be beneath their carved loincloths.

'Blessed and holy St Sebastian, hear me and watch over this your faithful servant, as angels cleanse the world with their scourges and scythes. May the sinners be cut down and perish and the righteous be exalted.'

The baby was wailing loudly now, her face scarlet, fists flailing. Her mother should have returned long before this. I opened the door, peering out, but the mist was too dense to see even to the far side of my herb patch. I edged forward along the track. I would have to go down and chivvy the girl. She'd probably forgotten what she'd been sent for and was idling her time in chatter, oblivious to my needs and her own daughter's.

It was hard to breathe in the chill air and before I had

gone more than a few yards, my skin and clothes were soaked by the tiny droplets of water. The mist hung a few inches above the ground, so that I was able to see the path immediately beneath me, though nothing ahead or around me. Occasionally a post or a tree-trunk reared up out of the mist, looming so close that my heart pounded from the jolt until I could distinguish what they were. I kept thinking I had lost my way, for I was certain I'd walked long enough to have reached the shore, but then I'd glimpse the wall of a certain cottage or a marker stone, which made me realise I had not come nearly as far as I'd thought.

But as I descended, I became aware of a growing stench that was far stronger than the seaweed and rotting fish on the shore. It smelt like the grave pit up at the chapel. But I was walking away from that, not towards it, so it should have been growing weaker. The mist must be dragging down the foul humours.

The path levelled out and I glimpsed the great round smooth pebbles that marked the edge of the shoreline, but the fret was even thicker there. The tide must be far out, for the lapping of the waves was no more than a distant whisper.

I heard pebbles rattling, as if someone was walking across them, and glimpsed a dark shape moving before the swirling white mist enveloped it again. That sickening smell, it was worse here and getting stronger.

'Goda! Goda, is that you? Answer me, girl!'

Again I heard the rattle of pebbles. The smudge of a figure appeared, sending the mist whirling as she moved towards me.

'Goda, have you forgotten your baby? She's as hungry as I am. You must have gathered a dozen—'

But the woman emerging from the fog was not Goda.

'I have not forgotten the baby, Matilda. Nor have I forgotten you.'

Janiveer was standing in front of me, her sodden skirts clinging to her legs, her dark hair hanging in wet strands about her face, as if she had just walked out of the sea.

'You have something that belongs to me, Matilda.'

'So, you're back,' I said coldly, though I confess my heart was thumping a little from the shock. 'I can assure you, Janiveer, I have nothing of yours. I would never bring myself to touch anything that a witch had owned. But, in any case, you own nothing save the clothes you were wearing when they foolishly pulled you from the sea. And the whole village rues the day they did that.'

'I will give them cause to curse that day a hundred times over if you do not give me what is mine – the hand of Cadeyrn.'

I snorted. 'So it seems you are not quite the seer Sara seems to think you are. If you were, you'd know the dwarf and some of the villagers came to my cottage in the middle of the night to steal it from me. I knew that creature was lying when he said he would give it to you, and I was right! He kept it for himself, didn't he? If you want it, you'd best find the dwarf.'

'Will brought me the hand you gave him, as he told you he would. But what he brought was not Cadeyrn's hand but the hand of another.'

'Then the dwarf must have switched them,' I snapped. 'They're foul, deceitful creatures. As I told you, he wants the saint's hand for himself. No doubt he thinks he can sell the relic for a good price to some abbey or cathedral. He'll have it hidden away in that cave he skulks in, like the animal he is. That's where he takes all the things he steals. Go to his cave, Janiveer, and see if I'm not right.'

So saying, I hurried back up the hill towards my cottage. I could feel those cold, evil eyes upon me all the way home, as if her malice was stalking me to my very threshold. It made my skin crawl. As I fumbled for the latch on the door, my fingers brushed against a wet cobweb that clung to my wrist. Its weaver scuttled across the back of my hand. I dashed the spider against the wall and hurried inside, slamming the door behind me.

I leaned against it, panting, my legs trembling from the fast climb.

Goda, gutting fish at the table, glanced up in alarm.

'Whatever is it, mistress? You look like you seen a corpse walking.'

'Janiveer's returned. The sea-witch is back in Porlock. She walked in on the tide. Did you see her down at the shore?'

The knife clattered from Goda's hand on to the table. 'The one that cursed the village? What does she want?'

'When she was here last time she said she wanted the life of a man, woman or child who had been born in Porlock Weir. And today, when I saw her on the shore, she spoke of your baby, Goda.'

Not stopping to wipe the scales and fish guts from her hands, Goda snatched up her daughter and pressed her fiercely to her chest. 'I'll not let her take her. I'll run and hide in the forest.'

Clutching the child, she tried to push past me to the door. But I barred her way, edging her back.

'She's a witch. They can smell out children as a hound can smell a deer. She'll find you however deep into the forest you go, and out there all alone, you'll have no one to protect you.'

'What am I to do?' Goda wailed. 'Suppose she comes here? How'll we stop her?'

'She doesn't need to come here,' I told her. 'If she can call the pestilence to the village and kill so many without even touching them, she can cast a spell to kill your child whenever she chooses. There is only one way to stop a witch and destroy her spell. You must draw her blood.'

Goda shook her head vehemently, backing away from me. 'I – I can't. I wouldn't dare. Suppose she curses me. You do it, you!'

'It wouldn't break her spell if I did it. It is your daughter she seeks to kill, a child of your body, so you are the only one who can stop her.'

I crouched and dragged out the box from under the bed. From it, I took a knife, sheathed in leather. Drawing the blade carefully, I laid it on the end of the table, the only part not covered in guts and scales. The steel glinted in the firelight.

'You must use this. It's as sharp as a razor shell. It will take only the lightest touch to draw blood. But it must be on her forehead, above her breath, to break any curse she puts on your child.'

Goda reached out to touch the blade.

But I caught her wrist. 'Careful. I told you the blade is so sharp you'll cut yourself badly if you touch it.' I slid it back into the leather sheath, and pushed it across the table at her.

She shook her head, backing away. 'If she would hurt my babby when there's neither of us done her any harm, what will she do to us if I cut her?'

'Once you have drawn her blood, the witch will be power-less to hurt you or your child ever again. She will never be able to work her evil against you. You'll be safe.'

She stared at the sheathed knife as if it might rise up and fly at her. 'But it's 'gainst the law to go cutting anyone. When that sailor stabbed the pedlar at Sybil's brew-house, Cador arrested him and they hanged him at the assizes.'

'You're only going to scratch her,' I assured the girl. 'Why, this knife is so sharp, she won't even feel it. And even if Cador still lived, he wouldn't arrest anyone for a mere scratch.'

I moved around the table, picked up the knife and tied the sheath around her waist by its leather strap. 'Don't go using that knife to cut the fish, else you'll blunt it. When you see Janiveer, just walk up to her, pull out the knife and strike. You can be away before she even realises what you've—'

The silence outside was shattered by the clanging of the church bell. It was not the slow, measured tolling of the death knell – no one had rung that since the pestilence pit was dug – or the summons to Mass, but a frantic and urgent tolling as if someone was trying to rouse the whole village. I flung open the door and hurried outside, Goda close on my heels. The mist was beginning to lift, and below I caught glimpses of the wet sand glistening out in the bay. The bell was still ringing, but more slowly now, as if whoever was heaving on the rope was tiring.

I hurried down the hill, Goda trailing after me, but we were nearly at the bottom before we stepped out of the mist and into the strange white light below it. A small knot of women stood on the foreshore staring out into the bay, and a few old men came limping towards them, summoned by the bell. The mist still drifted in patches over the wet sand, but between white swirls I could see something huge and dark. It was a ship, a crayer, beached far out on the sand and tilting over at an angle. The sail that hung from her single mast was shredded and tattered. But there were men on board, some leaning over the side, others up in the castle.

The gulls had at last taken to the skies as the mist began to lift and they circled the mast of the stricken ship, screaming, but they weren't landing and little wonder, for I suddenly knew where that terrible stench was coming from. As I watched I realised that not a single figure on board that vessel was moving. It was a ship of death.

Chapter 61

Sara

Fiddle-fish bring good fortune to a vessel if they are dragged behind it on a line till they disappear, but if that line be cut before the fish are gone, the ship's luck shall be cut with it.

Meryn hopped a pace closer on his crutches, his withered leg dragging behind him. He jerked his chin towards the stranded ship. 'Next tide'll lift her and smash her into the fish weirs. 'Tis a miracle she were beached afore she ran into them last night. Weirs'll be destroyed and those corpses'll be scattered all over the beach. She'll have to be burned afore the tide comes in.'

Sybil turned to look at me. 'Then it's us'll have to do it.'

'And just how will you get out there with enough pitch to set fire to it?' Isobel demanded. 'Last time the pestilence struck, the menfolk went out to fire the ships. If my husband was still alive, he'd know—'

'Well, he isn't,' Sybil retorted. 'So we'll have to do the thinking.'

'Mud-horses,' I said. 'If they can carry eels back, they can take barrels out.'

'Have you ever used one?' Isobel asked.

439

'Seen menfolk do it since afore I could walk. Can't be that hard,' I said impatiently, but it was.

Spinning looks easy to them who've never done it. My Elis laughed once that it must be the simplest task in the world if a woman could do it. So I made him try. He soon stopped laughing when he found he couldn't spin a half-foot of yarn that wasn't either as lumpy as a dish of beans or so thin it broke.

We managed well enough rolling the tar barrels down from the watchtower and lashing them to the runners of the mud-horses. But when I stepped out on to the wet sand and tried to bend forward over the frame same as I'd seen the fishermen do, I found I couldn't lie flat and put my feet on the ground at the same time. The mud-horses were built for the height of men, not us. And when my feet were touching the ground, I couldn't push the sledge forward, for the barrels were too heavy. I felt someone wriggling in beside me. Katharine leaned against the other spar. Between us we managed to get the runners to slide, but that mud-horse juddered and jerked over the sand as if it were a living beast. The men used to make the mud-horses fly. We could only crawl.

The frame dug painfully into my breasts, and my legs felt as leaden and unwieldy as tree-trunks before we had gone more than a few yards. Looking around me, I saw that the other women, too, were working in pairs, but making no more progress than we were. Sybil, being taller than the rest of us, was making better weather of it, but not much. We were all too weak from the flux.

'Stop,' I called to Katharine. 'At this rate we'll not reach the ship afore the tide starts running in. We'll have to push it like a barrow. But you hold on tight, case there's quicksand. If you feel the ground going from under you, get your foot on that runner.'

She nodded grimly. It was hardly much faster when we were walking behind and pushing, for our feet sank into the sand as the mud-horse resisted, or it would suddenly shoot forward, leaving us sprawling. I daren't glance up, for each time I did, the ship seemed further away than ever. Only the foul stench came closer, carried on the strengthening breeze. My back and legs moaned in pain, and my feet were so numb from the cold wet sand that a dozen viperfish could have stung them or razor shells slashed them and I'd have felt nothing. I just kept forcing them forward, one foot at a time.

Then, just when I thought I couldn't take another step, the great rough timber wall reared up in front of us, covered with clumps of barnacles and weed. We stared up. Three men hung, face down, over the side, thrown there when the ship had rolled on the sand bank. Their faces were black and swollen, dried lips drawn back over their teeth, like snarling dogs. Their eyes, filled with blood, glared down at us, like the demons in the chapel. For a few moments none of us could move. We'd lived with the grave pit for weeks, but the sight of these men looming over us was more terrible than any corpse we'd buried in the village. We might have been standing there still, if Sybil hadn't roused us.

'No time to waste,' she grunted. Her face was mottled red and white, and streams of sweat ran down either side of her nose. 'Tide'll be on the turn. No! Don't go pulling the barrels off, they'll sink into the sand. We'll have to burn them on the mud-horses. Push them in till they're touching the timbers.'

We gave one last push, ramming the mud-horses as far

as we could under the curve of the ship's timbers. Sybil pulled a flint and iron from the pouch that hung at her waist. The spark came easily enough, but the tar wouldn't catch.

'No good! We need straw or kindling or summat.'

She gazed helplessly around at the expanse of wet sand. There was nothing dry enough to burn.

Katharine turned around, her back towards me, and struggled to unlace her kirtle. 'Front of me is all wet, but the back of my shift should be dry enough. Help me rip it! Hurry!'

She pulled down the kirtle and, using my knife and teeth, I tore a long strip from the top of her shift. Several of the other women copied us, tearing cloth from any part of their garments that was still dry. We splashed along the row of barrels, stuffing the rags into the tops. The wind was stronger now, but Sybil, shielding the barrel with her body, managed to get the first rag to light, then another and another.

We waited, our sleeves pressed over our mouths and noses against the stench, until the flames leaped up from the first barrel, licking along the tarred seams of the timbers. The other barrels caught quickly and the flames, fanned by the strengthening wind, raced along the caulking between the ship's timbers and began to rear up towards the sloping deck.

I glanced at the waves breaking out on the edge of the bay. 'Tide'll be turning any time now, and that wind'll push it in fast. We'd best hold hands going back, case someone falls.'

My legs were trembling with weariness and some of the other women could barely stand, but we couldn't afford to rest. We linked arms and turned for the shore, trying to encourage each other.

'Be much easier going back without having to push the barrels.'

'Not far now.'

The heat from the burning ship scorched our backs. The wind was driving the thick, oily smoke over us, making our eyes stream with tears and our throats raw with coughing, but it was impossible to hurry on the soft mud.

An agonised scream made us whip round so suddenly that Katharine slipped and fell. We stared up at the blazing ship. One of the sailors was clinging to the rail in the stern. His clothes were afire and he was trying to beat them out. But his hands were burning like torches where the melted pitch from the timbers had stuck to them. He was howling and shrieking, then he flung himself over the side. The smoke was so dense we couldn't see where he'd landed. Then, as a gust of wind lifted it for moment, we glimpsed a blackened heap on the sand below the ship. It was blazing almost as fiercely as the tar barrels, but the man didn't move.

Katharine, kneeling on the sand, leaned over and was violently sick.

Chapter 62

Will

Riddle me this: Some try to hide and others to cheat, but whatever you do we shall always meet.

Janiveer appeared on the rise above the beach. I say *appeared* for that was the word that always came to mind whenever I saw her. One moment the spot was empty, the next she was standing there, like some ancient warrior queen, her dark hair streaming behind her. She was staring across the bay at the ship that blazed like a beacon in a pall of thick black smoke. Fragments of burning sailcloth were snatched up by the wind and tossed about like seabirds in a storm, carried up so high that those on shore began to glance anxiously at the thatch on their cottages. The mast lit up like a giant candle before it came crashing down on the deck, and even at that distance we could hear the crackle and crack of the timbers as the flames consumed the bodies of the sailors on the giant funeral pyre.

Janiveer stood motionless on the rise above us, her sea-grey eyes fixed unblinkingly on the ship as if she was willing it to burn. For a moment, I had the wild idea that if she looked away the flames would go out and the ship would be floating in the waves once more, with all the crew alive.

Janiveer had returned to the village and that same day a death ship had drifted into the bay. Had she summoned it, just to remind us of what she could do?

A wail distracted me. Goda was crouching on the beach, crying like a small child that her beloved Jory might be one of the seamen aboard that ship. Meryn, leaning on his crutches, clumsily patted her shoulder. 'And if he was, my maid, better this than you find his rotting corpse on the beach.' He glanced back up the hill towards the grave pit. 'You wouldn't want him dumped in with them. I don't reckon they'll ever rest easy.'

Goda's anguished wails redoubled. The man's words were plainly doing nothing to reassure her. I was about to step in and remind her that there were a thousand ships at sea, and at that moment her lover was probably supping his fill in a tavern on some distant shore, when I saw the Holy Hag making her way towards Goda, her face contorted with fury. I don't know what Matilda had to be angry about, but her fury was a summer's breeze compared to the storm that was boiling up in me.

I sprang into her path and stood there, arms folded. 'You wicked old hag. You sent me chasing after a mare's nest. You knew that wasn't the hand of St Cadeyrn. Where have you hidden the real relic?'

'There has only ever been one relic in that chapel, dwarf. Where would I get another? Now let me pass, you vile creature.'

She tried to sidestep me, but I skipped in front of her, dancing from side to side to block her way. 'Janiveer's returned, Matilda. She's searching for the hand. If she's the power to summon a ship of corpses, imagine what she'll do to you if she finds you've been keeping her ancestor's hand from her. Look at her, old woman! Look!' I pointed up to the rise where Janiveer stood, still staring out into the bay, as if she could command the waves to sweep in and drown the whole village.

The Holy Hag's eyes widened as she caught sight of the figure. Then, to my surprise, a pleased, almost cunning, expression crossed her withered face. Shoving me aside, she scuttled towards Goda, hauling her roughly to her feet. She bent close, muttering in Goda's ear. Whatever she was telling the girl, Goda plainly did not want to do it, for she looked terrified and tried to back away. But the hag shook her and gestured towards the burning ship. Goda stared at the flames. Matilda shoved her towards the path. I watched Goda walk up the beach towards the rise. Several times she glanced back at the ship, and each time it seemed to strengthen her resolve for she quickened her pace. She was not crying now, but her face was pale, her lips pressed tightly together.

As she reached the path, the wind changed direction and a cloud of thick, choking smoke billowed over me. God's blood, it stung the eyes worse than the smoke from a spit-roasted pig. I hurried back a few paces to get out of its way. When I looked again, Goda was running up the rise towards Janiveer. The woman either didn't see her, or was ignoring her, for she was still gazing seaward. I saw Goda pull something from her side and, in the same instance, I glimpsed the flash of steel. I heard Sara yell a warning, as Goda raised the knife.

I don't know if Janiveer heard her cry or merely caught sight of the blade. Goda lunged at her, lashing out wildly as if she was going to slash Janiveer's face wide open, but at the last moment, Janiveer stepped sideways, and seizing Goda's upraised arm, she jerked her forward, then pushed

446

her backwards. The blade spun out of Goda's grasp. Girl and knife tumbled over and over, down the grassy bank on to the path below.

The Holy Hag, screaming in fury, ran across, snatching up the knife that had landed a few yards away on the edge of the pebbles. From the way she was brandishing the weapon, I thought she was going to stab Goda. But she dragged the girl to her knees, standing over her. Matilda's face was scarlet with rage, her eyes bulging.

'You goose-brained whore, I should have killed you when I killed George.'

Goda's eyes widened in disbelief. 'Jory! You killed my Jory? No . . . no, my Jory's at sea.'

'*Your* Jory,' Matilda said savagely, 'was *my George*, *my* husband, *mine*! Did you really think I didn't know where he went to when I was in the chapel, whose arms he crept into when he thought I was asleep in bed? Sinners and fornicators must be punished! My George never went back to sea. Those ship's carpentry tools he kept sharpening and polishing every day he was ashore, he never once used them to mend anything in my cottage. But I put them to good use in the end.'

Goda scrambled to her feet, her face contorted. 'My Jory's alive and he's coming back for me and his babby. You'll see.'

'He's never coming back,' the hag spat. 'He's dead, you numbskull. Those candles you've been making were moulded in his back bones. Those needles you've been stitching with are splinters of his ribs. That bone goblet I gave you to drink from was made from his skull. He was always bone idle, but now at least his bones are working for me. And if you are wondering what I did with the flesh I stripped from

447

his bones, I fattened my pigs on it! Now his little whore will be punished too!'

She swung the knife high, aiming the blade at Goda's neck. I knew I'd never be able to grab her arm, so I bent my head and charged at her, butting her as hard as I could and knocking her to the ground. She gave a sharp cry. Struggling to push herself upright, she stared at her left arm in disbelief. As she had fallen, the force had pushed it across the blade held in her right hand. Blood was oozing out, but it wasn't a deep cut. She'd live, more's the pity.

Goda was standing on the path, shaking violently, silent tears streaming down her face. 'Jory can't be dead . . . he can't. I loved him. He hated her. She made his life miserable. He couldn't wait to go back to sea and be away from her. That's where he is . . . at sea. That's not his skull . . . it's not! I couldn't have drunk . . .' She ran across the beach, collapsing on to her knees and retching violently. I had to admit, I was close to doing the same thing myself. I'd eaten those piglets.

But no one else was paying any attention to Goda. The women had finally reached the beach and came staggering up to us. They stared down at Matilda. She was lying on the path grasping her arm, writhing in agony, and moaning that it was burning like the fires of Hell. The limb was swelling like a pig's bladder till it seemed the skin would burst. Matilda gasped for breath, her eyes bulging. Sara tried to help her to sit up, but she was as stiff as a wooden doll, unable to move. There was a ghastly rattle in her throat and then silence. Her face froze in a rictus of pain.

Sara stared up at us in shock. 'She's dead.'

She tried to close the lids over those terrible bulging eyes, but they were as unyielding as the rest of her.

'But . . . how could she be?' I said, utterly stunned. 'It was only a gash.'

'Aye, like the wound on Cador's thigh,' Sybil said. 'That blade was poisoned just the same as the one that killed him. Viperfish, that's what she used, and plenty of it. If Cador was murdered by any in this village, I wager it was her that did it, with that self-same poison.'

'I asked for a life to save the village.' Janiveer's voice rang out from above us. 'Matilda has given hers by her own hand. With her death, the curse will be lifted.'

Chapter 63

Sara

Sea anemones are called herring-shine, for they are transformed into shoals of herring.

What was to be done with Matilda's corpse? If that bitter-weed had caused strife while she was alive, she certainly had a way of causing even more when she was dead. Isobel was for chopping her into pieces and scattering them in the forest for the beasts to eat: she was certain that Sybil was right, and Matilda had murdered her husband to punish him for fornicating. But Sybil said it wasn't right to kill dumb beasts with a poisoned corpse when they'd done no harm. None wanted her laid in the graveyard along with their own kin, for fear she'd torment them and, besides, it wasn't right to lay a murderer in consecrated ground.

But there were other matters to be attended to first. Goda, half mad with grief at the thought of her Jory being dead, was howling for her baby left up in Matilda's cottage. But even when we took her up there and she could hear the poor mite wailing inside, she was too afeared to fetch her out, for the candles moulded in poor Jory's bones still stood around the saints and she near fainted at the thought of seeing them.

I brought out the babby, then Will and I searched the cottage, gathering up everything we could find made of bone – the needles, awl, candle-holders and that wicked-looking skull goblet, which I couldn't even bring myself to touch. We took them to the chapel along with the statues of the saints and the church linens. Harold laid poor Jory's bones in the linen chest on the holy cloths and dragged it up beside the altar, so he could rest till a priest could be found to bury his bones decently and say a Mass for his soul.

The villagers gathered outside Matilda's cottage as Will carried out the rest of her possessions. The bed, stool, plates, cooking pots, beakers and table all vanished at once. Some muttered that they should be burned, but in the end no one could afford to waste such things, though they did burn her clothes. None would have dared to dress themselves in those.

But no villager touched that barrel of pickled pork. When I'd woken that morning, if anyone had offered me so much as a single bite of good solid meat, I'd have sold my last pot for it, but when Will opened the barrel and told us to take our share, everyone shook their heads and turned away. Even the dwarf seemed to have lost his appetite for stolen pig.

Will cleared out the cottage from the cobwebs in the rafters to the mouse droppings on the floor, but even with every rag and scrap of furniture removed, there was still no sign of the hand of St Cadeyrn. Although we now reckoned we could guess whose hand the old hag had given us.

As for Matilda's corpse, what was to be done with it? She'd tormented the village when she was alive and no one believed she'd change her ways now that she was dead. Her corpse would walk, most were certain of that, and with a strength and malice that were a hundred times worse than when she'd lived, for she had taken her hatred with her into death.

All the villagers looked to Harold, for he was the only cleric we had and he was an exorcist, as the old hag had kept reminding him. But the lad refused even to look at her body, much less wrestle with her evil spirit, and who could blame him?

But while we were all arguing an icy voice cut through the heat of our babble. 'It was the evil of her thoughts and words that poisoned the village. It was her foul stench that was the sickness, her corruption that brought putrefaction. If you want to cleanse this village of the Great Pestilence, you must cleanse the village of all that remains of her.'

Janiveer was standing behind us. No one had noticed her arrive and uneasy glances passed between the villagers, though none dared walk away.

'So what's to be done? Burn her like the ship?' Sybil said gruffly, though she wouldn't look at Janiveer, not directly.

'Her spirit must be sent away from this place where it can do no harm. If you burn the body, her spirit will linger.'

I shivered, not at the thought of Matilda, but those corpses who'd burned on the ship, and that living man, blackened, screaming in agony, his very skin ablaze as if he was a flaming branch falling from a bonfire. Would his spirit haunt our bay and the lost souls of all those men on that ship?

Janiveer pointed in the direction of Kitnor and the forested cliff top that jutted into the sea. 'We lay her up there, between earth and sky.'

And since no one could think of a better place, that was what we did.

It took the best part of the following day to carry her up on a bier, for it was a steep climb, not made easier by the dense mass of trees and bushes. Janiveer led the way, though she did not help to carry the body. She had a large sack slung across her shoulder. It seemed heavy, from the way she kept shifting its position on her back, but no one asked her what was in it. I hoped it was spades to dig a grave, for we'd brought none with us.

When we finally reached the cliff edge, we laid the bier down, rubbing our aching backs and arms. Far below us the waves crashed against the rocks, and across the water, the land they call Wales looked so clear and close that I thought if I just took a single step I could reach it. Was a woman standing over there on that shore, staring back at me, or had the pestilence taken them all?

Sybil crouched and, picking up a bit of stick, scraped away at the leaves and dry grass. 'You'll not be able to dig a grave up here deep enough to bury a squashed eel,' she grumbled. 'It's naught but stones and tree roots. We should sling the old hag's corpse into the sea and let her wash up wherever it takes her. The current'll drag the corpse away from us.'

'The body must be laid *on* the earth,' Janiveer said, so firmly that not even Sybil dared argue with her, though she gave her a real sour look.

We tore at the grass and scrubby bushes until we'd exposed the bare ground. Then we lifted the old hag on to it. Her flesh was soft now, the body limp, but the arm blackened and still swollen as if it had been cursed by some terrible spell. We'd not washed her or prepared the body. She did not deserve that. We laid her down in the clothes in which she'd died, her leather pouch still hanging at her waist, the shoes on her feet, even the marriage ring on her finger, for none dared touch it.

Janiveer reached into the sack she'd been carrying and pulled out a round black stone, so smooth and polished you could see your face in it. She dragged Matilda's jaws apart and wedged the stone inside, holding down the dead woman's tongue. Taking a yew bough from the sack, she drew a circle three times with the sun around Matilda's body, muttering words in some foreign tongue, then laid the yew branch on the corpse's chest, folding her arms across it and binding them fast with a length of scarlet wool. 'The yew will lead her spirit away from this world into the realms of the dead. It will keep her from coming back to do evil,' she said. She pointed to a rock as big as a man's head, covered with moss. 'Will, fetch that and place it on her chest over the branch to hold her corpse in this place so it cannot walk.'

The dwarf is a tough little fellow, stronger than most men twice his height, but even so, I thought the veins in his neck would burst as he struggled to heave the boulder over to the corpse. He tried to lower it slowly, but it was too heavy and crashed down the last few inches. I saw him wince as we heard Matilda's bones crack.

Janiveer crouched at the edge of the cliff, her long hair flapping behind her, like the ragged wings of a bird. She opened her sack once more and dragged out a small wooden box bound in metal. It looked familiar, with its rusty iron bindings and tracks where the shipworm had bored into it.

I took a step closer. 'That's my Luke's box, the one he took from the sea the day the sun turned black. Where did you get that?'

She glanced up at me. 'It should not have been taken,

Sara, you knew that much. It must be given back to the sea, before she reclaims it and much else besides.'

She flung open the lid. The box was lined with lead, but as far as I could see, it was empty save for a small glass flask filled with a jumble of red woollen thread and pale fragments that might have been parchment or pieces of bone. The top of the flask was sealed with wax and a twig had been bound to it with more red thread.

Without rising, Janiveer shuffled on her knees back to the corpse. Pulling out her knife, she cut off a lock of the old woman's grey hair and then, to my horror, lifted Matilda's blackened hand and sawed off her forefinger at the base, slicing through skin and putrid flesh until we could see the shiny white cup of the joint. You'd think after all the dead bodies I'd seen these past months, nothing could turn my stomach any more, but the sight of her slicing the last strip of skin that held the finger to the hand made me retch.

Janiveer bound the lock of Matilda's hair and her blackened finger to a twig and then to a sprig of meadowsweet before laying them in the box next to the flask. Throwing back her head, she began to sing in a strange tongue that made your skin crawl to hear it. Then she closed the box, reached for the last time into her sack and pulled out three iron horseshoe nails. Using a stone as a hammer, she drove them through the lid into the sides of the box, sealing it.

She turned to Sybil. 'You wanted to cast her body into the sea. Help me throw this in and the Great Pestilence shall leave the village this very hour.'

Sybil hesitated. You could see she was loath to touch it, but in the end she grasped one end of the box while Janiveer picked up the other. They stood together on the edge of the cliff and swung the box, back and forwards.

'Now!' Janiveer called.

We watched the box fly out in an arc and tumble towards the waves. As it plunged into the blue-green water, a great plume of white foam shot up around it. The sea closed over the place and in the blink of an eye there was nothing to mark where the box had vanished. Far below us, the waves continued to hurl themselves at the base of the cliff, as if they would shake us all off into the deep, dark depths.

Janiveer, turning back from the sea, bade us collect all the rocks we could find and heap them over the corpse till it was covered. Matilda was a small woman, but even so, it took a long time to bury her under the heap of stones.

But finally, as the sun was setting, Janiveer announced, 'It is finished. Warn the villagers, warn travellers, warn your children that any man, woman or child who passes this way must add another stone to the murderer's cairn, else misfortune will follow them on their journey.'

All the grief, all the fear and misery of the past weeks suddenly welled up in me. I rounded on her in a fury. 'And what of my chillern, my sons, Janiveer? Shall they ever set a stone here? You promised you would bring them back, even if it is only for me to bury them.'

'Your sons are beneath the earth.'

I moaned, clamping my hand across my mouth to stop myself screaming. They were dead – the seer at Kitnor had told me so. Now she had said it too. I knew they were dead, but still a part of me refused to let go of hope. Until I saw their bodies, until I kissed their cold faces, I knew I would never be able to stop hoping. They say despair is a terrible thing, but hope is worse: it keeps you shackled for ever, like a dog in a wheel, always running, but never able to go anywhere, save round and round.

'Where are they buried, Janiveer?' I pleaded. 'You know! You can find them. If I could only see their graves . . . I'll ask nothing more. Twice now I've saved your life and you swore—'

'I made no such oath,' Janiveer said coldly. 'But I make it now. When I have the bones of my forefather, you shall have the bones of your sons.'

Chapter 64

Will

Riddle me this: What I catch, I throw away; what I don't catch, I keep.

The day they unblocked the road from Porlock Weir was the day I set off for the manor, determined that nothing and no one, not even Janiveer, would stop me taking Christina and my son away from that place. I couldn't afford to wait any longer. If the pestilence had ended in the rest of England too, then Randel might soon return to claim his bride. Worse still, if Eda had succeeded in getting word to Lady Aliena or to Sir Nigel, an assassin might already be on his way to the manor to ensure that Christina and my son were lying in their graves before they could bring disgrace to the family. They could all too easily claim that she had been another victim of the pestilence and no one of any consequence would question it.

I had still to work out the minor details, such as how I would smuggle Christina out without Wallace seeing us, but I was a dwarf, wasn't I? I had fooled Mistress Luck into helping me most of my life; all I asked was a last favour from her.

One thing I had decided, though: I was not going to

wriggle in through that stinking sewer again. On the other hand, I could hardly march up to the gate and demand entrance. But it occurred to me that Master Wallace would be anxious to bring in fresh supplies of food and fodder after so long a siege, so the gate might be opened many times before nightfall. Surely I could manage to slip in.

Just before I came in sight of the manor, I left the road and took cover in a grove of trees where I could keep watch on the main gate. Dawn was breaking, pink and silver across the bay. The first frost of the year had come early and even the fallen leaves were rimmed with white hoar that sparkled in the first rays of light. A honking made me glance up. A skein of wild geese flew, like an arrow head, over the cliffs from the sea. I hoped that was a good omen.

An ox cart rattled past me, piled high with hay. The manor's horses must surely be in dire need of that. It came to a stop outside the huge oak gates while the driver called out impatiently for the gatekeeper to open up. I'd never get a better chance than that. I ran forward as fast as my bow legs would scuttle. Staying hidden from the driver was easy for a short-arse like me. Climbing into the wagon was not. But a length of rope swung down from the side and I could swarm up a rope quicker than most longshanks can a ladder. Even so, I'd barely managed to cover myself with hay before the wagon began to roll forward. I say hay, but after the drought there was nothing sweet-smelling or soft about it. By the feel of it, it was mostly rank weeds and thistles – a great many thistles! Master Wallace was a bigger fool than I if he'd parted with more than a farthing for that load. My teeth rattled as the wheels shuddered over the cobbles. As the wagon came to a halt, I risked peering out. It was dark, and I realised we must be inside the huge barn where all the manor's crops were stored.

'You get atop, lad, fork it down,' someone called from the other side of the wagon. 'Jan, you make sure it's stacked loose so it don't overheat. His lordship wants only the best for his horses, especially today.'

His lordship? Was Sir Nigel come? I cursed myself and him. That would make it ten times harder to get Christina away, and I certainly couldn't risk him seeing me. I heard the scrape of metal on stone as someone dragged a pitchfork towards the wagon. I didn't fancy those sharp tines stabbing into my arse. The wagon stood close to the barn wall. It was the best cover I was going to get. I wriggled over the side and jumped, landing on the cobbles with a jolt that nearly forced my backbone through my skull. I scrambled under the wagon, just as the boy climbed up the other side.

The only light coming into the immense barn was through the open doors at the far end and the interior was so gloomy that you could have hidden a dozen dwarfs beneath the wagon without anyone noticing. But getting out of the barn was another matter. Any other man could have kept to the shadows and wagered on not being recognised but, with my shape and height, I hardly blended in with the burly farmhands.

I was still trying to work out my best route when the sound of a hunting horn, the clatter of hoofs and barking of hounds sent every man and boy running towards the courtyard. I hurried behind them and managed to slip out through the great doors while their attention was fixed on the commotion at the gate. Keeping close to the walls, I made for the stillroom, praying they would not yet have found a new Rosa to replace Janiveer, or if they had, she wouldn't have heard of the banished dwarf.

I was in luck. The room was empty, and since there was no fire burning, it seemed likely that no one was working there. I dragged a stool over to the casement and clambered up to peer out, searching for the stable lad who'd brought Christina to me last time.

Half a dozen men were dismounting their horses in the yard as grooms steadied their beasts and hounds milled around excitedly. I searched for the broad shoulders of Sir Nigel or any of his men I might recognise, but the party was already making for the inner courtyard. They vanished before I had time to get a clear look at any of them.

I clambered down and opened the door a crack, trying to spot the lad I could trust, but all the boys were scurrying around, unsaddling the great horses, which reared and tossed their heads in the melee. Then, to my horror, I saw the stout figure of a woman in a scarlet-and-white gown gliding across the courtyard like a ship in full sail. I'd only encountered her a couple of times when I was in Sir Nigel's employ, but Lady Pavia was a woman once seen, never forgotten, and she was heading straight for the stillroom. I stared wildly about, searching for a hiding place, then squeezed behind two barrels in the corner. I pulled a sack across the gap over my head. The room was unlit and the fire out. I hoped the shadows would be enough to conceal me, provided she didn't search too thoroughly for whatever she had come for.

The door opened and closed. Footsteps crossed the floor. They stopped. I could hear her heavy breathing and hoped she couldn't hear mine.

'Please show yourself, Gaubert. It is most disconcerting to find myself addressing a table.'

For a moment I thought she must be talking to someone else – it was so long since anyone had called me Gaubert.

'I asked some of the more trustworthy boys to keep watch for your return. Ever since one of the stable lads let slip that you had been here asking for Lady Christina, I guessed you'd be back.'

So the little brat had tattled after all. If I got out of here alive, I'd make sure the cook knew all about the weasel in that basket. But there was little point in remaining hidden now. I squeezed round the side of the barrel and made a perfunctory bow. Lady Pavia nodded and seated herself on a stool, which completely vanished beneath her ample rump so she seemed to be perched in mid-air.

She regarded me with a mixture of pity and puzzlement. 'I confess I do not know what Christina ever saw in you, but as my late husband, Hubert, used to say, *Affection blinds sight as surely as it deafens reason.* That may indeed be so, but I have decided to believe that what passed between you and the girl was nothing more than a game you both invented in a moment of idleness to vex her elders and your masters. You would do well to believe that too, Gaubert.'

I opened my mouth to reply, but she held up a hand to silence me.

'You should know that Sir Randel is here, and this very morning Father Cuthbert will baptise *his* baby son before he takes his wife and child to London.'

'No, he can't!' I blurted out, before I could stop myself. 'Oswin is not—'

'If a man stands before a priest and declares he is the father of his wife's child, then he *is* the father. That child will bear his name and inherit his lands and titles.'

'But the birth,' I protested. 'It was only six months after

462

her wedding night. And she knows for certain Oswin cannot be his son. She swore to me he was drunk the night he came to her bed—'

'And fortunately so drunk he is still unable to remember what he did. The child was born early, and as I explained to him, such things happen, especially when the girl is young and her hips are slender. I did not see any need to tell him just *how* early his son came into this world. I may have given the impression that Christina has only recently been delivered. Men, particularly new husbands who have spent the best part of their lives on the battlefields, can be excessively ignorant about such domestic matters. They could no more tell the age of an infant than they could stitch a rose. That's why they can so easily be fooled by bloody sheets.

'Sir Randel is not a man to start discussing his wife's confinement with serving maids, but just to be sure, I have persuaded him to start out with Christina on his journey today. The Lady Aliena will say nothing once she knows that Randel has publicly declared the child to be his. The only other person who knows the truth of the matter is Eda, and she is banished from here.'

'And on her way to tell all to Sir Nigel,' I said. 'I couldn't stop her.'

Lady Pavia smiled sadly at me, as if she was talking to a backward child. 'Neither Sir Nigel nor Randel will choose to believe her. No one in this land will. They would laugh at the very idea that a beautiful young bride could ever cuckold a handsome, noble, wealthy husband with a dwarf who doesn't even own the clothes on his crooked back. They would no more believe Christina would desire you in preference to Randel than that the Virgin Mary had lain with an ape. And you should both be on your knees giving thanks for that. Christina is Randel's wife and he has returned to claim his family.'

'But she doesn't love him,' I said desperately. 'She is terrified of him. He will make her life wretched.'

Lady Pavia sighed. 'If that were a bar to marriage, every noblewoman in England would be in a nunnery. Christina will learn how to please him, once she sets her mind to it. She must. As my husband Hubert always said, *Marry for love and love will flee. Marry for money and love will follow.* And if it does not, at least she and the child will be alive, and the boy will have a chance to grow up and make his own future.'

'So I should stand aside and hear my son call another man *father*?'

'You will never hear your son utter that word or any other, Gaubert. You will not set eyes on them again.' Lady Pavia rose and took a pace towards me, gripping my shoulder. The stones in her many rings dug painfully into my flesh.

'By some miracle the baby was born straight and as well formed as any natural man. As he grows, will a boy like that want to look down at a hunchback fool for a father, or up at a noble knight? What will he want his father to teach him – how to grimace and prance to make other men laugh, or how to win their admiration for his prowess in the saddle and his skill with a sword? Be grateful that your son will live to call any man *father.*'

Something in my expression must have told her I was not at all grateful, for she snorted in exasperation. 'Are you really such a fool as to believe that Sir Randel would simply shrug his shoulders if his wife ran off? You think him cruel? Can you imagine the depths of cruelty he would be capable of if a woman – his own wife – humiliated him in such a fashion? You may not care if he takes your life, Gaubert, but what of hers and the boy's? Randel will hunt them down if it takes the rest of his life. He is a powerful and wealthy man. He could pay an army of informants. Wherever you hid Christina and the child, he would discover that place. And when he found them, we both know he would see that they suffered all the torments of Hell to assuage his wounded pride. You should spend the rest of your life praying he never has cause to suspect. The only way you can protect them now, Gaubert, is to walk away.'

Fake dwarf I may have been, but I knew then that I was all too real a fool. How could I have thought for one moment that I could steal Christina from the manor? It was only fear that had made her beg me to take her away, not love, never that.

Did she ever gaze down at Oswin and see what I might have been? Was there the tiniest trace in his unmoulded face that reminded her of something she'd glimpsed beneath the gargoyle mask of mine? Or did she see only his long straight back, tiny mouth, rounded skull and feel nothing but relief? I knew at that moment that of all the names others had thrust upon me in my life, *father* is one that I could never own. I was grateful for the darkness of the stillroom, for I could not bear Lady Pavia to see the tears that stung my eyes. Even a fake dwarf has his pride.

'I will not . . .' I cleared my throat '. . . trouble the Lady Christina again.'

'That would be wise for both your sakes,' Lady Pavia said. 'Then let this be an end to it. Come, I will escort you to the gate myself, in case the steward should see you. He will not impede you if I am there.'

I opened the door for her and followed her out into the

icy morning air, taking care to keep her great bulk between me and the manor hall. A few of the servants gazed at us curiously, but most were too busy staggering from kitchens to hall, stables to barns, laden with sacks, kegs or great platters of food to notice who was passing in the throng. We had almost reached the gate when a voice rang out.

'A dwarf! Lady Pavia, you are a jewel. Just what we need to bring my son luck and good fortune on this day.'

Randel was bearing down on us, slapping his leather gloves against his thigh. He was tall and muscular, his face more tanned than when I'd last seen him, his beard and hair gold-streaked by the sun. It suited him, though his thin, hooked nose and close-set eyes still reminded me of a hawk. He evidently did not remember me. Hardly surprising. He'd have taken more notice of the features of a hound or horse than any servant, and I wasn't as well groomed or well fed as when I'd been in Sir Nigel's livery.

'Wherever did you find the creature, Lady Pavia?' He stared down at my filthy rags. 'He'll need a wash, though, and something more fitting to wear.'

Lady Pavia pulled me away from him. 'He's just a beggar. I was about to send him on his way.'

'But he's more than ugly enough to bless the christening. Frighten the devil himself away with that face.' Randel prodded me in the chest. 'Dance, can you, dwarf? Tell a few riddles?'

My jaw clenched.

'Come on, dwarf, show me what you can do or is it the whip you need to make you skip?'

I minced a few steps like an old whore, plying her trade. 'I am a father's child, a mother's child, but no man's son. Who am I, m'lord?' I asked sullenly.

'A daughter, fool. That one's as old as the ark. If your wits are so blunt, it's plain to see why you're in no man's service. No matter, it's your crooked back that'll bring us luck, not your tongue.'

Randel gazed around the courtyard and caught the eye of a passing kitchen maid. He beckoned her over. 'You, girl, take this creature and see what you can do to make him smell sweeter and dress him in some clean clothes. Doesn't matter what, so long as he doesn't give my guests fleas and lice. Then bring him to stand outside the chapel.'

He cuffed me across the head with his leather gauntlets. 'Play your part well, dwarf, and you'll get a belly full of good meats before you go on your way, and maybe a coin or two, if you please my wife.'

The girl led me to the back of the kitchens where she bade me strip and brought me a pail of cold water, soap and a horse brush she had borrowed from one of the stable lads. Shivering on the cobbles, I scrubbed my skin with the hard bristles till it was raw, not from any desire to be clean, but to scrub away the burning humiliation and misery. I crouched there naked until the girl returned, bringing oil perfumed with lavender and rosemary to rake through my hair and beard to kill any lice. *Rosemary for remembrance.* Then she watched with mocking amusement as I pulled on the assortment of clothes she'd found for me. Green-and-red hose, a yellow tunic that was so long it dragged on the ground like a woman's gown, and a man's hooded half-cloak, which trailed behind me so that I looked like an old crone on her way to market.

She stood back, hands on hips, giggling at the effect. 'That'll bring a smile to the Lady Christina's lips. Summat needs to. Her face has been as frozen as a wooden poppet's ever since her husband arrived. If I was wedded to a man like that, I'd be grinning from now to the feast of St Stephen.'

'Does she know I'll be in the chapel?' I asked.

'Outside it,' the maid corrected. 'They'd not allow a goblin like you inside a holy place.' She laughed again. 'No, orders are the Lady Christina is not to be told. It's to be a surprise for her.'

The maid, wrinkling her nose, picked up my rags between thumb and forefinger. 'These can go on the gatekeeper's fire.'

I snatched them back. 'I'll be wearing them again as soon as I leave.'

Even if I froze to death, I would not return to Porlock Weir dressed in that mocking garb.

The pealing of a small bell sent several doves flying up from the courtyard. The maid grabbed my shoulder. 'Hurry, that means the child has been named. They'll be coming out soon.'

She dragged me towards the tiny chapel and pushed me forward so that I stood near the door. One of the stable lads was hauling vigorously on the bell rope outside, no doubt in the hope that he'd be favoured with a coin for his effort.

The door opened, and Lady Pavia squeezed out. She was evidently searching for me. She bent low and murmured, 'Act your part well, Gaubert. Remember your promise.'

She drew aside as Sir Nigel's three wards and their elderly chaperon ambled out. Catching sight of me, the girls broke into peals of laughter. 'Come quick, Christina, look! It's a little bearded lady.'

One shoved the other aside. 'No, muttonhead, it's a dwarf. Does it bite?' She jabbed her finger near my mouth.

I pretended to snap at her hand and barked. She squealed in delight.

Then Christina was standing in the doorway. I'd vowed I would not look at her, but I couldn't help myself. She was dressed in a russet gown, the colour of autumn leaves, trimmed with brown fur, and over it wore a thick fur-lined cloak of forest green. Her hair was braided in two thick plaits down the sides of her face, looped up at the jaw-line and covered with a gossamer-fine veil, held in place by a narrow gold coronet. For the first time, she looked like what she was – a nobleman's wife. She gave a tiny gasp as she caught sight of me, staggering slightly, and pushing her hand against the door frame to steady herself. For only a fleeting moment our eyes met, but it was long enough for me to see the terror in hers.

Randel, my son cradled in his arms, emerged to stand beside his wife. 'There, my beloved, see the surprise Lady Pavia has found for us, a real dwarf to bring our son good fortune.'

He pushed past her for she seemed frozen to the spot. 'Turn around, dwarf, let my son touch your crooked back for luck.'

Staring at the ground, I did as I was bade and felt Randel bending over me as he pressed Oswin's tiny fingers against me. The child whimpered. It was only a baby's touch, so why did his little hand burn me as if it was a red-hot brand?

'You too, Christina,' Randel ordered. 'As the child's mother you must rub the dwarf for luck. There's no need to be afraid. I know he revolts you, for he's a hideous fellow, but he won't bite, will you, dwarf? Come along, do it to please me. You wouldn't want to lose your good fortune, would you?'

There was something harsh and menacing about the way he spoke those words. Had I been mistaken and he'd recognised me after all?

I steeled myself for her touch, but in truth I barely felt it for it was as fleeting and light as the flap of a butterfly's wing. But I wished I would feel it for ever.

The young wards giggled and crowded forward, pushing Christina aside and patting my back hard for luck, as if they were petting a boisterous hound.

'Come,' Lady Pavia said briskly, 'we must take your young son back to the great hall. This chill air will do him no good and, besides, his christening feast awaits us.'

The girls were immediately diverted and set off back along the path, their chaperon hobbling behind them.

'Are you going to bless my son, dwarf?' Randel demanded. 'I have named him Walter. Father Cuthbert tells me it means *ruler of men*. My son is destined to become a great knight, what think you to that? I shall have a sword in his hand just as soon as he can walk and see him schooled to a horse before he is out of clouts. Meanwhile, I suppose we could put a saddle on you, dwarf, and he could ride you as his hobbyhorse.' He looked at Christina and laughed. She smiled as if her lips shared the joke, but in her eyes there was nothing but misery and despair.

I spread my arm, making a mocking flourish of a courtly bow. 'I give you a dwarf's blessing, young Master Walter. May you receive what men are given, but kings can never buy. May you fall in that which you can feel, but none sees with his eye. May you know what a poor man treasures, but is never owned by a lord. For it is stronger by far than iron and cuts deeper than any sword.'

I thought I heard Christina give a sharp little intake of

breath, like a sob, but I dared not look at her, for I saw Randel's gaze dart suspiciously from one to the other of us as if he was searching for something he couldn't quite name.

'A strange blessing,' he said coldly, 'but, then, you are a queer little beast.' He tossed a coin into the dirt at my feet. 'For amusing us, dwarf.'

Then still holding my son in one arm and taking Christina's hand with the other, he led her away. She did not look back.

Chapter 65

Sara

*The first fish of a catch must be nailed alive to the mast
as a thank-offering else no more will be caught.*

Some say Janiveer brought an end to the pestilence, others
that it burned itself out as it had the first time it came. I
know only that, from the day we buried Matilda under the
cairn, there were no more deaths from that fever. We thought
the evil had passed and we had survived. But we were
wrong. The sea-witch had not finished wreaking her vengeance on the village. What we had seen was only the promise
of what she could do. The worst was not over. It was yet
to come.

We took turns at filling in the grave pit though it took
us many days for we were weak. Young Harold did his best
to say a few words that might make their bodies rest easy
in their grave even if their souls were in Purgatory. But he
couldn't say Masses for them. At least I saw my Elis buried,
though I couldn't bear to think of the torment he might be
suffering in the next world. But I couldn't bury my boys.
Where their souls were wandering, I didn't know.

They say the spirits of unbaptised babies become butterflies, and the spirits of drowned fishermen become gulls,

but where do the spirits of young lads go? Sometimes at night, when the moon was bright, I went to the edge of the forest and stared through the dark trunks. I was afraid of ghosts, but how could I be afraid of the ghosts of my own chillern? I longed to glimpse them, even if they were nothing more than wisps of mist. I called to them to come to me out of the darkness. But though I heard creatures running through the bushes and saw birds startled out of their roosts, flying up in the moonlight, I never saw the ghosts of my sons.

We who were left in the village were learning to live again. We made ourselves new mud-horses, the frames set at a height the women could reach. The first thing we did was take stones out to repair the furthest weir where all the biggest fish were caught. We slid past the blackened timbers of the burned ship, half sunk in the sand. None of us could bring ourselves to look at it at first, but after a few tides had washed in and out, carrying away the charred bodies and the stench, it became naught but another wreck to add to the many that rotted in the bays along those shores.

There was still no flour and there'd not be any grain to harvest the next year if we couldn't repair the hoes and tools, for most were broken from digging graves and for water. Bald John, though he'd been near death, had started to recover from the pestilence the day after Matilda was buried, but his arms and legs had turned black, and his hands had rotted away soon after. He lived, if you could call it that, but he'd never work the forge again, that much was certain.

Sybil said firmly there was as much use him wishing his hands would grow back as there was fishing for mackerel down a well. She persuaded his wife to help her drag Bald John to the forge, whether he would go or not. He still had a tongue, Sybil said, and she had the brawn, so he could tell her what to do. It wasn't easy to persuade him, but Sybil and Cecily kept at him night and day till they wore him down.

The two women set to work under his instruction, simple tools at first and they mostly went wrong, shattering at the first use for the metal wasn't tempered right. The curses that came flying out of that forge were hotter than the fire – Bald John bellowing in frustration at their clumsiness and Sybil yelling back at him for not explaining it well enough. But they were mastering it, even Bald John grudgingly admitted that.

Most of the village women had taken to cooking together at the bake-house. It was easier to prepare a common pot and to feed the orphans and old 'uns at the same time, for many had lost all their family. There were others who wanted feeding as well, travellers, not from our village, who edged in like stray cats, trying to reach any place they could find shelter or work. We'd no work to offer them, but we made them welcome as best we could till they moved on, though all we had to share was the cauldron of fish.

One woman arrived pushing her aged mam in a wheelbarrow, another with two small chillern clinging to her skirts, their arms thin as sticks and their stomachs bloated. Then came an old man and woman clinging to each other, as if each was the other's walking stick. They all moved on after a day or two, but Janiveer remained. We'd glance down at the shore as we ate, watching the flames of her fire on the beach leaping up in the darkness. Sometimes

474

we'd see her too, or the black shadow of her, standing on the shore, staring out at the sea, or pacing round and round those flames, her hair and skirts streaming out behind her as if she was swimming in the sea, not walking on the shore. Sometimes she seemed to swell up till she was twice the height of any normal woman. Sybil said it was a trick of the firelight, but all the same, I crossed myself and saw the others doing so, too. We wanted her gone.

That night, there was a raw edge to the wind, and no moon or stars to be seen for the clouds hid them. We ate by the light of the fire in the bake-house yard, for the candles and rush lights that remained were too precious to waste. A young girl with moon-crazed eyes had wandered into the village, her belly swollen with a babby. Drawn by the smell of the pot and the warmth of the fire, she edged into the yard and the women made room for her by the fire, though she was so near her time, she could barely lower herself to sit on the ground. She gulped the hot fish broth as if she feared we were going to snatch it from her, her gaze fixed on Will the whole time, as if the rest of us were invisible.

He wouldn't look at her, but sat hunched over his bowl, staring miserably into the firelight. You couldn't seem to get a cheerful word from him. All through the sickness, he'd always had a riddle to tell or a trick to make a child laugh, but now that others were beginning to see hope returning, it seemed to have run out of him.

The wind moaned through the deserted cottages and the waves crashed on the rocks, but I could have sworn there was another sound, too, that night, like many high voices singing, but sadder than that, as if the sea itself was keening.

It made my skin prickle. Several of us glanced uneasily towards the far end of the bay where Janiveer's fire burned. We could see her ragged silhouette, like some monstrous seabird, perching on the edge of the water.

'Looks like Janiveer's going for a swim,' Sybil muttered.

'Wish she'd swim back to where she came from,' I said.

'Don't reckon she's calling up another death ship, do you?' Katharine asked fearfully.

Will craned his head to peer at the shore. 'She said the pestilence is over, and that much I do believe,' he added dully.

'You speak the truth, Will,' Janiveer said, stepping into the pool of light cast by the fire.

We gaped at her. I stared back at the shore and, just for a moment, I thought I could still see her dark outline standing by the sea, her long hair whipping around her head in the wind. Then I realised there was nothing on the beach save her fire. Had I seen her there at all?

'The pestilence is indeed over, but death draws close again in a different guise. I have a riddle for you, Will. *It has no mouth, but cries. It has no wings, but flies. And eats—*'

'The wind,' Will interrupted. 'Even a lord can answer that one.'

'*And eats no meat, but grows*,' Janiveer finished. 'It grows. Out there, far across the sea, the wind is gaining strength. Soon it will be greater than any wind that has ever reached these shores. It will tear down trees and bring great churches crashing to the ground, and the waves it whips up will smash all in their path. This village will be destroyed, as easily and swiftly as the first wave of the flowing tide sweeps away a house of sand built by a child.'

Katharine moaned, burying her face in her hands and rocking. The others were muttering, half fearful, half

476

angry. Only Goda remained silent and unmoving, as if her body was there but her spirit had wandered somewhere else.

'Pay her no heed,' Sybil finally burst out, darting a furious glance towards Janiveer. 'She's still after that relic. Thinks to frighten us into giving it to her.' She raised her voice, though even the owls in the forest must already have heard her. 'We've told you, we don't know where the hag hid Cadeyrn's hand, if she ever had it. Why don't you ask Father Cuthbert, wherever he is? If anyone knows, he must.'

Harold shifted uneasily, shuffling back a little so that his face was in shadow. I hadn't raised two lads without being able to spot the look of a boy trying to hide something. Could he have taken it after all?

'Aye,' Isobel said. 'Get you back to wherever you've been hiding yourself, sea-witch, and leave us alone. You've brought the village enough troubles.'

Janiveer's expression did not change. She stared back at us, unblinking. One by one all the furious faces that had been glaring at her turned away as she looked at each of us in turn. None of us wanted to meet those eyes.

'I warned you of the Great Pestilence. You did not believe me. You would not pay me what I asked to protect you. And your menfolk died because you would not listen. When I was given the life I asked for, I charmed the pestilence from among you and threw it into the sea. Now I warn you again of danger, and again I am willing to save you, if you are willing to pay my price.'

Will's head snapped up. 'Pestilence burned itself out like it did before. You knew it had! You charmed nothing.'

'You are bitter because you lost your lover, but your love

was false if you'd sooner have seen her in her grave instead of another man's bed.' She turned away from him, her eyes glittering in the firelight. 'You can take your chance, as you did with the pestilence, but when the wind rages and the seas surge over your houses, it will be too late. You have three days to decide. Will you pay my price or will you risk your lives and what little you still possess?'

The women were silent. Why didn't they ask her? I pushed myself to my feet and stood facing her across the flames.

'What do you want of us, Janiveer? Cadeyrn's hand? Sybil's right. We've searched Matilda's house ourselves and none of us could find it. No one here knows where it is.'

I tried not to look at Harold, hoping I spoke the truth. I dreaded to think what the sea-witch might do to him if she discovered he'd been keeping it from her.

'The hand of Cadeyrn is mine. You cannot pay me in coin I already own. The great wind will bring the hand of my forefather to me. That is why I wait.'

'Then what, Janiveer?' I said. 'Another life as you demanded before?'

For a moment she did not answer. No one spoke or moved. The only sounds were the waves sucking on the pebbles and the wind sobbing through the empty cottages. The blood-red firelight and dark shadows shifted back and forth across her face as if she had a thousand faces, some young, some ancient, all cruel.

'Not just a life, Sara, a soul. A soul who will take the place of Cadeyrn, whom you trapped here when you separated his bones and offered them to your god. A soul who will suffer all the misery and torment he has suffered. A soul who will descend into the icy caverns of the dead, there to remain for ever and alone in the howling vortex of its darkness. A soul who will pay for all eternity for the blood your ancestors spilled when they betrayed the warrior king.'

Chapter 66

Will

Riddle me this: What doth the contented man desire, the poor have and rich require, the miser spends and the spendthrift saves and all men carry to their graves?

The woman appeared from nowhere, standing in the entrance to my cave, her rags billowing in the wind, like seaweed in a streaming tide.

'You'll protect my baby,' she said. 'Creatures like you can keep us from evil spirits and make the sick well. You're a . . .'

She did not need to say the word – *dwarf, goblin, beast, half-man*. Whichever you choose, it means less than human. And any creature who does not quite belong in this world must belong to another. We stand in the doorway between the kingdoms, straddling the divide, with one bandy leg in the human realm, the other in that of phantasms and faeries, so it follows that we must be able to turn the fates, to curse and bless. Bring us your infants to touch for luck, but know that our hand is not a saint's hand, but the hand of a gallows thief.

The woman crouched and laid her baby, not in a manger, on the floor of my cave. It squirmed at my feet, naked and

480

whimpering, wrapped in a bloody goatskin, like an offering to a grotesque little god. I vaguely recalled seeing a heavily pregnant woman by the fire when Janiveer warned us about the wind. Was it the same woman? Her face was hidden in the shadows of the cave, and only the whites of her eyes shone in the firelight, restless and wild as the crests of the waves crashing against the rocks.

She wasn't from Porlock Weir, that much I knew. Just another traveller who'd fled her village when the pestilence came, driven mad by hunger and the terror of death. Did the child's father still live? Maybe the woman herself didn't know who he was – a sailor with silver in his pocket, a lustful priest, a drunken packman: all might have walked away as I had done, not knowing their seed had taken root in her. Perhaps she had come looking for him or, like so many women in the village, had sat by his bed and watched him die.

The child's cries grew louder. I stared down at him as he thrashed his fists, so very small, so very straight and perfect. 'Take him!' I shouted. 'I can't care for him. I can't care for any child.'

But the cave was empty, as if a wave had washed in and swept the woman away. Only the baby remained. I carried him to the cave entrance and stared out into the darkness. The waves foamed white, thundering on to the pebble beach. Clouds raced across the moon. Janiveer had spoken the truth. The storm was coming, and I was glad of it, a storm that would wipe away all the stench and decay, the misery and pain, a storm that would bring a cleansing death to us all.

I lifted the child high in my arms, holding him out to the sea and wind. 'Come, what are you waiting for? Do your worst! Take me. Take us all. Sweep all away and make an end of it!'

A huge black wave reared up and crashed down, like a sea-serpent striking. White foam boiled over the glistening rock and sucked back, as if it was pulling its prey down into the depths.

'Ninth wave that was,' a voice from the sea said. 'My granddam always said the ninth wave'll take you. Hurry afore the next one.'

Two wet white hands clawed over the lip of the cave. The drowned were rising from the sea. The dead were crawling out of the depths and on to the land. Still clutching the baby, I backed away. A hooded head rose up, the firelight glistening on the bone-white visage beneath. It heaved itself on to the floor of the cave. Hands flung back the hood. I stared. Sara was standing in front of me and behind her, clambering up from the rocks below, came Harold.

They hurried to the fire at the back of the cave, kneeling and spreading their hands over the blaze to warm them.

'Don't know how you can abide living out here with only the sea for a neighbour,' Sara said. She jerked round as the baby gave a thin kitten-like wail. 'Wherever did you find that little mite? He'll catch his death in this place.'

She struggled to her feet and lifted the baby from my arms. Dragging an old sheepskin from the heap at the back of the cave, she snuggled the child in it and took him back to the fire, where she sat rocking him.

'Why have you come?' I demanded.

'You heard what Janiveer said. There's a storm coming,' Sara said. 'Don't know if she's the power to call it up or calm it, but one thing I do know. I'll not let her take another life from this village. It's revenge she wants and she'll not

482

stop till we're all dead. She reckons to make this a village of ghosts like Kitnor, where not a soul can ever rest easy in their grave. Even the ships that come here will be damned. She's not natural, not human.'

'Like me?' I said bitterly. 'You think, because I'm not human either, I can get rid of her for you, is that it?'

Sara gave a grunt of laughter. 'You're a queer one, all right, but a sprat is smaller than a cod, which doesn't make it any less a fish, nor you any less a man. Fact, you're more of a man than most twice your size. That's why we came. Harold here, he thinks he knows where the old hag hid that hand.'

'You heard Janiveer,' I said. 'Giving her the hand will not make her leave. She'll take it and take her revenge too.'

'I know that,' Sara said impatiently. 'But only *if* we give it to her. Harold and me have been talking. He reckons there's another way we could use that hand.'

I glanced at the lad, who was drying his skinny legs in the heat of the fire. He kept his head lowered as if he wanted no part of any of this. I'd wager a cartload of herring that if he'd told Sara anything about where the hand was hidden, she'd forced it out of him.

'So what's this great plan of yours, Harold?'

He darted a glance at us both, before staring dismally into the flames again. 'I know what needs to be said, right enough, learned it by heart, and what needs to be done to keep her from working her spells, but I've never had to do it. It's true I exorcise the chrisemores when their fathers bring them to the chapel for baptism.' He gazed over to the child lying in Sara's lap, sucking her finger knuckle. 'Babbies, they do no more than cry, but the sea-witch . . . I'll not be able to face her alone!'

483

'You'll not *be* alone!' Sara retorted, sounding so like the Holy Hag that Harold flinched. She shook her head in exasperation and turned to me. 'We need you to distract Janiveer while Harold does what he must. She'll not be able to stand against the three of us together.'

'She's the descendant of a warrior king,' I said. 'And I warrant she has more powers than ever he could command. She could stand against the king's armies if she had to.'

Sara glared at me, then reached over and briskly patted Harold's arm. 'But you'll have Cadeyrn's hand, her own blood and bone, to use against her. She'll not work her magic against that.' She looked at me again, her eyes full of fire. 'You'll help us? You'll come with us tomorrow night, won't you, Will?'

I waddled over and took the sleeping baby from her. Wrapping him even tighter in the sheepskin, I carried him to the mouth of the cave and stared out at the dark waves racing towards us. I hated Janiveer. Every muscle and bone in my crooked body was screaming its loathing of her. I'd allowed myself to listen to her. I'd believed her. I'd trusted her. If I'd taken Christina and my son when I'd first returned to the manor, I'd be holding him in my arms now instead of a stranger's child. I could have looked after them, kept them safe, made them happy. God's blood, I wanted Janiveer dead almost as much as I wanted Christina back in my arms.

But why should I help the villagers? They'd tried to hang me – Sara, all of them. And if they survived, would they treat me any differently? No. I'd still be vermin to them, living out my days like some scavenging crab on the seashore, to be mocked and tormented by their brats, to be accused the moment there was trouble. I had lost Christina, lost my

484

son. I had nothing left! So let Janiveer do her worst. Let the wind rage and the waves drown us all. That was what the world needed, a great flood to sweep it all away. Better that than a living death. They had their fool to dance them to the gallows, so let the executioner do her work. Let the witch make an end of it all.

Chapter 67

Men fear death as children fear the dark.
Medieval Proverb

'Get those doors fastened afore the wind rips them off,' Master Wallace bellowed, though he might as well not have bothered for none of the men or boys fighting their way across the courtyard heard a word he shouted.

But they could see as well as he could that if the doors to the stables weren't secured the wind would get beneath the thatch and lift the whole roof off. Inside the stables, the horses reared and bucked against their tethers, rolling their eyes back, desperate to be set loose. They sensed the danger better than their grooms could see it. The men tried to ram timbers against the doors to hold them shut, but they were working in the dark for the torches had long since been snuffed out, and even the gateman had extinguished his brazier for fear that the wind might whirl burning fragments on to the thatched roofs of the courtyard buildings and set the whole manor ablaze.

In all the commotion, no one noticed a solitary figure slip through the door of the darkened stillroom, a horn lantern hidden beneath his cloak. Once Father Cuthbert was safely inside and had managed to close the door again by throwing his whole weight against it, he set the lantern on the table and gazed round. The light barely illuminated the dim smudges of jars and boxes on the lower shelves, but the priest dared not risk lighting more candles for fear that the flames would be seen through the chinks in the shutters.

The letter Lady Pavia had dispatched with Randel, informing Sir Nigel of Sir Harry's death, would surely reach him any day now, if it hadn't already. Master Wallace had been only too willing to agree that Sir Harry had suffered the fatal cut by accident. The last thing he wanted was to be forced to admit that a murder had taken place while he was in charge of the manor. But Father Cuthbert knew that Lady Pavia had a more suspicious mind than any of the king's sheriffs. He was sure she would have voiced her doubts about his death in that letter to her cousin. Sir Harry's corpse was already in the ground and, Father Cuthbert devoutly prayed, would be too decayed for any coroner to examine, but the tongues of the servants were still very much alive and wagging hard. And the bloodstained knife, *his* knife, was still lying wherever Rosa had hidden it, like a buried caltrop waiting for a careless step.

Father Cuthbert had searched for it in the stillroom twice before, but each time the new maid had caught him and he'd been forced to invent some tale of having a bellyache for which he needed a cure. If she stumbled across the stained knife now, with his sign upon it, she was certain to remember his visits. He had to retrieve it.

He had persuaded Lady Margery to summon the stillroom maid to the solar, convincing her that her slight headache required immediate attention before it proved fatal. He prayed that Lady Margery's many ailments, which she could and would discuss at length, might occupy the girl for a good hour. But, even so, the priest knew he must make

487

haste, for the maid might return at any time to fetch some unguent or herb for the old woman.

He had searched many of the shelves before, though not all of them, but after long hours lying awake in a sweat of anxiety, he had convinced himself that if the knife was in or behind any of the jars or boxes on the rest of the shelves, the maid would have found it by now. Anyone taking over the running of a stillroom would surely have examined each jar in the first few days to learn what herbs and cures were stored there and which needed replenishing. So there was little point in wasting time searching the remainder of the shelves.

He lifted the lantern, sweeping the floor with the candlelight, searching for any signs that the beaten earth had been disturbed. He pushed aside chests and rolled out kegs to peer behind them.

He was kneeling on the floor, groping beneath the straw pallet of the maid's bed, when a mocking peal of laughter burst out right behind him. He jerked round, his heart thumping, but he was alone and the door was still fastened, though rattling violently as a gust caught it. He shook himself. It must have been the wind whistling over the cracks, or through the thatch, though the noise had sounded uncannily human.

A movement above his head made his heart race again. He held the lantern as high as he could, fearing that some imp was peering at him from the rafters, but it was only a bunch of dried herbs swaying. The draught howling in beneath the door or through the cracks in the shutters must have stirred it although, of a great many objects hanging from the beams – ladles, animal bones, bunches of feathers, dried snakeskins, herbs – only that one bunch was rocking

488

quite so violently. Doubtless a mouse had just scurried over it, that was all.

But all thoughts of mice and imps were elbowed aside by another more insistent one. That was it! Why hadn't he thought of looking up there? That was where the witch had hidden it, up on those beams or on the tops of the walls where they met the thatch. Even when the door was opened to bright sunshine, anything up in the eaves would remain in permanent shadow, and none of the servants coming to the stillroom in search of a cure for a headache or a soothing syrup would ever think to find it there. It would be the perfect hiding place for the knife.

Hob sat propped in the corner of the cave, his head lolling forward on to his chest. Beads of sweat ran down his nose, but he was shivering. He coughed, his chest heaving as he struggled for breath as spasm after spasm racked his thin body. He flopped sideways and Luke hauled on his sleeve, trying to drag him upright. Hob cried out as his bruised back was dragged across the rough wall.

'Sit up, Hob,' Luke whispered, darting an anxious glance towards Uriel. 'You'll not cough as much then.'

But Hob whimpered, struggling feebly to lie down. 'Tired, Luke, tired.'

'I'll hold you. But you have to stop coughing, Hob, else Brother Praeco'll think the demon's still in you and beat it out again.'

It was easier to hide Hob's coughing when the cave was full of the bustle of people eating or praying, but most were lying silent around the fire now. The only sounds in the smoky chamber were the snores and farts of the sleepers, their groans and rustles as they turned over on the rocky floor. It must mean it was night – at least, Luke supposed it was – but there was no day or night down there, only firelight or darkness.

Luke wriggled his arm as gently as he could around his brother and pulled his head against his shoulder. As Hob coughed, he pressed his grubby hand over the child's mouth, trying to stifle the sound, but it only made him cough more. His brother didn't seem to remember much about that terrible night, except the pain. Hob said it was the demons who'd hurt him. Luke said nothing. He knew it *was* a demon, a demon inside him. He tried to tell himself that he'd done it to save Hob, or they'd both have been cast out from the Chosen Ones, like that man Alfred, and what lay waiting for them up there was a million times worse than any beating.

But sometimes, as he fought from nightmare into waking, Luke found himself whispering that he hated God, which terrified him, for then he knew the demon was devouring him from the inside, like a great worm. What if he shouted those words in his dreams? What if he couldn't stop them? He fought to keep himself awake. He dared not sleep, for fear the demon would wake.

Brother Praeco was still in his own quarters in one of the smaller burial chambers back along the tunnel. Raguel was with him. Luke knew he liked her best and hoped she would keep him occupied for many hours. Phanuel would never tell the Prophet that Hob was still coughing, but Uriel most certainly would. He lifted his head, trying to peer over to the niche where she lay. He could just make out her hunched body. She seemed asleep, but you could never be sure.

Hob coughed again and someone sat up. Luke groaned, as they slid towards him. 'Here, let him sip this,' the figure whispered. 'It's warm. It might soothe him.'

490

It was Phanuel. She pushed a horn beaker into his hands and, with an anxious look towards the sleeping Uriel, slithered back to her place close to the fire.

Luke held the beaker to his brother's lips. At first the boy resisted, but then he swallowed a sip or two.

The sound of grating stone above made those on the ground stir and half struggle up. A blast of cold air shot into the cave, sending clouds of ash and burning sparks flying about the chamber. The Chosen cursed and slapped themselves as the sparks fell on bare skin, clothes and dry bracken. The wind roared above the hole as if a great dragon was flying overhead. Moments later, David clambered down the pole ladder, and the stone was pushed rapidly back into place by hands somewhere above in the darkness. He stepped over the prone bodies and hurried down the tunnel.

'God preserve us,' Friar Tom muttered. 'I pity those saints on guard up there. Sounds as if the whole world is a-wailing and gnashing its teeth.'

Brother Praeco emerged from the tunnel, his face red and sweating, buckling a leather belt around his robe. Raguel came scurrying after, carrying his huge cloak of animal pelts. She was clad only in a thin shift and as she struggled to help the Prophet don the heavy cloak, she passed between Luke and the fire. The firelight glowed through the fine linen of her shift. Luke felt his face grow hot, unable to tear his gaze from the curve of her breasts and buttocks beneath the transparent cloth.

David coming up behind, must have seen the lad's expression, for he glanced sharply at Raguel's body, then bent down and grabbed the front of Luke's shirt, jerking him so suddenly to his feet that Hob's head, which had rested on

491

Luke's shoulder, banged against the rock wall. The little boy yelped.

'You, lad, come with us.'

Luke felt Hob wrapping his small sweaty hands about his leg.

'Stay quiet. I'll be back soon, I swear,' Luke whispered.

But his brother clung to him.

David wrenched Hob away and shoved Luke forward. 'Don't keep the Prophet waiting.'

Smoke and ash whirled about the chamber once more as the stone trapdoor was dragged aside, and hands reached down to help Brother Praeco clamber up through the hole. David pushed Luke ahead of him. Luke straddled the ladder, his stomach twisting in knots, his legs as wobbly as a newborn colt's. He stared helplessly down at his brother. Tears were streaming down little Hob's face.

'Don't cry. Don't let them see you cry,' Luke mouthed at him.

But David was already prodding him from below, driving him upward, up into the Great Desolation.

A gust of wind flung Sara off balance and she cried out as her shoulder struck a tree. She stood a moment. She felt as if her breath was being sucked from her mouth by the force of the wind. Maybe it would be easier to walk once she was inside the shelter of the forest, but she was afraid to enter. The dark tangle of trees on the rise above her was in constant motion as if they were not solid at all but a huge rolling wave.

She stared back at the village. Before the sun had set, most of the women had already struggled further up the hill with what little they possessed or could carry. And it was as well they had, for the tide was already thundering towards the shore. In a few hours the sea would be crashing over Aldith's house again and all those down near the beach, as it had the night Janiveer had been swept ashore. But were the villagers any safer on the hillside? The wind was tearing the thatch from cottages, sending boards and shutters spinning through the air as if they were autumn leaves. Would a single building be left standing by morning?

Sara pushed herself against the wind, inching forward through the forest towards the cliff top. Several times, she fell to her knees and had to claw her way up again. The wind howled through the branches, cracking them as if they were twigs. The dry ground shook beneath her feet as somewhere a tree came crashing down, its own branches smashing through those of other trees as it fell. Sara stared fearfully up at the dark canopy towering over her. The earth had been parched for so long it could not anchor the roots, and half the trees were dying. Who could tell which might fall next?

What was she doing there? Janiveer might not even come, and if she did, how could a boy like Harold stand against her? Sara could hear her mocking laughter, see the scorn in her face. It was useless. She should turn back, find somewhere to shelter till the wind had blown itself out. What was the point of surviving so much only to be crushed in the forest?

She turned to retreat, but as she did, she glimpsed a flash of something bright between the thrashing bushes. She strained to peer into the darkness. There it was again, a glimmer of light, red and yellow. A fire! Harold must already be up there on the cliff top. He'd lit the fire as they'd agreed. He was scarcely older than Luke, but he had guts, did that lad. She knew how terrified he must be, yet still he'd come. She couldn't leave a boy to face that witch alone.

Noll grabbed Luke's shirt and hauled him up through the hole. Moments later, David clambered out behind him. Luke could see nothing of where he was, for the dim red glow of the fire flickering in the chamber below illuminated only the edge of a stone floor, but he guessed they must be in some kind of building or courtyard. Then the stone was pushed back into place and the light vanished.

Luke, like Hob and all the new initiates, had been led down into the chambers blindfolded. He remembered the sensation of walking over grass and weeds, then over flat stone, so he'd always imagined that the cave must lie beneath a building, but now he was not so sure. The wind roared around him, almost knocking him sideways, and as his eyes adjusted to the darkness, he thought he could see clouds racing through the night sky. Yet there were walls too.

'Master, see the roof is already torn away and—' David leaped aside as something heavy crashed to the floor, exploding into fragments.

'Outside! Quickly,' the Prophet commanded, stumbling the few paces to one of the walls. He groped for a handle. As he dragged the door open, the wind barged through the gap and he tottered backwards. Regaining his balance, he pushed his way outside. Luke, Noll and David wrestled with the blast as they struggled to follow. Brambles tore at Luke's breeches and loose stones rolled under his feet. After the fug of the cave, the wind bit through his clothes, chilling him to the marrow. He wrapped his arms around himself, huddling in the lee of the three men. Indeed, they were all

494

having to press themselves tightly together just to be heard over the roar.

David had his mouth close to the Prophet's ear, but he was still forced to shout. 'Master, the whole church could come down and the Chosen will be entombed alive. We need to move them.'

'No!' the Prophet bellowed. 'They are hidden in the cleft of the rock, as Moses was, until God's wrath passes over. Like Noah in the ark, they will ride unharmed through flood and tempest, and when the world is cleansed of the stench of sin, God will build his new kingdom with the Chosen.'

Noll tugged on the Prophet's sleeve to get his attention. 'But, Brother Praeco, the church was already weakened and crumbling. If it collapses, it could even crash through the roof of the cave below. They'll all be crushed. We must bring them up, just until this wind abates.'

The Prophet, his long beard and hair swirling up towards the sky, gripped Noll by the shoulders, shaking him harder even than the wind. 'Do you have so little faith? Would you betray me as Peter denied Jesus at the hour of his greatest test? It is written the saints will be sealed by the Blood of the Lamb until the tribulations are past. If the church collapses then that is the seal that will protect them.'

'But we could never dig them out.'

Luke pushed forward, tugging hard on the Prophet's cloak of pelts. 'Master, my brother is down there. Please let me fetch him. He'll be afeared without me. Please!'

Brother Praeco seized the boy and pushed him round to face the wind, holding him tightly against its force. Luke's eyes watered, and his face and hands stung from the twigs and grit it dashed against his skin. He shivered in his thin shirt. He felt the coarse beard of the Prophet whipping against his cheek as the man bent close behind him, bellowing into his ear.

'Listen to it, boy, feel it. That is no ordinary wind. That is the blast from the seven trumpets blown by the seven angels as they prepare for the Day of Wrath. It is here at last. The terrible day is come!'

Pushing in front of Luke and the two men, Brother Praeco raised his arms flinging them wide in the darkness. '"*Et dicunt montibus et petris cadite super nos et abscondite nos a facie sedentis super thronum et ab ira agni.* And they say to the mountains and the rocks – Fall upon us and hide us from the face of him that sitteth upon the throne and from the wrath of the Lamb. For the great day of their wrath is come!"'

Sara fell to her knees and crawled the last few steps towards the heap of stones that marked Matilda's grave. The storm was blowing from the sea, but the grave was so close to the cliff edge that she was afraid a sudden gust might knock her over the edge. Harold crouched by the fire. Even though he had dug a shallow pit for it and built a wall of stones around it to protect it, the red and orange flames were whirling like imps in Hell. Sparks spun up into the night to be instantly extinguished. Sara wondered how long the fire could remain alight. If it went out before Janiveer came, they'd have to face her in darkness.

Harold's face was pinched and pale in the gusting firelight, but he smiled wanly in relief at seeing Sara.

'Did you find it?' she asked. 'Was it there?'

'Moved some stones,' he mouthed at her, 'but . . .' He grimaced, shaking his head.

Sara crawled forward. A small pile of stones lay to one side of the grave. There was a hole in the cairn, roughly where she guessed the centre of the hag's body to be. Clenching her jaw, Sara peered down. She could see the large stone Will had dropped on the old woman's chest. She prayed they would not have to move that. She lifted out another of the smaller stones. The firelight was too dim and restless to see anything properly. She pulled a burning stick from the fire, but even though she tried to shield it with her hand, the flame was snatched away before she could even bring it close to the stones.

Harold was staring into the dense mass of trees. 'Heard someone moving. It could be her!'

'You'd not be able to hear anyone in this wind,' Sara said. Then, seeing Harold's expression growing even more alarmed, she added, 'More like it was a tree falling.'

He was right to be worried, though. If Janiveer arrived before they'd found the hand . . .

Sara drew her knife and, gritting her teeth, plunged her hand into the hole in the cairn, feeling around. Her fingers encountered the coarse cloth of Matilda's skirt. It felt unpleasantly wet and sticky. She tried not to think about that. Then she brushed against something soft and fish-cold. Her arm? The flesh was swollen. It was all she could do not to jerk away. She pushed higher, and then she found it – the leather belt. She gripped it with one hand and wriggled the knife in beside it. Sliding the blade under the belt, she began to saw. Mercifully the belt was not a thick one and her knife was sharp. The leather soon gave way. She tugged.

The belt slipped upwards. She seized the corner of the soft leather pouch that hung from it and tried to lift it, but it wouldn't move.

'Harold, help me. It's stuck. Lift the edge of that stone, while I pull.'

Shuddering, he put his hand where hers had been. She tugged. The pouch suddenly jerked free, sending her sprawling on the ground.

The leather bag lay between them on the stones, but neither was willing to pick it up.

'Is it in there?' Harold asked.

Turning his face away, he began piling the stones back into the hole as quickly as he could, as if he was afraid that Matilda might creep out through the gap.

Sara tugged at the drawstring, then upended the bag on the ground between the cairn and the fire. Something that resembled a great black spider came slithering out on to the ground. She glanced at Harold. He nodded grimly.

'The ancient mothers told me it would return to me with the wind,' a voice said.

Janiveer stepped from the shadow of the trees, her hair streaming wildly behind her. 'Bring it to me! The hand of Cadeyrn is mine.'

Luke gingerly edged a few paces back from the men, then bending low, he ran into the night. He took care not to head directly for the church, but away from it, towards the shelter of a ruined stone hut. He crouched there, trying to snatch a breath from the wind, but he dared not wait too long. At any moment they might see he was missing and guess where he was going. Keeping low, he dashed towards the corner of the church, creeping along close to the wall, feeling with his hands until he reached the open doorway and flung himself through. The church was tiny, smaller even than the one at Porlock Weir, but the darkness inside was impenetrable. He couldn't even see the floor, much less the stone trapdoor in it. Sinking down on all fours, he swept his hands over the flags in front of him, inching forward.

They were covered with dried dung, leaves and twigs that had blown in over the years, but he was certain that somewhere there would be a patch that was clear of debris, for surely each time they moved that stone it must be swept aside on that spot, unless the dust and rubble from the roof had already covered it. But he was trying hard not to think about that, or about the beams creaking ominously over his head.

He ducked as a shower of loose stones fell just inches from his head. It was all he could do to stop himself fleeing back outside, but he couldn't leave Hob trapped down there. He shivered as the wind hammered on the door of the church, and he heard them nailing the last board over the window in the cottage, blocking out air and light, shutting him in, walling him up alive with his father's rotting body.

Think! Where had he been standing when he first climbed out of the hole? The shriek of the wind seemed to fill every space in his head. He couldn't even remember which way he'd been facing. The whole world was in darkness. Was that how it was now, always dark, no day, no night, nothing but the howling of that wind?

He jerked in pain as his hand raked across something sharp on the floor. He rubbed his stinging palm and felt the warm slipperiness of his blood ooze between his fingers. Tears of frustration burned his eyes.

'Devil's arse!' he screamed. 'Devil's fucking arse!'

His heart began thudding: he was suddenly afraid that

the men outside might have heard him. Another lump of stone crashed down. He must find it. Where was the hole? Where?

Then he saw it, a line of red in the blackness, thin as a vein in a horse's ear. For a moment, he couldn't understand what it was. Then, in a flash, he realised. He scuttled towards it on his hands and knees, frightened to stand up in case he lost sight of it. He ran his uninjured hand over it. Now he could feel the gap and glimpse the feeble glow of the fire beneath shining up through the crack between the floor and the trapdoor. His fingers touched something even colder than the stone – an iron ring set into the top.

He scrambled up, and spreading his feet as wide as he could to brace himself, he hooked his fingers in the ring and pulled. The stone was heavy, but it lifted just a little. He heaved again, this time trying to drag it sideways. Stone rasped over stone and the crack of red light widened into a narrow oblong. He let go of the ring and scurried round to the open side. Sitting on the floor, he braced his feet against the edge of the stone and pushed as hard as he could. The stone slid backwards so suddenly he almost slipped over the edge and had to fling his arms out to stop himself.

A sea of faces peered up at him.

'Hob! Hob, are you there?'

From that height, he couldn't see the walls on either side of the chamber below, but he thought he heard his name. His brother's cry tailed off in a paroxysm of coughing.

'Hob, you must climb up here. Master wants you. Come quickly now.'

He saw movement below him. Hands were pushing Hob towards the bottom of the pole ladder. The boy doubled

500

over in another spasm of coughing. Luke lay on his belly and thrust his arm down through the hole.

'Climb up, Hob. I'll grab you.'

But the boy stared fearfully upwards, shaking his head. 'Can't . . . too high . . . and I don't want to see the master.'

There was a loud crack from one of the beams above and it swung down from the roof into the church, sending a cloud of dust swirling around Luke. The beam swayed back and forth in the wind, like a gallows corpse.

'Hob, you have to climb up here! He won't hurt you this time, I swear, but you must come now. Hurry!'

Hob hesitated then grasped the rungs, but he had only taken one step when a hand grabbed his shoulder pulling him back down.

Uriel stood at the bottom of the ladder, peering up at Luke, her mouth pursed and her eyes pinched hard.

'What does the Prophet want with the boy?'

Luke swallowed. 'Don't know,' he replied, as casually as he could. 'Just said I was to fetch him quickly.'

'If he wanted the boy brought to him, he would have sent David or Noll, not you. Where is he? Where is the Prophet? I shall speak to him.'

'No!' Luke's mind had gone numb, but he'd invented so many excuses to get out of trouble before that his tongue started babbling before he even knew what he would say.

'The master's praying, said he wasn't to be disturbed. He says the Day of Wrath is beginning and you all were to stay safe down here, 'cept for Hob. He needs him. The master said . . . he said the Blood of the Lamb –' Luke struggled desperately to remember the exact words '– would seal his saints against the tribulations. So you all have to stay here . . . sealed.'

Muttering and cries rose up among the disciples in the chamber below, like a colony of seabirds suddenly disturbed. Several fell to their knees and began to pray, each trying to raise their voice above those of the rest of the Chosen, clamouring for God's attention. Others pressed towards the ladder, staring anxiously up through the swirl of smoke and ashes, as the wind flew, shrieking like a demon, across the hole.

Raguel pushed her way through the knot of disciples and crouched down, pulling Hob on to her back.

'Hold tight, Hob, and close your eyes.'

She grasped the ladder, but Uriel thrust her arm in front of her. 'Where do you think you're going? You heard the boy. The Day of Wrath is upon us and the Prophet commands that we must stay hidden in the cleft of the rock where the Blood can protect us.'

Raguel pushed the scrawny arm aside. 'He also commanded the boy be brought to him. The demon the master expelled has left the child too weak to climb. I'll take him up. Then I'll come back. Unless you want to carry him up on *your* back, dear sister?' And before Uriel could stop her she had started up the ladder.

Hob's eyes screwed shut and his arms were wrapped round Raguel's throat so tightly that he was half strangling her. Luke was afraid she'd stop breathing before they got halfway to the top.

He reached down. 'Hob, come on, take my hand, I'll pull you up.'

But the boy only tightened his grip. Climbing the pole ladder was not easy, and Luke knew that doing it balancing a weight on your back must be harder still. Several times Raguel swayed backwards as if she was about to topple

502

off, and each time her foot missed the rung Luke's heart lurched.

As they neared the top, she rasped, 'Here, lift him off me before he chokes me.'

Luke braced himself. Lying flat on his belly so that he could reach down, he grabbed the boy under the armpits, but Hob was still clinging to Raguel and Luke couldn't lift him. Raguel heaved herself up another rung and Luke, rising to his knees, managed to heave Hob over her head to land with a thud on the floor. The boy yelped as his elbows hit the stone.

Raguel, her feet still on the ladder, leaned over the edge of the hole, gasping for breath. Luke pulled Hob to his feet, then turned back to her.

'Come on!' Luke cried. 'Grab hold of me and I'll help you out. Hurry before—'

He jerked round as fingers like bars of iron dug into the flesh of his shoulder so viciously he thought they would crush his bones to splinters. A shriek made him glance back towards the hole. The Prophet, his face lit by the hell-red glow of the fire beneath, towered over his young wife. With one great fist he seized her hair, yanking her head back while his other arm locked about her throat, the muscles bulging as his squeeze tightened.

'Run, Hob, run!' Luke yelled, but he barely had time to push his brother aside, before a fist slammed into his belly and he crumpled to the floor.

Father Cuthbert stood on the stillroom table, sweeping a kindling stick along the top of the beams he could reach from the centre of the room. Piles of dirt, loose straw, mouse droppings and dead flies showered on to the floor and rained down on the bald patch of his tonsure. He shuddered as he felt the scurrying legs of a beetle or spider running across the back of his neck, and dashed it away. But though a couple of tiny rolls of parchment, a lead seal and even a little drawstring bag tumbled down, Father Cuthbert didn't bother to examine any of them. He guessed they were merely charms or amulets set up there to ward off evil. Certainly none of them was big enough to contain a knife.

He was leaning out as far as he could to try to reach the furthest beam when the voice rang out so unexpectedly he almost fell off the table.

'Don't think you'll escape unpunished, priest!'

The voice grated like stone being dragged over stone, the sound so low he couldn't be certain he'd heard the words correctly, except that whoever had spoken had been close by, almost beneath his feet.

'Who's there? Come out and show yourself!'

Blood pounded in Father Cuthbert's temples. His feet seemed frozen to the table. He bent forward, trying to peer beneath it, but terrified that, even as he looked, a hand might reach up and grab his ankle from behind. He stood still, listening for any sound of movement, but he could hear nothing save his own hard breathing and the gale raging outside.

He raised the lantern, shining the feeble mustard light into every corner, but the stillroom was as empty as it had been before. Shaking, he dropped to his knees and awkwardly clambered down. Once more, he swept the lantern light around the room, even edging towards the kegs to peer cautiously behind them. He tried to tell himself that no one could possibly have crept into the room in that storm without him hearing the door open and feeling the blast from it.

With shaking hands, he lifted the thick oak beam and slid it through the brackets to brace the door. It made him feel safer. At least he could be certain that no one could enter now.

Father Cuthbert had lost all track of time. He couldn't tell if he'd been in the stillroom for minutes or hours. Every sense was urging him to leave, but the thought still gnawed like a worm in his mind – suppose the knife was lying on top of one of the walls. He couldn't leave knowing it might be up there. It had to be! He was certain of that now. Just another few minutes and he'd have it in his grasp.

The table was too cumbersome and heavy to drag round the room. Besides, he'd never get it close enough to the walls without moving all the boxes and kegs, and there wasn't time enough for that. He remembered having noticed a small rough-hewn ladder leaning near the back wall, broad at the bottom, tapering towards the top, constructed, he supposed, for a stillroom maid to carry out to the forest to collect wild fruit or leaves from the trees.

He leaned it against the wall, and climbed up a few rungs. It creaked alarmingly under his weight and he dared not mount another step. He stretched up, feeling along the top of the wall. But there was nothing except piles of dirt and bird dung. Clambering down, he moved the ladder and tried again.

It was on the third attempt that he felt it, something hard wrapped in a cloth that was stiff. He tugged it down. The white cloth was covered with a dark stain that had made the linen folds stick to each other. Hardly daring to breathe, much less waste time climbing down from the ladder, he feverishly tore open the wrappings. In the gloom he could barely see what lay inside, but his fingers curled around the handle of a knife. It felt all too familiar. Relief flooded through him. He had found it!

A sudden hammering sounded at the door. The maid had returned. She was trying to get in. Hastily thrusting the knife deep inside his shirt, Father Cuthbert tried to scramble off the ladder, but he moved too quickly. His weight tipped the ladder sideways. The priest crashed to the ground with a scream that the maid heard even over the storm.

The stillroom maid struggled to open the door, but eventually realised it had been braced from the inside. She ran to the grooms, who were still trying to calm the maddened horses. It took her a while to get them to stop and listen to her, let alone make sense of what she was saying. It took far longer still for them to realise that no amount of battering against the stillroom door would break that stout beam. In the end, they had to open the shutters, smash the casement frame and push the smallest stable boy through, while he squealed that they were ripping off his skin.

The lad found the priest lying twisted on the ground, staring up at him. A pool of dark, warm blood was soaking into the earth floor below.

As he later told his pop-eyed companions, with not a little exaggeration, a knife had sliced so deep into the priest's belly that only the very end of the handle was sticking out.

'If I'd been able to get to him sooner, I might have stopped the bleeding,' the maid tearfully told Master Wallace, as she sipped a steaming beaker of mulled ale in the great hall. 'What possessed him to brace the door?'

'May as well ask what kind of fool carries an unsheathed knife inside his shirt,' a groom muttered. 'My father always used to say, the only reason men go into the Church is that they haven't the wits to survive outside.'

'That'll do,' Master Wallace snapped. 'Man's dead. Show some respect. Though I can't pretend he'll be much mourned,' he added. 'All the same, it doesn't seem right, him being a priest and shriving others, that there was no one to say the words of consolation as he passed over.' He crossed himself. 'St Barbara keep us all from a sudden death.'

But Master Wallace was wrong in that, as in much else. Father Cuthbert did not die alone. The words of consolation he heard were carried to him from the sea and borne to him on the wind, but they did not bring him peace.

I will return the knife to you, when you return to me what you have taken. I always keep my promises, priest, always.

Sara could feel Harold's fear pulsing in her own throat as they stared up at Janiveer, but she dared not take her eyes from the sea-witch.

'You found the hand. That was *clever*.' Janiveer spat the word at them like a curse.

Sara's chin jerked up. 'Harold is a clever lad, brave too,' she added, hoping that the boy would believe it. 'He knew Matilda always kept that skull goblet of hers in the pouch at her waist. He'd seen her take it out when she thought she was alone in the chapel. But he remembered her bag was still on her belt when we buried her and there must have been summat inside from the way it flopped heavy when we moved her. Only it couldn't have been the goblet 'cause we'd already found that in her cottage, so he got to wondering what else she might have put in that pouch that she wanted to keep safe even more than the goblet.'

'Well reasoned,' Janiveer said. 'And now you will give it to me.'

'You want it, you'd best come and take it,' Sara said. She was willing Harold to begin, but she could see from the corner of her eye that he couldn't move.

'Oh, I will take it. You can be certain of that. But first I will take the soul I demanded. My forefather, the greatest warrior of all my people, was betrayed by your kin, not once but daily for hundreds of years. It was not enough that they killed him. They stole his bones and, without them, his spirit could not leave this place and journey to Tir na Marbh, the Land of the Dead. His spirit remained alone, separated from his ancestors and brothers, and now one of your kin will take his place, as he is called back across the seas.

'You, Sara, you have sons. At this moment, they both hang between life and death. You reminded me that you once saved my life. So I will make a bargain with you. I will take the soul of one of your sons, but the other I shall return to you alive. I will bring him back from under the earth and restore him to you and he shall live. You may choose, Sara. Which of your sons shall I keep and which shall I return to you?'

Janiveer drew the bear tooth amulet from beneath her gown and pulled it over her head, dangling it in the guttering firelight. The silver tip of the bear's tooth glittered as it swung wildly in the wind. She crouched and pulled a burning stick from the fire. The gale snuffed out the flame the moment it left the safety of the pit. Janiveer, digging the stick into the dry ground, scratched the outlines of two figures standing side by side, one taller than the other. Kneeling in the lee of the cairn, she dangled the bear's tooth between the two figures. It began to move, swinging in small circles, widdershins, against the sun. As if her hand had turned to stone, her fingers never moved, yet the circle grew ever bigger as the tooth spun faster and faster from its cord until a ring of silver hung in the air.

'Choose, Sara! Whose soul shall I take? Will it be Luke's or will it be Hob's? Which of your sons shall pay the price? Who shall descend into the realm of darkness? Choose, Sara, or I swear you will lose them both.'

'Stop!' Sara begged, unable to tear her gaze from the silver circle. 'You can't ask me to choose. How can I?'

'Who else should choose except the woman who bore them in pain and blood? Who else but a mother should decide which of her children lives or dies? They are her flesh, her blood, her bone.'

'Bone, Janiveer?' Will's voice rang out. 'You are almost as fond of those as the Holy Hag.'

Will was standing just inside the fringe of the trees, cradling a bundle wrapped in sheepskin in his arms.

'It took me a long time to realise who had left those symbols in my cave, Janiveer. *She sent me a bird without any bone. She sent me a cherry without any stone. She sent me a briar without any rind.* Except the bird you put there was nothing but bones and the cherry was a stone. So how does the last line go – *She bade me love a leman without any love.* It was the riddle of the faithless lover you set out for me. Why, Janiveer? Was it just to torment me?'

'You plucked me from the sea, Will, and I always repay my debts. If you really had the wisdom of the fool you would have understood that Christina was faithless, and when you'd learned that she was at the manor, as you were bound to do, you would not have gone looking for her, or discovered you had a child. I was trying to spare you pain, dwarf. But men seek out pain, as a dog goes running to dung.'

'But I know another ending,' Will said. '*She bade me love my leman without any longing.*'

'Only the dead in the Blessed Isles have no more desire, as Cadeyrn shall know.'

She looked down at the two figures she'd gouged into the earth, and the bear's tooth once more began to circle above them.

'This child was birthed here in this village,' Will shouted, thrusting out the bundle he was carrying. 'You want a soul, take his!'

Will darted forward and pushed the baby, wrapped in skins, into Janiveer's lap. She was thrown off balance by the sudden weight of the child, and as she reached out to steady herself and the squirming baby, Will snatched the bear amulet from her hand and darted around the back of the cairn, teetering between the stones and the cliff edge as the gale raged about him.

'Now, Harold!' he urged. 'Say it now. She is powerless without this.'

Harold stared at the glittering amulet in Will's hand. Then he clambered to his feet, trying to stand firm against the battering storm. He pulled a wooden crucifix from inside his shirt and thrust it high into the dark sky, but the wind almost ripped it from his grasp. He pressed it hard to his chest.

'*Crux sacra sit . . .*' his voice trembled '. . . *mihi lux.*'

Janiveer threw back her head and began to laugh.

'Go on, Harold,' Sara urged.

He swallowed hard. '*Non draco sit mihi dux.*' The firelight guttered wildly across his chest and face, as if he was being attacked by a thousand scarlet vipers.

On the other side of the cairn, Janiveer rose. Clutching the newborn baby in one arm, she pointed up into the starless sky. Her finger drew three circles. Then she snatched a handful of the smoke billowing up from the fire and tossed it towards the sea, like a fisherman casting a net.

For a moment, nothing changed, though Will, Sara and Harold all stared wildly about them, sure that something was about to happen, though they could not tell what.

Clinging so hard to the crucifix that his knuckles gleamed white in the firelight, Harold struggled to continue: '*Vade retro*—'

He broke off with a startled cry, gaping at the raging black sea below. The tide was running in fast. The great waves reared up as they galloped towards the shore. They crashed over the skeletal timbers of the burned ship in the bay below. The tips still jabbed out above the sea, like the fingers of a drowning man stretching frantically towards the air. But now each of the blackened tips of those timbers that was visible above the waves was burning, like a candle, with a crackling purple-blue flame. Even as they watched they saw the same unearthly fire begin to dance along the top of each wave, so that the whole bay was ablaze with cold blue flame, which raced towards the cottages on the shore.

David gripped Luke's arm, dragging him from the ruins of the church out into the storm. Luke thought he heard Raguel screaming behind him, but her cries were either silenced by her husband or drowned beneath the shrieking wind and thrashing branches. He twisted his head searching for Hob, but every bush and branch was writhing around him, as if they had been transformed into a pit of serpents.

Run, Hob, run, Luke willed him.

Leaves and dirt, stones and twigs flayed his skin and made his eyes stream. From somewhere in the darkness came a huge crash. The ground shook. Luke glimpsed a vague outline of a fallen tree, as he was dragged past it. The roots, torn from the earth, clawed up at the sky. The trunk had fallen on to one of the stone huts, smashing it like an eggshell.

A flash of lightning split the sky and Luke thought he saw a man standing in the shelter of a tree, his ragged clothes and hair whipping in the wind. The flash of light only lasted a moment, but the image was seared on to the boy's eyes long after the darkness closed in again. For though the man was standing, he had no face, no eyes, only a grimacing skull with shreds of dried tattered flesh still clinging to it. His body dangled from two iron spikes impaled through his shoulders.

David pressed his mouth close to Luke's face, bellowing into his ear. 'See him, did you? That's what happens to those who desert the Prophet. Alfred hangs there as a warning to all traitors.'

Luke gagged. When Brother Praeco said Alfred had been cast out, he'd thought he'd been sent away. He'd never imagined they had killed him.

Luke's legs were shaking so much he could barely move them. He stumbled and fell painfully on to one knee as a bramble wrapped itself around his ankle, but David didn't stop long enough to allow him to get to his feet. He dragged him forward like a sack, scraping him over rubble and thorns and pulling him into the shelter of a ruined wall. There

David dropped him, planting his boot on Luke's back, pinning him to the ground.

An icy fear drenched him. They would punish him. There was no doubting that. Would he be left out here to face alone the terrors the seven angels would unleash? For a moment, he found himself praying for that – he might survive the anger of angels – but if he was taken back down there to face the wrath of the Prophet, he knew for certain they would kill him, as surely as they had murdered the man crucified on the tree.

He yelped as a sharp stone hit his cheek, but the wind snatched away any sound. He felt the boot lift from his back. David hauled him to his knees. His hand grasped Luke's chin, jerking his head backwards until he was choking. Luke grabbed David's wrist, trying to drag his arm away, but he was no match for the burly disciple.

The wild-bearded face of the Prophet loomed over him, his long hair whirling about his head. Brother Praeco slowly raised his hand and Luke, fearing the blow he knew was coming, tried to duck, but David held him too tightly. But the hand, when it finally descended, caressed Luke's face almost tenderly.

'My son, my poor son.' He fondled the boy's hair. 'You should not have disobeyed me. You should have had faith in me, your father, to protect your brother. Haven't I always protected you both? Instead, you dragged him out here undefended, into the Great Desolation, into the terrible darkness of God's judgment. And God's anger cannot be tempered once it is unleashed. Your brother was struck down. A tree crashed down on the hut where he was hiding. See, over there . . . Hob is dead, Luke. Though God was merciful and he died instantly. Before this terrible Day of Wrath is ended, every man and woman left in the world will be begging God to slay them as swiftly.'

'No!' Luke could scarcely croak out the words. 'I'll not believe it. I won't! Hob's alive, I know he is. I just know!'

The Prophet patted his head, as if he were a small child to be appeased. 'You will know the truth of it soon, Luke. For God has called upon me to make a sacrifice. I must slaughter a lamb and smear the blood upon the lintels of God's house, so that the Angel of Death will pass over His Chosen Ones.'

He glanced up at David. 'The night you brought them to the cave I believed it was the younger brother God had delivered into our hands who was intended for the sacrifice, but the Lord showed me I was mistaken. That is why He allowed the she-devil to enter the boy and stayed my hand so that I could not cast her out. The lamb must be without blemish.'

He looked down at Luke again, running his finger tenderly across the boy's cheek and down the soft skin of his throat. 'It was the elder brother, the firstborn, whom God always intended I should offer to Him. I should have known. You who have become my beloved son, Luke, you are the precious lamb I must sacrifice to prove my faith.'

The Prophet's tone changed abruptly. 'Bind him!'

Luke struggled desperately, but even as he did so, he sensed Noll coming up beside him. David gripped him, almost snapping the bones in his arms, as Noll wound the rope about them, pinning them to his body. Noll grabbed his ankles, bringing him crashing to the ground and the two men lifted him, as if he was already a corpse. Luke wriggled and thrashed, but he could not break free.

They carried him across the rough ground back to the church, jolting him as they stumbled over stones in the darkness. For one wild moment, Luke thought they were taking him back down into the crypt. They couldn't really mean to kill him. The master spoke in stories, in wild images and strange words that were not really true, just a way of talking. Luke caught a glimpse of a dark, huddled shape lying close to the thin crack of red light on the ground.

'Raguel!' he screamed. 'Raguel, help me!'

But if she heard him, she didn't move.

David and Noll swung him upwards and brought him down with a thump on to the cold, hard stone. He could just make out the outline of a window above him and knew he was lying on the altar. The moment they released him he kicked out, flipping his body like a stranded fish. He rolled sideways, trying to fling himself off. But Noll seized his feet again and David's great hands gripped his shoulders, pressing him hard against the stone.

Luke saw the massive bulk of the Prophet, in his cloak of pelts, pacing towards them, the badger's head snarling on his shoulder. He caught the glint of a steel blade in his hand. Then Brother Praeco seized his hair and jerked his head down, so that the back of Luke's neck was stretched over the edge of the altar.

The Prophet roared up into the great black void above. '"And they shall sacrifice the lamb in the evening and take of the blood and pour it upon both the side posts, and on the upper door posts of the houses wherein they shall eat of the flesh of the lamb that night. And when I see the blood I will pass over them and the plague shall not fall upon them when I smite the land."'

He raised the knife high in both hands. Luke saw the blade flash above him and screamed.

*

'The sea is afire!' Harold wailed. 'The witch is burning the sea.'

'No, Harold,' Will shouted. 'It is St Elmo's fire, nothing more. It's a good omen, a blessed omen. It means you will succeed. Finish the words, Harold, you must finish them.'

But the boy couldn't tear his eyes from the cold blue flames crackling far below.

'Look at *me*, Harold,' Will yelled. 'I have the amulet. Without this, she is powerless.'

Janiveer laughed. 'I do not need that. You can throw it off the cliff, if you wish, little man. You think that will quench those flames? Look, they are racing towards the shore. Soon those burning waves will destroy every man, woman and child left in that village. There will be nothing left, Harold, nothing! You will have failed. But I can stop this. Sara, give me the soul of your son, and I will still this storm and spare those lives. Just say it, Sara, just speak the name. One name is all I ask!'

Sara stared down at the sea, then across at the storm-savaged village. Without warning, she leaped to her feet. Snatching up the hand of Cadeyrn, she stumbled the few paces to the cliff edge and held it out over the raging sea.

'That amulet might mean nothing to you, but I reckon this does. You'd not have your precious forefather going into the Blessed Isles without his axe hand.'

Sara cried out as a gust of wind punched her so hard she almost fell over the edge. Will grabbed the skirt of her gown, hauling her towards him. But, fighting down her terror, she defiantly flung out her arm again, holding the hand into the maw of the gale.

'It's my betting,' she shouted, 'that so long as his hand

remains here under the sea, his spirit'll be trapped here too, just like the old hag's in that box down there below those burning waves.'

Janiveer, still clutching the baby, bounded forward, like a great cat, stretching out to grab the hand from Sara. The two women struggled on the very edge of the cliff. Suddenly, Janiveer let go of her and thrust the baby out into the wind, so that it dangled over the cliff.

'Would you kill another mother's son, Sara? Give me the hand, the hand for this child.'

Sara hesitated. Her face full of despair, she glanced help-lessly at Will. Slowly her arm moved towards Janiveer, holding out the blackened hand towards her.

'No!' Harold yelled. He bounded across the stones, and darting between them, caught hold of the baby, jerking the child backwards and almost knocking Sara over the cliff. For a moment she teetered on the very edge then flung herself sideways, falling on top of Will and knocking him to the ground.

The underside of the old sheepskin in which the child was bundled was slippery with age and grease. The howling infant slid back down the dry grassy slope, crashing into the cairn. A weighty stone, balanced preciously on the others, rocked wildly and, as a violent gust caught it, the stone toppled off, smashing down on to the child's leg, pinning him to the ground. The baby shrieked in pain.

Janiveer took a step towards Sara and Will, who both lay winded, still tangled around each other. She tried to grab the hand, which Sara was still clutching, but Harold caught a fistful of her hair, jerking her back. Janiveer turned on him, her face contorted with fury. She seized him by his shirt, lifting him off his feet as if she meant to hurl him from the cliff. But before she could move, the earth beneath them gave a violent shudder.

Sara stared down at a long crack racing across the parched ground. She realised what was happening faster than Will. Grasping his arm, she heaved herself backwards, yelling out an incoherent warning to Harold.

With a rumble louder even than the roar of sea and waves, the edge of the cliff fell away. Rock and earth, grass and stones hurtled down, splashing into the thundering waves below. Sara, still lying on the ground, felt the rush of air and empty space beneath her feet. The full weight of the dwarf was suddenly dangling from her arm. For a sickening moment, they were both sliding into nothing, then Will twisted his body as only a jester could, and flung himself back on to the solid land, pulling her with him.

When they shakily staggered to their feet, still clutching each other, they saw that, except for the wailing baby, they were alone on the cliff top in the darkness. Harold and Janiveer were gone.

Something smashed furiously into the back of Brother Praeco's legs.

'Leave him alone!' it yelled.

The Prophet's knees buckled and he pitched forward, sprawling across Luke, but the knife was still gripped tightly in his hand. He whirled around, but the small figure had already scuttled back into the darkness, though Luke could hear stones rolling as he ran across the rubble. Relief and terror seized Luke in equal measure.

'Get out, Hob. Run!' he screamed.

'Silence!' Brother Praeco clamped his hand across Luke's mouth.

Luke tried to bite him, but the Prophet squeezed his jaws together so hard, Luke thought his teeth would splinter.

'David, keep a tight hold on the sacrifice.' Brother Praeco leaned towards Noll, lowering his voice: 'Fetch the boy. He's still in here. I can hear him moving.'

As soon as his feet were released, Luke struggled and thrashed with all the strength he could summon, but David pressed his full weight down on Luke's chest and arms till he could barely breathe. He could hear Noll stumbling around, cursing as he banged into fallen stones. Somewhere another great beam crashed to the floor.

'Master,' David said urgently, 'we must finish this now. The wind is building behind that wall. If it collapses . . .'

'It will not,' the Prophet growled. 'God has instructed His angels to hold back the winds until the Chosen are sealed. But we must hurry. The trumpets will sound with the coming of dawn. The blood must be daubed on the door and the lamb consumed before the first blast sounds.'

Luke heard someone blundering about in the church, louder this time, clumsier. The men heard it, too, and lifted their heads. Was it Hob? Was he hurt? Was he trying to get back to the altar? The Prophet turned his attention back to the boy lying on the slab. He slid his sweating fingers over Luke's face to his forehead, pressing his head backwards to expose the throat.

Luke tried desperately to wrench himself free. *Mam, don't let him kill me! Make him stop! Help me, Mam!*

There was a roar, which came not from the wind but from somewhere inside the church. Luke glimpsed a shape blacker even than the night, lurching towards the altar. It reared up, filling the space behind Brother Praeco. David must have seen it too, for he suddenly released Luke, hurling himself away from the monstrous demon. The shadow swelled, uncoiling itself until it towered above the Prophet. Sensing the movement behind him, Brother Praeco half turned, staring upwards into the face of the thing looming over him. He shrieked.

Luke, feeling the hands lift from him, flung himself towards the edge of the altar. He glimpsed the flash of eyes, a scarlet mouth and teeth like daggers. The Prophet tried to run as the demon embraced him from behind, clasping its great paws around him, crushing him. One of the Prophet's arms was trapped at his side, but he lashed out wildly with the other, striking with his dagger, stabbing as hard as he could into the huge paw. The creature roared in pain and, loosening its grip, slashed at Brother Praeco's face with its huge curved claws. Bone, brains and scalding blood splattered across Luke's head and neck as he threw himself on to the floor.

The fall knocked the breath from Luke's body and sent a flash of white-hot pain ripping through his shoulder. But as he lay, fighting to draw the breath back into his lungs, he felt a shaggy pelt brush his skin as the beast plunged down on all fours, lumbered across the church and out into the night.

There, among the ruins of Kitnor, the great bear reared up once more, raking its claws across the bark of the newly fallen tree. Then, with a final roar, it vanished into the chaos of wind and darkness. Luke felt something wet fall on his face. He couldn't understand what it was at first. Another drop fell, and then another. Rain began to patter down on to the parched forest. The drought was finally ended.

Chapter 68

Sara

On the last day of Lent a red herring is carved to resemble a man on horseback riding away. The herring is eaten to say farewell to forty days of fish, bid welcome to meat.

Something icy touched my foot in the darkness. Wet fingers, cold as death, closed around my ankle. Her face stared up at me from the darkness below. She was clawing her way back up the cliff face. I tried to shake her off, but her grip was too strong. Her long hair whipped around her head in the wind. *Choose! Choose!* The locks of her hair were snaking about my legs, binding them so that I couldn't move.

The cry woke me with a start and I was half on my feet, moving towards the child, before I'd even opened my eyes. A babby's wail will always wake a woman who's once been a mother, however far she's travelled into the land of dreams and nightmares. But I was so exhausted, it took me a moment to realise it was Goda's little 'un who was wailing, not my own chillern, not my Luke and Hob.

I sank back on the floor of the chapel, shivering. *Choose,* she had said. How could any mother choose? But if I'd chosen maybe . . . maybe one of my boys would be safe, one would have survived. I had failed them. After all I had done I hadn't been able to save my sons. I couldn't think about it now. I didn't want to think or feel ever again.

My limbs ached and my head was pounding, but I was too afeared of the dream to try to sleep again. Besides, the women curled asleep around me were already beginning to stir. Most of us in the village had taken refuge from the storm in the chapel during the night, for no one dared to stay in the cottages down by the shore and I could not return to my house for it was still a burned-out shell. Last night's wind had torn part of the thatch from the chapel roof and puddles of rain had gathered on the floor at one end, but the rest was dry enough.

Sybil lumbered to her feet. Raking the dirt and mouse droppings from her long grey hair with her fingers, she bound it up in a length of cloth. She strode to the door and flung it open, peering out. A chill breeze rushed in. Swollen clouds, the colour of lead, were rolling in from the sea.

'Wind's died down and it's stopped raining for now,' she announced. 'But not for long by the look of that sky. We'd best get moving. I reckon most of us'll be living in here for a few days yet, till we can put our own cottages right. We'll need to patch the hole in that roof. I'll go and see if there's anything we can use to keep the rain out. Some of you had best get down to the shore and pick any fish that got tossed up last night.'

Several groans went up.

'Aye, but fish is still better than an empty belly. And I've been thinking, if we fill a good few panniers we can take them to the manor, as long as we can round up any of the widgebeasts to carry them. I know we've had our fill of fish, but I reckon they'll not have tasted any these past months, so they might be willing to barter for some with a bag or two of grain or meat, if there's any to be had.'

Katharine was already blowing on the embers of the fire that the villagers had built close by the altar. She glanced up. 'We need to fetch wood too, if there's cooking to be done.'

'There'll not be much dry kindling to be found after that land-lash,' Meryn said, using the corner of the altar to drag himself up on to his crutches.

Sybil gave a snort of laughter, shaking her head. 'For months we've had any amount of good dry wood to heat our pots, but no water to boil in them. Now we've water aplenty to boil and no dry wood to heat it.' She gestured at the painting on the chapel wall of Christ on His throne staring down at us all. 'Sometimes I reckon it's Him that's the jester.'

Katharine stared anxiously around the chapel. 'Where *is* Will?'

Others peered round, too, as if he might be lurking in a corner, but there was no sign of him and nowhere that even a dwarf could hide. I'd thought he'd followed me to the chapel last night, the howling babby wrapped tight in his arms. But the night had been so dark, and with the rain dashing into my eyes, I'd barely found the way myself. I'd no notion where or when I'd lost him. I prayed that he was safe, that little 'un too, for I guessed his poor little leg had been broken by that stone. So much pain and him barely come into this world.

The chatter of the women was growing ever louder, as they all began to discuss what needed doing and who would do it. It was like being trapped in a byre with a flock of gulls. I dragged my damp shawl around me and picked my way over those still sitting, towards the open door.

'I'll go up to the forest,' I said to Sybil. 'That wind will have brought some branches down. Trees might have kept the worst of the rain off them where they grow close.'

Truth was, I needed to get away for a little, try to untangle the wool inside my head.

I found myself on the path leading towards the forest, the same one we'd taken to Kitnor. But that seemed another lifetime ago. The track that had been so dry then was a river of mud and rain now, strewn with twigs and leaves. I gave up trying to clamber up the slippery grass banks to avoid the deep puddles and splashed through them, my skirts already wet and caked with filth after struggling down from the cliff top.

I stared down at the waves surging far out at sea, grey-blue now and cold, the colour of her eyes. Was she dead? Was she really dead? Unless I saw a corpse, I dared not believe it. But I had seen her corpse once before, lying on my table, with Elis and Daveth, Col and Hob and Luke watching her – all gone now. All gone. We'd thought her dead then, but she had lived and they had died. She had come from the sea, the ninth wave, and taken everything I loved.

The high-pitched mew of a red kite made me look up. It was flying towards Kitnor. A narrow shaft of sunlight had broken through the heavy clouds, making the wet trees glisten. Someone was standing at the edge of the forest gazing down towards the village and the sea beyond. The sunlight was dazzling and I couldn't see him clearly for the lower half of his body was hidden behind the rise of the path.

'Will?'

The figure turned his head and retreated back into the shadow of the tree.

'Will? Is that you? Wait!'

Picking up my sodden skirts, I hurried up the rise . . . then stopped. Two boys stood under the tree, thin, ragged boys, one taller than the other. Their huge hollow eyes stared out from masks of dirt and dried blood, like the ghosts of men slain in battle. We gaped at each other. Their faces were so familiar, yet so strange. They didn't move and, for a moment, I was afraid that if I spoke or took a single step they would vanish like wraiths back into the forest.

'Mam?' The dull, feeble cry was so faint I could barely recognise it, but it was enough.

Tears blinded my eyes as I stumbled towards them, holding out my arms. They had come home. My sons were alive and they had come home to me!

Epilogue

Will

Riddle me this: What walks on four legs in the morning, two legs in the afternoon and three legs in the evening?

'Father, tell me a story.'

Young Adam sits on a low stool by the hearth, his hair gleaming copper in the firelight. He is supposed to be mending the fowling nets but, like most boys, he spends more time dreaming than working.

Though only ten summers have passed since he was born, he is already slightly taller than me, but he doesn't seem to notice. There are few at Kitnor to remind him of what a man should be, and the boy himself walks with a bad limp. His thigh was broken the night of the storm when the stone from the Holy Hag's cairn fell on it. The leg mended crooked, shorter than the other. So, like me, he rocks from side to side as he walks. Fate fashioned him into his father's son, or maybe it was Janiveer. I will never know the truth of it. But we have little use for truth here. Truth is only one story among many.

Most of us creatures and outlaws who, over the years since the pestilence, have settled in Kitnor are not what passes for human in the world beyond. Some are wanting a limb or an eye, a nose or a tongue, while others have more than they should. There is a man with a bulging blind eye in the centre of his forehead and a woman with two good arms and two withered ones that hang from her back like featherless wings. Some came into this world already malformed in their mothers' wombs; others, like me, had deformity thrust upon them for money, for crimes or simply for the amusement of others.

We even have our own holy man. Friar Tom, we call him. His wits are all but fled for he thinks we few are the only survivors of a world that the angels destroyed. He occupies himself with preaching sermons to the trees and holding Mass in the ruined church, which none but the goats attend, for men taught us all long ago that we are not made in God's image. But Friar Tom takes the goats' bleats as amens, and they gobble up the holy bread he solemnly offers them, so he is content.

We repaired the round stone huts, and mine is certainly drier and warmer than the sea cave, though not as spacious. The valley is sheltered and the crops grow well here. I cleared a patch for a garden to grow worts and herbs. And, like the others, I rear our chickens and goats, and fatten our pigs on the mast in the forest – I always had a hankering for sweet roasted pork. Did I ever mention that? Though I will admit it took a few years before even I could bring myself to cook it again.

What makes a happy man sad, and a sad man happy?

Why, *time*, of course, for all things pass. Just as the time of happiness passes, so does the time of sadness.

And in time saplings sprang up to hide the scars in the earth where the old trees were torn from it. Few outsiders ever stumble on this valley, save for the kites that wheel overhead. Villagers round about warn travellers that Kitnor is haunted by hungry ghosts and shrieking demons, and we are glad of it, for they leave us in peace.

'Father, the story!' Adam demands impatiently.

'Let me see,' I say. 'Did I ever tell you about the plague charmer who once came to a village far away?'

His eyes sparkle in the firelight. 'Never, Father, never. Tell me that one.'

We laugh. We both know I have told that story more times than he has eaten pigs' trotters, but still he never tires of it, and maybe the tale has changed a little over the years. Like children, once born, stories have a way of growing by themselves.

'Once upon a time, in a land far away, a village was suffering from a terrible plague. Many were dying and there was despair among the living for no one knew how to stop it. Then one night, when the moon was full, a strange woman walked out of the sea and into the heart of that village.'

'Maybe she was a selkie or a mermaid,' Adam interrupts.

'She was not of this land, that was certain, for the very tides of the ocean ebbed and flowed in her eyes. And this woman said she could charm the plague away from the village for a price. The villagers promised to pay her what she asked, if only she would stop the plague. So she cast a spell and the plague was swept up from the land, like dust in the wind, and carried far away. Those who were sick recovered and no one else fell ill. Then she returned to the villagers and reminded them of their promise, but they said, "How do we know you charmed away the plague? It would have burned out whatever you did." And they would not pay her. The woman was angry and she cast a spell to charm their children away from them.

'Only one tried to stop her, a man called Harold, who was scarcely more than a boy himself, but in her rage the plague charmer cast a spell to drive him off the cliff into the sea, hoping to drown him. But so brave was he and so pure was his heart that as he fell he was changed into a magnificent kite, and before the waves could claim him, he spread his great wings and soared up into the sky where he could for ever watch over that village.

'The plague charmer led the village children to a steep hillside. The kite saw where she was taking them and he tried to warn the villagers, but they could not understand his mewing cries and, thinking he was trying to steal their food, they drove him away. The plague charmer led the children through a door in the rock on the side of the hill into another world, a place of water and fire, where they saw and heard many strange and wondrous things. And the creatures who lived in the world offered them food and drink, and they ate and drank. And no sooner did the food touch their lips than they forgot their homes and their mothers. It seemed to them that only a day had passed when a hundred years had gone by.'

My son wriggles in horrified delight. 'You should never eat faery food, should you, Father?'

'And you remember that next time you go foraging. Toadstools are faery food and they make you very sick, don't they?' I say. I try to look stern, but it's hard when your mouth is always grinning.

He grins back. He knows exactly how to divert me from a scolding. 'And how did the children escape, Father?'

He knows that too, but I tell him anyway. 'After many years of flying back and forth searching for the lost children, the kite was crying his strange tale from the sky when the

529

King of the Forest, a great bear, heard the song of the bird and understood its meaning. The King of the Forest was angry that the King of the Underworld should steal from his domain. So he descended into the dark caverns and there challenged the King of the Underworld to combat.

'So fierce was their battle that the earth above trembled as they smote their battle-axes against their shields and trees came crashing down at the roar of their battle cries. The clash of their swords could be felt beneath the earth for miles around, so that all the villagers, huddling in their cottages, trembled at the sound. They fought all through the night, but finally at dawn, the great bear slew the King of the Underworld and burst out of the rock on the side of the hill, leaving a great cleft in it, which is there to this day.

'The kingdom beneath the earth vanished and the lost children found themselves alone in the cold, dark forest. Eventually they found their way back to their village, but they had been gone for so many years that everything had changed. They knew no one and no one knew them. And they sat, day after day, staring out at the sea, as if they were in a trance from which they couldn't wake, and the villagers called them the children of the dead, for they had come home without their souls.'

Historical Notes

In the spring of 1361, the Great Pestilence returned to London with a vengeance, only thirteen years after it had first struck England. King Edward III ordered measures to prevent its spread, including banning the slaughter of animals at Smithfield, but nothing could contain the deadly epidemic. That year, on the Eve of Ascension on 6 May, the sun vanished in a total eclipse at midday, which many in England saw as an evil omen, coming as it did after many strange sightings already witnessed over France and in other parts of Europe. These 'omens' added to the sense of fear and foreboding among the people. The royal family and court fled to safety at Beaulieu Abbey in the New Forest, but even such isolation could not protect the king's own daughters, Mary and Margaret, who were both destined to die of the pestilence in September of that year.

In a cruel twist, the second wave of the Great Pestilence seemed to be attacking the young and fit – adolescents, working men and the wealthy. Three times as many men were dying as women, while the old and infirm were left unscathed or recovered. There have been many attempts to explain why this outbreak of the plague should have caused the disproportionately high death rate among fit, working-age men and young people. Women and the elderly appeared either not to contract it or to survive it if they did. Some have argued that women's deaths were under-recorded, but the many eye-witness accounts of communities being left with few able-bodied men to work the land or in the trades show this not to have been the case.

One theory is that those who survived the second plague had developed some kind of immunity from having been exposed to the Black Death in 1348, but if this was true, you might expect more or less equal numbers of adult men and women to survive the plague of 1361.

It is also interesting that the plague of 1361 appears to have flourished in hot, dry conditions as opposed to the wet and cold of 1348, and there are marked differences in some of the key symptoms between the two plagues recorded at the time. While eyewitnesses in mainland Europe recorded the presence of buboes on victims in 1347, mention of this very obvious symptom is curiously absent from many accounts of the disease when it finally reached Britain in 1348, which suggests the plague had either mutated or three different forms of the disease – bubonic, pneumonic and septicaemic plague – were spreading simultaneously. It is now thought to have been pneumonic plague which dominated in Britain in 1348, spread from person to person by coughing. The wet, cold conditions would have been perfect for transmitting this form, causing people to huddle indoors in close proximity for long periods.

But during the second outbreak in 1361, eyewitnesses in England record the characteristic painful swellings in the armpits and groin, which we now associate with the bubonic plague, or Black Death, transmitted by rodent fleas. So, was the plague of 1361 a mutation of the same one that had entered Britain in 1348 or was it a separate disease?

One possible theory that has been put forward for the differing death rates between men and women in the second outbreak is that the form of the disease that struck in 1361 required the iron from its human host in order to multiply rapidly. Working men generally have more iron in their bodies than women of child-bearing age, the infirm or the elderly. In poorer families what little red meat there was would have been given first to the working men and boys, as is often still the case in developing countries, because it was vital for the survival of the whole family that the men remained fit and strong.

The bacillus would therefore have been more virulent in men and also in the wealthy classes, who ate far more fresh red meat than the poor and would therefore be likely to have had more iron in their blood. As women tended to have depleted levels of iron, due to menstruation, the bacillus would not have been able to multiply so rapidly, and their own immune system would have had a chance to fight it, enabling them to recover.

The plague died down in the autumn of 1361, although, as we now know, it simply lay dormant and would return many more times in future centuries, as it still does in countries such as the USA, though we now have the means to treat it. But in 1361, the shattered communities were to face yet more disasters, for the year that had begun with a terrible drought saw storms and gales batter the country throughout that autumn and winter. They culminated on St Maurus Day, 15 January, when the worst hurricane ever to strike England in recorded history swept across the country, ripping off the towers of great cathedrals and smashing all in its path. Known as the St Maurus Wind, it changed the shape of the British coastline. Cliffs crumbled, spits and peninsulas vanished and harbours were destroyed, while the debris was swept ashore elsewhere to block river mouths and ports, and create beaches where there had been none before. That year, England lost many ancient trees and historic buildings.

Porlock Weir and Kitnor

Porlock Weir is an ancient fishing village at the foot of Exmoor and is famous for its medieval fish weirs, the traces of which are still visible. It is now a very popular and picturesque tourist spot.

Kitnor, now known as Culbone, is a village in an isolated forested valley or coomb further along the coast. The church there, St Beuno's, is said to be the 'smallest complete parish church in England' and many people still visit it by walking from Porlock Weir along a new footpath created through the forest. The church is mentioned in the Domesday Book and sits 400 feet above the wild and dramatic Exmoor coast. It has many original features including twelfth-century walls. Parts of the nave are Saxon, dating back to before 1066.

It is believed that this valley was first inhabited in AD 430 by seven monks from a Celtic monastery in Wales, who sailed across the sea by boat and gave it the name Kitnor meaning *the place of the cave*. The monks lived as a community of hermits in individual stone beehive-shaped huts, the ruins of which were used and reused for centuries, long after the monks left or died out around 518.

In around 1265, about a hundred years before the setting of this novel, Kitnor was used as a place of banishment for heretics, witches and the mad, who lived in the stone beehive huts surrounding the church. The men, women and children survived well over the next forty years, repairing the church and building a thriving community, in spite of having little contact with the outside world. After they left, the place fell into ruins, but in 1385 it was again used as a penal colony, this time for male criminals banished there for months or years for such crimes as theft and adultery. Left to fend for themselves, many committed suicide. It was closed as a penal colony in 1478, but in 1544 became a leper colony.

Centuries later, thirty-eight East Indian charcoal-burners were sent to live in Kitnor. They had been taken prisoner during the British Raj and were sent to what by then had become known as Culbone to live and work for twenty-one years, before they were granted their freedom. Twenty-three lived long enough to leave Culbone, but they could never afford the passage back to India.

Stone Markers

The Culbone Stones, which Will and Sara stumbled across, are ancient, some carved with the symbol described in the novel. They were probably erected around the time of Stonehenge and may once have led the way to a stone circle in the area or even to Kitnor itself, since the valley was believed to have been sacred in ancient times. Indeed, that might have been what originally attracted the Celtic monks to come to the place when they saw the fires of the old gods burning in the darkness, since they would have been visible from the coast of Wales, just across the narrow stretch of sea. The Culbone Stones are currently on private land, but public access via a footpath is permitted once a year to view those that are still visible, though archaeologists believe many more may have fallen and lie hidden beneath the soil or dense undergrowth.

Sir Nigel Loring

Nigel Loring was born between 1315 and 1320. In 1335, he served in the Scottish campaigns and was sometime esquire to the Earl of Salisbury. In 1340, during the Hundred Years' War, he was knighted for 'conspicuous valour' at Sluys, although his armour and weapons had been stolen on the evening before the battle, and in 1341 a tournament was held in his honour, attended by Edward III and Queen Philippa.

Around 1343, Sir Nigel married Margaret, daughter of Sir Ralf Beaupel of Knowstone, Devon, and it is possibly through this marriage that he acquired the Manor of Porlock in Somerset. He appears not to have spent much time in Porlock, if any at all, for it wasn't until 1366 that he applied for a charter to hold a fair there. In 1345, Sir Nigel was sent on his first diplomatic mission to Rome to arrange a dispensation for the Black Prince to marry Margaret of Brabant, a marriage that never took place. Shortly after, Sir Nigel entered the service of the Black Prince, becoming a lifelong confidant and friend. He was one of the founding knights in the new Order of the Garter. In 1351 he became chamberlain to the Black Prince, a post he held for twenty-four years and at the battle of Poitiers he acted as a member of the prince's personal bodyguard.

He became lord of the manor of Chalgrave in Bedfordshire which he inherited from his father in 1346. It was a substantial and wealthy property. Also, after each of the campaigns and envoy duties he performed for the prince, he was generously rewarded with gifts, lands and properties right across England, including the manor of Drakelowe, and revenues from tin mines in Cornwall and estates in Devon. He was appointed steward of the lordship of Macclesfield and, in addition, received revenues from several churches. The income from all these rights and properties must have been vast. Sir Nigel retired from military service in 1370 on an annual pension of 100 marks (£1,200). He died in 1386. The manor house of Porlock burned down in the nineteenth century, but stood on what is now the site of Court Place Farm.

Brother Praeco and the Chosen Ones

Throughout the history of the major world religions, cults have emerged from time to time that follow a particular pattern, often referred to as *apocalyptic* or *millenarian* cults. There were many of these in the Middle Ages, arising at times of pandemics, economic crisis or other catastrophes, such as flood or famine, when itinerant preachers roamed the land warning that the end of the world was nigh and denouncing the corruption of the Church, king and sinful populace. Some preachers were ignored or arrested, but others were able to collect bands of fanatical followers.

Each movement was different, but most had the following elements in common.

The cult centred around a charismatic leader, well versed in religious text and imagery. In the case of medieval Europe the imagery was frequently taken from the Book of Revelation, also known as the Apocalypse of St John, found in the New Testament, which the leader used to explain current disasters and justify his extreme actions. He was able to convince others that he had personally received a divine message or revelation.

Cult members believed they were living in the 'end days' when God would destroy the sinful or unbelievers in a series of cataclysmic events or in a great battle, which would wipe out all those who refused to accept the truth of their message. Only the true believers would survive to enter a new, purified world in which they would be rewarded by God for their faith and sacrifice. So strong was the belief that they would be divinely rewarded that members could be persuaded to commit acts that resulted in violence or even in their own suicides. Bizarrely, though cult leaders preached against sin and immorality, and claimed that was why God was destroying the world, the robbery, rape and murder of non-believers by cult members was sanctioned by some leaders both to protect the group and to punish those who did not believe.

Leaders were able to convince the group members to accept their view of the world by separating them from the rest of society, often confining them in an isolated place and using a combination of positive persuasion and terrible threats. Extreme millenarian cults still arise from time to time today and some have ended with mass suicide such as occurred in Jonestown, Guyana, 1978 or murder as happened in 2000 in Uganda by leaders of the 'Movement for the Restoration of the Ten Commandments of God'.

In this novel, Brother Praeco refers to *the four horsemen of the Apocalypse*, described in the Book of Revelation. Most medieval people would have been familiar with these references, having seen the terrifying depictions of these riders in psalters and in wall paintings. They knew that the horsemen symbolised the catastrophes that would destroy men in the end days. Down through the centuries preachers have ascribed different meanings to the horsemen to fit the events of the time, but in the Middle Ages the rider of the pale horse was thought to represent *death and disease*, especially pandemics. The red horseman was usually interpreted as *war and bloodshed*. The black horseman was *famine*, and the rider of the white horse was the *Christ* figure come to judge the world and sweep away corruption and evil. When Brother Praeco referred to 'the pale horseman', his disciples knew it was another name for death.

Bears

Although the wild bear is believed to have been hunted to extinction in Britain by the twelfth or thirteenth century, bears were a familiar sight in medieval Britain. In 1252, the King of Norway sent to King Henry of England the gift of a 'pale bear', probably a polar bear, which was housed in the Tower of London, but which the sheriffs of London were obliged to provide money to feed. They had the bright idea of tethering it on the banks of the Thames where it could fish for itself, which drew many fascinated spectators.

But a far more common sight was the brown bear: no medieval fair or great celebration would have been complete without a dancing bear. Bears were also trained to appear to tell fortunes by choosing certain objects such as stones or bones from a selection scattered before them. Those bears were perhaps the luckier ones, for many more were used in the lucrative 'sport' of bear-baiting. Bear pits were constructed outside the town walls, where tethered or loose bears would be set upon by dogs. The dogs would be trained to snatch ribbons or flowers stuck on the bears' heads with pitch, or simply to fight them. In spite of Edward III's attempts to discourage it, this was a favourite pastime in the medieval period and many fortunes were won or lost betting on the outcome. By the reign of Henry VIII 'many herds of bears' were kept for this purpose in towns across Britain. Elizabeth I was so addicted to this 'sport', she forbade the performance of plays on Thursdays as they clashed with the bear-baiting. In 1620, the town of Congleton, Cheshire, had raised money to buy a new Bible, but when the town bear died, they used the money to pay for a new one instead.

Given the huge number of bears kept in captivity and being led round the country from fair to fair in medieval times, it was inevitable that occasionally bears would escape and turn feral. They would not have learned how to hunt or forage, and would have known humans as a source of food and also of pain, so raids on isolated homes in search of food, with attacks on people, dogs and livestock, were bound to occur.

According to folklore, if a person kills a bear, the bear's ghost will continue to haunt that spot and terrorise all who encounter it. There were reports of the ghost of a bear that had been killed haunting Martin Tower in the Tower of London. It was seen by a guard on duty there, and so terrified him that he collapsed and died.

Vade retro satana

The invocation that Harold tries to use on the cliff top is known as the *Vade retro satana* ('Get thee behind me, Satan'). It was the medieval Catholic formula for driving back any form of evil. It is believed to have originated with the Benedictine monks, but some of the phrases within it are based on the words of Jesus as recorded in the Gospels, when he was tempted by Satan during his forty days in the wilderness. This invocation was regarded by the Church as a spoken sacrament. In its full form it reads: *Crux sacra sit mihi lux. Non draco sit mihi dux. Vade retro satana. Numquam suade mihi vana. Sunt mala quae libas. Ipse venena bibas.* It translates roughly as: 'The Holy Cross be my light. The dragon will not lead me. Get thee behind me, Satan. They will never tempt me. Who proffers evil to me, let him the poison drink.'

This formula was used throughout the Middle Ages to repel or disarm witches and sorcerers. In the witchcraft trials of the seventeenth century, people accused of witchcraft were forced to confess they could not perform a spell in any place near a cross where these words were written or spoken. Since the late eighteenth century, the initial letters of each word of the invocation have been added to St Benedict medals or to crucifixes to protect the wearer.

Medieval Riddles

All the riddles that head Will's chapters were told in the Middle Ages. Many medieval riddles are no longer asked now, because the world they describe is so different from our own. For example:

Riddle – Which saint does most good for the church?
Answer – The saint in a glass window for he keeps the wind from blowing out the candles.

But some riddles, such as *Which came first, the chicken or the egg?*, are still quoted today. The medieval answer to that one was, *The chicken, for it was made with the birds at Creation.* That is probably not the answer most modern readers would give.

Here are the answers to the medieval riddles posed in the chapter headings

Riddle – How many calves' tails would it take to reach from the earth to the sky?
Answer – Just one if the tail is long enough.

Riddle – What is the distance from the surface of the sea to its deepest part?
Answer – A stone's throw.

Riddle – How may a man discern a cow in a flock of sheep?
Answer – By looking.

Riddle – What brings ill fortune to him who rides and good fortune to him who flies?
Answer – A dead horse for it is a misfortune for his owner, but a feast for the ravens.

Riddle – How many straws go to make a goose's nest?
Answer – None, for having no legs they cannot go anywhere.

Riddle – Which man killed a quarter of all the people in the world?
Answer – Cain when he slew Abel.

Riddle – How many hoof prints does an ox leave in the last furrow when it has ploughed all the day?

Answer – None. The ox walks in front of the plough, so the plough being pulled behind always obliterates its footprints.

Riddle – Which craftsman builds the house that will stand the longest?

Answer – The sexton, for the dead will dwell in what he builds until the Day of Judgment.

Riddle – If you say my name, I vanish.

Answer – Silence.

Riddle – I saw a man who never was, who smiled and wept, and walked and talked, but uttered not a sound.

Answer – A man's reflection in water.

Riddle – What is the widest stretch of water, yet the safest to cross?

Answer – The dew.

Riddle – Little man clad all in red, with a stick up his backside and a stone in his belly.

Answer – A hawthorn berry or a cherry.

Riddle – I never was. No one ever saw me, nor ever will. And yet that I will be is the hope of all men while they live.

Answer – Tomorrow.

Riddle – Put me in a bucket and I shall make your burden lighter.

Answer – A hole.

Riddle – Some try to hide and others to cheat, but whatever you do we shall always meet.
Answer – Death.

Riddle – What I catch I throw away; what I don't catch, I keep.
Answer – Lice.

Riddle – What doth the contented man desire, the poor have and the rich require, the miser spends and the spendthrift saves and all men carry to their graves?
Answer – Nothing.

Riddle – What walks on four legs in the morning, two legs in the afternoon and three legs in the evening?
Answer – Man, for he crawls when he is an infant, walks upright in his prime and walks with a staff in old age.

The last riddle is one of the oldest ever recorded. Ancient Greek legend has it that it was the riddle the Sphinx asked Oedipus Rex. The Sphinx challenged travellers with riddles, strangling anyone who failed to give her the correct answers. All the travellers were killed, until Oedipus arrived and answered correctly. The Sphinx was so incensed that she killed herself.

In the novel, Will asks Christina, '*What does a wife give to her husband that he never sees? What does her husband wear that he never feels?*' The answer is *a cuckold's horns*. In the Middle Ages, the image of a man with horns, echoed in an insulting hand gesture, meant that, unknown to the man, his wife had been unfaithful, making him a cuckold. This insult is still used today. In July 2009, the Portuguese economy minister, Manuel Pinho, made the gesture to an opposition MP during a debate and caused uproar in the Portuguese Parliament.

The term *cuckold* comes from the French name for the cuckoo. The female cuckoo lays her eggs in other birds' nests for them to hatch and rear the chicks. There are many theories as to why a cuckolded man should be symbolised with horns. Some link it to rutting stags who compete for females, others to the ancient Roman practice of presenting returning soldiers with horns to honour them for their long service on the battlefield. But what began as an honour gradually came to imply that other men might have been performing services in their wives' beds during their absence. Shakespeare associated the cuckold's horns with Actæon, an ancient Greek huntsman, who was turned into a horned stag by Diana and torn to pieces by his own hounds. Another suggestion is that, just as an animal cannot see its own horns, so a husband may be blind to his wife's infidelity, even if it is obvious to everyone else.

The visual riddle that Will finds in the cave is an old medieval one, which in the twentieth century was used as the basis of a folksong. Medieval audiences loved double-entendre riddles in which one answer was innocuous, the other sexual: *She sent me a bird without any bone.* Answer – *An egg* or *a penis.*

She sent me a cherry without any stone. Answer – A *cherry blossom* or *a woman's sexual organs.* This was not a reference to the hymen or a woman's virginity as 'cherry' wasn't used as euphemism for either until much later.

She sent me a briar without any rind (bark). Answer – A *leaf bud* or *any obstacles to sex, such as a lock or a jealous husband.*

She bade me love a leman without any love. Some versions say *without any longing.*

In the first case, this line refers to a faithless lover; in the alternative it refers to a lover who has obtained the object of her affections, therefore has no need to 'long' for him.

Porlock Legend

The inspiration for the spirit box came from a legend about an incident that is supposed to have occurred several centuries after this novel is set. The story goes that a wealthy but evil pirate, known as Lucott or Luckett, was buried in the churchyard at Porlock Weir. But his spirit would not rest. He haunted the church night and day, even tormenting the priest and congregation during holy services. Twelve priests in succession attempted to exorcise the ghost, but he mocked them and they all fled in terror. Finally, a priest from the village of Watchet was summoned. He confronted the evil spirit and struck a bargain with him. He would pose three riddles to the ghost and if the ghost failed to answer any of them he would be forced to obey the priest, but if he guessed all three correctly he would carry the priest down into the grave with him.

The ghost of the wicked pirate could not resist a wager, so he agreed and the two of them withdrew to play their deadly game alone. The spirit easily guessed the first two riddles, but the answer to the third riddle was *the Holy Trinity*, and while the spirit knew the answer, he also knew that if he uttered those words he would be dragged down to Hell. He could not give the answer to the riddle and the priest won.

The priest ordered him to mount a donkey and ride it into the sea. But as he passed, the spirit struck the priest, blinding him in one eye in revenge, because the priest had tricked him. The priest threw an iron box into the sea and made the ghost climb inside. The cleric then locked the box and pushed it out into the waves where it sank. He warned the villagers that the box must never be pulled from the sea and opened for then the evil spirit would return seven times stronger than before. The priest returned to Watchet, having saved Porlock Weir, but he paid for it with his eye, and the dead eye burned like the fires of Hell for the rest of his days on earth.

It is interesting that this tale bears many similarities to the ancient Nordic Sagas using riddles to win control over the night-stalkers and ghosts who torment the living. Another feature similar to the ancient sagas is the concept that spirits and the undead cannot be banished without their agreement and co-operation. This is a pre-Christian idea and one not taught by the Western Church. Both of these elements from the 'elder faiths' have found their way into a much later Christian legend.

Glossary

Acolyte – The highest of the four Minor Orders of clergy. Acolyte comes from the Greek meaning *candle-bearer* and the acolyte's primary duty was to carry the candles when the Gospel was read or when the Host was elevated during Mass. The acolyte had to be aged fourteen or over and his other roles included preparing the wine and water and assisting the priest in the celebration of Mass. For the church services he wore an alb (ankle-length white robe) bound with a girdle and an amice (linen neck-cloth). In poor churches or chapels, the badly paid acolytes even performed the duties of the deacons, who were in Major Orders, by baptising infants and giving the consecrated bread to the people.

Beller – Dialect word meaning to bawl or wail.

Bless-vore – Dialect word for charm or spell, usually one for healing.

Brock – Traditional English name for a badger, from the Celtic *broc*. Some place names containing the word *brock* seem to be a corruption of *brook*, but others refer to a place associated with badger setts, such as *Brockhall* and *Brockholes*, which come from the Old English *brocc-hol* – badger hole.

Cadeyrn – Pronounced *cay-der-rin*. An ancient Celtic name derived from the Welsh *cad* meaning 'battle' and *teyrn* meaning 'king' or 'ruler'. The most famous person with this name was a fifth-century king of Powys in Wales, also known as Catigern, son of Vortigern.

Chasuble – From the Latin *casula* (little house); the distinctive outer garment worn by priests at Mass, often Y-shaped and decorated with strips of embroidery known as orphey. The colour of the cloth depended on the liturgical season. Today green is used for most of the year, but in medieval times the colour sequence was not fixed and there was much variation between parishes. When so many days were dedicated to martyrs, the most frequently seen colour in many parishes in the Middle Ages was red.

Chickenwort – *Stellaria media*, a common weed with white star-shaped flowers, otherwise known as *chickweed, chick whittles, tongue grass* and *white bird's eye*. It is rich in copper and was a popular medieval vegetable, eaten both cooked and raw, and used medicinally as a poultice for boils, eye lotions, an ancient slimming aid and for digestive upsets.

Chrisemore – A dialect name for a newborn baby that is yet to be baptised. This was a dangerous time when the unbaptised baby might be possessed by demons or stolen by faeries and replaced by a changeling. Some people refused to utter the name of the child before it was baptised for fear it could be used by evil spirits, so the baby would be referred to as *chrisemore*. Since it was believed all babies were 'born in original sin', when the child was brought for christening the parish exorcist would expel the evil from the infant in front of the door of the church before the baby, now cleansed, was brought inside for baptism.

Colewort – The medieval cultivated cabbage, similar in appearance to modern *collard*. It was small, loose-leaved and far less bitter than its wild ancestor. Leaves could be picked from the stem as needed without having to cut the entire plant, and after the first crop, if the stem was left in the ground and a cross was cut in the top, it would often regenerate, giving a second crop, so it could be harvested even in early winter. That made it a very important plant for food and medicine. *Coleworts* or 'worts' were either eaten alone, shredded, boiled and tossed in butter, or added to the pottage pot. 'Worts' were believed to improve eyesight and ease palsy, gout and ulcers. They were also a cure for the ill-effects of too much wine.

Crayer – A small single-masted boat resembling a barge, which was used to carry cargoes in northern Europe, usually hugging the coastline or crossing the Channel. Depending on size, at this period they could carry between ten and seventy tons. Over the next century the size of the vessels increased, along with their capacity. Although their crew would have been armed and would have fought if attacked, the vessels were slow and clumsy to manoeuvre, so easily fell prey to French and English privateers.

Darnel – *Lolium temulentum*, a weed grass that infested meadows and grain crops. It was disliked in the Middle Ages because it was thought to poison livestock and if the seeds got into the harvested grain, and were accidently eaten, they were said to cause shaking, staggering, vomiting and blurred vision, as if the victim was excessively drunk. It could prove fatal. But we now know it is a fungus that often infects this plant that causes this poisoning, not the plant itself.

Darnel was a medieval symbol of deceit and evil, because it looks like wheat until the ears of grain form, hence its other name *False wheat*. It is possible that it is the weed referred to in the Gospel of Matthew as *Tares*. However, it was used medicinally, for example, when pounded up with salt and radish roots it could be applied externally to treat leprosy sores and ringworm.

Devil's eye – *Vinca*, a wayside plant also known as *periwinkle*, *blue buttons* and *sorcerer's violet*. Chaucer called it *parvenke*. It was thought to be used by witches and sorcerers in their spells because it grew on graves and was therefore associated with death. It was also bound around the legs to ward off cramp. Medicinally it was used to treat nosebleeds, toothache and abscesses.

Dulse – Edible seaweed, most commonly *Rhodymenia palmata*, with broad reddish-brown fronds. In coastal villages it was gathered from rocks at low tide, dried and chewed between meals for its salty flavour.

Dwale – From the Old French meaning *mourning*. Dwale is the medieval name for the plant *Atropa belladonna* or *deadly nightshade*. Atropa was one of the three Fates of Ancient Greece who cut the thread of life with her shears. In low doses, dwale was regularly used as a sleeping draught, but on several occasions in history, it was employed to poison the water or food of enemy soldiers, either killing them outright or rendering them drowsy and helpless, so they could easily be overpowered and slain.

Frica – It was a common medieval belief throughout Europe and Scandinavia that sickness and illnesses were caused by seven (sometimes nine) female demons, all sisters, whose names were variants of *Frica, Ilia, Restilia, Fagalia, Subfogalia, Iulica* and *Ignea*. These demons posed a great threat to unbaptised babies, but they could also enter children or adults in a variety of ways. For example, they lurked between the leaves of multi-leaved vegetables, such as lettuce or cabbage, and could be swallowed by someone eating them without having first driven out the demons by cutting a cross in the stalk. If anyone consumed food or drink that had been left under a bed at night they, too, were likely to be infested by one of the seven sisters, who would make them ill. Medieval amulets written on parchment or lead were often inscribed with the names of the demons, banishing them by the power of the Holy Trinity or the Holy Cross. The charms were carried or worn to ward off sickness or to cure someone who was ill.

Gatty – Medieval diminutive of *Gertrude* and Matilda's name for her cat. St Gertrude of Nivelles (626–59) is the patron saint of cats. She was abbess of a double monastery and is often depicted with either a cat or a mouse. Gold and silver mice were brought as offerings to her shrine. She may have been invoked to help rid people of plagues of mice, but in the Middle Ages mice also represented the souls of the dead, so this emblem may symbolise her role as patron saint of the newly dead, who spend the first night of their three-day journey into the afterlife under her protection. *Gyp* was an affectionate term for a pet cat in the Middle Ages, which in later centuries was replaced with *Pussy* or *Kitty*.

Green sickness – A serious and often fatal anaemia, frequently caused by what in modern times would be labelled *Anorexia* *nervosa*. It was a common ailment in the Middle Ages among the extremely pious who regularly mortified the flesh by starving themselves. It was also said to be an affliction of the lovelorn. In the medieval period, green sickness was thought to be particularly common in young people.

Gypon – A close-fitting sleeved tunic worn over the shirt, reaching to the knees, though shortening to hip-length as the century progressed. It was often padded for warmth and protection, or simply fashion. From around 1370 onwards it began to be known as a doublet.

Hand of Glory – It could be used to open any lock, render a thief invisible and put the occupants of a house into a deep sleep so that the house might be robbed or the women raped. It was made from the hand of an executed felon, cut off while he was still hanging on the gallows. The blood was squeezed out and it was embalmed, using saltpetre, salt and herbs. Sometimes a candle made from the fat of a hanged man was pushed between the fingers, or the fingers themselves could be lit and used as the candle. Once lit, the room would be filled with an unearthly blue light; those asleep would be unable to wake, and those awake unable to move. The flames could be extinguished only with milk or blood. The belief in the *hand of glory* was so enduring that a thief was apprehended with one as late as 1831.

Harbour – A term used in medieval hunting. The hound (*limer* or *lymer*) used for locating the quarry for the hunt would track the scent of an animal such as a stag or boar on a long leash. They usually worked in pairs, with the handler, known as the *valet de limier*, following on foot, until they had *harboured* the quarry. The huntsmen would then release the *running hounds* or *raches* and the quarry would be *unharboured*, that is, set running for the huntsmen and hounds to chase until it was brought to bay and slaughtered.

Heller – Dialect word meaning a naughty or wicked child, a brat.

Horse bread – The poorest-quality bread baked in the home. It would be made from a mixture of grain and pulses, ground into coarse flour by hand, using a quern. It might include peas, beans, wheat and rye, and even dried roots, such as bulrushes, which could be used to bulk out the grain flour in hard times.

Janiveer – Old dialect word meaning *January*, and used in a number of weather-lore sayings. The month of January was named after the Roman god Janus, whose name means *doorway* or *gateway*. He is the god of beginnings and transitions. His image is often found on ancient gateways and bridges, with two heads facing in opposite directions, one to where the traveller has come from and the other to where he is going – the past and the future.

Jory – A West Country diminutive of *George*.

Knee holly – *Ruscus aculeatus,* a short prickly shrub, also known as *knee-holme* and *pettigree*. The stems and leaves made a tough scouring brush for cleaning cooking pots. The seeds inside the scarlet berries were ground with the leaves to make a poultice for broken bones. The roots, ground in wine, were used to treat headaches, menstrual pain, jaundice, and bowel and kidney ailments. In later centuries the plant was known as *Butcher's Broom* because it was used to scrub butchers' slabs and to encircle or cover any meat on display to prevent mice getting on to it.

Lady Day – Vernal or spring equinox.

Lymer – See '*Harbour*'.

Minor Orders – From the age of seven, freeborn children could be received into the Minor Orders of the Church, and as a sign that they were now in Holy Orders, they were tonsured. Many boys and young men took Minor Orders without any intention of becoming a priest, simply to get an education. Many also did it to gain 'Benefit of Clergy', which meant that if they had been accused of a crime, such as theft or murder, they could demand the right to be tried by the far more lenient ecclesiastical courts that did not impose the death penalty.

There were four Minor Orders. The lowest was the *ostiarius*, sometimes called a *porter*, whose duties were similar to a modern verger. Then came the *lector* or *reader*, whose task was to sing the lessons. Next was the *exorcist*, who had to drive out demons from the mad and exorcise babies at the church door before they were baptised. The highest was the *acolyte*. In small churches, the acolyte's duties often encompassed all four of the roles of Minor Orders.

Unlike clergy in Major Orders, who were committed to Holy Orders for life, if anyone wanted to resign from Minor Orders and become a layman again in order to marry or pursue another occupation, all he had to do was let his tonsure grow out.

Mud-horse – A long wooden sledge, with runners that lay flat on the ground at the back and were curved high at the front, with a waist-high wooden frame set on top of the runners. These were built so that a fisherman could travel over soft mud and wet sand at low tide, to retrieve fish and shellfish from nets, weirs or wicker traps that might be set a mile or more out in the bays.

The fisherman would stand at the back of the sledge and bend forward over the frame so that the top half of his body was lying along it, distributing his weight, then propel himself forward with a skating motion of his feet. He would suspend baskets or sacks from the wooden frame to hold his catch, which ranged from shrimps to conger eels. He could also safely sit a child on the frame in front of him to help harvest the catch.

Mud-horses have been in continuous use in Britain since Saxon or even Roman times up to the present day. Before the Second World War, twenty or thirty mud-horses would have been seen out in some of the bays along the coasts of Somerset and Devon. Now only a couple of families still work the nets in this way.

Mynedun – Known today as the seaside resort of Minehead, built beside the hills known as East and West Myne. The name may be a corruption of the Welsh *mynydd*, meaning 'mountain'.

Nisseler – Old dialect word meaning small and weak. *Nissel-dredge* or *nissel-tripe* were also used in different parts of the West Country for the runt or the smallest of a litter.

Nug-head – Dialect word for a blockhead or stupid person. A *nug* was a formless lump of wood before it was carved or shaped.

Pied hose – Men wore thigh-length stockings with pairs of eyelet holes around the top so they could be laced to strings, known as *herlots*, that dangled from the underside of the gypon. It was fashionable in this period to wear a hose of a different colour on each leg or alternatively a pair of *pied* hose, meaning multi-coloured.

Pollax – The medieval name used by the English for the long-handled war hammer, from which we get the modern expression 'he was poleaxed', meaning the news or an event stunned him. The *pollax* was a heavily weighted hammer on a long shaft that could be swung or thrown, with a slim axe-blade on the opposite side to the hammer face. The weapon was principally designed to deliver a crushing blow, while the axe-blade could be used to slash the tendons of the enemy's arms or legs to cause a man or a horse to fall to the ground.

Polypus-fish – Octopus. The term *octopus* wasn't used in science until the sixteenth century and didn't become a word in common usage until a century or so later. In earlier centuries, these creatures were called *polypus-fish, poulp, preke, poor-cuttle* and *devilfish*, but today *devilfish* usually refers to one of the species of giant ray.

Praeco – Latin for a messenger, a herald, a crier or a prophet.

Pumpes – Pork meatballs, in which ground pork was mixed with cloves, mace and raisins, moistened with almond milk and stock and rolled into balls known as *pellettys*. They were then fried. A runny sauce of thickened almond milk or meat stock was added and the dish finished by sprinkling it with sugar and mace, and decorating it with edible flowers, such as those of wild marjoram, ramsons, chives or thyme, which would have added to the flavour.

Rampin – A Somerset dialect word meaning *furious* or *raving mad*, possibly a corruption of rampant.

Red herring – A term that can be traced back to at least the thirteenth century, and is probably from much earlier. It refers to a herring that has been gutted, split in two and smoked, causing the flesh to turn a dark ruddy brown. Today it is more commonly known as a *kipper* but a true red herring was more heavily cured than a modern smoked fish.

Spirit boxes – It was a common belief that if you wanted to rid yourself of an evil spirit you lured it into a box, which was then often buried under moving water, as spirits were thought unable to pass through that. But if you just wanted to rid yourself of an illness or a run of misfortune, you would place some token of it in a little box, such as a stone or a snippet of cloth that had been touched to the affected part of the body. You then left the box on a road or under a tree where a passer-by would find it. If they were inquisitive enough to open the box, the illness or bad luck would leave you and attach itself to them.

Tabor – A small hand or snare drum, consisting of a round wooden frame and two skins, which could be tightened by rope tension. It was usually fastened by a strap to the forearm and beaten with a stick held in the opposite hand. The *tabor* would be played vertically, allowing the hand of the arm to which the tabor was strapped to be raised to the mouth, so that the musician could play pipes at the same time. 'Pipes and tabor' were generally used together, with the musician operating as a one-person band.

Twibill – Also spelled *twybill*, from the Old English *twibile*. It was a T-shaped tool with two long blades and a short wooden handle forming the leg of the T. The top was made of iron, and sharpened into chisel-like blades at both ends. The two ends were of different widths or shapes. At one end of the iron crosspiece, the flat of the blade ran parallel to the handle, like an axe, while at the other end of the cross piece it was at right angles to the handle. The twibill was an important medieval tool used in woodworking, both on land and by ships' carpenters, to roughly shape wood and to gouge out deep mortise joints – it was quicker to scrape out the shaved material using this than with a straight chisel and mallet.

Viperfish – *Echiichthys vipera*, now known as *Lesser Weever* or *Sting-fish*. *Weever* is thought to be a corruption of the Anglo-Saxon *wivre* meaning *viper*. It feeds on shrimp so often lies concealed in very shallow water under silt or sand. It has a set of dorsal spines linked to poison sacs. If trodden on or threatened, it stings.

The sting is agonisingly painful, and produces swelling, stiffness and numbness, which can last for days. It causes a fast pulse rate and breathing difficulties and can result in temporary paralysis. The sting of a single fish is not usually fatal, unless the victim has a pre-existing heart or lung condition or goes into anaphylactic shock, but if the poison of several fish is extracted, a lethal dose can be produced.

Whispering and pistering – Old Exmoor expression meaning to gossip or tell tales in secret, especially spreading the kind of stories that would cause harm.

Widdershins – Turning or circling anticlockwise, against the sun, as opposed to *deiseil*, which was turning clockwise or with the sun. Deiseil was believed to bring a blessing or good luck, but widdershins – going against nature and the heavens – was thought to bring bad luck, misfortune, even death. It was used in spells intended to curse or to summon demons. Medieval housewives were careful to perform even insignificant tasks, such as stirring a pot, clockwise, or deiseil. Millstones in mills were made to turn deiseil. We retain vestiges of this belief today – port is passed clockwise round the table, even though most people are right-handed, and beating the bounds of a parish is done on a clockwise circuit.

About the Author

Karen Maitland travelled and worked in many parts of the United Kingdom before settling for several years in the beautiful medieval city of Lincoln, an inspiration for her writing. She is the author of *The White Room*, *Company of Liars*, *The Owl Killers*, *The Gallows Curse*, *The Falcons of Fire and Ice*, *The Vanishing Witch* and *The Raven's Head*. She now leads a life of rural bliss in Devon.